Agnes Canon's War

Agnes Canon's War

a novel

DEBORAH LINCOLN

Blank Slate Press | Saint Louis, MO

Blank Slate Press
Saint Louis, MO 63110

For information, contact
Blank Slate Press at 3963 Flora Place, Saint Louis, MO 63110.

Manufactured in the United States of America
Cover Graphics: Shutterstock, iStock (Getty Images)
Set in Adobe Garamond Pro and Exmouth
Cover Design by Kristina Blank Makansi

Library of Congress Control Number: 2014946275

ISBN: 9780985808662

To my mother, Elizabeth Robinson Lincoln
and to the memory of my father, Max Lincoln, with all my love.

Main Characters

Agnes Canon

Jabez Robinson

Charlie, Sarah Belle, Harrie Lee - Agnes and Jabez's children

Eliza Wetmore Robinson - Jabez's first wife

Sam Canon - Agnes's cousin

Rachel Canon - Sam's wife

Billy Canon - Sam and Rachel's son

Julia - Billy's wife

Nancy Canon Jackson - Sam's sister and Agnes's cousin

John Jackson - Nancy's husband

Elizabeth, James, Rebecca, Johnny - Nancy & John's children

Tom Kreek - Elizabeth's husband

Book One

"One of the most favorable signs of the times,
was that the ladies had been persuaded to give up corsets."

~ Margaret Fuller, *Woman in the Nineteenth Century*, 1845

1

April 1852

Agnes Canon saw a woman hanged on the way to the Pittsburgh docks. The rope snapped taut, and a hiss rose from the watching crowd like steam from a train engine. The woman dangled, ankles lashed together, hooded head canted at an impossible angle, skirt flapping lazily in the breeze. A sharp pang of sorrow shot through Agnes though she knew little of the woman's story.

Rumor had it she'd bludgeoned her husband while he slept, and more than a few in the milling crowd muttered that he well deserved it.

The prison squatted beyond the road in a hollow of wasteland, stone walls lit by a streak of afternoon light breaking through a low overcast. Agnes and Elizabeth, perched on trunks stacked in the wagon bed, were level with the gibbet, and Agnes couldn't tear her eyes from it. Most days, Elizabeth, Agnes's cousin, had a flash about her like a hummingbird in the summer sun, but now she turned, wan and trembling.

"Agnes," she said, her soft voice shaky. "Shouldn't she have run away? Like you?"

Agnes shuddered as the woman's body disappeared and the crowd roared. "Shouldn't have married the man in the first place." Her papa had accused Agnes of being selfish, but her act of defiance in rejecting a loveless marriage proposal now seemed pitiful.

Twisting around from the wagon's bench, Sam Canon, another cousin, glowered at Agnes from under willy-worm brows. Sam took a dim view of

Agnes's venture and had expressed more than once the opinion that she should have stayed home and married Richard Wiggins. "There's a lesson, cousin," he said in his baritone. One of his longer speeches. He clicked to the mules, and the cart resumed its descent toward the harbor. Agnes rolled her eyes at Elizabeth and seized the wagon's rail as it lurched downhill.

They'd bounced about in the back of the wagon, atop trunks and carpetbags and hundredweight sacks of rice, near ten hours. Seemed like ten days. Sam appeared to direct the wheels over the largest cobbles and into the deepest ruts for the entire thirty miles. The wagon listed to port, the iron-shod wheels were out of round, and altogether the two women felt well churned by the time they reached the Pittsburgh harbor.

Flatboats lined the docks like cows at milking, and steamboats puffed and pawed at the wharves. A stench of fish, burning coal, and animal waste laced the air as the shouts of stevedores echoed over the roar of steam engines. Under a lowering sun, their flatboat rode at anchor amid swarms of gulls and trash, a wormhole-riddled floating box that was to be their home all the way to the Mississippi River.

Children scampered underfoot and men tossed barrels and crates and wrestled animals while the women struggled to generate a warm meal in a rising wind. Agnes hauled and prodded the last of her bags and trunks into whatever nooks the others had not yet claimed, her status as spinster guaranteeing a crowded bunk below deck and forward with the children. Her height, unusual for a woman, would mean cramped nights. The river's dampness invaded the tiny space, the water lapped just inches from her pillow. She thought it was the loveliest cubby-hole she'd ever seen.

Elizabeth, settled into a tiny cabin already furnished by her husband, Tom Kreek, fetched Agnes and in the dimness of the evening, Agnes could see that her cousin's face had not regained its color. She wondered whether it was the effects of the hanging or the smells of the boat that bothered her. Perhaps both, but she laughed and teased her for her daintiness.

They followed Tom to the stewpot and poured themselves hot coffee as evening deepened. Agnes's legs and back ached with the journey, the fetching and carrying, but it was a satisfying weariness. The three of them carried their full plates to a row of hampers in the bow and watched the dimpled expanse of river fade into smoky promise downstream. A hundred lights, haloed with the softness of evening air, flickered into being on shore, while behind them they could hear the children squirming and complaining on their way to bed. A cob-webby mist rose from the water and settled on Elizabeth's hair like dew on a black rose as Tom hung a tannin-stained hand across her shoulders. Elizabeth leaned into him and pulled her shawl close, her eyes lit in satisfaction.

Despite their differences—Elizabeth being a married woman of twenty and Agnes an aging old maid of eight and twenty—they were best friends. Elizabeth was Sam Canon's niece and so Agnes's cousin once removed. Favored with youth and beauty, Elizabeth journeyed in the company of her parents and siblings and that most prized of a woman's blessings, a husband. But her domesticated manner hid a quick mind and an iron will, and she ruled her husband without his ever suspecting. She also sympathized with Agnes's restlessness as none of her sisters had ever done, and Agnes treasured their friendship the more for it. Yes, Agnes knew the occasional spurt of jealousy which she tried to conquer with common sense, but she admitted to herself that she was not always successful.

Unlike Elizabeth, it was not satisfaction but impatience that clutched at Agnes. Impatience to put behind the tedious lot of an unmarried schoolmarm. Impatience to be gone from the plodding life that pinched like last year's boots. Gone from the old farmhouse, weathered to the color of leftover porridge, its soul vanished along with her mother. Agnes longed to clutch the brilliance of the westering sun on the river, grasp the future, and pull it to her like a lover.

Agnes had buried her mother with her favorite Margaret Fuller. When it was her turn to step up to the casket, press her lips against her mother's cold forehead and bid her good-bye, she slipped the small volume from the sleeve of her dress so no one would see —especially her father—and tucked it beneath the coverlet. It rested by her mother's side, the side away from the infant who had killed her and who himself lay stiff and cold, cuddled in the crook of her arm.

Mother had given Agnes the book the year before, upon its publication. "Our secret," she said, and it signified for Agnes that she truly was special to her of all the daughters. Agnes had torn out the frontispiece so she would always have the inscription: *To Agnes. Be good enough and strong enough to give up corsets.* She signed it, *Your Mother, Ann Jones Canon, Christmas 1845.*

3

She was ill even then.

Agnes relinquished her place to the next sister in line and joined her father in the first pew. A weight pressed against her heart, as one by one, the remaining six sisters kissed their mother and took their seats. Their father glanced over them, then turned a stony stare to the casket. Seven healthy daughters, followed by three sons, none of whom lived to see his third year. And each one of those three seemed to steal the flesh from their mother's bones, until she had no more to give. The last one took her, the wife Daniel Canon had loved but never understood.

Two days after the funeral, Agnes's father gathered his daughters in the parlor and took his seat in his great armchair. "Let us understand one another," he said. He was a big man, six and a half feet from foot to forehead, with shoulders wide as an ax-handle's length. His voice thundered when the mule defied him or in church at the "amen," but in the parlor his voice was soft, and that was when they knew they must listen closely.

"I'll be understood now she's left us," he said. "I aim to do my duty by you long as you lodge under my roof. Then you will marry, be obedient wives, give me grandchildren." He fixed them one by one with a look they knew well. "Your ma held strange ideas, but she would be shamed if you was to do else." At the time, the sisters ranged in age from mid-twenties to fourteen, and since none of them had yet received an offer, they were uncertain how they might please him.

As the years passed, the suitors did not materialize. One by one Agnes's sisters left for nearby villages to take up teaching positions, the only profession open to them. Agnes alone attracted an admirer. Richard Wiggins. He taught with her in the academy at Union Town and pursued her for some months. His mind was not acute, he favored foods with a great deal of garlic, and he endorsed families of no less than a dozen children. He was short.

Somehow Agnes's father learned of his interest, and after a family meal on a Sunday, called her into the parlor. She was apprehensive. Being alone in conversation with her father was a rare occurrence. He took his customary seat and pulled out a clay pipe. She sat, hands folded in her lap as she'd been taught, while he ministered to the pipe.

"I congratulate you, daughter." He squinted through the smoke.

She looked up at him. "I'm not sure what you refer to, Papa."

"Your marriage." He pulled the pipe from his lips and glared. "I'm told you've been made an offer."

"No, I have not." She twisted her hands and looked away.

"But you expect one."

"What exactly have you heard, Papa?"

"Girl, don't provoke me. Richard Wiggins has been courting you and if he ain't already, he intends to make you an offer. Sure you reckon that?"

"Mr. Wiggins has been attentive, but I don't believe he intends to make an offer."

"He most surely does. He told me so hisself!"

That caught Agnes up short. For Richard to speak to Papa without approaching her was more despicable than she expected even from him. She took a deep breath.

"Papa, I will soon be twenty-eight years old. Well beyond the age when a man needs to approach a woman's father for permission. He should have come to me first." She could not look her father in the eye, so she gazed past his shoulder to the mantel. The fire roared, and she grew over warm. "If he had, I would have refused him." A log tumbled and threw sparks up the chimney. "If ever he does offer, I shall refuse him."

Her father said nothing, and the silence drew out between them. Then he leaned to the hearth and tapped the bowl of his pipe on the stones. The heavy scent of burning tobacco filled the room. He propped the pipe in its holder and stood.

"You will marry."

She stood as well. "I will not."

"You're a fool," he said, his voice so low she could scarce hear him though they were but a foot apart.

"Perhaps I am, Papa, but I will not marry where there is no love and less respect."

"Don't be addlepated, girl, that's childish notions."

Agnes said nothing. Her father puffed out his lips, backed up a step and ran his hand through thinning hair.

"Agnes, what's a woman for but for children?"

For so many things, but there was no point in saying it. The disappointment in his eyes angered and pained her, and she looked away. He turned to go. When his hand was on the doorknob, she spoke. "Papa, would you deny me the love you and Mother had between you?"

Without turning, he said, "That ain't enough," and left the parlor, closing the door behind him.

5

In the fall of 1851 farm prices plunged, fields lay fallow, and livestock were slaughtered to save the cost of feed. Agnes's cousins, led by Sam Canon and John Jackson, determined to sell out and set off for the rich, virgin farmland of the Missouri frontier. Elizabeth played the role of Agnes's advocate with her father and uncle, and between the two women, they convinced the men that Agnes might accompany them. Agnes spent hours crouched by her mother's grave talking to her about it, dreaming, and taking leave. And then she counted her savings, sold her treasured set of Walter Scott's tales and packed her trunk. When she approached her father to tell him her plan, he stared at her long and hard as if memorizing her features, then turned his back and strode off without a word.

On a lovely April day in 1852, Sam pulled the wagon up in front of the house, and Agnes's sisters crowded about with kisses, tears, and good wishes. Her father remained in the barn and did not wish her good-bye or God speed.

Agnes sighed at the memory and tried to let the anger and disappointment at her father melt away like the setting sun. Soon the clouds shifted, and a star appeared, then another and another. Elizabeth settled her head on Tom's shoulder, and he kissed her temple. Agnes dipped her head and looked away and thought of the woman they'd seen hanged that day. Never again would she watch the stars blink on, feel the mist on her cheeks. She had no future.

Agnes did.

2

They left with the dawn, the company lined up along the bow or crowding the cabin roof, some in tears as Pittsburgh disappeared into the brilliant orange and purple sunrise. Day after day they slid down the Ohio, the going wretchedly slow. The names of towns—Bellevue, Sewickley, Aliquippa—were familiar at first. Then the river swung south and west, and Wheeling glided by, with its pall of smoke and its refuse floating in the current, and after it the hamlet of Parkersburg. The lindens budded in delicate greens and yellows and the willows dragged limp branches on the water. Farms along the way stretched up the sloping banks, their tidy black furrows ready for seed. With river traffic raging around the clock, they daren't remain on the water after dark, so each evening they tucked in along the sandy beaches and stretched their legs on land.

One day, just beyond Parkersburg, they pulled to the bank at a lovely cove shaded with maples where a creek rippled into the great river. Nancy Jackson, Elizabeth's mother, shepherded her younger children out of the boat and settled herself out of sight of the men. Though her eldest was twenty and her second, Sarah, nearing womanhood, her young ones were little more than babies, the last an infant at the breast. Agnes brought her a plate of cold chicken and sourdough bread as she unfastened her bodice for the baby to feed.

Nancy was sister to Sam Canon, and Agnes had never been easy with her. Her conversation limited itself to children and household; Agnes doubted she'd ever read a book. She'd convinced herself Nancy didn't deserve her husband, that a man as quick-witted and active as John Jackson required an equally adventurous wife. Tall and lean, eyes gentle, smile affable, more than twenty years earlier John had poled up the Ohio River from the west, into their lives and into Agnes's imagination. He spoke to her of great distances, of wilderness and freedom, and early in her teens, she'd formed the notion that Nancy had hogtied him to the chimney corner and bore babies to bind him there. So Nancy and Agnes were never close friends. But today she set her plate at her side and took Agnes's hand to pull her near.

"Remember," she said, stroking the baby's cheek, "the glade below our house? Where we had a tea party? You were just a bitty thing. Guess I was, oh, maybe eighteen. Just met John." Her eyes looked past Agnes, into the long ago. "I pretended you were my little girl. We took a hamper, ate cream horns and cheese straws along by that crick where Pa fished for trout."

Young as Agnes had been, she remembered that tea party. They'd played house, Agnes most unwillingly acting the role of baby, much like her grandmother's cat when she dressed him in an infant's christening gown and rocked him in her sister's cradle. He endured the insult just so long, then whipped out his claws and with a howl disappeared, dragging the gown behind. Agnes had felt like howling at Nancy's tea party, but then she wouldn't have gotten any cream horns.

Nancy reached up and pulled at a willow wand, the buds in soft green whorls. "John and me, we buried our little babes there, the first two, on the rise. Just above the creek? You remember? John and me, we were young." She smiled at the infant now in her arms. Agnes stared at the river, its current traveling west. "The hardest part of this trip is leaving those babies behind."

The child stopped sucking and screwed up his tiny face, and Nancy put him up to her shoulder. The baby's bellow withered to a whimper, and the tiny hands clutched at his mother's collar. Nancy had forgotten Agnes.

3

Jabez Robinson dropped his valise and his medical bag from the roof of the stage, scrambled down beside them and pushed his locked hands over his head, cracking his back. For the hundredth time he wished to God they'd figure out how to finish the rail connection to Cincinnati. Two hours from Columbus to Xenia by train, a full day on top of that damned rickety stage crammed together with a half dozen other men. Not a propitious way to start a long journey.

But he soon let go his peevishness and turned to the town spread before him in pleasantly warm April weather. Cincinnati, already a sizable town, rolled west along the banks of the great river, three-story buildings facing the shoreline and the melee of humanity that swarmed there. Steamers lined the docks and fed the hodgepodge of shacks, tents, carts and open-air stalls that sold, bartered and fenced every kind of goods imaginable. Jabez pulled a thin cigar from his coat pocket, struck a match against a roadside outcropping, pulled the smoke into his lungs and grinned. Nothing better than a sunny day, a good smoke, and the always-fascinating bedlam of half-civilized humanity spread around him for his enjoyment.

He slung his valise over his shoulder and picked his way along the rutted street that bisected the embankment, muddied and pockmarked by hundreds of hooves and boots. Piles of skins, blankets, canvas, saddles, barrels of pickles, salt pork, fish, herds of sheep and goats, yards of dress goods, piles of potatoes and early peas, coffee and farm tools, much of it just off the steamboats, crowded the marketplace. Horses snorted and dogs whined in the heat of mid-afternoon. The press of travelers, mules, cattle, leather-clad frontiersmen, hunters, traders, Negroes and Indians flowed around him. He counted six discernible languages amid the prattle.

"Raisin pie! Shoofly pie!" a raspy voice called.

"Fresh eggs! Brown eggs!" another cried.

A weathered creature lifted a hide of rank fur with bits of skin clinging to the leather, a poorly-tanned buffalo robe like the one he'd brought back from California. A sun-browned man with a ring in his ear offered a handful of gold coins to a young red-headed fellow for a girl Jabez took to be the young man's wife. The redhead's temper flared and he knocked the coins to the ground, but the wife, a beautiful girl with jet black hair, laughed with delight and pulled him away.

Jabez found himself trailing after the couple along the row of vendors, amused by their wide eyes and obvious wonderment at the carnival around them.

"You'll need a churn in the far west, lady!" A filthy mitt clutched at the girl's sleeve.

"Cheeses! Cheeses will keep 'til Missouri and beyond." A plump matron held up a round the size of a dinner plate to the young man's nose.

Jabez turned off between the stalls and found the rooming house where Doctor Wetmore, his teacher, mentor, and future father-in-law, was accustomed to stay on visits to town. He'd spend the night here and catch the steamer to St. Louis the following morning. He signed in, left his bags and, impatient to stretch his legs after the tedious trip, wandered back into the street. He could smell the river and the stench of dead fish and mud from the boarding house stoop, so he turned his face to the breeze that blew from the west and headed back into the crowd. He felt the old stirring in his blood, that yearning to be on the move, on the road, open land ahead of him and crowded cities at his back.

He stopped to inspect a bolt of yard goods. "Look mighty fine on your wife, will it not?" the seller asked him.

"I'm not yet married," Jabez said, but thought of Eliza and how she would love it. An early wedding present, perhaps. It was cream-colored watered silk, with a rose pattern, delicate like Eliza. Fragile. She would want it for her trousseau. Appropriate for Columbus, maybe not so useful in the little Missouri town where he planned to take her. Also like Eliza. But no matter, he liked to buy her things, she'd waited so long for him.

He nodded to the cloth merchant and pulled a five-dollar gold piece from his pocket. As he waited for the cloth to be wrapped, he spotted the red-headed boy and his beauty. They were joined now by another couple, a tall woman with a heavy fall of chestnut curls and a younger boy with the fuzz of the adolescent on his upper lip. His physician's instincts led him to analyze details of appearance more than was probably acceptable to strangers, and he tried not to stare. But for some reason, the group fascinated him. There was a resemblance between the two women in the slope of the brow and the shape of the eyes, but there likeness ended. The second woman had at least four inches on the other, and on many of the men she passed, and walked with a sway and a grace that hinted at confidence. He noticed her hands, especially—her fingers were long, slender, and expressive when she talked, like a pianist who sensed the world through the magic of her touch. She had none of the classic beauty of the other, obviously younger, woman, but she was certainly striking. Intriguing.

The boy with her planted himself in front of a caged parrot and engaged it in conversation. The tall woman reached to pet the rich pelt of an otter, and The Beauty admired a green silk shawl with a deep fringe. She called to her husband, but he stood in conversation with a fellow in brocade waistcoat and buff hat, stroking a brace of pistols mounted with brass, nestling in a mahogany box. The boy joined them and ran a finger tentatively down a sleek barrel.

"How much?" Jabez heard him ask.

The man sized him up. "Too much for you, kid." The boy knotted his fists and scowled. Jabez remembered those years when it seemed forever before he'd be a grown man. He smiled to himself and turned away, feeling guilty for eavesdropping.

Ahead, an open-fronted tent sported a banner that read simply: BOOKS. Now here was a place Jabez could never pass by. Stacks of books teetered on tables, on the ground, in barrels. Maps hung from pins in the canvas walls. The bookseller stood at the entrance, rocking from heel to toe, a fat cigar stuck to his lower lip, hands jammed in his pockets. Jabez poked among the tables and lost himself in shuffling through the books, the tall woman and her friends forgotten. Novels and histories, classics and religious tracts, everything from Plutarch to medical texts to Mr. Barrington's *Kate Wynward* were piled in no discernible order. He picked up Cooper's *Dictionary of*

Surgery, but it was an older edition of one he already had, so he put it down.

He glanced toward the door to see the tall woman and the boy slip into the tent. The boy made a beeline for the maps, the woman for a barrel of novels. He watched her sideways, didn't want to distress her by staring, but he found himself curious about her selections. She picked over two or three, then leafed through a fourth. He was too far away to see what they were.

The boy was engrossed in the maps. He flattened the corners of an ancient chart depicting California as an island and read aloud the labels on another that divided the vastness of the north among tribes of Natives. Then he reached out a tentative finger and traced the route of the *Alhambra* past Rio de Janeiro and around Cape Horn at the southern edge of the world on a chart hand drawn on the back of a ship's bill of lading. The boy turned and beckoned to the woman.

Jabez strolled over to them. "I took that route," he said and touched a spot on the map labeled Tropic of Cancer. "We were blown off-course here by the wildest blow you'd ever want to see. Added a week and a half to the trip." He ran a hand down his trim beard and smiled.

"You rounded the Horn?" The boy tapped the tip of the southern continent.

"Oh, yes, that was the best part. Cold—cold as death and twice as frightful." Jabez pulled out another cheroot and a lucifer match, struck it on the rusty hoop of a barrel and lit up. "The whole company was sick for days, crew and all. Seas higher than the crow's nest." He embellished slightly, but the boy's face lit up.

"But you got through?"

"Obviously."

"And you were in California?"

"I was. Two years."

"You dig gold there?" The boy glanced back at the map where gold strikes were marked with exes.

"In a manner of speaking." Jabez held the cheroot away and knocked off ash. "I doctored in the camps." He moved to another map, one that showed the strikes around Sutter's Mill, and pointed. "Easy enough to let other men do the work and relieve them of their dust in return for services."

"But didn't you do some panning yourself?"

"Well, of course, no man can resist prospecting when there's gold washing out of the hills like snowmelt. But I like doctoring better."

Jabez enjoyed story-telling, and the boy was an eager audience, but the sun hung low, and The Beauty and her young man had joined them.

"Billy, come away," the tall woman said. "We still have purchases to make."

Jabez smiled and bowed to her. "Madam. You and your brother will find California delightful."

"Cousin, sir." She smiled at him. "And we do not plan to go on to California."

"Agnes, he's been there ... panned for gold and went around the Horn and everything!" The boy held out his hand. "Billy Canon," he said. "I'd sure be pleased to hear more."

"Jabez Robinson. I'd be pleased to tell you." He shook, then turned to the tall woman. Agnes.

She tipped her head. "Good day to you, sir."

"Hey!"

A shout from the bookseller and everyone whirled to the street. A commotion rose from the east end of the stalls. A half dozen boys scampered, eyes wide, faces flushed and laughing. Behind them a mule leaped and bawled, harnesses flying. Its back legs slammed against its wagon, skittering into a tent filled with tin goods. The driver disappeared beneath a cloud of canvas and a crash of pots and pans. The beast lurched into a row of barrels. Brine splashed, pickles flew, and the vendor screamed obscenities. Another wild roll of the haunches, a thrust of the hind legs, and books scattered. The redhead plucked The Beauty from the street. The mule planted its hooves straight-legged into the dust and shuddered to a stop within a foot of Agnes. Jabez could see the blood in its eye. She and the mule stared at each other. The mule snorted.

And then she reached out and grasped its bridle, whacked it hard with the flat of her hand between the eyes as if it were the old family plow mule. It wrenched its head, and the two young men grasped each cheek piece.

Jabez threw an arm about her waist and hauled her, none too gently, out of the way. Billy Canon twisted the ungainly head down and back, nose to withers. The mule quivered and nipped but could do no more than screak like a rusty-hinged door blown back and forth in a high wind. The driver appeared with a loop of rope. A toss about an ear and over the broad nose, and the protests subsided into brays and bleats and a wild rolling of the eyes.

The tall woman twisted out of his hold and scurried away, her cheeks a brilliant rose. His arm had remained about her waist a shade longer than necessary. Cigar clamped between his teeth in the midst of a broad grin, he applauded.

"Bravo, madam," he said, laughing. "And what were you planning to do with the beast once you had possession of it?"

Billy, breathing hard, narrowed his eyes at Jabez. The boy appeared possessive of his cousin's honor. "Agnes, that was mad. Don't ever do that again."

She glared at them both. "I'll act as I see, Billy Canon. I've handled mules before."

Billy grunted. He nodded curtly at Jabez and stalked away.

Agnes turned away, too, then back. "Thank you." She bobbed her head once. The sensation of her waist within his arm, her shoulders pressed against his chest, lingered. Tall as she was, her head had come to his chin.

He bowed deeply and smiled, watching her go.

4

Billy, who was Sam's son and at sixteen nearly a man, stood in the stern, balancing himself with one hand on the cabin roof, ready to push with a length of tree limb as John eased the flatboat away from the bank. Billy and Agnes made a team. She stood behind him, ready to loop the anchoring line as he pulled it in, dripping, across the widening gap. At the other end of the deck, Elizabeth and Tom waited, reeling in the bow line. Billy stabbed at a boulder and missed, and Agnes dropped the line to grip his shirt before he tipped into the river. He was solidly built like his father, though no more than her height. She couldn't have held him had he toppled.

He pulled back, red-faced, and grinned. "That's me, missing the mark."

"My life's tale," she murmured, looping the line.

Billy sent her a look and leaned over the rail again, jabbing his pole into the shallows as they swung into the current and headed west. Until Pittsburgh, Agnes had never visited a real city, and now she'd seen Cincinnati, with its massive buildings and high steeples and crush of noisy, odorous, fascinating travelers. Along with Billy, Elizabeth, and Tom, she'd toured the marketplace, marveled at the quantity of trade goods, ate chicken on a stick, encountered a peckish mule. And a strange man took liberties, thinking she was about to be stomped by that same mule, when all she did was treat it as she used to treat Maud, her papa's mule. Agnes only remembered him, the man that is, because he was so much taller than she was. Not many towered over her like he did. His eyes were as black as she'd ever seen and his beard reminded her of the otter pelt she'd found in the market. His voice carried the distinctive tones of northern New England, where the *Rs* disappear and one syllable words become two. His hands were browned by the sun, the fingers long and supple....

But she forgot him soon enough. All she could put her mind to was the next big town, St. Louis and maybe, some day, San Francisco—the world was opening up. Billy, besotted with the prospect of visiting new worlds, talked of little else. His mother, Rachel, feared he would take off for parts unknown before he was grown, and she held Agnes to account for his crotchet.

The days were long and sultry as they slid on down the Ohio, the sun high by seven in the morning and the western horizon colored lavender and peach at half past eight in the evening. The breeze over the river held its chill until noon but by dinner time they welcomed it as it kept off the flies and the heat of the sun. The evenings were fine and the breezes gentle, and Agnes loved to sit up after everyone else was abed, listening to night sounds. The boat bobbed against the shore like a cradle and fireflies darted in and out among the trees and caught in the tall grasses. Many a night, Elizabeth and Tom would wander into the forest with a blanket, to return with the dawn. Agnes often watched them go.

At Cairo they abandoned the flatboat and took passage on the *Belle Gould*, a sidewheeler with spark-spitting stacks and an odor of greasy cooking that permeated the cabins. The motion and the smells sent both Rachel and Elizabeth to their bunks. Rachel soon rallied, but Elizabeth remained closeted in the tiny cabin they shared with her two sisters, retching until there was nothing left to expel. Agnes spent her afternoons wetting cloths in the basin and folding them over her forehead.

"Your complexion needs attention, Lizzie," she said. "It's green."

Elizabeth groaned. "Don't tell me. The thought makes my stomach heave."

"Good thing Tom can't see you like this. There'd be no more wandering into the underbrush for you."

"Isn't that what put me into this predicament?" Elizabeth squeezed her eyes against another roll of the ship.

Agnes pulled back to look at her midsection. "No, really? You think so?"

"I'm sure of it. I've never been sick with motion before and I feel it in my breasts." She rolled to her side and took Agnes's hand. "A woman knows." She attempted a smile.

"Well." Agnes's breath hitched. A wisp of longing and something like jealousy seeped through her, but she pushed them aside. Elizabeth looked so afflicted.

"My dearest friend, I congratulate you." she said softly and massaged her temples. "Does Tom know?"

"No one knows but my mother. And Aunt Rachel. She guessed as soon as I began vomiting. I'll tell Tom once I'm presentable again." She heaved onto her back and dropped a limp arm over her eyes. "Thank goodness the men are bunking down in steerage. I couldn't face any of them right now. I wonder if they know how miserable they make us?"

"I could use a little such misery at times." Agnes stared out the tiny round window without seeing. "I watch you and Tom and wonder what it's like."

Elizabeth raised onto an elbow, a sly smile on her face. "When you put it like that, it really is worth it." She dropped back onto her pillow. "What's between a man and a woman in the privacy of their bed…." She giggled.

"I don't expect ever to find out."

"Many a woman would like your freedom."

"I can't imagine what it would be like to put myself at someone else's command. The way your mother does everything your father tells her. Including giving up her home and heading into the wilderness. You know she can't be happy about that."

"She's happy just being with Papa. She doesn't consider any other way. You and I will never be so domesticated."

Agnes took her hand. "You've domesticated Tom instead. He's more likely to do your bidding than you his."

"And I love him for it. What you need is a husband who will be your equal."

"Not much chance of a husband at all, at my age."

"There are ten men for every woman west of the Mississippi. They'll be tripping over themselves to get to you." She raised herself, clutching her belly, and swung her legs to the floor. "What about that man in Cincinnati? He had an eye for you."

"What man?" Agnes rinsed the basin into the slop bucket and poured a glass of water for her.

"The one at the book stall. He was exceptionally nice looking and was quick to get an arm around you."

"Too glib by far. And I'll never see him again, anyway." Agnes hadn't thought of him since, well, since last night, but she wasn't going to tell Elizabeth that.

"He was certainly no Richard Wiggins, tied down to his fusty old schoolhouse." Elizabeth took the water.

"No. He even smelled of, I don't know, something wild. Fresh."

"There will be others. Oh dear." She paled and sank back onto the bunk. "Leave for awhile, Cousin, won't you? Go roam the deck and investigate the passengers. There must be bachelors among them, don't you think?"

Agnes pulled a face and stood. "I'll send Sarah in with biscuits. You need to feed that child."

Elizabeth groaned, and Agnes left, shutting the door behind her.

Under the enervating June heat, the passengers on deck did little but sit while the *Belle Gould* steamed up the Missouri through a wilderness unlike the tame Ohio River Valley. Elizabeth continued ill and refused to eat so that her frock hung from her thin frame like a nightdress. Even the children suspended their romps and games and raised their voices only to be cross with one another.

Agnes turned her attention to the Missouri River itself, so often had she read of it in newspapers and fliers back home. Thick mud obscured its bed, snags lay in wait, and the current seethed around ghostly, half-submerged wrecks. Where the channel changed on the river's whim, tree roots drowned in the suffocating water, their skeletons washed into the flow. Sand emerged here and sank there so that even the most experienced pilot was often caught off guard. Mists hovered so thick on the river that the boat's crew frequently tied up for fear of catching on a newly formed sandbar or a hidden snag. Agnes didn't fancy sinking into those dirty waters, and at times believed the demands of the captain's schedule drove him up the river at real risk of disaster.

Two days out of Kansas Town, as the steamer picked her way through a fog into which she had no business venturing, the one-armed man from steerage appeared on the stairs and approached Agnes's family. The man was large, even taller than Agnes's father, and his empty right sleeve swung at his side. A coarse black beard sprouted from his neck, crept over his chin, across his cheeks and into his ears. Beard, brows and matted hair left little room for features, though Agnes felt in gazing on him that he gazed back and through her. Dressed in coat and pants surely never washed and boots with years of caked filth, he strode across the deck and glared down at the children. James, Nancy's eight-year-old, scuttled between his mother and Agnes, hiding among the folds of their skirts.

The one-armed man stuck out his left hand toward Sam. "Name's Bigelow," he said. "Reuben Bigelow."

Sam stood up from his deck chair, set down his coffee cup and took the hand. "Have a seat, Mr. Bigelow?"

"Naw." Bigelow propped himself against the rail, pulled out a plug and bit off a chaw. His scent permeated the cramped space.

"Coffee?" Rachel asked.

Bigelow grunted and shook his head.

Elizabeth, her complexion resembling a tinned oyster gone bad, pressed a hankie to her nose and mouth against his smell.

"That's Tom in five years," Agnes whispered to her. "The wilderness influence, you know."

She moaned and glared. Her sense of humor had not returned.

Sam swallowed his coffee. He set down the cup, and still Bigelow hadn't spoken.

"Something we can do for you, Mr. Bigelow?" he asked. "My young'uns been pestering you?"

"Understand you're looking for a place."

"Thought about settling along the Missouri. Maybe north of Independence. Not too far into Injun territory," Sam said.

"I got a place. Holt County. Hundert and fifty, sixty acres." He picked at his nose.

"Good farmland?" Sam asked.

"Sell it to you. Two dollars an acre."

"Improved any? Buildings?"

"Got a good enough house, I guess." Bigelow glared at the women, and they drew back from his smell as if it traveled toward them on the sheer force of his gaze.

"Are there settlements nearby?" No farmer, John planned to teach school or work at the law.

"Lick Creek's there."

"Lick Creek. Got a salt lick does it?" Sam asked.

"Naw. Folks named it thought the land warn't worth a lick."

"Huh." It was Sam's turn to be silent. He peered at Bigelow. Sam measured a man by his eyes, but Bigelow's hairy features nearly hid his.

Bigelow chewed and spit.

Rachel shuddered ever so slightly.

"Why do you sell?" Tom asked.

"Belonged to my wife's folk. Ain't got use for it; got a place of my own."

Sam stared over the river for a moment, then said, "Won't buy sight unseen."

"Seems fair." Bigelow stood up and offered his left hand again. "We can ride out of Kansas Town." He turned and towered over little James. His bulk blocked the light, and he looked down on the boy from his great height, his smell overpowering. He reached into a coat pocket.

James squeaked and sank against Nancy's knees.

When the big man's hand emerged it clutched something. He dropped it into James's lap and was gone.

The boy let out a rush of air and groped in the folds of his untucked shirt until he retrieved an arrowhead, finely chipped and fashioned of a deep black stone.

5

At Westport Landing, the group followed Bigelow off the steamboat and into Kansas Town, the village that threatened to take the overland traffic from Independence. Sam and John planned to leave the women and children in the settlement while they inspected Bigelow's farm. Kansas Town was Cincinnati *redux*, as joyfully unrefined but in its infancy. The fresh and clean juxtaposed with the filth of mud and animals. Raw, unfinished structures grew next to shanties in various stages of collapse, bustle and rush everywhere. The town crackled with its prime occupation and preoccupation, that of sending Americans across the plains and into the unknown. On Main Street alone, Agnes counted fourteen hand-lettered signs hawking indispensable goods for emigrants at the lowest prices. From the top of the high street she marked three wheelwrights' shops and two purveyors of canvas. Handbills tacked to a stable's wall advertised everything from oxen to Smith and Wesson revolvers to guides for hire.

Bigelow paraded them the length of the avenue, ankle deep in dust and powdered horse droppings, until they clustered before the only hotel. Two stories, stone below and wood above, painted a once-glorious red now washed by the sun, it promised crowded quarters, perhaps mattresses harboring bugs, but all that little concerned them. The sign captured their attention, faded but readable, above the central doors:

MISS FLORENCE'S
HOUSE OF PLEASURE

Nancy pinked and turned away, tugging at Sarah's sleeve. Rachel squeaked an "Oh, my," and covered her lips with her fingers. Elizabeth rolled her eyes at no one in particular and sank onto the top step, Tom squatting next to her. Agnes laughed, and John grinned at her. Sam turned to Bigelow.

"It's a bordello, man!" he snapped. "Would you have us leave our women here? For the love of God."

Bigelow's expression hid behind his beard, but he shrugged his massive shoulders, palm out.

"Only place in town, Mr. Canon," he said, "and besides—"

He was interrupted by a whoop and a bang as the front door slammed open and a woman hurtled out the doors and off the porch, flinging her arms around the huge man's neck and wrapping her legs about his torso.

"Reuben Bigelow—you're back!" and she planted a smacking kiss in the midst of that shaggy beard.

The beard parted in the first smile Agnes had seen from him, and he unwound the woman's arms. "Maggie girl! Ain't you looking grand?" He held her off enough to take her measure, up and down.

She sported a mane of the most unusual color, hennaed in streaks of varying shades ranging from cinnamon to carmine. Her complexion, resembling a fine-grained vellum with a spot of rouge on each cheek, betrayed her age as being somewhere beyond the forties. Her peasant blouse and skirt, the kind pictured in travel books as native to the Mexican states, showed off once-supple curves running to fat.

Bigelow beamed and slung his arm over the woman's shoulders, squeezing her to him.

"Maggie, I bring you a whole passel of boarders, but they're wanting a classy establishment, now. You convince 'em you're out of the business and run a respectable place."

Maggie stepped back and curtsied, holding her blue skirt with both hands. "Sure and I give up that life many a year ago, don't you mind that sign. I'm Maggie O'Day and I'm a reputable business woman. Just ask anybody here in town." She waved toward the street. "And besides, there ain't no other lodging between here and St. Joe. Come on along, you can inspect before you pay." She turned with swaying hips and disappeared through the wide doors.

Sam lifted his eyebrows at Rachel, who shrugged. John led Nancy by the arm and climbed the steps, and Agnes followed. She liked the look of this place, and the proprietor fascinated her. The others trailed after, Tom Kreek muttering that Maggie O'Day ought to be painting over the sign if she laid claim to respectability.

The interior, dark and blessedly cool, looked to be threadbare but dust free and painstakingly clean. Agnes imagined the red velvet and gold braid on the settees and at the window would do any Philadelphia hotel proud. A board floor blotched by years of spittle and clay was scrubbed to a sheen. Her stomach rumbled at the aroma of fresh bread and bacon. Rachel and Nancy inspected the rooms and found the beds clean with linens supplied— and no indication of single females in residence. That settled the question, and they signed their names in the book. Sam, John, Billy and Bigelow ate a quick lunch, stowed the baggage and returned to the steamer, heading north to Holt County and the town of Lick Creek. Tom remained behind to mind the women and children and because Elizabeth insisted.

That evening, Agnes tucked the children into their first real bed in weeks. No matter that the women and children shared a single room and two beds, as many to a bed as possible, they were true beds, with feather mattresses and sheets and a roof above that didn't rock and sway with the current.

"Agnes, is this our new home now?" Rebecca, Nancy's next-to-youngest, asked. A sleepy hand wound a honey-colored curl round and round.

"Not quite, darling, but we're close," she said, kissing the worried forehead. "Your pa will find us something very soon."

Elizabeth stood at the narrow window, watching Maggie's colored man lead a buggy horse across the yard. "Our new home," she murmured. The hand she laid on the window frame was thin, nearly translucent with the last of the evening light behind it.

"Elizabeth, come to bed. You're not well," Agnes said, touching her shoulder.

She shrugged her off and pulled away.

"I am perfectly well." She sent her a black look. "I'm tired, that's all. I'm tired of dirt and movement and of living amongst a crowd." She sank onto the bed and curled her arms about her knees. "I can't even be with my husband in the night." The hotel was crowded, and Tom shared a dormitory room with a dozen other men.

Agnes pulled the curtains against the growing dusk and lit a candle. The room was stuffy and close.

"I think it's poisoning me, Agnes," she said, her voice low, but not so low the other girls could not hear. Rebecca sat up, her eyes large and frightened.

"Your sister's only talking, sweetheart. There's nothing wrong with her."

"And how would you know?" Elizabeth flopped over, her back to Agnes, face to the wall. "You've never had something like this inside you. And you never will."

Agnes bit her tongue and sat on the bed undoing her boot laces. "That's no way to talk about a baby. What does your mother say?"

"She says it's what a woman must do. If I die from it, well, that's only my lot."

"Not very encouraging."

"You don't understand."

Agnes could scarcely hear her, she'd buried her face in the pillow. "It doesn't matter whether I do or I don't." She blew out the candle and slipped into her nightdress. "You are the only one who can lift your spirits."

Elizabeth stiffened beside her and didn't answer, and Agnes lay awake long into the night.

In the days of waiting that followed, Agnes became better acquainted with Maggie O'Day. The woman showed no shame about her history and seemed to care nothing for the opinion of anyone else. She displayed a natural talent for housewifery and especially for cooking; the smells from her kitchen that first day did not disappoint. They feasted on fried chicken and roast pork, fresh corn and wild grapes and blackberries. What she could do with blackberries! Blackberries and warm cream, blackberry pie, blackberry pastries, pancakes light and airy and covered with fresh butter and blackberries. Sweet potatoes and turnips were on her table at every meal, new peaches, plum puddings and milk for the children.

She fed the group and the other boarders with the help of one Negro girl and her man, who lived out back in a rough cabin of squared logs. The man stacked firewood and tended a capacious garden, milked the cow and did the odd jobs while the girl worked in the kitchen, scrubbed the floors and hauled the bath water. One day Agnes asked Maggie right out whether they were slaves.

"Servants, we say down here," she said. She stood at the oak table in the center of her kitchen, flour everywhere, rolling out circles for pies. Agnes watched her, balancing her mid-morning coffee and leaning against the window frame.

"But you own them?"

"'Deed I do. Pinched and set aside for years so as I could get a good pair." She looked up and gave Agnes a wry smile. "You Yankees don't approve, do you?"

"There is a great deal of objection where I come from to treating people as property."

"Think it's depraved, do you?"

"Certainly degrading. Both for the Negroes and for the owners."

Maggie scooped up a handful of flour and sprinkled it over her dough. "You think them darkies know about degraded? They was born degraded. It's their natural state." She leaned into the rolling again. "Now I ain't saying you can't raise yourself out of the degraded state given the right circumstances. You want to get out of that state you do it from the inside. You just set your mind to it."

She straightened and poked the rolling pin in Agnes's direction. "Just like women. Us women're born degraded, and it's up to us to untangle ourselves. Each and every one. Don't get no help from anybody else."

Agnes lowered her cup. "I don't believe I was born degraded."

"Sure you was. You're a woman, ain't you? All that fine education and what's it for? To serve a man, birth his babies, like your cousin there. She ain't feeling any too special just now." She peeled a round of dough from the tabletop and fitted it into a block-tin pie dish. "Poke up that fire, will you?" She nodded toward the stove.

Agnes did as asked and added a scuttle of peat.

"Now take me, for instance. I worked at a profession that most folk consider the worst a woman can do. I started out at fifteen to keep food in my belly and clothes on my back. It didn't make me no different than I was before, I figured. It don't degrade me if I don't let myself be degraded."

"But how did the men treat you? Didn't they treat you like ... well, like dross?"

"Sure, some of them did. Some of them hit me. Wanted to do worse. I just didn't allow it." She turned to face Agnes, leaned against the table and folded her floury arms over her chest. "To a man, a woman's biggest sin is selfishness and a woman who don't let herself be bounden to a man is selfish. That's all there is to it. I decided what was going to happen to me. No one else. It made me good money and it got me what I wanted." She gestured around her kitchen. "Here. Place of my own, place where I can cook, which is what I love most to do." She smiled wickedly and laid a finger along her cheek, leaving a wide streak of white. "Even more than I love to roll around with a man."

"What about children? Surely they must have come."

"Didn't want any so didn't have them. I know how to be rid of that sort of trouble. Fact is, I could help your cousin in that way if she was a mind to."

Agnes wondered if her complexion drained away, because Maggie chuckled at her and turned back to her pies, stirring coarse white sugar into a mix of rhubarb and wild strawberries.

"No," Agnes said. "I don't think there will be any need for that kind of intervention."

"Tell the truth, I had a baby once. Didn't get to it in time, so thought I'd see what it was like. It was a girl so I give it away. If it'd been a boy I might have kept it. Can't imagine why any woman'd want a daughter, knowing what's in store for her."

"You might have taught your daughter what you've learned."

"It's a rare woman who can do what I done. Made myself up, I did. My name ain't Maggie O'Day, just something I made up when I was ready to be somebody else. Hell, I ain't even Irish. Made myself French, once, called myself Marie Saint Ives. But I couldn't say it like the Frenchies do, got caught out by one of them French traders from up north. So I changed it again."

Agnes shook her head. "You're a caution, Maggie." She nodded out the window, where the black man was wielding a hoe. "You freed yourself, why not free them?"

Maggie glanced up, her expressive face now a mask. "There's freedom and there's freedom. They tried to make a slave out of me and I wouldn't let them." She folded a top crust over heaping berries and picked up a knife to crimp the edges into a delicate ruffle. "Let the Nigras figure it out for themselves."

How might they figure it out for themselves, Agnes later wondered as she watched the Negro girl clean the front parlor, when they're not allowed to learn to read nor take leisure time for study? Perhaps, individual by individual, the world would someday change. Meanwhile, Agnes struggled for her own brand of freedom. Her sin, the selfishness of independence.

6

Sam and John, with Billy trailing behind, trudged up the muddy path from the steamboat landing in Kansas Town. Billy was full of tales of the river trip and the farm they'd found and couldn't wait to tell Agnes. And Elizabeth, if she'd listen. He knew if Lizzy hadn't been sick and made Tom stay behind, his pa would have left him with the women. And Jesus, that would have been boring. He wondered what the heck Tom had done the whole time they were gone, over three weeks. Lizzy wasn't in any shape to keep him entertained. But Agnes, he knew, would have explored the town and searched out anything of interest, and he wanted to hear about it.

But even before they got to the hotel, his pa sent him off to scout out mules and wagons for the trip north. Sam decided to buy the animals in town and go overland to Holt County. He'd need the animals on the farm, and it'd save steamboat fare. John went along with the idea, and Billy noticed that John usually agreed with Sam. Billy didn't and all too often had to bite his tongue.

It took three days to round up the wagons, pack their goods and head north, which gave Billy and Agnes plenty of time to catch up. They left Kansas Town and ferried across the Missouri, heading cross country toward a settlement called St. Joseph on a track through the prairie grasses. There were plenty of birds, prairie hens and wild turkey, quail and geese. Billy, walking along next to the rear wagon, kept his Kentucky rifle in one hand. He was a good shot, better than Sam even, and he brought in a brace of quail and one of the big Canada geese on the second day. That was the day they passed through fields of hemp and tobacco worked by Negroes, the first field slaves Billy had ever seen. The slaves watched the group pass with blank eyes, their movements automatic, with the mildly curious attitude of a herd of milch cows in pasture. Agnes, walking beside him along the dusty track, stared back at them until they'd passed them by.

"Maggie O'Day said they're born degraded," she said, "and it's up to them to raise themselves up, figure out freedom on their own." She pushed her bonnet back and swiped at her sweaty forehead with a hanky. "How can people treated like cattle possibly figure it out for themselves?"

Billy walked backwards to watch the field hands move slowly along the rows of crops. He remembered stories his ma told of Negro slaves in Maryland, where she grew up. The idea of being owned, or owning another human being, gave him a sick feeling.

Early in the evening of the third day they pulled the wagons into a grove above a creek and set the mules and the milk cow—named "Maggie" with much giggling by the younger children—free to graze the prairie grasses. The mood of the family was hushed and reverent, feeling the vastness and emptiness of the plains. The oaks and beeches around them were of another time, ageless, impervious, dwarfing them beneath their fat limbs and imposing trunks.

Soon as the mules were unhitched and hobbled, Billy grabbed his rifle and slipped into the high prairie grass along the creek. The grove of trees bent away from the creek and opened up, making for good turkey habitat, and it wasn't long before he heard them. He moved back to the trees, slipping from one to another until he located the sound and plotted his movements. He'd learned early on that turkeys could spot movement from a long way off, and once they did, they'd be gone.

A big tom strutted from behind a rocky ledge and Billy froze. The tom pecked and gobbled, turned tail and wandered back behind the rock, and Billy sank slowly to the ground, his back against a big tree. He was hidden now, as well as he could be. The tom wouldn't see his silhouette.

He brought his gun to his knee, stock to his shoulder and sighted. And waited. The tom reappeared, his neck stretching out and pulling back. Billy counted, one, two, then the neck stretched again and he shot. Clean shot, perfect. Right through the neck. Dinner enough for the whole crew. He wished his Pa had seen that shot.

Evening had faded by the time they finished their turkey feast, the fire banked to a glow that shone on the cool blackness beneath the trees. The children huddled together for warmth in makeshift beds near the wagons, Sarah and Agnes on either end of a little row of warm bodies. Billy rolled up in his blanket on bare ground away from the others, relishing the silence and the solitude of the dark. Over the fire, off through the tangled branches of the trees, a great white light rose, coloring silver and purple the scraps of cloud that hung on the eastern horizon.

Billy dozed; embedded rocks made for cranky sleeping. Something, a sound in the night that jarred, combined with the stiffness of limbs waked him. He sat up, trying to pierce the blackness left behind by the setting moon, now low in the western sky, its light no longer penetrating. He reached for his boots. A mule nickered behind the wagons, another responded. They moved restlessly, blowing and stamping. By the wagons, a deeper blackness moved, a stick cracked, and a figure muttered "Hell," under his breath. John.

"Billy's the best shot," he was saying. "Get him up."

Billy was already up, pulling his rifle from the wagon. The way the mules were acting, there was something out there.

Agnes scrambled out of her quilt, tugging on her boots. Trust Agnes not to miss the excitement, Billy thought. Sam struck a match and lit a shaded lantern. The light caught her eyes, dancing with excitement.

"What is it?" Her whisper, loud in the night chill, made Sam jump.

"Quiet," Sam said to her, low under his breath. "Stay here." He motioned to Billy to follow and headed for the creek. Agnes ignored Sam's order and trailed along.

"What is it?" Billy asked, low as he could. He needed to know what he was up against. If it was one of those big cinnamon-colored bears, a grizzly, the kind that rose eight feet tall on their hind legs, they'd be in trouble.

"It's big," John said. "I can hear it down by the creek. The wind's blowing its scent up here. The mules know it's there, but it may not have spotted them yet."

"It must be on the other side," Billy said. "It doesn't know we're here yet." He'd gone into hunter mode, stealthy and silent on the carpet of duff underfoot. Sam and John fell into single file behind him, and Agnes brought up the rear. The animal moved carelessly, not as if it were on the hunt, brushing against the dry leaves that covered streamside brambles. The brass fittings on Billy's rifle glinted, the darkened lantern sending just enough light in front of his feet to keep him from stumbling.

The animal had sensed them now, and Billy could almost feel its tenseness, its surprise. He brought the rifle to his shoulder. They knew where it was, in a thicket not two dozen yards away, but they could see nothing. The brambles did not stir. It was motionless in the last of the moonlight. Then Sam drew off the lantern's hood, and the wide circle of light swung out over the stream and through the undergrowth. A glimpse of a long tawny body frozen in a crouch, ears pricked forward, glowing eyes blinded by the strangeness of the lantern lighting up out of all its experience. Then a *rowr*, surprised, challenging, and a leap and a scramble through the bushes, the swish of a long and sinewy tail, and the majestic cat was gone, like an apparition, through the shadows of high prairie grass.

They let out their breaths as one. Billy looked at them, shamefaced. "I couldn't shoot," he said. "Never saw anything like it before."

Agnes touched his arm. "I'm glad—"

"Shoulda taken your chance," Sam snapped and stalked off. Billy glared after him.

"I'll build up the fire," John said. "Billy, build another one over the other side of the mules for fear it circles back. Keep that rifle handy and stay awake."

Billy and Agnes gathered up an armful from the pile of sticks the children had collected, and they soon had a blaze going at the far edge of the grove. He sat in the fire's light on bare ground, rifle next to him, hands dangling between his knees and sulked. "Nothing's ever good enough for him." He glowered at the flames.

Agnes squatted next to him and poked at a log. "Every sixteen-year-old since Cain has complained about his pa not understanding him."

"That doesn't help."

"I know, but don't let him put you out of sorts. He's proud of you, you know. He couldn't say enough about the turkey."

"He said exactly three words: 'Nice job, son.'"

"Well, for Sam, that's downright voluble."

They were quiet.

"At any rate, I'm glad you didn't shoot it. I've never seen such a magnificent animal."

"It was something, huh? I like to hunt, and I'm good at it, but sometimes, I just can't pull the trigger." He leaned over to the wood pile, picked up a branch and threw it in. "Last fall I was hunting up along Frazer's Ridge, you know that place back behind Hans Meuer's spread? I was by myself and I couldn't find a deer to save my life. Not a track, no scat, nothing. I stopped to take a—" he caught himself and looked at Agnes sideways. "Well, to take a break, and when I looked up there was a stag standing there, top of the ridge, outlined against the sky. Must have been ten points on that rack, six feet across. I never saw anything so big in my life. And it was staring at me, just standing up there staring. And I couldn't move. I had my rifle in my hand and couldn't aim it." He glanced over at Agnes with a half smile. "After a while he turned around and disappeared over the ridge. I went home empty-handed." He looked back at the fire. "Couldn't kill it."

Agnes squeezed his shoulder. "That means you're a civilized man, Billy. You can pick and choose. You did the right thing then and the right thing tonight." She pushed herself up, using his shoulder for a boost. "Your pa'll see it that way tomorrow, you wait."

"No, he won't, but Ma will." He grinned, in humor again. "She'll bring him around."

"Good-night then, Billy. Keep us safe from beasties."

"Night, Agnes."

He watched her until she slipped back into her bedroll next to Rebecca, then threw another branch on the fire. Sparks shot up into the treetops. The beech trunks, wrinkled and enduring, looked soft to the touch in the firelight. He wondered what they had seen, here in this grove. Maybe other travelers, maybe the ancient people who roamed these plains, untold generations passing by, coming and going year after year. He listened for sounds of the cougar, but there was nothing but the peepers at the creek and the occasional buzz of a mosquito. He dozed by the fire, the predawn air chill. His head snapped up at a rustle in the camp, and he saw Agnes leave her bedroll again and make her way to the creek.

He waited a few minutes, to give her time to do her business, but when she didn't return he rose and followed her to the creek's edge. The footing was tricky, but the darkness was melting into that subtle grayness that was no longer night but not yet dawn, and he found her sitting cross legged on the top of a mossy boulder, her hands tucked beneath her armpits for warmth. She looked down at him and patted the rock next to her, so he climbed up, folded his legs and wiggled until he was comfortable. From where they sat they could see over the prairie to the east, back toward Pennsylvania and civilization. The black of the sky overhead shaded into deepest blue, then into rich azure at the horizon. A single star hung in the east, its brilliance fading. A faint line of red-gold grew, low down along the tops of the grass.

"It's daylight in Pennsylvania," she said. "Papa will be in the barn doing the milking. Mattie's slopping the pigs. She hates that job but there's no one else to do it." She wrapped her arms around her knees.

"You sorry you came?" Billy said.

"Not at all. I miss them. But I'll see them again, some day." She glanced at him. "And now I need to do this."

"Yes, you do." He took her hand and squeezed it, let go. "I'm glad you're here."

7

August 1852

A welcome mizzle of rain had begun falling in late afternoon when Jabez arrived at the roadhouse along the east bank of the Missouri. He was on the return trip to Ohio, with a ticket on the next day's steamboat for Kansas Town. He'd spent most of the past two months in northwest Missouri, in the town of Lick Creek, finding a home, buying the basics, re-establishing his medical practice.

He'd discovered Lick Creek back in '43, when he thought Eliza was lost to him and he left Columbus at loose ends. It was brand new back then, two years a town, and already cholera was showing its ugly presence. His services were sorely needed, though he wasn't fully credentialed, and he'd set up practice with Doctor Norman.

Two years later the army called, his own restlessness called louder, and he took ship for the southwest and the war for Mexican territory. But he always hoped to return to Holt County when it was time to settle, and in the back of his mind he never let go of the idea that Eliza would be with him when he did.

A figure met him at the roadhouse door, arms folded over a stout belly. *"Fastyr mie!"* Henry Banks's voice echoed across the yard in the accents of the Isle of Man. "Ye're welcome, Doctor, welcome," he said and thrust out his hand.

Jabez shook and swung his cases inside the door. The welcome aroma of boiling beef and hot coffee wafted out. Henry always had the stew pot on and never failed to give him a hearty welcome. He'd been one of Jabez's first patients nine years ago when the cholera struck. One of the lucky ones.

They entered into a smoky warmth, lit by lantern and cook stove, damp and humid in the August rain. A heavy table ran the length of the space, two men sitting on benches and shoveling stew into their mouths with hunks of black bread. Jabez recognized them, Ora Juwitt from up by Hemme's Landing, and Willard Bigelow from Lick Creek. Both of them very young, both of them trouble, both of them already half-drunk.

He ignored them, nodded to a stranger tipped back in a chair by the door pulling on a pipe, and sat to table, ravenous. By the time he finished, dusk had fallen and Henry had lit a fire in the hearth to chase away the damp. The sounds of wagons and the creak of harness drifted in under the steady drum of rain, signaling more guests. It would be a crowded night. Jabez retreated to a dark corner by the fireplace and pulled out a cigar.

Henry checked the stew pot, grabbed a lantern and opened the door.

"Have you shelter?" Jabez heard a man's deep voice, "and a hot meal?"

"You can bunk in the barn. Ladies in the storeroom," Henry said. Ladies. That meant all the men would be bunking in the barn, Jabez thought. Sounded like lots of them.

They crowded into the single room, blinking and stretching and filling the space. The stranger slipped out behind them, the two drunk boys ogled the women.

There must have been four or five women and a gaggle of kids. One of the women, taller than the others, dropped onto the bench and looked dumbly about her. Jabez started. He recognized the woman from Cincinnati, the book stall. And her friend, the black-haired beauty.

"There, you, Juwitt, and you, Willard, off ye go, make room for the ladies!" Henry flourished a butcher knife so expertly about their ears that the two boys scrambled away from the table without protest, taking their flask with them. Henry was an amiable host, and he set the women and children to table in quick order, placing steaming beef and vegetables in front of them.

The warmth of the food went a long way toward reviving the younger travelers, but the older women were visibly tired, almost crotchety. The black-haired woman was no longer quite so lovely, her face pale and drawn, her eyes dull in the firelight. The tall woman, Agnes, he remembered, began to look about her with interest, and for some reason he pushed back into the shadows, his features hidden. He kept an eye on Juwitt and Willard, though. Willard's eyes, the color of newly-dead fish, were glued on the black-haired woman. Jabez drew on his cigar, and Agnes glanced toward him and then away.

The women had nearly finished eating, the children yawning, by the time their men came in from settling their stock. Jabez recognized the red-haired boy, married to the Beauty, and Billy. And to Jabez's surprise, Reuben Bigelow followed, bringing with him that particular odor which trailed along with him wherever he went. Jabez liked Reuben. The big one-armed man was a character around Lick Creek, uneducated, rough, ready for a fight, but good-hearted under all. Jabez wondered if Willard was there to meet his pa or if it was just the boy's unlucky day.

Bigelow leaned over to light a straw at the fire, touched it to the pipe clutched in his teeth, drew deep. "Henry," he said, "This here's the Canon clan." The big man turned from the fire, made to introduce the men around and caught sight of the boys against the wall. So, Willard's unlucky day. Reuben's single hand rose slowly and pulled the pipe from his mouth. "Wil Bigelow," he said, the sound low and deep in his chest. "What you doing here, boy?"

The boy shrank away. "Hey Pa," he said and laughed, a high cackling sound.

Bigelow dropped his pipe and wrenched the flask from Willard's fist. "Ain't I told you keep away from this stuff?" He threw the flask across the room. "And you, Juwitt. I told you keep a distance from my boy." With a massive paw he grasped his son's shirt collar and lifted him clean off the floor, hustled him to the door and planted a boot on the boy's behind. Willard landed face-first in the mud of the dooryard.

"In the barn and sleep it off," Bigelow called after him. "You'll go home with me tomorrow so's I can keep my eye on you." The boy scrambled to his feet and scuttled into the darkness.

One of the children whimpered, no one else ventured a sound. Bigelow scowled at Mr. Banks.

"Henry, why in hell you let him come in here and drink?"

"*Yeesey*, let with, man, let with. I'll not be minding your boy for ye."

"Nothing but trouble, that one," Bigelow said. He stared at the floor and then drew in a long breath. "Well now!" and slapped his hand on the table. "You've food for a traveler, eh?" He helped himself to the stewpot.

While the new arrivals settled down to dinner, Jabez stood, pitched the butt of his cigar into the fireplace, settled a hat on his head and headed for the barn. He felt Agnes watching him as he left. He chose an empty stall with particularly clean straw and rolled up in his blanket. Willard, stretched out just inside the door, already snoring; Juwitt followed not long after. Jabez settled in and slept.

A woman screamed and Jabez was on his feet before he was fully awake. Around him men were scrambling out of bedrolls. The red-haired boy, the one married to the Beauty, was out the door first, in his stocking feet, blundering through the deep darkness towards sounds of scuffling in the barnyard.

One of the Canon men lit a lantern. Willard was over by the privy, grappling with a woman, the redhead's wife. The husband grabbed him by the shoulder and spun him around, swung a fist. Willard ducked. Then the boy, Billy, was on Willard, yanking him to his feet, pinning his arms behind him.

The woman trembled, her bodice torn and her eyes glazed in the lamplight. A man Jabez figured to be her father went to her and wrapped her in his arms. "Go ahead, Tom," he said. "Fetch him a lesson."

The men formed a circle around the three boys, their silhouettes dancing in the glare of the lantern. Billy grasped Willard while Tom swung and connected with Willard's chin. Jabez heard a distinct crack. Tom nursed his knuckles and breathed hard, then sunk his fist into the boy's belly. Willard doubled over, and Billy hauled him upright again.

Reuben stood at the edge of the light, left arm across his chest, hand gripping his empty sleeve, breathing hard, face unreadable behind his beard. Juwitt stood next to him, swaying, the vacant look of a far-gone drunk on his face. The watchers kept silent while Tom got off a blow to the ear and another that must have blacked an eye. Billy let Willard sink into the mud. Then the girl's father stepped into the light and clasped Tom's shoulder.

"That's enough now," he said. "I guess he's been taught."

Tom reached with bloody hands for his wife and pulled her against his chest. Jabez turned to see Agnes, wide-eyed, standing right next to him.

"Boy's drunk as a boiled owl," he said to her. "Help get her inside, but keep her next to a window. She needs fresh air." His medical bag was in the barn, but he didn't think he'd need it.

"What did he do to her?" Agnes asked. She turned toward him and her eyes widened still further; she'd recognized him.

"He didn't hurt her, too drunk to do much. He's a trouble maker and can't hold his liquor, but he's harmless."

In the strange light, dull red blotches hollowed the Beauty's cheeks against a pasty complexion. Tom lifted her, carried her into the inn, Jabez following with Agnes trailing after. Tom lowered himself to the bench, settling his wife on his lap. Jabez knelt next to them and took her hand. He held her wrist, touched her forehead with the tips of his fingers.

"I'm a doctor, ma'am," he said. "Are you dizzy?"

She nodded.

"Elizabeth," Agnes said. "Her name's Elizabeth."

"Have you been bleeding, Elizabeth?"

She stared at him blankly, then shook her head.

"Cramps? Nausea?"

She sighed, closed her eyes and shrugged.

"You need rest and fresh air, but you'll be all right. You've had a scare." He stood. "How far along is she?" he asked Agnes.

"I beg your pardon?"

"She's with child. Do you know how far along she is?"

Tom spoke up. "At least three months. Maybe closer to four." He rocked Elizabeth, nestling her head against his shoulder. "It wears on her mind. It's changed her something fierce."

"Not unusual. Childbirth on the frontier can affect a woman like that." Jabez looked back at Agnes. "Her first one?" She nodded. "She's strong. She'll do all right if she gets some rest."

"We'll be there tomorrow. At the farm, I mean," Agnes said. "The journey will be over."

"Well, maybe you'll call on me when it's time." He turned to Tom and stuck out his hand. "Name's Robinson, Jabez Robinson. I'm going to Ohio to fetch my wife, but I'll be back before the baby comes."

"Tom Kreek." Tom took his hand briefly.

Jabez turned to Elizabeth, touching her forehead again. "No fever. She needs to sleep. See if you can't get some fresh air into this room." He turned to the door. "Don't worry about the boy. Reuben will handle him." He stopped for a moment and looked at Agnes. "Good night."

He turned back into the night. The rain had stopped but a heavy mist muffled the night. The barnyard had emptied. A smile tugged at the corner of his mouth as he thought about the tall chestnut-haired woman, remembered the feel of his arm around her waist. So the group is settling in Lick Creek, he thought. Life is full of strange coincidences.

8

Lick Creek perched between timber and prairie, rising from the roll of the earth, the roofs of its buildings low to the ground. Heat shimmered over boardwalks as they approached from the west and swung along the north side of the town square, the street deep in dust, past frame and brick buildings, some white-washed, some ramshackle. A large fresh-built courthouse dominated the square. Agnes noticed a forge, two stores, a saloon. The sound of an out-of-tune piano floated from a home at the far edge of town, a lace curtain fluttered from an open window. Then they were through the little settlement and out the other side.

They moved through a landscape drooping in August heat, underlain by the scent of fertile prairie soils and the muted tints of grasses. The wrinkles in the land smoothed, and a broad plain rolled before them. In the center of an untilled meadow, a homestead nestled in a swale. The house of unplaned logs, with deep overhangs, faced south, the sunlight picked up the honeyed gold of peeled wood. The barn united two substantial structures under a single roof, a courtyard in the center. The lone tree, a weather-beaten maple casting a pool of welcome shade, overspread the yard.

Agnes, riding in the front wagon behind Sam and Rachel, felt like an intruder as her cousin reined in the team and twisted to face his wife. His profile was impassive, but his left hand twitched against his knee.

Rachel sighed, surveyed the scene before her. Agnes thought about the clapboard house Rachel had left behind, painted white, with shutters and a second story. But her husband wanted a new start in this rough place, and so she would want it, too. Rachel's forehead relaxed and her eyes crinkled about the corners. "It's beautiful, isn't it, Sam?" she whispered. "I love the distances. I think we will do fine here." Sam's shoulders relaxed. He lifted the reins and clicked to the mules. Agnes let out the breath she didn't know she'd been holding. She wanted Rachel to like it, she wanted them all to like it, because the prairie was the most beautiful place she'd ever seen.

Religion. Agnes always marveled at how inexorably it followed folks wherever they went, and more, how no single religion would do. Wherever half-a-dozen families congregated, at least three different religions sprang up, neighbors and acquaintances classified by denomination. In Lick Creek, the Baptists met in a tent by the cemetery southeast of town and no matter the weather, baptized the congregation in the clear, frosty creek that flowed through the high plateau. Their revival style reached fever pitch one summer when the Reverend Joab Powell came through, saving souls by preaching damnation. For six weeks that summer, the faithful flocked to meeting through the sticky Missouri nights. Then one day they found him dallying with the daughter of Mr. Foster, the lawyer, and he with a wife rumored to be waiting in St. Joe. The spell broke, and the good Baptists of Holt County turned on their preacher and drove him out, an indication of how quick to turn these people are, like a summer storm that comes up in no time at all.

The Reverend Mr. William Fulton preached the Old School Presbyterian and never gave the townsfolk reason to find fault. Mr. Fulton owned the only ice-cream freezer in town, and the Sunday afternoon ice cream socials in the Presbyterian churchyard brought everyone together, Baptists, Calvinists, Methodists, even a few atheists.

The Methodists were a divided group with the Germans meeting in the old log school building that was condemned for classes but good enough for German Methodists. Their hymns, muffled in frosty air by the improperly chinked logs, rang familiar, though the guttural German words rumbled as if they spoke in tongues.

The Methodist Episcopal service was the one Agnes's family chose, and, upon arrival, they nearly doubled the size of the congregation. Agnes later discovered that the townspeople eagerly awaited the first Sabbath to see

41

which of the denominations they would choose. She understood bets were placed around Ed Poor's forge.

As their wagon crawled into town that first Sunday, Agnes saw a face at a window, a man in a door, the flicker of a curtain. On the boardwalk, a smallish woman who seemed to have been drawn from a collection of circles—round face, round shoulders, full brown skirt, round black hat—leaned on a cane as they passed. Agnes pasted on a smile, but the round woman didn't smile back, instead watching them with the judging look in her eyes Agnes had come to recognize as particularly Missourian. Missourians were a judging race, she'd decided. Rachel nodded to the woman, Nancy fussed with the baby, Elizabeth had refused to come. Agnes held on to her rigid smile as the wagon plodded down the street.

The Episcopal Methodists met at that time in William Zook's store. Zook's Mercantile was weathered clapboard, dusty and dim after the brilliance of August's sunshine. Inside, figures materialized out of the comfortable gloom, roosting on planks placed between crates and barrels or leaning against the walls among stacks of goods. The folk gathered for the Methodist service were like the little round woman: shades of brown and black, unreadable faces that showed neither curiosity nor interest. Not much warmth here, but no coldness either. Talk was subdued, half-whispered. Men shuffled in the dimness, and additional planks materialized. Women shifted on their seats. Children, cross-legged on the floor, appraised each other as their tribe will, one step removed from a pack of dogs sniffing about a newcomer. The Canon and Jackson women settled onto benches, their men blending into the group against the wall. The bustle quieted. No one spoke.

"Let us pray. Amen." The Reverend Marvin's white face floated in the gloom behind the counter. "Dear Father, grant us thy blessings on this thy day of rest." His voice trilled thin and high, not the booming voice the preacher at home had used to pin his congregation to their seats of a Sunday. "Bless this harvest that we are gathering." His Adam's apple worked above a limp white collar, his black suit merged into the shadows. His hands, long and bony, smoothed the leather cover of his hymnal, stroking up and out in rhythm with his words. "And bless these good townsfolk…." Agnes turned her head to the side and slit her eyes open to peer around the room without seeming to raise her head. Several of the women used the same method to survey the newcomers. These were to be their neighbors, maybe friends, maybe not.

"And bless the newcomers in our midst, for they shall bring us strength and new blood to wrench our homes from the wilderness. Amen."

"Amen," the congregation said.

"The doxology, please." The Reverend Marvin shifted his view from the counter to the ceiling, his eyes sliding over the congregation, and lifted his hands before him, fingers resting together, the tips just touching his chin.

The singing echoed. Someone along the wall had a fine voice, deep and resonant.

Praise father son and ho-lee ghost.

James dropped his black arrowhead, and Nancy laid a hand on his head.

Ahh-

The bass voice in the back was very low, more a rumble than a note.

me-e-e-nnn.

This congregation loved the Amen.

Agnes settled onto the hard plank. She understood Methodists and knew the sermon to come. There was a saying in Pennsylvania, whenever it blizzarded no one was out but crows and Methodist preachers. The Reverend E.M. Marvin was predictable, comfortable, dependable. Agnes was glad they hadn't chosen the Baptists.

9

That fall, Agnes often turned to the land in her moments of solitude, the feel of it, the smell of it, the excitement and the life in it. She sensed in the fields and meadows of her new frontier home a long-term promise. As autumn moved in, it became a land of brilliance and brightness, the trees jeweled towers of red and gold, lingering on and on under a sky startlingly azure, the stars almost touchable.

Then the heavy cloud cover moved in, weighed down and pressed them into their cabin. The wind drove out of the west filled with prickles of ice to sting faces and tear at clothes. The creek was rimmed with ice, delicate traceries surrounding half-submerged branches and whiskery reeds, crackling out from the bank so that each morning's drawing of water required more care, boots braving the frigid mud, foot prints frozen in place for the season. Then one late evening, the snow arrived.

Day after day, the Great Snow of '52 blew in. It began the sixth day of December, trapping everyone indoors like beavers in a frozen lodge. John, whose family lived in the front half of the barn, strung a rope from house to barn and from house to privy. The children, particularly James, who hatched scheme after scheme of escape, were forbidden to go out alone for any reason. The snow refused to relent, forming hills where there were none, wind-sculpted swirls that climbed to the window sills. They rationed hay for the animals and wood for the stove and persevered as best they could.

By Christmas week Rachel was drawn and thin, Nancy snappish with the children, Sam even more silent than his wont. On those rare days when the storm abated for an hour or two, Billy disappeared, rifle against his shoulder, on snowshoes crafted from hickory and buckskin. But game was scarce. John buried himself in books, and by Christmas had read through all they owned only to begin again. Elizabeth's waist thickened, her clothes tented about her, the light in her dark eyes gone, her hands resting heavily in her lap. They tired of the snow, tired of the perpetual dusk, tired of each other. The days sidled by, maddeningly similar, agonizingly dull. Agnes read, plied her needle, and waited.

Then the storms ceased and the nights began to retreat, and there were days when the temperature soared with false spring, and sap began to rise in both maples and humans. On one of those days in early February the school board rode to the farm in search of a new schoolmaster. William Zook led them, head uncovered in the balmy air, wispy hair lifting in the breeze, a small brown mare struggling with his weight. Levi Zook, brother to William, rode next alongside Peter McIntosh, proprietor of the town's rival store, who spoke to the Zooks only on school business. Another man whom Agnes did not know rounded out the delegation. She sat on the porch, peeling last year's potatoes, reveling in the sunshine, and watched them trot down the hillside, a welcome sight. John, splitting wood by the big maple, stopped to greet them.

"John, morning," said William Zook. He nodded to Agnes and began the descent from horseback. He reminded her of an old mama bear backing out of her honey tree.

The others waited and watched. The business would commence only when William was safely aground.

"Morning, William." John put out his hand, tipped his hat to the others. "Levi. Peter."

"Rufus Byrd, Mr. Jackson. Pleased." The stranger stretched out his hand.

"Womenfolk survive the storms all right?" William pulled a stumpy cigar from an inside pocket.

"Yes they did, thank you kindly. Won't you step in? Have some coffee?"

"No, no, we've come on a bit of business." William bit off the end of the cigar, turned his head, spit. He searched for a light.

"William, you'd leave a man to freeze before you'd think to bring a match." Levi produced a match from an inside pocket and struck it against his boot sole.

Cigar lit, William took a deep breath, let it out slowly. Everyone waited.

"We're thinking you would be the best man for the school," William said, through a curtain of smoke. "Young ones are appearing in Lick Creek faster than flies on carrion."

"Mr. Collins is yet the schoolmaster, I thought," John said.

"Aye, that's so, but we've too many for him now. He'll stay at the Mad Dog Creek schoolhouse over west of town while we start up another for the families here in east county."

Mr. Byrd chimed in. "The authorities in Jeff City's taxing us for education, so by God we're going to spend our money here!" He seemed to be an excitable little man, who, despite the warm day, kept his round head wrapped in a furry cap, leaving his long narrow neck exposed.

"Well, I'd be pleased to look into the situation," John said slowly. "Do you foresee a full term?"

"Soon as the roads are passable we can get you twenty scholars," said Levi. "That's a dollar a scholar a month. Twenty dollars." He beamed. That was a substantial wage.

"'Course they'll be needed for spring plowing in April," said William. He coughed, inhaled again, let out the smoke with a soft aahhh.

"And you can do your lawyering at the same time," said Mr. Byrd. "There's a right nice house up close against the school that I can let you have for a nominal sum."

John looked from one to the other. "Make it one dollar fifty a scholar," he said. "I'll need Miss Canon to assist."

Three-fourths of the school board looked to William Zook, who took his time with the next puff on his cigar.

"Think we could do that, yes sir," William said, and they all looked to Agnes. She smiled, raised the hand that held the paring knife in a half-salute. The men shook hands all around, William Zook tossed the last of his cigar into a melting bank of snow where it sizzled, stuck his foot back in the stirrup and grasped the pommel of his saddle. He threw a leg over the old brown mare, and off they went, back to town.

John turned to Agnes and grinned. "Looks like we're in business."

When John and Agnes first opened their schoolroom on a late winter morning, they found thirty-odd scholars squirming or sprawling or abiding quietly on scarred oak benches. The Jackson children took their places, the girls still and expectant, James carving at the seat with the point of his arrowhead. Billy, hands jammed in his pockets, stood with Agnes against the wall at the side of the room.

Reuben Bigelow, taking full advantage of the new public education system, sent a whole passel of children to Mr. Jackson's classroom, probably as much to remove them from the house during the season of enforced idleness as to educate them. An older boy slumped at one end of a bench twirling a whittling knife between his fingers, five stair-step brothers and sisters lined up next to him. A muslin shirt stretched across his broad chest, meaty wrists protruded from unbuttoned cuffs, a thick shock of blond hair slicked to one side. His teeth tumbled one against another like neglected tombstones. He looked to be fifteen or sixteen, so tall that when he'd entered the classroom, he needed to duck his head at the door.

Billy nudged Agnes and nodded toward a lanky, wiry boy lounging against the window sill. "Recognize him?"

She shook her head.

"Bigelow's boy from the roadhouse. The drunk one."

"Willard Bigelow." John stood at the front of the room, reading from a list.

Willard stared at John without moving, said not a word.

John peered at him over his spectacles. "Willard Bigelow."

"Yeah," the boy muttered.

"You will answer 'yes, sir,'" John said. If he remembered Willard from the roadhouse, he showed no sign.

"I ain't here but to mind the family," Willard said. His eyes narrowed over cheeks dusted with beard. "I'll be leaving soon as I know they're settled."

"But Wil," the seated blond giant said. "Pa says you need schooling." His anxious eyes flitted between Willard and John.

Willard snorted and tossed his head. "Not me."

John gazed at him for a moment, not in a challenging way, and Willard soon flushed and lowered his eyes.

"Jacob Bigelow."

Willard's brother turned red and mumbled, "Yes sir."

John went to the next. Several names down the list, he called out, "Earl Kunkel."

47

Willard Bigelow leaned forward and brayed like a donkey. A titter ran around the room, and a small child in the front row, hand halfway in the air, started, dropped his arm and rounded his shoulders as if to protect himself from a blow.

John scowled. Billy stood, took his hands from his pockets.

Willard sat back and leered. "Donkey's arse."

Earl's ears turned crimson. He stared at the floor.

John jabbed a finger at Willard, then a thumb at the door. "Out."

Willard stayed put and grinned.

"Out," John said again.

No movement. Billy tossed Agnes a look, wandered over behind Willard, put a hand on his shoulder. "Mr. Jackson said to leave."

Willard shrugged him off and straightened. He was taller than Billy but he read something in Billy's face that he didn't care to deal with. He shrugged, looked casually over at his brother. "C'mon, Jake, let's go."

Jacob hissed at him. "Pa'll skin us alive!"

Willard ignored that. "Let's git."

Jacob squinted at John, looked down at his own big hands, hesitated a moment, and then snapped the knife shut. He stood and the two ambled out, taking their time. The children let out a collective breath and wiggled uncomfortably. The Kunkel boy huddled on the bench, staring fixedly at his knees, cheeks wet. John cocked an eyebrow at Agnes. Off to a solid start, she thought.

But the remainder of the day succeeded beautifully. Earl Kunkel slowly relaxed, the children kept to their best behavior. That evening, Reuben Bigelow drove his buckboard into town and closeted himself with John at the house, and the following day, Jake returned to the classroom. The Holman School settled down to work, and Willard disappeared from Lick Creek.

10
March 1853

When John moved his family to town, Tom and Elizabeth settled into lodgings above Mr. Baxter's haberdashery, leaving room for Agnes to board with the Jacksons in the clapboard house next to the school yard. She shared a cozy chamber under the slanting eaves with Sarah and little Rebecca. Sarah took on the role of teacher's aide, and they soon dropped into an easy routine. At the end of each school day, they stowed the readers and the geographies on the shelves, washed the slates, swept the floor and banked the fire before leaving for home and dinner. John often stayed late to mark papers or meet with a client of his burgeoning legal practice. Holt County citizens proved to be a litigious group.

On a blustery afternoon, Mr. Kunkel, Earl's father, appeared in the schoolhouse door, hat in hand. His scrap with Mr. Bigelow over the ownership of five acres of bottom land that adjoined their two properties was legendary around Lick Creek. He'd had enough of arguing with the pig-headed old codger, he told John, and intended to sue. With clouds boiling low on the western horizon and the lurid light of the setting sun promising a gale, Agnes and Sarah were anxious to be gone. They donned their coats and left John huddled with his client.

They were mere steps from the schoolhouse when a vicious blast of wind whipped plump rain drops under their bonnets, and by the time they'd ducked into the front parlor, the wind gusted so strong the flames in the lamps wavered. The younger children clustered around the table with plates before them as Nancy poked at the cook stove fire. Agnes and Sarah began to shake out their bonnets and cloaks, but before they could hang them on their pegs, Nancy straightened and turned to them, her brow creased and her face pale.

"It's time," she said. "Elizabeth's pains began this morning." Agnes and Sarah looked at her stupidly. "I kept her here today while Tom went to Forest City. Sarah, I need you to go fetch him, he should be back to Baxter's by now. And Doctor Norman. Find Doctor Norman." She went to a window and pulled aside the curtain. "And Agnes, go back to the schoolhouse. Tell John I need him here." Her hand trembled. "There's something terribly wrong."

Agnes caught a glimpse of Elizabeth through the bedroom door, her face gray, mouth twisted. *Oh dear God, don't let her die.* Agnes hadn't prayed since her mother died, and knew that whatever happened would happen, prayer or no, but she thought again, *Dear God, don't let her die.*

Sarah dashed out the door, heading to the tailor's shop, with Agnes right behind her. Halfway to the schoolhouse she realized she'd left her cloak. Thunder rolled overhead, the air fizzed and sputtered with electricity. Agnes threw open the schoolhouse door and called out. John dropped a sheaf of papers and raced back to the house leaving Mr. Kunkel wide-eyed.

Agnes changed into dry clothes and went to the children who'd been left to fend for themselves, the baby fretting like a fledgling swallow. She picked him up and rocked him, watching Nancy dab at her daughter's cheeks with a cloth. *Dear God don't let her die.* Sarah and Tom ducked in from the storm, scattering raindrops and shivering. Tom sank onto a chair at Elizabeth's bedside and took her hand. She moaned again, her eyes closed.

"Doctor Norman's gone," Sarah said. "Off to Saint Joe for two weeks." *Dear God.* "I sent Paul Norman for Doctor Robinson. He's new. Mrs. Norman said he'd help." I hope you'll call on me when the time comes, he had said to Agnes. She remembered his elegant hands and long, strong fingers.

Doctor Robinson either could not be readily found or took care to finish his dinner before braving the storm. The clock struck nine before she heard his knock, muted by the wind, and opened the door to him. Her impression was of blackness emerging from blackness, dark frockcoat smelling of wet wool, hat pulled low over his eyes, head ducked to the wind. All she saw of his face was glistening beard, sparkling in the lamplight with drops of water. His figure filled the doorway.

He shed his hat and coat and surveyed the parlor. Johnny slept on Agnes's shoulder, the children huddled at the table, schoolbooks open and ignored. John had fidgeted with the fire until they all simmered in the rain-soaked atmosphere like chickens on the boil. The bedroom door stood ajar, and Elizabeth's moans seeped through.

"Evening, folks," Doctor Robinson said. He shook hands with John. "Understand there's a baby on its way." He set a heavy mahogany box on the floor, its brass fittings catching the lamplight.

Tom stumbled into the parlor, exhaustion lining his face. He ran his fingers through bristly hair. "Robinson," he said, voice thick with fatigue. "She's in a bad way."

The doctor rolled his cuffs to the elbows, poured water from the kettle into the basin and plunged his hands in. "Has the young lady been ill the last few weeks? Confined to her bed?"

"She seemed healthy enough." Tom dropped into a kitchen chair, rested his forehead on a shaky hand. "She just never took to it. Seemed real unhappy about it."

"Happens sometimes with the first." He shook out his hands and took the towel John offered. Agnes's eyes strayed to the bed in the next room.

Elizabeth cried out, for what seemed like the hundredth time. The bedroom door opened, and the doctor emerged. Sarah had bundled the children off to bed. Nancy and Tom kept watch at the bedside. John had stepped out back for a smoke, one of many he'd indulged in this long evening. Agnes sat alone, watching through the dark hours, counting clock strokes, listening for the strike, half hour, then quarter, then hour then quarter again that marked the seconds of her life, and yet no child, no end to it. In the deepness of night the storm had faded, thunder distant as a dream.

Robinson, shoulders sagging, shirt limp with perspiration, poured coffee from the white-speckled coffeepot. He sat on the stiff settee, leaned forward with hands on knees and took three deep breaths, in through the nose, out through the mouth. Then he sat back and pulled out a small brown cigar and gestured toward Agnes.

"Do you mind?" The question was not perfunctory. He waited until she shook her head before striking a light.

They sat in silence as he took in the cigar smoke, breathing out through the nose, eyes closed, and his shoulders began to relax.

"I'll need your help in there." He took a deep draught of the cigar.

"Of course."

"Mrs. Jackson's exhausted, and Mr. Kreek's worse than useless." He held the cigar in front of him and studied it, putting one booted foot over the other knee.

"How will it turn out?" she said, confident he knew, that he could foresee such things.

"Mrs. Kreek will make it. The baby, we'll just have to see." He sipped coffee. "It's quite large...."

He stared at the glowing tip of his cigar, his lips moving as if he reviewed what must be done, then knocked away the ash and stood. Elizabeth shrieked again, the sound of a dying rabbit. "We'll need more cloths, another sheet folded thick. And water." He went to the stove, opened the door, knocked up the fire and lifted the teakettle. It was full, still warm. "Good." He disappeared into the bedroom.

For the third time, Agnes turned up the wick on the lamp. There were but three of them in the room, Elizabeth, the doctor, and Agnes. Nancy huddled glassy-eyed on the settee in the parlor. Tom slumped at the kitchen table, head cradled in his hands. Elizabeth's closed lids lay deep in shadowed pools. Her pale skin put Agnes in mind of her mother when she lay in her casket. The lamp quavered and smoked, the stench of sweat and blood and illness saturated the room. The mahogany chest stood open next to the bed, brass instruments picking up the flash of the flame and reflecting off the walls in eerie patterns. The doctor chose one, impossibly long, with curved blades.

"Sit by her head, please, Miss Canon," he said. "You will need to hold her shoulders but keep her propped against the pillows. She must be half-reclining."

She turned her back to him, concentrated on Elizabeth. Sweat steamed on her forehead, and Agnes swabbed it once, left the cloth there, took her shoulders. Elizabeth moaned, her eyes remained closed. The cloth slipped down along her cheek, lay damp against her neck. Her body jerked once, and the doctor muttered. Elizabeth's lips opened, a silent scream, her face contorted into something hideous, something so unlike Elizabeth, strange and inhuman. The doctor swore softly; it seemed not impiety but a challenge to death. Brass hit against brass as he selected another of those wicked instruments. Tears flowed from under Elizabeth's lids, and Agnes realized that she was conscious to the pain and the fear. She had hoped she was not. Again brass against brass.

"Now be prepared, please, Miss Canon." The doctor's voice was hoarse. Agnes drew in her breath. "Elizabeth, dear Elizabeth," she whispered. *Dear God dear God dear God.* Elizabeth moaned then, deep and unnatural, and convulsed. Agnes threw herself across her chest and cradled her. She sagged, wracking breaths heaving, and slipped into unconsciousness.

The doctor sat motionless for moments, then he sighed, a sigh very close to a sob. There was no cry, no whimper, no other sound. The light sputtered and hissed. He and Agnes were alone with that small death, and it filled the space between them.

"Miss Canon," he said gently.

She lifted herself, took the cloth and laid it over Elizabeth's forehead.

"You must take the child, please." He always said please when he gave instructions. "I must see to Mrs. Kreek." He looked away, then up at Agnes. "A girl."

He held in his hands a bundle, wrapped in one of Nancy's towels, a heavy muslin with embroidered flowers at the edges, now thick with blood. Agnes took her and cradled her, bloodying her bodice, choking as she looked at the tiny, still being. The skull was broken, crushed like an eggshell, the marks of forceps clear on the temples. John and Nancy must not see this, nor Tom, nor anyone, until she was cleaned, fixed, prepared. Agnes took her to the basin and began to wash.

11

Jabez rocked, the tap of his right boot putting the chair in motion. The rocker sounded a *nck nck* against the porch boards, regular as the tick of a clock, a soothing click that worked on the rigid muscles throughout his body. *Nck. Nck.* He concentrated on his breathing, visualized it, the air sucked into his nasal passages, into the lungs, washing over each capillary, bathing the blood, moving from capillary to artery to heart, surging over the body to drench every nerve with tonic like the flow of water through a mighty river system. He closed his eyes and imagined the tingle of the cells as they encountered oxygen-flushed blood and slowly relaxed, sank into repose. *Nck. Nck.* Then he turned to the muscles and willed them to let go, the pads of his feet, the long soleus of the calf and the thigh, the femoris. The latissimus dorsi stretching from hip to collarbone along the spine took attention. Then the trapezius, the deltoids, the biceps, the fingers. Each digit in turn, smallest, ring, middle, index, thumb.

He took abundant pride in being thus able to control his body. The more he knew about the structure of the human body, the interconnections of muscle and bone, the pathways of feeling and sensation, the more certain he became that he could master the mind as well, that pleasure, pain, the sense of duty, all that enriched life could be controlled and enhanced. He approached the body as a sculptor approached a finely veined block of marble or a potter approached a high-grade porcelain clay.

The rocker moved rhythmically, its *nck nck* the only sound but for the sough of breeze in the new-hatched leaves of the maples in the square. The storm had hushed the night-speaking crickets and the peepers, and ragged clouds skittered across the sky. He had been summoned from his dinner at the height of the storm to attend one of Doctor Norman's patients, John Jackson's daughter, whose pregnancy had often been a topic of discussion between him and his colleague. The young woman had withdrawn from husband and family to a place of deep melancholy, so that the delivery augured poorly from the first. Indeed, given the mind's influence and power over the body, the pregnancy was doomed from its beginning. And the birth had been difficult, the child unable to free itself, and so he had destroyed it.

He pulled from a vest pocket a Havana cigar and a lucifer match. The light flared inside his cupped hands, and the satisfying smoke wreathed his head and seeped into his brain as well as into his lungs. The child's head was distended, chin and occiput hung up on the pubic bones. Extracting it alive required ripping open the mother's belly. He knew of doctors that performed such operations—they called it the Caligula birth for the damage it did to the mother—but he loathed the thought of it. He'd performed the procedure once, long ago, when a young Spanish woman was brought to the army post by a clutch of black-clad old women and a priest. No more than sixteen or seventeen, she'd been in labor for many hours. He'd palpated the young mother's belly, examined between her legs and found that the head of the child was of a size that nothing short of disembowelment would save it. And so, at the insistence of the priest who declared the child to be the only concern, he disemboweled the young woman. Without laudanum, without opiates, with only a shot of brandy, one for her, one for himself, he extracted the child from the belly of its dying mother. The child lived, at least as far as he saw it, bundled up and spirited away along with the violated body of the child-mother.

Tonight's decision was simple, once he put aside the hopes and anguish of the family: the young husband, red hair spiked with sweat and rain, the grandparents with young ones themselves, the intriguing Miss Canon. The child's head crushed, the body withdrawn, the mother saved for future children.

The sky brightened, that hour before dawn when one doesn't so much see the sky lighten as instinctively know it is happening, when the edges of the clouds are distinguishable and the outline of a branch appears. Eliza stirred in the bedroom behind him. Through the open window he heard her rise, take the straight chair with the needlepoint cushion from its place by the hall door and set it next to the sill. She leaned out, rubbed his shoulder, ran her hand down his arm, squeezed his wrist.

"Time to sleep, my dear," she said. He shifted his chair so he could see her form, dark in the shadows, the edge of the lace curtain framing her profile like a mantilla. Her white satin nightgown was loose at the neck and fell open, the pale light caught the curve of her breast. The mole on its underside was dark as an ink spot.

"Not tonight," he answered. He slipped his hand over hers and intertwined their fingers so the knuckles lined up, large and small, brown and white, a matched set. He traced them with the finger of his free hand.

"You lost the patient," she said, a statement rather than a question.

"I lost the baby," he said. "I saved the mother." He ran an index finger over the back of her hand, up her wrist and around to the soft cupped underside where the pulse beat. He pressed against the vein, feeling the life flow. A sense of passage seized him, and he wanted to grasp the pulsing life and freeze it for all time.

They had been like this once before, years and years gone by, standing on a porch on a breezy spring night with the scent and sound of reawakening life all about, and he had held her hand. Now, a stiff breeze blew aside the clouds, and the waning moon appeared for a brief look. Jabez felt time circle around, out of its familiar linear path, to repeat itself.

He pulled back and looked at Eliza through narrowed eyes. "You were wearing a blue gown." He kept her fingertips trapped in his hand. "The blue gown with black lace. And your hair was in those horrid ringlets." If he squinted enough he could almost raise the two images, side by side, Eliza as she was then and Eliza as she was now. The passion for her that once consumed him was now a memory, but Penelope-like, she had waited for him, and he loved her for that, in a deep secret place that nothing could touch.

"How do you remember that? It's been, what, ten years?" Her teeth flashed in the reflected light of the moon. "I wanted so much to go away with you." She rested her forearms on the window sill, her chin on folded hands. "But off you went to meet your lovers."

"Lovers?" Jabez raised his brows.

"The army and the gold fields. Two fancy ladies. No decent woman has a chance against them."

"Every man tires of whores eventually." Jabez stroked her hair, once thick and lustrous, now dull and thin, the scalp visible.

"Do you know," she said softly, "I should like to walk with a cane. As an old woman, to walk with a cane. Canes are so … authoritative."

It seemed their entire acquaintance was a long farewell. They both knew it, they treated her death as an event in their futures to be scheduled and planned. It hung between them like the next Christmas dinner or a business trip to St. Louis. But they never talked about it.

12

Agnes first met Eliza Wetmore Robinson at the child's burial. She and her husband stood at the graveside in cold sunlight and a stiff March wind, clouds like snowdrifts floating against hard blue sky. It was a small group, Agnes and Billy, his parents, Nancy and John, Sarah and the Reverend Marvin. Elizabeth remained abed, and Tom carried the tiny pine coffin himself, perched on his shoulder. The cemetery was a lonely place to leave the child, its black walnut trees catching the clouds in their uppermost fingers and its hilltop looming over an empty prairie. So Doctor Robinson and his wife were welcome, and Agnes found their presence a solace.

Mrs. Robinson's childlike expression, her waifish frame and fragile features, contrasted sharply with her husband's powerful energy. Her eyes, an extraordinary cobalt, eclipsed her other features, and an exotic black lace mantle covered thin, dull hair. She whispered to her husband occasionally throughout the service, gloved hand on his sleeve. After the final prayer was offered and the mourners had filed past the grave to drop in a handful of dirt, dust to dust, the doctor introduced his wife to everyone.

"Miss Agnes Canon," she said, as she shook Agnes's hand. "My husband tells me how helpful you were the night of the child's birth."

"He was very skillful," Agnes said. "Without him we might have lost Elizabeth."

"My husband is an excellent doctor with wide experience." She watched his broad back as he walked ahead, in conversation with John. "The loss of a child has always affected him, though, more than any other death. He's seen many over the past ten years."

"You've recently arrived, I understand?"

"From Ohio, near to Columbus. It was a dreadfully cold journey." She laughed, a husky sound. "I was not well, and poor Jabez nursed me throughout our honeymoon. We've been married but six weeks." Her gaze swept the gathered family, moving in a cloud of black bombazine and wool toward the cemetery gates. "He tells me he met your family last fall when you arrived in Holt County."

"He was kind to my cousin. She fell ill when we stopped at Iowa Point."

"I'm so sorry. I haven't asked about Mrs. Kreek." She stopped, laying a hand on Agnes's arm. "How is she? My husband intends to keep a close eye on her."

"She keeps to her bed, but she's improving. Truly, she seems better than she has been all winter. She's talking with us again, and eating." Agnes opened the low iron gate, and Mrs. Robinson swept through in a rustle of black taffeta. "It's as if her body held a corruption, a contamination. Do you think it's terrible to think of a child that way?" This had been troubling Agnes greatly, and she was astonished to find herself saying such a thing to a stranger. She'd spoken of it to no one else.

"We all must contend with our own private devils," Mrs. Robinson said softly. "Perhaps this was your cousin's." She turned to Agnes. "Do you have private devils, Miss Canon? I know I do." She turned away again. "I suppose everyone does."

There was something bewitching about this woman, as if she reached across chasms that others are too dull or stupid to detect.

"Perhaps devils drove me here, drove me west," Agnes said.

"Oh, you understand! So few do when I rattle on." Her forehead wrinkled in concentration. "Perhaps not devils that drove you here, but something else, the converse. Angels, perhaps. Everything has a mirror image, don't you think? Every action a reaction. I've thought about this often." She gestured with black-gloved hands. "There are good forces and there are evil forces. It's our responsibility to encourage the one and reject the other." She laughed again, a rush of sound as if the pressure of her thought had been released, steam escaping from a valve.

"I've been reading Mr. Andrew Davis. The clairvoyant?" She glanced at her husband, then leaned in to Agnes with a conspiratorial smile. "Don't tell the doctor. He doesn't believe in such nonsense." They had reached Missouri Street, the corner by Ed Poor's smithy. The sound of the forge and the work of the blacksmith, the busyness of the town flowed over them, in contrast to the silence of the cemetery. Doctor Robinson shook hands with John and Sam.

"I'm so pleased to have met you, Miss Canon." She gave Agnes her hand, her smile brilliant. "Please let's continue our conversation," she said. "I would so like to know you better."

Agnes wanted to know her, too. She was captivated. By the contrasts between the faded woman and her vital husband. By her exquisite, otherworldly charisma. "I'll tell Elizabeth that you and your husband were here."

"Oh yes, please," she said, as if she'd forgotten Elizabeth again. "And when she's well perhaps I may visit and get to know her, too." She released Agnes's hand, bowed to Rachel and Nancy, and turned away.

Agnes often thought of the doctor and his wife. She watched them from the schoolyard or from the upstairs window in the Jackson house as they walked in the evenings or rode out in the doctor's buggy. Two halves of one thought, as Margaret Fuller said, dark and fair, tall and slight, one bursting with energy, the other languid. They chatted when she chanced to encounter them in Zook's mercantile or the Irvines' bakery.

And then for a fortnight she saw nothing of Mrs. Robinson. Word spread she was indisposed.

That year, spring burst out overnight. A soft south breeze snaked its way over the prairie, melting the crusty patches of dirty snow like butter. The orchards responded with a wash of green, promising a sea of blossom. Doors stood open, and bedding flapped on the lines. Farmers plowed and harrowed and planted their fields to corn and wheat, the black soil of the prairie sending up a dank smell, steamy and rich as the warmth of the sun soaked in.

The rising spirits of the winter-bound citizens of Holt County responded, and like a spring freshet found an outlet in the form of a dance. The arrival of an itinerant fiddler, an Irishman of some fame, provided the excuse, and the Cottiers offered their barn, an ambitious structure supporting an ambitious farm.

Agnes and the Jackson family, the Canons and the Kreeks arrived to find the interior brilliant with lanterns swinging from rafters and hooks, and the Cottiers, man and wife, standing in the doorway. The Zook tribe debarked from wagons and carriages, William and Daniel and Levi, their wives interchangeable, small, lively and plump. Aldo Beaton, bachelor, had waylaid Billy, who but half attended Mr. Beaton's words, his eyes fastened on a bevy of young girls. The Baxters sat with the Kunkels, and Jace Biggers, the banker, stood deep in conversation with Doctor Robinson. Rufus Byrd and Mrs. Byrd buzzed about, and our old one-armed friend Bigelow lurked diffidently in the shadows, accompanied by his wife, our first sighting of the elusive Miranda. Willard and Jake Bigelow slouched behind the punch table, dipping from the spiked bowl. Mrs. Robinson sat with the elderly ladies, handkerchief pressed to her lips against the dust.

They'd scarce said their hellos when the fiddler climbed onto a platform in the corner and tucked his instrument under fleshy jowls. A waif of a child with deep eyes and a shock of untamable hair moved to the front of the platform and folded his hands. The bow drew back, the strings sang once and were still. Tom Kreek and the men talking orchard business around the punch bowl quieted, the children hushed. John shed his jacket and grinned down at Nancy. Billy headed for the girls. Another note, slow and mournful, then a third, then a flurry of tones that spoke to the blood and moved faster and faster. Boots tapped, young people looked sideways at each other, Ben Cottier seized his wife by the hand and swung into the middle of the floor. John followed with Nancy, the spell snapped and the reel took over the entire company.

Agnes found herself whirling in the arms of Aldo Beaton, past Sarah and the Ramsey boy, past Billy with a pretty girl she'd never seen before. The fiddler's arm flew. The boy, tambourine in hand, leapt about the stage in time. The dancers stamped and whirled and raised a cloud of chaff that set the onlookers to sneezing and wiping their eyes. Even old Rufus Byrd, his absurd round head bobbing on its neck like a dandelion too big for its stalk, clumped by with his rotund wife, her cheeks glowing. Abruptly, the reel came to an end with a commanding twang of the bow. The dancers stumbled to a stop, laughing, gasping and surging en masse toward the punchbowl.

"You're a right fine dancer, Miss Canon," said Aldo Beaton as he steered her, hand on her elbow, toward the punchbowl. "Did you learn that in Pennsylvania?"

"I can't tell you how I learned that. We never had such dancing in Pennsylvania."

"We danced it in the Virginia mountains," he said, ladling punch into her cup, "but I was just a boy and don't remember it quite so lively. My ma could dance though, she was known through three counties."

"The fiddler's a master."

"It's witchcraft, cousin!" The crush had spun her up against Tom Kreek, big hands wrapped around filled tumblers. "The Irishman has bewitched us with his fiddle." He gestured toward his wife, ensconced in a chair next to Eliza Robinson.

"I'll have Elizabeth up and dancing, too, before the night's out, you wait and see." And off he went. Beaton, however, hovered. The warmth of the barn amplified the scent of his hair oil. He bore an unfortunate resemblance to her erstwhile suitor back in Pennsylvania, and when he turned to speak to Mr. Cottier, she edged away.

And bumped into Doctor Robinson. In deference to the heat his jacket was gone, but his white shirt was crisp and clean, his waistcoat a stylish cut, well-fitted across his broad chest. He laughed, and she had the distinct understanding that he knew she attempted escape. He positioned himself between her and Mr. Beaton and dipped a cup of punch for himself. "Must I rescue you from another mule?" he asked, raising his cup to her in a toast.

"Hush," she hissed. "He'll hear you."

"Then we'd best move away." He grasped her elbow and pulled her beyond the table. "There now. I even succeeded in holding onto you again."

"Really, sir, very improper." She sipped at her punch, thinking she flirted where she shouldn't.

"Not so improper at a dance."

"Is Mrs. Robinson not dancing?"

His expression sobered, his eyes flicking to his wife.

"No. No, she's not well. I was pleased she agreed to come tonight."

Now the fiddle interrupted, two introductory notes to set the mood, then a rill and something astonishing. The fiddler's boy, arms at his sides and upper body held still, eyes fastened on a point on the far wall, shifted his feet. His lower body moved, a separate being altogether from his upper body, nailed boots clicking in time to the jig, gaze distant as if seeing the far valleys and villages where such dancing was invented. Doctor Robinson and Agnes shifted with the crowd toward the platform. The fiddle flowed in and out, weaving a story without words.

The music faded, and the child's feet stilled, his reedy voice melting into the fiddle's song. The fiddler allowed his note to die away on the evening and stood back as the boy blended words to the memory of the tune and sang, unaccompanied.

Oh Shenandoah,
I long to hear you,
Away you rolling river,
Oh Shenandoah,
I long to hear you,
Away, I'm bound away
'Cross the wide Missouri

The words called to something deep inside, wild and free and lovely, the tune like the wind in greening treetops. Then it melted into a whisper and gently died, and with a shiver Agnes returned to the brilliance of lanterns in a homely barn, Doctor Robinson by her side.

"I envy him," she said, the first thing that came to mind. "Roaming the west, unfettered—what an education. Fortunate child!"

"Not so very fortunate, I think. I knew that old man in California. He takes on boys like a hurdy-gurdy man takes on monkeys." He watched the singer head for the punch bowl. "Perhaps he's better off than he would be starving on a farm in Ireland, but he's bound to the old man."

"Do you mean he kidnapped the child?"

"Not at all. The boy probably went with him gladly enough just to survive. The child is chattel, Miss Canon. The old man owns him, to do with what he wishes. It's the way for many children."

He glanced at her face. "But I've spoiled the evening for you, let me make amends. Whatever the old man is, he's a master of the violin." And he bowed over her hand as the fiddle slowed into a sweet melody, a simple version of a Strauss waltz. Agnes curtsied, and he swept her onto the dance floor.

She was electrified, as if a power source flowed through him and out his fingertips to hers. Dancing with him she grew graceful and light. His scent, soap and cigar and sweat, made her giddy. She reached high to place her hand on his shoulder and wondered what it would be like to feel that rich beard against her forehead.

He looked down at her from his height, his eyes somber. "I'd like to ask a favor of you," he said.

"Of course."

"Would you visit my wife?" He glanced toward Mrs. Robinson, one of the few not dancing. "I mean, come to the house. She's no longer able to join me when I call on patients. She's lonely."

"She doesn't look well."

"There's a cancer that began in the breast some years ago. Her father was a doctor, and he managed to treat it at the time, but it's back, and it's spread beyond anything I can do." He spoke in a rush, as if getting the words out quickly would lessen their horror.

Agnes shivered. Mrs. Robinson's devils were gathering. "Yes, of course I'll visit," she said. "I'm so sorry."

The music ended, and he released her waist, touched her elbow. "Come say hello to her. She's looked forward to seeing you tonight," and he guided her toward the seating arranged along the wall. He bowed to them both and took up his post behind his wife's chair.

"Miss Canon." Mrs. Robinson smiled, squeezing Agnes's hand. Her recent indisposition had left her visibly weaker, her complexion a dull gray. Agnes dropped onto a hay bale and dabbed at her forehead with a handkerchief.

"You dance beautifully. You and my husband make an enchanting couple." Her eyes were bright with fever, her smile genuine.

"I enjoy dancing. I'm sorry you don't feel up to it."

"I haven't recovered from an illness." She continued to grasp Agnes's hand. "I've suffered from it off and on these past twelve months." The doctor turned his head away, watched the fiddler rosin the bow.

"But I'm much better this evening." Mrs. Robinson shifted to face Agnes. "I enjoyed talking with your cousin. She seems in good spirits."

"She improves daily." Agnes searched through the crowd until she spotted Tom's red hair blazing among a cluster of young couples, Elizabeth on his arm, smiling at his stories. "She's changed, though. She's not as lighthearted as she used to be."

"The time is yet short. I expect she'll soon have other children." Agnes looked up at the doctor for confirmation, but his attention was elsewhere. "I'd like to know her better. I fear we must hurry the acquaintance, though." She withdrew her fingers and picked at the black velvet ribbon that circled her wrist. Her husband laid his hand on her shoulder.

"I'm sure you'll soon be in health again," Agnes said.

Mrs. Robinson laughed. "Of course you're right," she said. She patted her husband's hand. "Isn't she, Jabez?" He smiled down at her, his face shadowed by the tilt of his head. Her eyes shone as she gazed around the room, over the gathered company, at the knots of farmers and shopkeepers, women and children. "But here I've brought a touch of gloom to your evening, my dear Miss Canon. And you've been dancing so well. You must be enjoying this after such a trying winter. The young Irish boy is enchanting ... I've heard of such characters roaming about the west, children singing for their supper. Do bring him to me, Jabez." The doctor nodded and stepped away to fetch the child.

Agnes moved from her hay bale to make room for the boy, who looked down at his hands while Mrs. Robinson asked questions about this and that, and he mumbled "Yes'm" and "No'm" and refused to look at his questioner. It ended when she pressed a coin into his hand, which he clutched and after shooting a glance at the fiddler, plunged into his pocket. As the old Irishman drew the bow across the strings once again, she looked up at Agnes. "Do come see me, Miss Canon," she said. "I so enjoy talking with you. I don't expect to get out much for a time."

Agnes said she would and shook her hand. Mr. Beaton claimed her, then, and for the next round of dance, the fiddler launched into a frisky tune, and soon after the Robinsons said their good-byes and left. The evening concluded shortly thereafter with a gentle dance, the tune a remnant of that music of fifty years ago. Doctor Norman and his wife stepped through a dignified set, a stately forward and backward movement, light touch of the hands, a curtsy, raising memories of a time when the century turned and drawing rooms were filled with young ladies in high-waisted narrow silks and gentlemen in knee breeches.

13

Agnes began to call on Mrs. Robinson, sometimes with Elizabeth, sometimes alone. School recessed for spring plowing, and she required a pastime, Elizabeth required diversion. Agnes wasn't proud of her reasoning, but she hoped Elizabeth's association with someone truly ill would shake her out of her melancholy, a strategy that proved successful. And perhaps she sought more conversation with the doctor, a motive she kept strictly to herself.

On their first visit they found Mrs. Robinson in her parlor, a copy of *Wieland* open on her lap, a sad and bloody novel for a woman in her situation, Agnes thought. She wore a heavy wool morning dress and a shawl about her shoulders though the room seethed with an over-generous wood fire. She didn't rise when they came in, but held out her hand with a happy smile.

"Miss Canon, Mrs. Kreek, how wonderful of you to visit me!" She waved her hand to the settee. Her girl, a young farm woman hired by the doctor to cook, took their cloaks and the basket of tarts Agnes had purloined from Nancy's pantry. "It's been so long since I've had the pleasure of talk with ladies." She wriggled into the nest of her chair like a child delighted with new playmates.

They chatted about the weather, which led them to comment on Mrs. Byrd's carriage as it passed by splashed to the sideboards in mud, then to the doctor's rushing off that morning in his buggy through the puddles to tend a suspected case of the measles. At that point the servant brought in a pewter tray with coffee and the jelly tarts arranged on a plate of bone china, and Mrs. Robinson poured and passed. Then they went back to the measles, which led them to the topic of their health: Agnes's ("Excellent, thank you"), Elizabeth's ("Improving daily, I thank you"), and Mrs. Robinson's ("Not sanguine, I'm afraid"). Mrs. Robinson studied her hands, clutched in her lap, then looked up at Elizabeth, her face open and cheerful, as if they talked about how to bake a cider cake. "The doctor has little hope for me, so I'm doing my best to prepare." She smiled.

Clumsy as always, Agnes said, "By reading *Wieland*? A book about child murder and suicide?"

She laughed, not the least offended. "It's a bit grim for my situation, I suppose. But the spirit world is often in my thoughts, and death isn't something that frightens me." She pouted at the book on the side table. "But these are particularly vicious deaths."

"I've never read it," Elizabeth said.

"Don't," Agnes said. "It's not something one reads when one's recently lost…." She ducked her head. It seemed she could say nothing without blundering.

Elizabeth patted her hand. "Recently lost a child. I know, dear, don't fret. We can't avoid the fact forever."

"My dear Mrs. Kreek," Mrs. Robinson said. She swung her feet from the footstool and leaned forward. "I've thought many times since that awful night that you would find comfort through the use of a medium."

"A medium what?" Elizabeth asked.

"A medium … you know … one who speaks to the spirits?"

Elizabeth and Agnes looked at each other, then back at Mrs. Robinson.

"Oh, I know," she said, her pale features flushing. "It's difficult to believe at first, unless you've experienced it." She leaned back and laughed. "I began to patronize a medium in Ohio while Jabez was gone to the west. I was terrified, you see, that something dreadful would happen to him, and I would never see him again. Then I met a woman who speaks to the departed and thought I'd try it so that even if he were taken from me I wouldn't lose him."

She paused, her gaze on the rain that trickled down the window glass to pool in a depression on the sill. The wind gusted and a branch of lilac rapped on the pane.

"And have you attended a ... what is it called? ... a séance?" Elizabeth appeared intrigued.

"Several. I was never successful in contacting my mother—she's the only person I really wanted to speak to—but several others spoke to loved ones."

"And what is it they say?"

"They talk about the next world, who else is there, whether they're happy." She looked up. "They all seem to be happy."

"I've read there's a great deal of fraud among mediums," Agnes said.

The front door opened and closed, and they heard the doctor's step in the hall. A gust of wet air shivered the fire. Mrs. Robinson touched a finger to her lips and raised her eyebrows. "We'll change the subject, now. My husband will laugh at me." She turned anxious eyes to him.

The doctor greeted them absentmindedly and disappeared into his surgery. They spoke no more of spirits, and soon after, Agnes and Elizabeth took their leave.

"Well, what did you think of the spirits, Agnes?" Elizabeth asked as soon as the door closed behind them. She tugged her hood close about her against the rain.

"I tend to agree with the doctor." Agnes said. "It's a passel of nonsense, but if it makes her feel better about her illness, there's no harm."

"I liked the idea. Do you suppose I can contact my baby?" Her smile was wistful, but she winked at Agnes.

The gloomy day beamed bright again. Elizabeth would be well.

Over the next few weeks, Elizabeth grew stronger as Eliza grew weaker. Agnes continued to call during the morning hours when the doctor attended patients, and Eliza was alone. Agnes was drawn to her, like a dull moth drawn to a guttering candle. Eliza often lounged in a dressing gown, stretched against pillows or writing letters at a delicate desk, her girl bringing her coffee or tea. One day late in April, Agnes found her on her knees before a leather and copper-studded chest tucked in the corner of the parlor. A swath of fine black lace flowed from her hands, a bolt of intricate tracery that shadowed her bare forearms like spider webs.

"Agnes, look at this." She held it up. "Spanish lace from Mexico City. Jabez brought it to me from his time in the army."

The shawl was exquisite, soft as eider down. Exotic.

"And these." She pulled from the chest a handful of silver and turquoise, the finest jewelry Agnes had ever seen, necklaces and armlets and brooches. "Indian, from the southwest. He was there as an army doctor, you know, back in forty-six." Agnes hadn't known. "Then later he traveled to California and worked in the gold fields." She slipped a circlet of silver, dull and blackened with age, over Agnes's wrist. "We were apart for ten years."

Agnes twisted the bracelet to study the deep etchings. It was lovely. "Such a long time."

"I had no choice. My father refused his permission."

"Your father didn't care for him?"

"On the contrary, he cared for him very much. Jabez came to my father as a student." She stroked the lace as if it were cat's fur. "But he hadn't earned his medical degree, and my father wasn't certain he would ever make a proper living to support a wife."

"So he sent him away."

She laughed. A harsh sound, unbecoming. "They had a vicious row. Much too much alike, those two. Father knew Jabez was a rogue, a wanderer. And he was. He wandered into the army, through the camps, all about the west, before he finished his schooling and came back for me."

"You waited."

"Yes, ten years. And now it's too late."

Agnes was impatient with her. "You give up too easily. You resisted the cancer once before. Do it again." She tossed her head and stared out the window. *What a trial she must be to her husband,* Agnes thought. *And I don't care if that's mean.*

"Agnes, please. You're strong. You don't understand weakness." She turned back to the trunk. "Here." She handed her a bundle of letters tied with a velvet hair ribbon. "Here's the record of those ten years."

Agnes wouldn't take them. "Those aren't for me to see."

"I suppose not." She set them on a table next to an untouched breakfast tray and stroked the black lace absently, eyes turned inward to a distant memory. She seemed weary, enervated, her dark eyes shadowed, her skin pasty. Agnes left soon after, both of them vaguely dissatisfied with the other.

When next she visited Eliza, the trunk of memories no longer haunted the parlor, but the stack of letters covered the table at her elbow and littered about her chair like fallen leaves. She half-reclined against a mound of pillows, a quilt shielding her from the April breeze that puffed lace curtains.

Without greeting, she handed Agnes a letter and picked up another. "Read that one," she said, her voice weak. "He's had so much opportunity. How fortunate for men to be able to move about the world on a whim." Eliza seemed unconcerned about sharing private correspondence, and Agnes wanted very much to know more about him. So she read.

December 12, 1848

My dearest girl. We've rounded the horn, and saw Fuego in the distance. I can tell you that the storms of this voyage are not much exaggerated. They come up with the suddenness of a tiger, lying in wait behind mountainous seas and under lowering skies, until they leap upon this tiny chip of a boat without warning. We encountered three such storms before we fully rounded the tip of the continent and made way up the western coast. I've treated three cases of scurvy with little patience for those who refuse their limes, set two broken bones, pronounced a boy of sixteen dead after a fall from the mast and watched as his body, sewn into his hammock, slid into an icy sea. These among a host of minor ailments and mishaps.

The coast itself is a jewel-green belt of trees and mountains, with a strip of pearly white beach bordered by the deep green and turquoise of the ocean. We put into Valparaiso for water and supplies and I found for you a beautiful rosewood box inlaid with abalone, made by the native people of the region. We followed the coastline north in calm weather and you filled my thoughts as the moon turned from half to full and began again to wane. We have touched down in a tiny harbor in Peru, with two weeks yet to go before California and I mail this now, hoping it reaches you with all my love,

Jabez Robinson

This was wandering on a grand scale. Even John Jackson, in Agnes's opinion the epitome of the adventurer, foundered in comparison.

"I don't know what happened to the rosewood box," Eliza said. She handed Agnes another letter. "Here you see what a talented doctor he is."

April 16, 1849
Grass Valley, Calif.

Dear Eliza, I am writing late at night in a canvas tent with rain rolling in beneath the flaps and turning the floor to mush. Lamplight flickers about me and shadows advance and waver and I can only wish that you were here to share this all with me, it is so lonely. Tonight I took off a man's leg. It was crushed when timbers from a mining shaft collapsed. The hurry and rush for gold is such that men take little care how they construct their operations and I fear hundreds will die from accidents easily preventable.

The gore and blood and disease of the mining camps are equal to that I saw in the southwest during the war with the Mexicans, brought about by both greed and thoughtlessness. My patient this evening finally collapsed under the weight of laudanum and pain. Whether he will awake I do not know. I am the only doctor for nearly a hundred miles either direction and I see it all—accident, childbirth, all manner of disease. I dare say no professor in medical school back east shall ever have the temerity to refuse me my credentials after this. Tell your father I think of him often and wish for his assistance and advice daily.

With all my love,
Jabez

"He walked from his home in Maine to Philadelphia, only to be refused admittance to medical classes," Eliza said. "I think he still carries the grudge. My father agreed to tutor him. He was an apt pupil, but not a satisfactory son-in-law until he had been … seasoned, I think Father said."

"Did he ever approve of your marriage?"

"Only after Jabez returned home and took his degree."

"Holt County must appear very tame to him after … after all this." Agnes waved the letter.

"It's a compromise. It's not Worthington, Ohio. He can't take me to California. He'll surely go when I no longer hold him here."

Agnes hadn't the heart to chide Eliza for dreariness. She simply accepted what was. Soon enough her husband would be free to wander where he pleased.

Agnes visited Eliza daily after that. She seemed like spun sugar dissolving in the soft spring rain. Sometimes Agnes passed the doctor as he left to visit patients or returned with his arms full of hams or chickens or whatever payment he received for his services. He always threw her a grateful glance, never mentioned his wife, left her hurriedly with a few inquiries about her health and family. His energy and the space he filled in the world seemed to expand as his wife's contracted. Eliza and Agnes continued to read the letters, but only when they were alone, without Elizabeth or the occasional visitor. Agnes took to calling the doctor by his given name, in her imagination, fancying that she understood him, that they were in sympathy. She wondered what occurred to him when he returned after years away and found the fragile creature to whom he'd committed himself. His letters recounted operations and battles and fist fights, even murders, mixed among descriptions of a country so beautiful it stopped her breath to read about it. The words grew into a thread linking Agnes to Eliza, to Jabez, into the past, a continuity of lives, and it seemed Eliza bequeathed him to her so that the unbroken chain in which she was a necessary link remained whole.

May came in a burst of blossoms, apples and peaches and pears turning the plains and valleys into a paradise of bloom. The scents of the prairie, fresh turned earth and young grasses, the hurry of animal life, the newness of the breeze washed over the tiny community with the sound of birdsong, and in the small frame house on Missouri Street, Eliza quietly let go.

Agnes sat with her one morning as she lay on a cot in the freshness of the parlor, window open to the sound of bees busy in the apple tree, against Agnes's advice exposed to the spring draft. Propped on pillows so she could see across the fields, her papery hand held a letter, the one they'd read several times about Jabez's boyhood in Maine, his father and all those sisters and brothers. Eliza loved it especially because it painted him as a child, and she liked to imagine a son of her own just like him. She lifted the letter in Agnes's direction.

"If I'd had a son I would have named him after my father. Charles Wetmore. Charles Wetmore Robinson. Father would like that. I wish I'd had time for a son." She turned to the window. "Agnes, have many sons. And let them be rogues. I like rogues." She smiled, her look far away.

Soon Eliza slept, her breath deep, sounding stronger than it had for many days. Her chest rose and fell gently. Agnes leaned back in the chair and closed her eyes. The hum of insects dulled her thoughts, the sunlight warmed the room and raised the sweet smell of lilac. She dozed and dreamed a forgotten dream, and when she awoke, she was alone. Eliza's form lay yet on the cot, but a sense of solitude prevailed. Agnes sat for some time, then rose to find the doctor.

14

Jabez had taken Eliza with him to visit patients, whenever she felt well enough, and when she grew too weak to go out, he was grateful for the townsfolk who visited. He remembered with amusement his first meeting, in Cincinnati, with the lively Miss Canon and remembered with admiration her assistance the night of Mrs. Kreek's delivery. She and his wife were so very different. Agnes Canon, statuesque, with aristocratic cheekbones, her chestnut hair flashing copper highlights, shouting health and well-being. Many times he arrived home to find they'd been sitting together, and he often tried to engage her in conversation, but she would pack up her work bag and hurry out, with a sideways look at him that may have been embarrassment.

As the end approached, he found excuses to be away from the house. The more he saw of death—violent, as in the southwest, tragic, as in the gold fields, gentle, as it came for Eliza—the more he sickened of the waste and the tragedy. Life itself was his religion, and to maintain and restore life was the reason he drove himself in his work. Being unable to stop death's incursion into his own home left him helpless and angry. Having faced every other challenge, physical and mental, in the past forty years with enthusiasm, he could not face this.

So someone else was with Eliza when she died, and he was relieved and comforted to know that that someone was Miss Canon. He buried his wife in the cemetery on the hill, not far from the Jackson baby, not far from where they had all stood together at that small grave, and he grieved.

Book Two

"…there is a reason why the foes of African Slavery seek more freedom for women; but put it not upon that ground, but on the ground of right."
~ Margaret Fuller, *Woman in the Nineteenth Century*, 1845

15
July 1853

Agnes walked ten steps behind the cradler, a rhythmic motion: step and stoop from the waist, reach and gather the long yellow stalks of wheat, pull them close, shake them straight, flick the twine about the bundle, once, twice, twist and tuck the ends in the ancient binder's knot, toss the sheaf to the side, step and stoop. Each sheaf improved, tidier than the last. Her movements became swifter and surer, her fingers recalling the motion, a skill she learned as a very young child and repeated summer after summer, one in a long line of children following the reapers in the heat and the dust. Only then she detested the chore. Now it was a pleasure, a contest, a challenge thrown down over July's harvest picnic.

The Missouri farmland was still nearly virgin, the sweet heavy smell of rank vegetation, unbounded growth, an overwhelming richness of the prairie. Sam's broad back ahead of her strong and straight, his muscled, competent arms swinging the cradle in a trance-making rhythm. The blade sang in a whisper through the ripe stalks, laying them neat and sure for her to gather and bundle, bind and toss, a lengthening swath through a field of gold like a moon path across a gently rolling lake. Over the waist-high wheat to her left, Billy cradled his path, and Jabez followed, stooping, gathering, bundling, binding, the two teams moving in choreographed cadence.

Jabez watched as she tossed her bundle. She circled the stalks with a twist of twine, then stole a look to the side. He saw her, shook his bundle and wrapped it deftly, his sheaf tidy and regular. She straightened her sheaf, twisted and tucked, a perfect knot. His sheaf flew through the air, he stooped and gathered again. She stooped and gathered, shook and straightened, wrapped, twisted, tucked, tossed. He tossed as she tossed. He turned to grin at her, teeth flashing white through that silky dark beard, and her unwise heart leapt.

He'd lost time to smiling and Agnes picked up the pace, winning the unspoken race, the twine already around the next sheaf. He stooped, gathered, straightened, all in one fluid move, his long fingers working surely, swiftly, as if the coarse twine were suture and the ripe golden stalks flesh. She stumbled over the rough stubble, but her sheaf was gathered and bound and tossed a half motion before his. He laughed, a deep, delighted laugh and without looking she knew he'd thrown back his head, his eyes dancing.

16

Missouri Democrat. August 29, 1853. The weather off Cape Horn is brutal. California-bound adventurers who choose to sail the Horn at the very bottom of the earth rather than cross the plains and desert or the Central American isthmus often find themselves on their knees in prayer in the midst of a storm of wind and rain and mountainous seas the color of slate. Murderous headwinds packed with snow and sleet and waves twice the height of the masts bear down on ships for days on end, sometimes blowing them back to the Atlantic with the viciousness of the devil himself, sometimes taking the ship and all its souls to the bottom of the sea. Few men who survive the crossing dare brave it again, and the memory of the power of the winds and the seas stays with them all their lives.

"Sanctimonious drivel," Jabez growled, tossing down the newspaper. The journey he remembered was four months of pure, unadulterated hell: wormy food, stinking water, filth, vomit, lice, casual cruelties among passengers and crew. And overlying everything the constant smell of fear. Icy storms and mountainous seas were the least of it. Nothing romantic about it.

What amused him, though, was the juxtaposition of the account to a story about Missouri's two cantankerous politicians. Senator Atchison and Congressman Benton were at each other's throats this hot summer, railing about central railroads and Indian land, Nebraska and abolition and slavery in the territories. Here was a storm, Jabez thought, one that would make a squall off the Horn feel like a spring shower. He wondered if the author had seen the connection. If he hadn't, his high-strung editor had. Frank Blair never missed an opportunity to make Atchison look bad and Benton look good.

Jabez removed his collar and stared over the town square, parched and deserted. He'd changed his shirt after the last patient but already the back had soaked through and clung to his shoulder blades. Heat danced in waves off the brick courthouse; the building shimmered like a live thing. The high temperatures seemed to exacerbate the rhetoric out of Washington and St. Louis. He glanced at the newsprint, smudged by sweat from his hands. Atchison said he'd see Nebraska "sink in hell"—though the paper printed it as "sink in h---"—before he'd let it go free soil. Atchison was cracked. He'd go to war to get his way. Maybe if he'd had to fight in Mexico and Texas instead of so enthusiastically sending other men to do it for him, he'd be singing a different tune.

He rubbed a big hand down his face to shut out images of that war. Broken bodies scattered over dusty wasteland, crawling with vermin and scavengers. Boys barely old enough to shave slashed by sabers, mewling like kittens, leaking out their lives in a foreign land. A chronic absence of medicine, clean linen, even water. Amputated limbs in great rotting piles. He couldn't bear to think of it and yet the images haunted him.

Jabez dropped the paper to the floorboards, propped his boots on the rail and pulled out a cigar. He struck a match and puffed until the tip glowed, leaned back, raised his hand to the man cutting across the street toward him.

"Evening, Doc," John Jackson said, lifting his hat and swiping at perspiration with a forearm. "Don't get up." Jabez waved him into the other chair and pulled out a second cigar. John shook his head. "Too damn hot. How you can light a match when it's over a hundred out here is more than I can understand."

Jabez grinned. "It's all in the contrast. Pull the smoke into the lungs, and it appears cooler on the outside." He stood, stepped into the house and returned with a decanter and two glasses. "How's the family holding up in the heat?"

"Well enough. Suppose you've been called out to tend to folks?"

"Two cases of sunstroke today. Heat rash. Dehydration. Not much to be done about it."

"My wife keeps talking about how cold it was last winter." John took the glass of whiskey. "Can't believe the change. I know we had heat and cold in Pennsylvania, but nothing like this."

"That's Missouri. Can't do anything by halves." Jabez sipped and smoked and thought he detected the beginnings of a breeze.

John pulled a booklet from his trousers pocket. "Ever seen this?"

Jabez set his glass on the rail and took the booklet. *"A Manual of Freemasonry,"* he said. "I saw this floating around in the gold camps. Lots of Masons hunting gold." He flipped open the cover to the motto on the flyleaf. *"Ordo Ab Chao.* Order out of chaos." He looked at John and handed it back. "Well, that's what this country needs. Can Masons pull that off?"

"We can try." John pushed it back into his pocket. "You ever thought of joining?"

"My father-in-law was a Mason. He mentioned it once to me, but I never followed up."

"Sam Canon and I joined a lodge back in Fayette County. We're getting some of the other fellows together here, see if we can get a charter to start one up. Interested?"

"Maybe. What do you think a lodge can do?"

"Can't hurt to set up some structure. There's trouble coming." John put his glass carefully on the rail, squaring it precisely with the edge. "Can't help but think we're going to need a reason for men to stick together in spite of their differences. Masonry tends to do that."

Jabez nodded and rocked. The thought of those bloody, broken bodies flashed again. Any straw to grasp.... "What do I have to do?"

Jabez blinked in the dim light. He'd climbed to the second floor of the old courthouse building, a drafty wooden structure that Hank Sterrett had turned into a shop for women's dress goods once the new brick courthouse was finished. The raw October wind heaved through chinks in the walnut weatherboarding, and he shook rainwater from his hat brim. The stairs opened into a tiny chamber in the southeast corner. A single candle flickered from a sconce, and Jabez's first thought was that it was too close to the gimcrack partitions. A figure waited at the top of the stairs, back to the candle, face in shadow. All Jabez could see of him was a fringe of thinning hair, a gleam of shirt front and a patch of white at his waist. Without a word, the man stepped forward and led Jabez through a curtained door. The second room was lit by a spirit lamp and in the increased light, he could see that the man who clutched his elbow was Jacob Mosier, whom Jabez had treated for shingles in early September. The man gave no indication that he recognized the doctor, so Jabez bit off his greeting.

They stood in shadowy silence while a series of rappings, a shuffle of feet, an occasional cough, emanated from a back room. This is foolishness, Jabez thought. This must have been the type of thing Eliza had experienced at séances, another activity full of nonsense. Three more raps sounded, and Jabez coughed to disguise a laugh. Surely the spirits had established contact.

The knocks must have signaled action, as Mosier moved to open the door into the main room. Four men emerged, all in frockcoats with a swath of linen or leather at their waists. The room behind them reeked of sweat, stale tobacco and pomade. Jabez's view into it was blocked, and the door was drawn to after the last man. Bill Price, a miller from out Forest City way, led the group. Frank Cayton followed him, along with two men Jabez didn't know. None of the men acknowledged Jabez. Price stopped in front of him and folded his hands.

He cleared his throat and settled his glance over Jabez's left shoulder. "Do you seriously declare," he said without preamble, his voice solemn and deeper than Jabez remembered it, "upon your honor that you freely and voluntarily offer yourself a candidate for the mysteries of Masonry?"

Jabez nodded. "I do."

"Do you seriously declare, upon your honor that you solicit the privileges of Masonry by a desire for knowledge and a sincere wish of being serviceable to your fellow creatures?"

"I do." Jabez noted the definite similarity to the marriage ceremony.

Price turned and disappeared into the back room, closing the door noiselessly behind him.

Now Cayton stepped forward. "I'm Junior Deacon, Doctor Robinson," he said. It was the first hint that any of them remembered his name. "I must ask you now to remove your clothing."

Jabez's eyebrows shot up, and he looked to Mosier. Mosier's face remained impassive. "Just down to shirt and trousers, sir," Cayton said in his squeaky voice. "Please remove boots and stockings as well. And empty your pockets of change. Also, Jacob will hold your watch." Mosier held out his hand.

Jabez did as he was instructed and when he stood, barefoot and in shirtsleeves, one of the strangers slipped behind him and passed a kerchief over his eyes. Jabez started, a momentary sense of panic quickening his blood. His hands lifted to the hoodwink, but Cayton—he assumed it was Cayton—grasped them and pulled his arms to his side. "No need to be concerned, Doctor, this is all part of the purification process."

Cayton proceeded to unbutton Jabez's shirt, but left it tucked into the waistband, and another man slipped the shirt off his left shoulder and arm, leaving his chest half bared. Someone rolled his left trouser leg to his knee, pushed his right foot into a slipper. It was all horribly childish.

But then they slipped the rope around his neck. It settled over his head, and he smelled the pungent odor of sisal, felt the scratch of fibers against his collarbone. The tail of the rope dragged down his back and swayed against his calves.

"A noose?" he growled. The ceremony no longer seemed like child's play, and in the complete darkness behind the mask, his control slipped.

"No, no," the high voice of Frank Cayton came to him. "A cable-tow only. A lifeline, the silver cord." Jabez's mind drifted to scenes of men dangling, of a row of slaves lashed together by the neck. The rope lay hot against his skin. "*. . . or ever the silver cord be loosed,*" Frank said. "Ecclesiastes." He grasped Jabez by the elbow and guided him into the back room.

Jabez struggled, not entirely successfully, to beat back the sense of floating through a shadowy world of phantasms. More knocks sounded, he was led forward, halted, spoken to. His left breast was touched by something cold and sharp, and he thought of the scaler in his dental kit. Questions were asked. Frank Cayton answered for him at first, and then John's voice took over. Jabez's sense of comfort increased under John's guidance, and he responded as he was prompted though he had little comprehension of the meaning of the stilted phrases. Once he heard Sam Canon's bass tones, but most of the examination was conducted by someone he thought might be J.W. Moodie. J.W. had a curious hitch in his voice, the result of scar tissue from badly extracted tonsils. Once his guides manipulated his feet into an odd posture and lowered him to his knees. He swore oaths on what he supposed must be a Bible, and the hoodwink was stripped away.

The glare of three tapers surrounding an alter pierced his eyes. He was conscious of a mass of men filling the room, and once again he felt vulnerable. What if this was all an elaborate prank? Were they making fun of him? Was this a sort of hazing, the kind fellows do in those silly secret societies in eastern universities? Choler rising, he glared around the room, but there were no smirks, no muffled snickers, only a quiet and deep solemnity. John watched him with the expression of a proud father, so Jabez tamped down his suspicions and did what he was next instructed to do.

And then it was over, and Jabez was allowed to don his clothing and reclaim his valuables, and when he returned, the big room was cleared of alter and candles, rugs and trappings, and bottles of whiskey and beer had appeared along with plates of oysters and cheeses and pastries. The pastries were courtesy of Ira Irvine, the baker, who leaned against a wall talking to Frank Cayton. John slapped his shoulder and congratulated him. Sam, too, shook his hand and then Mr. Moodie and Bill Price and Jacob Mosier. Jabez surveyed the room. It was no more fey than any smoky tavern on a stormy night. Men laughed and joked and drank as if there had been no white aprons, no star-studded collars, no compasses balanced on open Bibles. Doctor Norman was there, along with Foster the attorney and Mr. Collins the schoolmaster. Galen Crow, who'd fulfilled some part of the earlier ceremony in his Tennessee voice, stood shoulder to shoulder with Rufus Byrd. The one an Atchison supporter, the other a Benton man, they rarely met without breaking into political argument. Two of the Zooks, the banker Jace Biggers, and Peter McIntosh lifted their glasses to the newest brother. Even Reuben Bigelow and Francis Kunkel abided each other's company for the sake of the brotherhood. Maybe there was something to this, Jabez thought as he accepted a glass from John and a cigar from Frank Cayton. In the outside world, most of these men harbored deep-seated grudges against one or another of their fellows, but in this room differences lay low or disappeared entirely. Maybe there was a straw to be grasped.

17

The first thing Jabez saw when he stepped through the Jacksons' front door was a small balsam perched on a table covered with cotton batting, its fresh scent filling the room. His acquaintance with Christmas trees was limited, his acquaintance with Christmas celebrations even more so. Back in Maine, the Robinsons ignored Christmas, and the festivity struck him as delightfully pagan.

"Welcome, Robinson!" John's voice lifted over the confusion of sound rising from a crowd of young ones clustered at the foot of the tree, racing up and down the stairs, or huddled under the makeshift table of trestles and planks that dominated the front parlor. "Make yourself at home, be right with you."

Jabez hung his damp overcoat and hat on the pegs behind the door and found his hands grasped on one side by James, on the other by Rebecca.

"Come see our tree," Rebecca squealed, eyes big and smile bigger.

James yanked, and Jabez feared for his finger joints. "See what we done!"

The boy pointed to the top of the tree, where his arrowhead, that shiny black stone that was never out of his possession, sat proudly lashed to the tip of the highest branch, point aimed to the heavens. "It's our star."

"A black star," Jabez said, kneeling. "Must be a first in the history of Christendom."

James looked doubtful but Rebecca nodded vigorously. "The first," she spit out through a missing front tooth. "We never had a Christmas tree before—it's the first!" She gazed up.

Jabez straightened. John, wrapped in a flowered apron, was at his elbow, extending a mug. "Try this," he said. "Tell me if there's too much rum."

Jabez took the eggnog and sipped. His eyes watered. "Just right," he said. "No such thing as too much rum."

"My sentiments," John said. He went back to the table, where two large bowls sat side by side, surrounded by a basket of eggs, a mortar of fresh-ground nutmeg and several jugs of milk. Tom Kreek sat across from him, providing helpful advice. "This bowl has the rum in it. The other's for the children and the women. Or maybe it's the other way around...."

Jabez dipped up a generous helping from the first bowl. "This is the adult version. All you have to do is smell it," and he took another long draught. "Good stuff, John. Didn't know you were so skilled."

Elizabeth slipped up behind her father and threw an arm around his waist. "Papa, don't make the women drink out of the children's bowl. I want some of that."

"No ma'am, not with that young'un in your belly." Her father patted her protruding stomach, swollen with new life.

Jabez scrutinized her over the rim of his mug. Her complexion was clear, even rosy, her hair shiny and healthy, her expression serene. There was no sign of the sickness that had haunted her first pregnancy.

Billy held out a mug. "I'll take her share."

John lifted a ladle, half-filled the cup. "Go easy on this stuff, boy. It's powerful."

Billy grimaced. "I've had worse."

"Your pa know that?"

"Does your pa know what?" Sam asked, kicking the front door closed behind him, a load of wood in both arms, snow melting off his boots and puddling on Nancy's flowered wool carpet.

"Nothing," John said and elbowed Billy.

Billy set down his mug and took the load from his father. Jabez pulled a chair away from the table and motioned Elizabeth into it. "Sit, Mrs. Kreek," he said. "That's an order from your doctor."

Elizabeth ignored the chair and sank into Tom's lap. "They chased me out of the kitchen," she said. "Not that I needed to be chased. My back hurts like the dickens and the smell of giblets is more than I can bear."

Jabez smiled and settled into John's reading chair next to the fireplace.

The children chattered among themselves while they snipped paper and tied ribbons into fantastical shapes to hang on the tree. Sam fussed with the fire, John with his eggnog. Elizabeth transferred her bulk from Tom's lap to the rocker by the front window, hummed and laughed and advised the tree trimmers. Cedar covered the mantelpiece and twined through stair rails. The smells floating in from the kitchen were enough to derange a sane man. Johnny, the Jacksons' youngest, adrift and underfoot on unsteady feet, went ashore at Jabez's knee, and the doctor scooped him up. He settled the child against his waistcoat, from which the boy dug out watch and fob and promptly put them in his mouth. Jabez drained his eggnog and accepted a glass of whiskey from John. This is how it should be, he thought. Eliza would have delighted in such a scene. He'd waited ten years for a home like this and in ten short weeks it had been snatched from him.

He watched Billy fashion snowflakes from pages of *The Democratic Review* while Rebecca hung on his knee. The boy would have a family of his own some day, but first he needed to explore, go adventuring. Jabez took a sip of his whiskey, set the glass out of range of the baby's reaching fingers. When regrets threatened to overwhelm him, regrets for the years that might have been spent with Eliza, he told himself that he never would have settled, never would have been a proper husband, had he not seen something of the world beforehand. That chapter was finished, nothing to be done about it. And now he was starting over. He'd started over many times, but at forty he was finding it something of a chore. He'd take it slowly. No hurry.

The kitchen door opened to the aroma of roast goose, and Agnes leaned into the room. "Clean up time," she called. "Dinner in five minutes," setting off a scramble of men and children for the washroom. "Oh, hello, Doctor," she said, catching sight of him behind the baby, and she bobbed a quick curtsy. Her cheeks were rosy with the cooking, there was flour on her chin, and her hair slipped in tendrils from its pins. She was very pretty.

Smiling, he pulled the watch from Johnny's sticky fingers and gave him a silver dollar to play with instead.

"Look, doc," Billy said, reaching across the sleeping forms of Rebecca and Johnny, book in hand. Dinner cleared, dishes washed, the family clustered around the Christmas tree and the square rosewood piano, John's Christmas gift to his wife. The tree's candles had been lit, Nancy had played and sung *It Came Upon a Midnight Clear,* and the candles had been extinguished. The children had received their gifts—a piece of candy, a book, a pair of mittens—and the two younger ones dozed on Nancy's lap.

"Mrs. Stowe," Jabez said, taking the book and turning it in his big hands. "*Uncle Tom's Cabin.* The book that'll launch a thousand ships." He winked at Billy. "Or a thousand soldiers."

"It's my present from Ma and Pa," Billy said, retrieving the book and flipping through the pages. "Ma says she remembers a slave being beaten to death back in Maryland on a neighbor's cotton farm."

Rachel, making the rounds with the coffee pot, looked up. "Those poor, poor creatures," she said. "I'm glad this book is getting people riled up."

"Thank the Lord the people of this county aren't so immoral," Nancy put in.

"The people of this county don't happen to have tobacco or cotton crops," Jabez said.

"Galen Crow brought in a gang of slaves to harvest his apples," Agnes said. She crouched on the floor, her skirts puddled around her, working through a wooden puzzle with James. "Their owner hired them out from Kansas City. Mr. Crow said it was cheaper than local labor."

"Were best he'd hired local," Sam said. "Local white boys need the work."

John set his coffee cup on the piano just as Nancy slid a saucer beneath it. "We'll have slaves a-plenty right across the river if Atchison has his way in Kansas," he said.

"Do you think there'll be fighting?" Billy looked to Jabez.

"Yes, I do," Jabez said. "There're too many hotheads on both sides to let the territories vote in peace on something as divisive as slavery."

"You don't think Kansas settlers will vote to organize free?" John asked.

"If there were such a thing as a legitimate Kansas settler who's there to grow wheat and vegetables and cattle, sure they would. But there's no such thing."

"Atchison says he'll send five hundred Missouri men into Kansas to vote pro-slave," Billy added.

"Then six hundred New England men will vote free-soil," Sam said.

"That's the point," Jabez said. "The real issue isn't slavery but sectionalism. It's whether one set of opinions prevails over another, one group of men has the power to tell another how to live. And the argument will be condensed into an area about the size of Holt County. A keg of gunpowder."

John tamped tobacco into his pipe. "I would agree if the subject were any other. If we were talking about an agrarian society versus an industrial society, or religion, say. But we're talking about slavery. We're talking about basic humanity, basic rights. Surely one group of men has the right to tell another group that what they're doing is wrong."

"Papa's right." Elizabeth said. Her gray eyes flashed in the lamplight. "Slavery's a national disgrace. We simply must do something about it."

"We're a laughingstock around the civilized world," John said. "Our influence and credibility are finished. The press in England and France ridicule us daily. It's bound to affect our trade."

"England and France look down their noses at the same time they buy up the South's cotton," Jabez said. "If the slave society were to dissolve today, they'd cry bloody hell from here to kingdom come when the price of cotton shoots sky high. Their manufactories can't survive without our slave labor." He nodded to Nancy. "My apologies, ladies."

"I wonder," Agnes said, "that America can hold together with north and south thinking so differently. It's like England and Ireland—very different cultures. And they're forever squabbling."

"That's it exactly," Jabez said, jabbing an unlit cigar in her direction. He was unaccountably pleased they were in agreement, and he smiled at her. "The question that'll split us is whether the country should be united at all costs. Or whether it should divide into separate nations, like in Europe." He poured himself a finger of brandy from the decanter at his elbow. "The result could be civil war, and the loss of life would be stupendous. Is anything worth that kind of tragedy? I think not."

"Then nothing's worth war?" Sam asked. He scowled at Jabez. "Man, I think you don't value your country."

"You question my patriotism?" Jabez said quietly, holding Sam's gaze.

Billy frowned. "Pa, that's not fair. He fought in the last war."

Sam's broad face reddened. "Watch your tongue, boy," he growled. It was Billy's turn to flush.

Jabez kept his eyes on Sam's. The man reminded him of the tedious New Englanders he'd known in Maine, and he hectored Billy abominably.

"The slave power—"

"Hogwash!" Jabez slammed his empty glass on the table. Rachel's head shot up. Children stirred. "There's no such thing as the slave power, there's nothing but a small class of rich spoiled landowners who can't abide the thought of change. They can't agree on anything—couldn't agree on Texas, couldn't agree on the Mexican War, couldn't agree on the Compromise—how in heaven's name can anyone call them a power? That's just abolitionist bug-bite and moonshine!" He dropped back in his chair and slapped his palms on his knees.

Agnes put a hand to her face. Jabez had the sense she was concealing a laugh.

Billy sent a defiant look to his pa and spoke up. "You think secession's legal, doc?"

Jabez's temper waned. He wondered who Agnes was laughing at and hoped it wasn't him. "It can be argued," he said. "I do think there are principles worth fighting for. I just don't see that union is one of those. Is it any better to be governed by eastern seaboard aristocrats a thousand miles away than to be governed by hereditary aristocrats in England? The continent's too big to be governed as one country. It must and will break into pieces." His voice softened. "The question is whether it can be done peaceably. I've seen war. I've seen what it does to armies and to the civil population alike, and I tell you, forcing these two sides to live with each other in a marriage of hellish proportions is not worth the carnage. The two sections must let each other go."

John studied his friend. "Then you side with the southerners?"

"I side with no one," Jabez said. "I'm disgusted with the whole lot. Politicians take up the torch so they may go electioneering. Northerners need a cause that'll allow them to form a new party and ride it to power. The south will decide it's being put upon and fight them every step of the way. Both sides are unprincipled, childish and hotheaded. I can't subscribe to that kind of irresponsibility."

Rachel stood. "Sam, we need to start for home," she said. "Billy, the horses please."

Jabez smiled at Rachel. "Your present dredged up more dissension than you bargained for, I'm thinking, Mrs. Canon."

"Yes, indeed, Doctor, more than we need on Christmas Eve I think," Rachel said.

"But isn't that what Mrs. Stowe had in mind?" Agnes asked. She stood, the sleeping James cradled in her arms. "Generating discussion?"

"I wonder," Jabez said, "if she also intended to generate war."

"It won't come to that," said Sam, "Right-thinking men won't allow it." His look continued black. "And Doctor, there'll come a time when you get off the horse on one side or th'other in this business. I hope to God A'mighty you make the right choice."

Jabez fixed him with a stare. "I know exactly where I stand, Sam. And I'll do everything I can to prevail."

18

April 1854

Ice crackled in puddles among the shadows, and on St. Joseph's main street, horse turds steamed as they melted the mud around them. Jabez pulled Jupiter to a stop in front of the first of a half dozen smithies and leaned on his pommel.

"St. Joe's grown since last I came through," he said to John, who reined in alongside. "I'm guessing they aim to give Kansas Town a run for its money."

John nodded and swung off his mount. "Full of free-soilers, I'm thinking." He backed up to his horse's left hind leg and picked up the hoof. "Damn nail broke right off. Be back in a minute." He handed the reins to Jabez and disappeared into the forge.

Jabez turned in his seat to look for the others. Sam and J.W. Moodie trailed a block behind, Billy and Galen Crow brought up the rear. The four men wound their way through wagons and oxen-carts, past shoppers and drovers. Under a lowering sky and a chill breeze, steamboats packed the Missouri River, lately freed of ice. On every side Jabez heard the flat, nasal accents of Boston, New York, Connecticut, Maine—the accents of New England. Free-soilers, like John said. Free-soilers and abolitionists.

John was back. "He can do it now. You want to wait or head on? I can catch you up."

Sam's big black stallion nosed up next to Jupiter and snuffled. "We'll wait," Sam said. "Atchison can bide his time."

Jabez settled onto a bench outside the smithy with a chunk of bread and a slice of cheese and watched Billy water the horses. Senator Atchison had requested a meeting with a delegation of men from Holt County, and Sam thought it'd be educational for the boy to ride along.

Moodie lowered his bulk next to Jabez. "Strike a flint and this place'll blow sky high," he said, pulling a chunk of dried beef out of his pocket. "Those fellows over there ain't looking too happy to have New Englanders amongst them." He waved his beef at a knot of men gathered in front of the dry-goods store. Jabez recognized the type, men he saw every day in Holt County, in the backwoods of Noddaway and the bottomlands of the Platte River.

Galen Crow squatted on his heels in front of them, drew a stag-handled knife from its sheath and carved into an apple. "Me neither. Them folks should stay home where they belong."

"Now Galen," Moodie said, "Doc here's a New England man himself. Ain't all bad."

"The doc didn't bring any foreign ideas when he come here," Crow said.

"Don't seem to me claiming a homestead and making a farm is exactly a foreign idea." Moodie pushed his hat to the back of his head.

"Them New Englanders might as well be Russians." Crow tossed his apple core at a stray cat and drew in the dust with the tip of his knife. "Don't you think so, Doc?"

Jabez brushed crumbs from his waistcoat and pulled a kerchief from his pocket. "I think there's trouble coming, boys, that's what I think."

They left St. Joe on the inland road and by sunset were a mile outside Gower. A graveled drive wound through low hills and across a smooth-shaven lawn. Thick stands of rhododendron fronted a two-story brick mansion, a balustraded balcony stretched the length of the second floor, paddocks and outbuildings nestled in the rear.

The men dismounted at the broad steps, and Negro boys appeared to take their horses. A black butler, in livery, stood at the open door, the faint sound of male laughter and the scent of expensive cigar smoke wafting onto the veranda. "Mr. Canon ... Doctor Robinson," a voice boomed from the hallway. "Welcome, welcome! And Mr. Jackson." David Rice Atchison, Missouri's senior senator, shook John's hand. "Congratulations, sir, congratulations on your appointment as school commissioner. The education of Holt County's scholars is in excellent hands." The Senator stood well over six feet tall, a heavy shock of hair sweeping above a high forehead. An embroidered blue-and-gold collar hung with gilded medallions encircled his neck, the badge of his office as Grand Master of the Clinton County Masonic Lodge. A half-smoked cigar waved from fleshy fingers.

"And Judge Canon." He turned to Sam. "I understand you're Holt County's newest man on the bench." Sam, unsmiling, took the offered hand.

"Mr. Crow, Mr. Moodie." He gestured to his companions. "Officers in our lodge. Holt County businessmen." Hands shook all around. "You know Doctor Robinson. John Jackson. My son, William."

"Yes, yes, of course, of course, delighted, sir, delighted." The Senator swept a hand down the hall, scattering ash as he herded his guests toward a room to the left. "Shed your wraps and join us in the library, gentlemen. There's a goodly representation of Missouri grandees gathered. You must meet them."

He ushered them into an overstuffed parlor where a fire cackled in a fireplace the height of a man and flashed off brass knickknacks, mahogany upholstered in rubbed velvet, crystal decanters. A tumbler of whiskey appeared for each of the new arrivals—refused only by Mr. Moodie, a teetotaler—before the men could take stock of the company. Atchison waved them to seats.

Four men relaxed with drinks and cigars in green velvet chairs. Jabez recognized one, hard to mistake: a man as tall as Atchison, probably tipping the scales at three-fifty. Albert Boone was famous as an Indian trader, a mining outfitter, and the owner of Westport's largest house and first bathroom. If Boone's here, thought Jabez, we're in for a rabid proslave lecture.

Atchison led off the introductions with Boone, moved to the next man remarkable in comparison as he was a small, pinched little man. "May I present Doctor John Stringfellow, gentlemen?" said Atchison. "You and he have something in common, Doctor Robinson, as he is of the medical profession himself." The intelligence among Jabez's medical colleagues was that Stringfellow was not a physician one would allow to attend one's family. The small man bowed slightly without rising. "Doctor Stringfellow edits the *Squatter Sovereign*; perhaps you've read it? If not, I suggest you do. Excellent paper, excellent."

Next to Stringfellow on the stiff settee was Jo Shelby, slight, precise, sporting a neatly trimmed and sharply pointed beard. Jabez knew him by reputation as the richest slaveholder in Missouri. Shelby acknowledged them with a wave of his hand.

Atchison turned to the man leaning against the chimney piece who bore a decided resemblance to Stringfellow. "And the doctor's brother, General Ben Stringfellow." The general smoked a pipe, a fragrant cloud lingering about his head. "We expect great things from him, in the contest to come, eh, General?" He cuffed the man on the shoulder, threatening to knock him off his feet.

Almost as an after-thought, Atchison turned to the window, and Jabez started when he recognized the figure standing in the shadows. The man shuffled into the firelight, his rough wool trousers and threadbare shirt a stark contrast to the rich clothing of the others.

"Bigelow?" John said. "Willard Bigelow?" He folded his arms across his chest, and Bigelow scowled, looking away. He was the last person Jabez expected to turn up in Atchison's parlor.

"Hey, Mr. Moodie. Mr. Crow," Willard mumbled. He nodded to Sam and Jabez and sipped his drink. He no longer looked the whining bully, sneaking shots of spiked punch at the barn dance. He'd grown into his height, close to six feet Jabez judged, fit and muscled, a hank of oily yellow hair flopping over his forehead. But most arresting were the eyes, Jabez remembered those eyes. Even in the shadows, they were strikingly pale, not quite silver, burning cold and white. A faint purplish scar ran from his left earlobe to the bridge of his nose. From having stitched up many similar wounds, Jabez knew it to be a knife slice healed without the benefit of medical attention. It hadn't been there a year ago. The expensive crystal tumbler in his hand was half-full of whiskey, neat, looking out of place in rough hands.

"So you know my friend." Atchison stepped to Bigelow and put a proprietary hand on his shoulder. Willard's eyes slanted in Atchison's direction, a fleeting smirk of distaste crossing his lips, then he shrugged off the hand by lifting the glass and swallowing the whole of its contents. "Wil's young, but he has at his command a whole company of good Missouri boys who ain't afraid to fight for the honor of the South, eh, boy?" The big man slapped Bigelow on the back. "Hails from your neck of the woods—one of yours, eh?" Without waiting for a response, he turned to the company. The boy, Jabez thought, could be the most dangerous man here.

"My friends," Atchison said, regarding the newcomers, puffing out his chest as he swung into his stump speech. "My colleagues and I have asked you as fellow Masons to join us this evening on a matter of great importance." He waved at the others in the room. "It is, of course, the Kansas question.

You may think that the settlement of the Kansas territory need little concern the citizens of Missouri. Certainly you may think the question of Kansas has aught to do with farmers and businessmen such as yourselves." He stopped for effect. "Well, my friends, you would be wrong." He took a pull on his cigar to emphasize his point. "Kansas is an extension of Missouri. Its climate and soils match those of the Missouri River corridor, its future is in tobacco and hemp, corn and hogs, just like that of the great state of Missouri. Its institutions and society should be Missourian. Its fields and prairies should be settled by those who bring southern honor, southern pride, southern values to the new west. In short, gentlemen, Kansas should be, must be, settled by slave interests."

He stopped there, red-faced, puffing with exertion, splashed another finger of bourbon into his glass and gulped. Sam and John stirred uncomfortably, Billy looked to Jabez. Jabez kept his expression carefully blank.

"Now, Senator," Sam said.

"Just a moment, though," the Senator interrupted. "There are other reasons, beyond the need to provide land for good Missouri citizens to farm. Let me enumerate them." He held up a pudgy forefinger. "One. The northern money power aims to dominate us, to impose the tyranny of its control on the south." His voice crescendoed. "Gentlemen, Faneuil Hall is coming to rule us. Do we stand by and allow that to happen? By God, I say no—never!"

Up went a second finger. "If Kansas was to organize as an abolitionist state, Missouri, our home, would be surrounded, surrounded, gentlemen. The abolitionists would be all around us. Our institutions, our property, our very way of life would be threatened with destruction."

The Senator's friends nodded, murmured their assent. J.W. Moodie glanced nervously at Sam. Jabez stirred impatiently.

"And third," Atchison held up yet another finger, heavy with a gold and jade ring, "and most important. We are playing for a mighty stake. The game must be played boldly. If we win, we carry our institutions to the Pacific Ocean. If we fail—well, gentlemen, we cannot fail. To fail would be to lose Texas, Arkansas, all the territories. And yes, to lose Missouri." His voice softened, now sad and gentle. His fierce black eyes pinioned each Holt man, one after another, challenging and inviting their alliance. "Gentlemen, I say we cannot fail."

Sam would not be still. "Senator," he said. "We ain't slave-holders. Holt County folks farm small holdings. We grow corn and hogs with free labor. Our own labor." He set down his whiskey glass with a thump. "We don't cotton to abolitionists, no sir, we don't hold that the Negro can live alongside the white man." He stood, planted his feet, forced Atchison to take a step back. "Sir, the course you take'll tear this country apart. I won't be a party to it."

One of the Stringfellows, the doctor, jumped to his feet. "We got to draw the line here, Canon." His face was fiery. "We got to fill Kansas with our own folk before Kansas turns into a swarm of lawless infidels and abolitionists. You can't sit back and watch it happen. They'll take your farm, too, wait and see."

John spoke up. "Seems to me there're more southerners in Kansas now than northerners. Maybe, gentlemen, we're jumping the gun here. Douglas's idea—and yours, too, Senator—allow settlers to vote their minds which way they want to go. Seems to me that's the way to bring the territories into the Union peacefully."

Atchison turned to him. "Ah, Mr. Jackson, there's the rub." He stabbed a forefinger at John. "My support of Stephen Douglas's bill came with the assumption that Missourians would pre-empt Kansas and there'd be no interference. If truth be told, the Senator and I had that very agreement." He straightened up, squared his shoulders. "But I am surprised, no astounded, shocked—by the news from Boston. That's the reason I returned home, even though I am sorely needed to work the House before its vote on the bill." He looked around. "Gentlemen, as we speak, the abolitionists in Massachusetts are organizing a mass migration to Kansas. They have chartered an emigrant aid society to fill the territory with their kind. Now, sir, I have opened this great country for Missourians, not for abolitionists, and I expect Missourians, all Missourians, to assert their rights."

Sam stepped to a window, hands in pockets, and stared out at the night. Mr. Moodie jumped in. "There ain't no indication that the northerners're abolitionists. They might just be farmers like us. God knows we could use some northern manufacturing know-how down here."

Atchison turned on him. "Any man," he roared, "who comes to make Kansas a free state I regard as an abolitionist, sir, a black and dirty fiend who aims to make the nigger the equal of the white man. Do you wish to see your daughters married to a black man? Do you wish to see your wives and children sitting side by side with black wenches in church? Nor do I. I'll not see Kansas vote free soil. That, sir, is our duty as southerners and the only way we preserve our freedoms."

Jabez stirred, stubbed out the cigar which had burned to ash under his hand. "And what is your plan, Senator?" he asked. "How do you intend to counter the northerners?"

"We are organizing. Even now, families with black labor are preparing to move soon as weather permits. We have dozens of boys under Wil, here," he nodded at Bigelow, "moving into Kansas to stake their claims. When the abolitionists arrive, they'll find the good land gone. And if they choose to stay anyway," he turned slowly to each man, "we will shoot, burn and hang. I assure you, gentlemen, the thing will soon be over. We intend to Mormonize the abolitionists."

Jo Shelby leaned forward in his chair, his beard trembling. His words were as pinched as his appearance. "Gentlemen, you must understand. We brought you here as brothers in Freemasonry. We're sworn to support one another, to provide succor to one another." His small hand stroked dove-gray trousers. "If you are not with us, then you are against us. Please consider."

John looked from Shelby back to Atchison. "What would you have us do?"

General Stringfellow stepped away from the chimney piece, pipe in hand. "We need you to organize men from the northern counties. We need names, men we can count on to cross into Kansas and stake claims."

"Spring plowing's coming up," Moodie said. "The men in Holt and Noddaway need to tend their farms, ain't got the resources to go gallivanting about Kansas."

General Stringfellow waived away the objection. "They'll be back in a week. All we ask is they stake claims. They can come back to tend their farms for the summer."

"But to prove a claim a man has to build and farm it."

"Don't concern yourselves with details," Albert Boone said. "We'll take care of it."

"We'll need men to vote," the general said. "As soon as elections are called, sometime in the next few months, we intend to take a thousand Missourians in to vote proslave. We need to raise at least fifty from your area."

John looked askance. "Those votes will never be certified."

"There's no residency requirement," Boone answered. "How do you think those northerners expect to carry a vote? They'll be bringing voters right along with their settlers. Once we carry the votes and get our men into territorial government, we can be sure the future of Kansas goes the right way."

John turned to Atchison. "Was this the idea behind popular sovereignty? That it would devolve into a contest over who packs the polls?"

Atchison snorted. "Don't be naive. Every election in this country is carried by a stuffed ballot box. We're simply ensuring the vote goes our way."

Jabez's eyes slid to Bigelow, lounging against the wall in the shadows. "Sounds like a recipe for violence."

"You may be right, Doctor Robinson. We ain't afraid of violence," Atchison said. He turned to his friends. "Right boys?" He grinned, and they nodded back at him.

Sam had had enough. "Senator, I won't speak for my friends here. Every man'll let his conscience talk. But you won't be hearing from me." He shrugged into his coat. "Evenin'." And he stalked from the room without acknowledging the others.

John stood. "Well, sir." He extended his hand toward the Senator. "It's been an interesting evening and an interesting discussion." He nodded to the rest of Atchison's group. "We'll discuss your plans among ourselves. If any one of us is interested in joining with you, I'm sure you'll hear." He left the room. After a moment of uncertainty, Moodie and Crow nodded to the company and followed him.

Billy hung back as Jabez stepped close to the Senator. "Atchison, you risk civil war. The cataclysm that results would dwarf any war ever seen on this earth."

Atchison's eyes narrowed. "We won't be tyrannized by the north."

"Then secede. Take the south out and form a new nation. Do it now while you can still do it peaceably. Because if you pursue Kansas you'll find the northerners just as willing to butcher their enemies as are you. And then it'll be too late."

"I'll consider your words. Are you with us?"

"I'll do whatever I can to keep us out of war. If that means working with you or against you, I'll do what's necessary."

Atchison took a long drag on his cigar. "I can see you would be a formidable opponent, Robinson. I've heard of you; I know something of

101

your past. You could be useful to us."

"Only in the effort for peace. I'll work for secession if that will ensure peace."

"What about you, boy?" Atchison turned to Billy, tipped his head at Willard Bigelow. "Sign up with Wil here and see some mighty fine action."

Billy turned a thoughtful eye toward Bigelow. The blond man stared back, one side of his mouth lifted, light eyes derisive. "I don't think so, sir," Billy said. He moved to the door and waited for Jabez.

"We'll be in touch." Atchison offered his hand. After a moment, Jabez took it. He and Billy nodded to the others and left.

The horses plodded in single file on the road beyond Castile. Noon was fast approaching, the day overcast and gloomy. They had endured a fretful night in a livery stable, no other accommodations being available in the vicinity of Atchison's estate. Jabez, in the lead, reviewed in his mind the discussion of the night before, giving Jupiter his head. As the road rounded an outcropping of rock, Jupiter suddenly snorted, shied, danced on the rein. A copperhead, possibly, waking from the winter and seeking warmth on the packed surface of the road. Jabez pulled up, and Sam, then Billy, rode alongside him.

From behind the rock, a rider ambled into the road. Another followed, then a third and a fourth. In a moment, seven horsemen blocked the path, leaning casually on saddle horns, ragged hat brims tilted over brows.

"Morning, boys," said the first, kneeing his horse forward, thumbing his hat back. Jabez looked into pale silver eyes. Willard Bigelow sat his sorrel mare easily, shotgun slung across pommel. Jabez felt the absence of his own pistol. No one of his party carried a gun, while the men in the road ahead ensured their firearms were conspicuous.

Bigelow threw a leg over his saddle, leaned a forearm on the horn. "You pass a nice evening?" The men behind him shifted in their saddles.

Sam assumed the role of spokesman. His horse danced under a tight reign. "Move, Willard."

"We need to talk, Judge," Bigelow said easily, a smile on his thin lips. "I don't think we come to agreement last night."

"Ain't no agreement asked," Sam said in a measured voice. "The Senator knows my mind."

"That ain't good enough," said Bigelow, straightening in the saddle. "As the man said, either you're with us or you're against us. Now, which is it, Judge?"

Jabez twitched Jupiter up, close enough to Bigelow to challenge him. "We told Atchison we'd get back to him. That's good enough," he said. Jupiter's head bumped into Bigelow's mare. The mare whimpered. "Now move your men and let us pass. You've no call to make threats."

Bigelow looked Jabez up and down. "Your answer better be the right one, Doc," he said. "We'll be calling on you. And your families. We expect you to be on the right side." His lips curved, dead-fish eyes cold. After a moment he pulled his horse around, signaled to his men, and disappeared into the brush.

19

April 1854

The new year sped by, and Agnes was well into her thirtieth year. Thirty years. How, she wondered, had she come to age so quickly? She felt as if she was of Billy's and Elizabeth's generation, rather than ten years their senior. A function of dependency on her relatives, she supposed. But she had a plan. She was setting aside money each month and soon, before too many years passed, would have enough for a small property of her own. Or perhaps she would use it to travel west. San Francisco. Oregon.

Though as she grew older, the appeal of traveling on alone waned. She found the society in Missouri much more liberating than back home—she could think and read and say what she liked and no one hissed or frowned at her. And too she found herself well attached to her relations. To the younger ones, especially. And there was another new one to love. Elizabeth's little John Andrew was born one month ago exactly, and he was a plump and rosy thing, much loved by his mother. His papa was ecstatic. Doctor Norman delivered, as Doctor Robinson was gone to St. Joseph or some such place.

Agnes had seen little of Doctor Robinson since Christmas dinner. That is, she saw him ride out on that big bay of his, but he had not visited the Jacksons' home. His medical bag always hung from the saddle horn, so she assumed he was on his way to see patients. She found herself watching for him from her bedroom window or from the schoolhouse door. The ladies had named him (but not to his face) Holt County's most eligible bachelor. Mamas from Forest City to Richville invited him to family dinners and

Sunday church socials. She had seen him at one or two, but instead of paying court to the young ladies on display for his benefit, he indulged in conversation with the men, always talking politics, a passion that Agnes thought the world should dread no less than religion for its power to do harm.

Agnes feared the doctor and Sam were contrary with one another. The town was much too small for two leading citizens to be in opposition and what with the Masonic meetings and so forth they were often thrown together. Though she understood something of the doctor's difficulty with her cousin as Sam had always been opinionated and appeared to grow more obstinate with age. He and Billy had had yet another falling out, and Billy had begun to talk of going to California after the weather turned. He and Doctor Robinson had become great friends, a circumstance that could not but irk Sam terribly. Billy often stayed in town, working for Mr. Zook in his store, and mixing with the men of the town in conversation. The doctor's patience for Billy's opinions and questions appeared limitless, and Agnes was a bit envious of the time they spent together.

Her mind ran often to the doctor, and she blushed sometimes to think he might be the reason—one of the reasons—she was no longer keen to travel away from Lick Creek. He was a gregarious and sociable man, and he appeared to delight in debating the great questions of the day. But his temper was quick and hot, and he had alienated several of the town's leading citizens, in addition to Sam. The Kansas question and the feud between Benton and Atchison and particularly the subject of slavery in the territories were causing dissension among the men in town, and Jabez made no secret of his strong feelings.

John often returned home from a Masonic meeting and told Nancy and Agnes stories of Doctor Robinson's latest speech on Kansas and slavery and abolition. At first he laughed about it, especially one evening last month when words escalated into fisticuffs between Peter McIntosh and little Rufus Byrd. Though Agnes was not certain fisticuffs was the word for a scuffle between a Scotsman well over six feet tall and a wizened little rooster a foot shorter. But now it appeared that factions were developing in their little town. Everyone seemed to have an opinion, but of course no one had a solution, and many were ready to take offense at someone else's opinion. John no longer laughed when he spoke of these discussions but was somber and his eyes showed worry. Agnes feared there was a dreadful quarrel coming.

Agnes's favorite walk led south and east, past the cemetery and down the back of the hillside on which it perched, into the undulating countryside crossed with rills and creeks, with outcroppings of granite, too stony and hilly for farming, not yet turned over to grazing. A serene weeping willow perched on the bank of a brook, trailing fronds into the water and concealing a nook carpeted with mosses and diminutive flowers. She loved to sit there, nearly hidden, listening for the rustling in the underbrush, pretending that the land was yet undiscovered and that she was one of those wild inhabitants who knew the secrets of every burrow, every hidden habitation.

It was late April and the light had that iridescent quality that meant night approached and day creatures should scatter to their homes, but she was loath to leave—she sat with her legs drawn up, chin on knees, idly plucking at clover, half-heartedly looking for a four-leaf. She'd been there for half an hour, waving off the occasional mosquito, listening for the last trill of the song sparrow, when the subtle scent of tobacco smoke floated by on a shifting breeze. She was startled and momentarily concerned, since unsavory characters often roamed about this part of the frontier, but it occurred to her that anyone planning something nefarious would not light up a cigar first, and besides, she thought with an inward smile that she detected the scent of Doctor Robinson's imported tobacco.

Then he sat up, peering around a clump of sassafras from across the creek. "Do you always talk to yourself?" he asked, knocking ash from his cigar.

Her mind raced back over her thoughts; she couldn't remember what she might have said. She stammered something, then bent her forehead to her knees and hid her face.

A shout of laughter rang from across the creek. "Come now, Miss Canon, I often talk to myself. Sometimes it's the only intelligent conversation I get in a day."

She looked up, tossed a stray lock of hair off her forehead. "Then you know my secret. I've spent the past nine hours with thirty school children, and I needed an adult to talk to."

"And will I do?" he asked, rising and crossing the creek in two broad strides. He settled next to her on the bank. "I will confess I didn't hear your words clearly, so your secrets are safe from me."

"I really have no very interesting secrets, Doctor, so it doesn't signify whether you heard or not."

"That's hard to believe," he said, drawing on his cigar. "A young lady must have at least a few mysteries. In your case, perhaps they involve a certain Mr. Beaton?" He looked at her sideways.

She sputtered. "Really, Doctor Robinson, whatever are you talking about?"

"I've noticed he's been spending evenings in your cousin's parlor. As a matter of fact, the last three times I've visited my friend John, Mr. Beaton's been sitting in my favorite porch chair."

"Aldo Beaton can visit whom he pleases. I'm certainly not concerned."

Doctor Robinson, looking innocently across the creek, grinned. "All right, so that's not your secret. What should be my next guess? How about your age? That's always a secret among young ladies."

"That's a secret I'll willingly share. It's too easily discoverable." She looked him square in the face. "I will be thirty in November."

"Ahh," he said, "a mature woman."

"Spinster is the word, I believe."

"Not at all, Miss Canon. Spinsterhood is in the eye of the beholder." He tossed a pebble into the creek, not looking at her. "Give me another."

"Really, sir, I'm sure I have a dull enough life that secrets aren't a part of it. What about you? What secrets do you hold?" She turned toward him. "I hear you've had some involvement in the Kansas business. Is that not much more interesting than my confessions?"

He studied the end of his cigar for a moment with a slight smile on his face. Then he turned to her. "No, Miss Canon, it's not at all interesting. I have had very little to do with the Kansas business and hope in the future to have even less." He took a last pull on the cigar and stubbed it out in the dirt of the creek bank. "That disaster must proceed without me."

"I suppose there'll be fighting...."

"I'm sure of it. I have seen—argued with—the two sides and neither is willing to give an inch." He lay back on the bank, crossing his arms beneath his head and squinting at the heavens, where the light faded. "The radicals from the north will demand equality of the races and the extremists in the south will insist on slavery from here to the Pacific coast." He sighed. "I see no hope for a peaceful solution."

"Surely the reasonable men in the north won't allow things to go that far. Not everyone is an abolitionist. Stephen Douglas appears to be a sensible man."

"Stephen Douglas is an opportunist."

"Really, Doctor Robinson, you make a very simplistic judgment."

"Not at all, Miss Canon. Douglas is attempting to make deals with devils on both sides. His first concern is to enrich himself by building a railroad. He'll do anything that promotes that project at the expense of what's best for the country."

"Oh, come now, Doctor, I can't believe Douglas would sell out."

"Then you're naïve, Miss Canon," he said. "He's already sold out."

She hissed and gathered herself to rise, but he sat up and smiled just a little and put out a hand to hold her in place. "My apologies. I have a vicious temper, and I let it control my tongue." He turned to face her, folding his legs Indian-style. "I think you're wise. I know you're well-informed." Agnes sank back down. "I'm afraid though that even well-informed people can only sit back and watch this train wreck."

His compliments were absurdly pleasing but his anger stung. "What would you do?" she asked.

"Secede. The slavocracy should break off, form its own country and its own society. Heaven knows, slavery will die of its own weight soon enough. If the north insists on union, then we'll be plunged into a war beyond anything we've ever seen before."

They were silent as the light died, deepening from an opalescent gray to a faint yellow, then to a soft indigo, her vexation dimming with it. "Do you think there will be war?" She chewed on a grass stem.

"Yes," he said. "I think there will be war."

"And it will start here, won't it? Among all this rich cropland and these honest farmers." She sighed. "What a travesty."

He cocked his head, studying her with dark, fathomless eyes. "Yes, Miss Canon," he said. "It will start here."

They sat there, he looking at the slowly appearing stars, Agnes looking into the creek as the water blackened with the mysterious tints of night, and neither of them spoke. It occurred to her that she felt comfortable, safe, with him there, though the future was uncertain.

As the dark set in, he stirred, stood and reached out a hand to pull her to her feet. "I'll walk you back, if I may. It's getting late."

They strolled together up the hill, past the cemetery and through town to Agnes's door. "I enjoyed our talk." He bowed over her hand. "Perhaps we can have another adult conversation some time." He smiled, turned, and left her on the doorstep.

She encountered him several times that spring, the mild weather extending into late June before the heat and oppressive humidity came. Her evening walks refreshed her, and whether she walked in the hope of meeting him again or whether those chance meetings were unexpected she couldn't say. When they met, they talked of many things. He asked her opinion of a young woman whose mama exhibited her for his consideration, and she told him that the young woman, Miss Baxter, was pretty and empty-headed. He continued to tease her about Mr. Beaton, and she fancied his teasing had an edge to it. He had seen her one Sunday morning leaving church in Mr. Beaton's company, Mr. Beaton taking her arm as if he had every right to do so. She told him that Mr. Beaton reminded her very much of a gentleman she had known in Pennsylvania. He raised his eyebrows at that but pressed no further.

They talked about Agnes's students, who was bright, who struggled, and he offered suggestions on how to influence some of the more recalcitrant boys. He asked about the Bigelow children and hinted that their brother was up to no good. She replied that the younger ones held promise, but that Jake may as well withdraw since he made no progress at any subject. And they talked of his medical practice, within the bounds of propriety, and she saw in him a fascination, a passion for the wonders of the human body and the infinite permutations of the human mind.

They also talked about the manner in which the townspeople were taking sides in the coming conflict—who was proslave, who was free state, the varieties of opinion that existed between those two poles—and she often saw flashes of his temper, which was capricious, blazing up suddenly with a growl and a flush of the face. He would raise his voice and roundly censure one man or another for his views, one faction or another for its actions, one section or the other for its obstinacy. Then his anger would dissipate as quickly as it arose, and he would laugh and change the subject. Agnes sensed, though, a deep and abiding frustration simmering in him.

Once the heat came, it came with a vengeance. The temperature climbed toward the nineties, and thunder storms drove in from the western prairies. The folks of Lick Creek conducted their business early in the morning or late in the evening and retreated into their homes mid-day. There was little to do for a school teacher without classes. She visited Elizabeth and her little John Andrew at their home on the edge of the cherry orchard. Elizabeth's waist once again thickened, and Agnes did what she could to relieve her cousin of the heavier housework. Billy had made good his promise, joined a cattle drive to California in May. His letters were few and far between, but when they did come she loved the tales he wrote of sleeping in the open, riding night guard, attempting—but rarely succeeding—to outwit thieving natives. And she treasured the maps he drew for her and the snatches of song he copied out. Worry for him became her constant companion.

In the evenings, when the heat abated, friends dropped by for coffee and cake and talk, and Doctor Robinson was occasionally one of the company, as was Mr. Beaton, unfortunately. They shared their newspapers and the gossip that drifted their way from Jefferson City and St. Louis. John and Sam, Doctor Robinson and Mr. Beaton, in agreement for once, denounced Atchison for promising to send his Missouri boys to Leavenworth and Lawrence to vote in the November election. They all wondered if Franklin Pierce, that amiable drunk in the White House, cared what happened in the West. Tempers flared over whether the Union was sacred or secession was legal, whether blacks should be resettled far from America or slavery should be left alone to die of inertia. Everyone agreed that northerners should stay out of Missouri and leave Missourians to manage their own affairs. But in spite of impetuous tempers and rowdy arguments, opinions remained fluid. The close group of friends, neighbors and relatives whom Agnes had come to love and respect were not yet captive to those uncompromising, unrelenting views that were soon to solidify into the hostility and hatred that would tear their little community into fragments.

20

August 1854

The big bay gelding picked his way carefully through the mud, instinct and the feel of the soggy ruts his only guide. Ancient beech limbs overhung this stretch of the pike between Platte City and Barry on the road to Kansas Town. During the day, in decent weather, the road was pleasant enough, the woodland open and carpeted with old leaves and little underbrush. But tonight in the midst of a raucous mid-July storm, it swam in inky darkness until the next bolt of lightning, when nightmarish shadows danced across the path. Thunder tumbled off the massive trunks, magnifying its roar thrice over, causing the horse to skitter sideways.

Jabez hunched over Jupiter's withers, hat brim pulled low over his eyes, impeding his view. Not that he could see beyond the horse's nose, anyway. Jupiter had been his close companion since he returned from California, and he trusted the animal's surefootedness. But the most accomplished horse might falter on a night like this, and with the rain dripping off his hat and under his collar, he was in no mood to trust either his or Jupiter's instincts. He pulled his riding cloak closer around his shoulders. Without it he was soaked to the skin, with it he steamed like a hothouse lily. He mumbled a string of oaths to himself, then addressed them to Jupiter and shifted in the saddle.

To take his thoughts off his sore and soggy rump, he replayed in his head the meeting that occasioned this journey. Three days earlier, just after Mrs. Watson, his housekeeper, cleared the dinner dishes, he had settled into the rocker on the front porch for his after-dinner cheroot. He worked through in his mind the operation he'd performed that day, in which he'd excised the badly infected tonsils of the Kunkel boy. The operation succeeded, and though the child was uncomfortable, he'd controlled the bleeding, checked the contagion. As he considered different ways of reducing pain, a gray mare towing an open buggy trotted up the street past Zook's store and stopped at his doorstep. A figure in dust-covered trousers and vest descended, leading with his posterior and puffing with the July heat. Jabez groaned to himself. David Atchison looked about him and flung the reins over the fencepost. His wide face, flushed and damp, split in a smile, and he lifted a hand in greeting.

"Robinson," he boomed, hand stretched out as he mounted the steps. "I've found you with the first try. Good day, sir, good day." He looked about him expansively. "Pleasant little town you have here."

Jabez stood, took the offered hand. "Senator. I'm surprised to see you here."

"Not a-tall, Doctor, not a-tall." Atchison gestured to the chairs. "Mind if I have a seat?"

"Of course not. Make yourself comfortable," Jabez said, turning into the door. "Mrs. Watson," he called, "Water and the whiskey, please." Turning to Atchison: "Have you had your dinner, sir?"

"I thank you, I ate on the road." The Senator settled his bulk into Jabez's rocking chair, which creaked alarmingly, and Jabez dropped into the second chair. Mrs. Watson brought tumblers, a pitcher, and the whiskey decanter, and Atchison poured himself a hefty shot without the benefit of water. Jabez took a smaller portion, offered the Senator a cheroot, which he declined, extracting a thick Partagas from his coat pocket.

They both lit up, blew smoke in the direction of the street, sipped whiskey, said nothing for a moment.

Casting about for conversation, Jabez started up. "You've been on the road for awhile, then?"

"Left Gower early this morning, Doctor, came as fast as my mare could go." Atchison blew a smoke ring.

"Well, then," Jabez said after a bit. "What can I do for you, Senator?"

Atchison shifted in the rocker; it creaked again. He helped himself to another two fingers of whiskey. "I've become aware, Doctor Robinson, that you are acquainted with, perhaps related to, a certain Doctor Charles

Robinson."

"I am. He's a distant cousin. I met him in California."

"And what are your relations? Are you on friendly terms?"

"I hardly know. We knew each other only superficially. He came to me for medical care after he was involved in a disturbance in Sacramento. I haven't seen him for years."

"Yet you are related to him, and you both practice the same profession."

"I'm related to a great many people, Senator, and know a number of doctors."

"Of course, of course." Atchison patted his sizeable belly. "Are you aware that this Doctor Charles Robinson has returned from California and is here in Missouri? And that he is leading that very Emigrant Aid Society that we spoke of last April?"

Jabez took pains not to show his disquiet. "No, I was not aware. This is the emigrant movement to Kansas that you were denouncing? I wasn't aware that he held abolitionist views. But then, as I said, I knew him very little."

"But you are acquainted. And related. And that is what brings me here." Atchison turned to face Jabez. "It occurs to me, Doctor, that you may be just the person to appeal to your cousin and preserve the peace." He leaned forward, drops of whiskey sloshing onto his waistcoat. "You indicated to me in April that you would work with us." He held up his hand to stop Jabez's interjection. "Ah, ah, a moment, sir. You told me you would work for peace, even for secession if that meant peace."

"And I will," Jabez said quietly. "What is it you have in mind?"

"A mission to this Charles Robinson. From me. And in utmost secrecy. I cannot, of course, be known to be dealing with the enemy." Atchison leaned back, puffed on the cigar. "What I want you to do, Robinson, is go to Kansas Town, meet with your cousin and convince him to turn back. Let him know that we in Missouri will fight to keep Kansas for our people, fight to keep it proslave. Let him know that if he attempts to settle, we will burn him and his abolitionist settlers out, we will show no quarter." He turned to Jabez again. "Tell him that, Robinson, and make him turn around. Send him back to Massachusetts with his tail between his legs. Do that and you will be hailed as a hero across the country!"

Jabez was silent. He knew very well that no action of his would turn back the coming storm. But was this an opportunity, a small one, to play a part in keeping the peace, to avert the terrible and terrifying cataclysm that he knew in his gut would come if the abolitionists tried to settle Kansas?

"You understand, Senator, that I have no claim to Doctor Robinson's notice or consideration? He may refuse to see me. Certainly he has no reason to agree."

"Ah, but I sense you are a born negotiator. You will be able to present the choices to him clearly and succinctly. I am counting on you to do that. And you have the obsession to succeed. Your passion will carry the day. I have confidence in you."

Jabez stood and leaned against the porch rail, his back to his visitor. He was proof against the Senator's flattery, but in one sense, Atchison was right: he did indeed have an obsession for peace. His memory flickered to a day stinking of gun powder and blood, horrifying with the screams of wounded men and horses, defiled by corpses strewn like wind-fallen apples, his own arms bloodied to the elbows with the results of that day's work. The abomination of the battlefield hung just past his conscience, never quite dissipating, as if he viewed the world through a screen door. He would do anything in his power to deflect that horror from invading his world again. He knew his influence was feeble in the scheme of things, but every man must do what he can. He did, at least, have access to one or two of the men whose power to avert catastrophe exceeded his. He would try. And perhaps, just maybe, he could make an inroad.

He tossed his cheroot onto the street where it winked and died. "All right, Senator," he said without turning around. "I'll take the commission. I'll speak to Charles Robinson. Nothing guaranteed, of course. But I'll do my best."

"That's all I ask, Doctor. That's all I ask."

Lightning flashed again. He and Jupiter emerged from the woodland, crossed a creek on a wooden bridge, drumming hooves echoing now-distant thunder, and headed across pastureland north of the village of Barry. Maybe he should have stopped in New Market, when the storm first blew up, and started out again in the morning. Or back in Platte City, where he might have billeted with an acquaintance from medical school who lived somewhere along the bluffs. But then he would not have reached Kansas City until late tomorrow afternoon and might have missed the emigrants.

He'd been delayed in leaving Lick Creek by the impending delivery of Mrs. Obediah Jones, who'd been so inconsiderate as to remain in labor for all of twelve hours before producing her eighth son and releasing Jabez to pack his saddlebags and head south. So he found himself in the midst of a storm, miles from his destination, at an hour close to midnight when he should by rights be tucked up in a warm, dry bed. He grumbled his string of curses again and kicked Jupiter into a trot.

Four in the morning rang from a distant Kansas City steeple as he came to the Missouri shore, the eastern sky tracing a line of dirty gray against the receding night. The rain had stopped, leaving behind mid-summer humidity. The air felt like damp cotton pressing against his nose and mouth, making breathing difficult. A miasmatic mist rose from the water, the river itself sluggish as if it too found the heavy air difficult to push against. He roused the old ferryman from the shack at the tip of Harlem Point, a swampy appendage that pushed into the river across from the Kansas City wharves. The ferryman, cranky at being pulled from bed before daylight, muttered abuses under his breath as he fussed with ropes and oars. Jabez ignored him, standing at the rail with one hand on Jupiter's bridle, the other fishing in his waistcoat pocket for a cheroot. He lit up, took a satisfying drag, blew a stream of blue smoke into the damp, and turned to watch the few lights on the wharves ahead draw closer. After a moment, he realized the ferryman was grumbling not about getting up early, but of having been up all night, something about "them St. Joe boys what wanted me to put in downriver in the dark."

Jabez inhaled more warm smoke. "I see I'm not your first passenger today."

"No sir, you sure as hell ain't. I got one side of the fight, then the other. Those boys what comes after midnight was backwoods boys from north of St. Joe they was. I can tell by the voice. They's hill boys and spoiling for a fight with them Yanks what showed up last week."

"And you consider me to be the other side of this fight?"

"Well you sure do sound like a Yank to me, friend. All them other Yanks talks through their noses just like you do. You ain't no Missouri backwoods boy, now ain't that right?"

"That's right, I'm not. But neither am I a Yank." He blew smoke downstream. "You say the Missouri boys asked you to land them away from the wharves?"

"They didn't do no asking. They told me where to land. I told them it were dangerous to float down past my usual place, but they don't pay no mind to that." The old man pointed to the far bank, at a spot well east of Kansas City. "And they was armed—big knives, side pistols. No way was I gonna nay-say them."

"Did they say why they wanted to land in secret?"

The ferryman yanked on an oar, steering the ferry around a sandbar only he could see. "No sir, they surely did not. But I heard them talking low like, one of them telling another the Yanks would know him if he was seen. Sounded like they's planning something the Yanks couldn't know about."

Jabez thought a moment. "How many were there?"

"They's six of them, almost more than I can handle on this here boat, them and their horses." The ferryman gestured about him as if the animals were still there. "They left a mess as you can see." He pointed to a pile of horse droppings.

"And did you know any of them? Anyone you would recognize again?"

"They's all strangers to me. But the one, the leader appeared to be, I'm not forgetting him again soon."

"How's that?"

"Scar clean across his face." The man slashed a finger over his left cheek. "And them eyes. They's silver-like, flat. Like something dead. I don't mind telling you, he give me the shivers. That boy's a mean one, and I seen mean ones afore. You be wanting to steer clear of him."

Jabez scowled. Bigelow had brought his band of good old boys from Atchison's Clinton County headquarters to take on the emigrants. Had Atchison set him up? If so, why? Or perhaps Atchison sent Bigelow's gang as back-up in the event Jabez's mission didn't succeed. If Charles Robinson refused to alter his plans, Bigelow may have instructions to commence the hanging and burning Atchison had threatened. Or Bigelow may be acting on his own. He appeared capable of it—at the April meeting, it was evident he had no liking for Atchison.

Jabez tossed his cigar into the river and leaned on his forearms against the railing, looking down into inky water. Once he talked to Charles, he would need to locate Bigelow and find out what was going on. If the radical—and violent—fringes on both sides were neutralized, bloodshed might yet be avoided. Charles must control his radicals, and Jabez would have to figure out how to control this particular band of southern hot heads, at least until the emigrants moved out of Missouri.

The ferry bumped against the wooden wharf at the foot of High Street. Jabez tossed a coin to the ferryman. "You didn't see me this morning," he said.

"Sure thing, friend," the ferryman said, tucking the silver into a grubby pants pocket. "I ain't one to get in the middle of nothing." He held the boat steady while Jabez led Jupiter onto the dock, then pushed off and was gone into the graying mist.

Jabez mounted the bay and directed him up the steep street into the center of town. Kansas City had grown like an invasive weed in the past two years, officially a city, no longer a town. In the pearly light of dawn, delivery wagons and mule teams rumbled down the main street, its deep dust temporarily settled by the storm. A sleek black dog ambled along the boardwalk, sniffing and marking, ducking away from a broom wielded by an early-rising storekeeper. The clean, rich scent of the surrounding prairie, mixed with odors from the stockyards, the fresh smell of horse dung, and the welcoming scent of baking bread, hung in the air, made heavier by August's humidity and the promise of another oppressively hot day. Two more sleeping and eating places joined Maggie O'Day's hotel, catering to the flood of emigrants headed for California, the Oregon Territory, and now Kansas. One of these, sided in rough green fir and named the American Hotel, was managed, according to Atchison, by a man named Jenkins, an employee of the emigrant company. Here Jabez expected to find his relative, so it was toward the American he directed Jupiter, hoping for a wash and breakfast.

The lobby of the hotel smelled of fresh-sawn lumber and whitewash. Nothing stirred, including the night clerk, who slept tilted back in his chair, snoring, one booted foot on the edge of the desk. Jabez looked around for a bell to ring. Seeing none, he dropped his saddlebags to the floor with more force than was absolutely necessary, and grinned when the clerk snorted and jumped, chair legs crashing down. The man, sleepy-eyed and sniffing, looked about him in a daze.

"Morning," Jabez said cheerfully. "Hope I didn't wake you."

The clerk mumbled something incoherent and pushed his hair out of his eyes with both hands. "Help you?" he said.

"I need a room and breakfast, and then I need your help locating a friend," Jabez said, drawing out a leather wallet from an inside pocket.

"Yes sir," the clerk said. He turned a log book around, handed Jabez a pen and reached for a key from the slots behind the desk. "Who's your friend?"

"Doctor Charles Robinson," Jabez said, scrawling his name in the book. "Know him?"

The clerk's eyes narrowed. "Yeah, I know him. Guess everyone in Kansas City knows him by now." He turned the book to read Jabez's signature. "What do you want with him?"

"I'll let him know that directly, thanks. Is he a guest here?"

"You a relative?" the clerk asked. "Jabez Robinson, Holt County. Didn't know the doc was expecting relatives."

"He isn't. I don't believe you've said whether he's here."

"No, I guess I ain't. You know, you ain't the only one asking for him tonight. He's a busy man."

Bigelow and his men had been here. Jabez's voice was casual. "Did someone else find him?"

"I ain't told no one where he is. I'll be asking him first who he wants to see." The clerk stood up and pulled out paper. "Leave him a note. I'll see he gets it."

"Good enough." Jabez jotted a few words to Charles, included his room number, and handed the note to the clerk. "I'd appreciate it if he gets it soon. Say, before anyone else sees him." He dropped several coins on the desk, picked up his bags and headed up the stairs to his room.

Two hours later, Jabez was digging into his third fried egg and second cup of coffee when a big hand came down on his shoulder. "Doctor Robinson," said a warm, deep voice. "We meet again, sir."

Jabez stood, wiped his beard with a napkin, and turned, hand out. "We do indeed, Doctor Robinson." He smiled. "And I hope it's under pleasanter circumstances." They shook. "How's the shoulder?"

"Good, good, I thank you." Charles Robinson was of a height with Jabez. He was slender, thin, balding, with close-cropped beard and deep brown eyes. Though he was several years younger than Jabez, his somber, lined face gave the impression of later middle-age. Jabez's practiced eye saw that he favored his left shoulder, the shoulder from which Jabez had dug a lead cartridge after the squatter battles in Sacramento four years ago.

"And you? What brings you to Kansas City?" Charles took the other chair at the small breakfast table and accepted a cup of coffee.

Jabez pushed aside his plate, poured himself more coffee. "I live now in northwest Missouri, up in Holt County. I've taken a decided interest in the settlement of Kansas, as have most folks who live along the border." He sipped. "I understand you're bringing in an immigrant group to settle up the Kaw River? You must still be looking for adventure."

Charles Robinson was a champion of causes. The trouble in Sacramento involved a squatters' association which he organized and then led into discord and riot. Indicted for murder in California but never brought to trial, he impressed Jabez as a man with a fierce dedication to certain principles laced with a misleading gentleness, a lack of humor, and a withering sobriety that reminded Jabez of bleak Puritan clerics of times past.

"No, sir, I am not." Robinson sighed and rubbed a slim hand across his eyes. "I hope to settle my folks peaceably and bring industry and enlightened government to this new state."

"You are of course aware that there are many across the south who oppose northern immigrants," Jabez said. "Men who will turn to violence to make Kansas a slave state."

"Of course I am," Charles snapped. He leaned forward. "We aim for Kansas to be free labor, Doctor. We're bringing newspapers and schools, churches, steam power. How can anyone object to that? We want to see the land between the Mississippi and California filled with men who work for themselves, with manufactories as well as farms. We'll plant the North's way of life across this continent." His long fingers creased a fold in the cotton tablecloth. "There will be no free blacks in these territories, but we will have no slavocracy either." His voice softened. His eyes, though, were intense, almost black, and they stared unseeing past Jabez's shoulder. "I view the slave power as degenerate, sir, and will devote my time and my energies to fighting its spread."

Jabez mentally compared him to Atchison. If these two were to go head to head, and it appeared they might, they presented polar opposites. One bellicose, fiery, rhetorical, bombastic, the other disciplined, intense, sober, almost reticent. Jabez sighed.

"There may yet be peaceable ways to go about winning your goal." Jabez picked up a teaspoon, tapped it on the table top and looked at Charles thoughtfully. "You must recognize you're dealing with a completely different culture here, maybe as different as the English are finding in India." He leaned forward. "You can't simply impose your moral views on a different society. For the slave interests, this isn't a moral issue. It's a matter of property rights. They object to being told what they can do with their property." Charles nodded once, briefly. "With time and patience, the value of that property will lessen to the point where it'll no longer be economical to maintain it. Can you not let the institution die out of its own?"

Robinson's expression was guarded, his eyes not quite hostile. "Will the slave power keep the peace? Will the slave power respect the rights of New Englanders to settle Kansas and Nebraska without interference?" He turned his palms up, as though appealing to Jabez's good sense. "Can we live together side by side while we await your natural solution? I cannot believe so, sir. Is Atchison not threatening guns and hanging? I know he is, I have sources close to him. He thinks Kansas belongs to him and his constituents and no one else need apply. Well, sir, we are here to gainsay that."

"I must tell you, Charles," Jabez said. "I was asked to meet with you by Atchison himself. He desired me to convey a warning." He turned the teaspoon end over end in his fingers. "But I'm here not as his messenger, I'm here of my own volition. I'm here to plead with you." He kept his voice low, reasonable, controlling the sense of foreboding that wanted to creep into his tone. "You and I have both seen war. We've seen violent death, we've seen homes destroyed and bodies mutilated." He took a deep breath. "What we saw in California and during the war with Mexico is nothing compared with what could happen if this blows up into full-scale war. The loss of life would be appalling. One part of the country or another would be destroyed for decades. Can you justify that?"

Again, Charles looked into the distance, a great sadness on his face. But when he looked back to Jabez, his features were resolute, determined. "Yes, I can. No one can justify allowing the slave power to extend itself beyond the south. Once released from its cage, there will be no putting it back."

"Will you meet with the Senator and negotiate before you proceed?"

"No sir, I will not. We have every right to stake our claims on the Kansas prairies, and we will proceed as planned. Do not attempt to interfere."

"If it comes to that, will you shoot to kill?"

"I'd be ashamed, Doctor, to fire at a man and not kill him."

"Then you will bring about disaster, violence, possibly the dissolution of the country, Doctor Robinson, and may you long wear that upon your conscience." Jabez stood, dropped his napkin next to his plate and bowed. "I pray you do not succeed." He pulled his coat from the chair, turned to walk away, turned back. "A warning, sir. There is a group of men in town, arrived last night and demanded to be put off the ferry south of town where they couldn't be seen." Charles raised bushy eyebrows in question. "They're led by a man named Bigelow. A Missouri farm boy. You'd know him by his eyes, pale and flat. Disturbing." He shrugged into his coat, settled the lapels. "I have a bad feeling about him. Watch your back."

Charles nodded and lifted two fingers to his forehead in a salute.

Jabez spent the morning sleeping and the afternoon riding to Westport to see a chemist who mixed a particular type of ague powder from willow bark. By evening he sat on the porch of the American Hotel, tipped back in a chair with his after-dinner cigar in his fingers, watching the parade of wagons and mules lining up on the road to Kansas. Charles's emigrants were on the move, preparing for the last leg of their journey and an early morning start across the border and onto the short-grass prairies of Kansas.

Groups of hard-eyed men idled about the edges of the caravan, thumbs in belt loops, knives and sidearms prominent. Jabez's eyes roved up and down the street, searching for any sign of Bigelow or of trouble between the two factions. Charles Robinson, much in evidence, moved along the line of conveyances, talking quietly with each family, exuding an infectious nonchalance toward the hostility around them. Judging by the malignant looks and rude gestures directed toward his tall, thin figure by the rowdies clustered in doorways and porches, he personally represented the northern invasion, the offense being offered by New England and the abolition movement, all that these southerners hated.

As night drew on, Jabez's disquiet grew into a strong sense of foreboding and intensified, hurried along by low hanging storm clouds and a bank of thunderheads along the western horizon. The atmosphere sparked with electricity, exacerbating the antagonism between the two factions. Emigrants huddled together in small groups, throwing troubled glances toward the townspeople. Some sent their women and children into the relative safety of the American Hotel lobby.

Jabez stood and tossed away the stub of his cigar. He slipped a hand into his coat pocket to reassure himself that his Colt was accessible. He'd taken to carrying it after the encounter with Bigelow's group on the road from the Atchison meeting. It gave him little comfort—he was, after all, one man against a tidal wave—but it was better than nothing. His thought now was to check on Jupiter, then take a stroll around town.

Gloom shrouded the alley leading to the livery stable; no windows opened on it, and lights from the street did not penetrate. He pushed through the door of the stable and Jupiter, stabled in the third stall from the door, nickered and tossed his head as if he, too, sensed both natural and human storms. Jabez stroked his neck and scratched his ears. "Shh, boy," he whispered, "nothing to worry about. Not yet, anyway."

Jupiter snorted and dipped his big head to push against Jabez's hand. A nervous whinny came from several stalls down. Jabez's hand stilled, he listened. Nothing. He mentally chastised himself for nerves. Thunder rumbled again, lightning followed at a discreet distance. He dished up a measure of oats from a barrel in the center aisle and poured it into the manger. Jupiter snuffled, bumped against him in gratitude, happy for both the company and the treat, and pushed his nose into the trough. Another horse snorted down the way, a sound of surprise and consternation. Jabez pressed up against the back wall of the stall. Probably the livery man, no need to be jumpy. But something wasn't right. Now there were footsteps, coming from the far end of the stables. In the light of a hooded lantern, the steps stopped at stalls, searched the corners.

"Clear," someone hissed. "Wil, over here." Jabez tracked their movements by the glow of the lantern as it moved toward the front door of the stables. Hand on Jupiter's shoulder, willing the big gelding to silence, he moved to the front of the stall and peered through the slats. Three men, no, four, huddled at the entrance, silhouetted against the milky gray of the deepening dusk. One lifted his hat, swiped a forearm over his brow.

"All right, boys, this is what we're going do," he said. His words were staccato, harsh. "Them boys on the street will follow our lead once we make a move. Jess and Fred are stationed at the edge of town, along by the border." He pointed to his right. "You, Virgil, and you, Hank, take the south side. Them boys from Independence'll do what you tell them to do." He gripped the shoulder of the fourth man. "Harlan, you stick to the north side of the street. If Robinson tries to make for the hotel, get him in the knees." He settled his hat again. "Leave him for me to finish off."

It was easy to tell who was speaking. Wil Bigelow's voice, with its nasal twang, continued.

"Harlan, Hank, you got the flares? Fire up them wagons once you hear Virgil's call." The shadow turned to the doorway. "Virgil, don't make no move until you hear my whistle. Boys, them Yankees don't know how to fight worth shit, but shoot if you get opposition." Bigelow moved back into the darkness of the stable. "It won't work unless we move together, so for God's sake don't move until you hear me."

A low murmur of assent came from the men clustered around the doorway, then each moved out, shadow by shadow. Bigelow stayed behind; Jabez could see him push each man off with a pat on the back. Bigelow pulled out papers and tobacco, rolled, struck a match, and lit up. Jabez watched him take a deep pull and expel a cloud smoke. Without Bigelow, Kansas City might still ignite. But if Bigelow purposefully struck the flint and steel, the town would surely go up like a bonfire, and the conflagration would engulf more than Kansas City. If there were any chance to avoid violence this night, Bigelow had to be silenced.

Jabez thought about the Colt in his pocket. He had never shot a man, and he had no wish to use the weapon now, even though a part of him knew Bigelow's death may mean the preservation of other, more innocent, lives. And a shot would bring the town down on the stable and set off who knows what chaos.

But he could use it as a club. He dropped his hand to the latch and gently, quietly, under cover of a low rumble of thunder, released it so that the stall gate cracked open on its hinges. Jupiter woofed through his nostrils, and Jabez stroked his nose to quiet him. Bigelow didn't seem to notice. He dropped his smoke into a water barrel, his back to the stalls, his attention directed toward the center of town. Jabez studied the still, dark figure through the opening in the stall door. Bigelow was probably a dozen yards away. Jabez had no illusions about his ability to overcome a well-muscled man twenty years his junior. He felt about him for something to throw, and his hand hit on the grooming brush he'd left on the edge of the trough. He picked it up and hurled it past Bigelow.

Bigelow jerked, reached for his sidearm, and spun toward the sound. Jabez threw open the stall door and used the butt of his Colt to knock him across the head. Bigelow fell with a low groan and rolled, scrambling for the revolver at his side. Jabez kicked his hands aside and, using the Colt again, struck him above the ear. Bigelow sighed, his eyes rolled up and he was out.

Jabez stood astride the man, breathing hard. "First, do no harm," he muttered. Then he smiled. He leaned over and pressed a finger against Bigelow's throat. The pulse was weak, but there—the man was out, but not in danger. Jabez looked about him. No one was the wiser. He hoisted Bigelow into Jupiter's stall, tied him at the wrists and ankles with a length of lead rope and gagged him with the man's own kerchief. Within moments, he had Jupiter saddled and Bigelow slung over the saddle horn, not particularly careful to be gentle. Once Bigelow moaned and showed signs of coming to. Jabez, knowing just the spot, pressed his fingers against the man's throat and he was out again.

Leading Jupiter from the stall, he stopped at the stable doors, checked that the alley was clear and moved into the night, now thick with a steadily falling screen of rain. He walked Jupiter to the rear, where the stables backed up to pastureland and beyond that to meadows and fields east of town. He swung himself into the saddle, hunched over against the rain. If anyone saw him, he trusted to the misty darkness to camouflage the burden flung across his saddle. He checked Bigelow's breathing, raspy, but steady. He wouldn't smother.

They cut across fields and meadows, through a woodlot and across a creek, until he came to an area where the rolling countryside began to climb into hillocks, granite outcroppings scattered along a wagon track. He dismounted, wandered a bit, exploring with his hands in the deep blackness of the storm and by occasional flashes of lightning, until he found what he wanted: a small overhang that offered some protection from the wet. Returning to the horse, he dragged Bigelow off and hauled him by the armpits beneath the overhang. He took out the folding knife he always carried in his pants pocket. Though he hated to lose it, he couldn't let the man lie here helpless for days. No telling when someone would come by this way. He left the knife close to Bigelow's hand, checked again to see that the man was still out, and satisfied that it would be a couple hours before he regained consciousness, mounted Jupiter and returned to Kansas City.

21

May 1856

The odor of smoke hung heavy in the spring air, reaching Jabez a mile or two east of Lawrence, Kansas, on the road from Franklin. The rumors rife in Franklin were apparently true, the acrid breeze out of the west told the tale. Lawrence had burned. Jupiter whinnied and balked at the scent, but Jabez kept him on a tight reign and nudged him forward. As he approached the outskirts of the village, he spotted smoke from breakfast campfires to the southwest, across the prairie in the direction of the Wakarusa River, but Lawrence stank of burned buildings, the smell of destruction.

A lovely May morning hid behind the gray pall that hung over the prairie. Jabez found himself once again in Kansas, summoned this time not by Atchison but by a Congressional committee which had traveled to the troubled territory to determine who should bear the blame for the turmoil of the past eighteen months. Last December, fifteen hundred Missouri hotbloods encamped south of Lawrence, capital of the free-soil movement. Atchison, almost certainly egging on the ruffians behind the scenes, summoned Jabez to serve as intermediary. The Congressmen, aware of Jabez's role, commanded his appearance at the hearings. But by the time he reached Franklin in late May, the committee had decamped in the face of a new Missouri horde which moved into position south of Lawrence, leaving Jabez with a wasted trip and a close-up canvass of the aftermath of the attack.

The high road fed into the village's main street. He passed a dry-goods shop, its plate glass window shattered, shards of glass scattered on the boardwalk and glinting in the dust of the road. A bolt of muslin lay trampled in the mud alongside a horse trough, canned goods and broken crockery cluttered the roadway. Ahead, a split wooden sign reading *Kansas State Free Press* swung by a single nail amidst blackened timbers and tilting walls. Newsprint fluttered in the breeze, type was embedded in the road underfoot. A woman in black jabbed at the boardwalk with a ragged broom, tears dampening her cheeks. Every building on Main Street showed the effects of the previous day's looting: cracked windows, spoilt goods, stove-in barrels, broken glassware. The office of the *Herald of Freedom* had suffered the same fate as its competitor.

Jabez halted Jupiter in the town square and leaned on the saddle horn. The remains of the Free-State Hotel crouched on the square's north side, concrete walls blackened and flaking, soot and cinders floating from shattered windows. Roof timbers filled the lobby, ruined furnishings smoldered. Just five months before, he had shuttled back and forth from the Wakarusa River to the third floor of this building, carrying messages between the governor and the free-state leaders. Charles Robinson and his colleagues labored in an upper room, struggling to reach a peaceful agreement with their enemies. In December they succeeded. In May, they lost. Their headquarters now were rubble, the town itself eerily silent, an occasional curtain lifting in the breeze, nothing but the cawing of the crows disturbing the hush.

Jabez dismounted and threw the reins over a broken porch rail. A cannon, a six-pounder, squatted in the street, aimed at the door of the ruined hotel. He ran his hand across the still-warm barrel. He recognized it as one of a pair owned by the Eldridge brothers, proprietors of the hotel, once displayed with pride at the hotel's entrance. He squinted down the street against the flash of morning sun off a jagged piece of tin plate, wondering about casualties. He carried his medical bag, as always. Or maybe the free-staters had cut and run, and no one got hurt. He hoped so. Even without deaths, the destruction of Lawrence would most likely ignite the country. Dead and wounded, even worse, women and children caught in the cross-fire would ensure a brutal reaction.

He caught sight of a shadow inside the broken doors of Brooks' haberdashery, a face in an upper window. A stocky, bushy-bearded old man rounded the corner of the gutted bank building, hooked his thumbs in a sagging waistband, and stared at Jabez. A jay screeched once, then quieted, the breeze rustled papers and new leaves along the street. He swung into the saddle, intending to talk to the old man by the bank and heard the jingle of harness, the creak of leather, the blowing of horses. It came from the direction of Blanton's Bridge to the south, toward the Wakarusa. A steady, deep thrumming signaled the movement of dozens of animals, and a column of mounted men appeared, rounding the base of Mount Oread. Jabez watched the lead riders advance into the center of town. The old man at the bank froze. Even from a distance, Jabez marked the contemptuous tilt of his head, the hostile set of his shoulders.

At the head of the column rode two giants, both on sleek well-kept stallions. Jabez recognized Albert Boone sitting tall. The other was David Atchison, slumping from what Jabez speculated was a hang-over. The two led their victorious men toward the ferry on the Kaw River north of town and the road home to Missouri. Behind them, three twelve-pounders and two six-pound cannon rumbled, pulled by big Missouri mules. Jabez recognized John Stringfellow and his brother the general, followed by Kickapoo Rangers and territorial militia, some sporting fixed bayonets. But the bulk of the troops consisted of ragged, insolent, jeering rowdies, men tagged "border ruffians" by the northern newspapers, recruited across the south for no other purpose than to cause mayhem.

Alongside these troops rode a familiar figure, pale eyes peering out from under a broken hat brim, lank yellow hair to his shoulders. Bigelow looked to left and right and caught sight of Jabez. He reined in the piebald horse he rode, causing the animal behind him to shy and snort, and wheeled out of the column. Jabez returned the intensity of his look from a block away. Bigelow put a hand on his sidearm, slid it part way out of its holster. Jabez held up both hands in an almost mocking gesture, signaling he was unarmed, though the Colt lay heavy in his pocket. Bigelow shoved his gun back into the holster, sent him a long look, then turned his horse and moved along with the column.

Townspeople appeared at windows, doors, on street corners. The mounted men directed the odd jibe or insult toward them, but the citizens of Lawrence remained silent, watching their attackers move through town and down to the river bank, where the ferry began the tedious job of moving men, horses and cannon across the river. Jabez inquired about casualties, and finding that the free-state forces had abandoned the town to destruction by the proslavers without argument, turned Jupiter east and headed back to Franklin.

Franklin, three miles south and east of Lawrence and held by the slave faction, took pride in its raw and joyful untidiness, its random stores and homes, its muddy streets. It boasted a single hotel, part brothel, part rooming house, which provided a place to stay for those who could not bring themselves to put up at the Free-State Hotel in Lawrence. Jabez had paid extra to keep his room and ensure he wouldn't return to find a half dozen roommates lodged with him. His foresight proved warranted. When he reached the town, he found the upper ranks of the proslave army in possession, all looking for a bed and dinner, most of them already three sheets to the wind.

Jabez had no interest in conversation or association with any of them; he planned to order a steak and make off with it to his room, settle in for the night, and leave for home at first light. But it was not to be, and before he made his escape he was accosted by the leader of the victorious army, the former Senator himself.

Atchison appeared to have recovered from the effects of drink and to be ready to begin another round. His large face flushed and split by a merry grin, the big man waved a whiskey bottle in Jabez's direction. "Well met, friend," he said, plumping himself down in the only other chair at Jabez's table. "I should have known you'd be where the action is." He signaled the serving girl for another glass and poured himself and Jabez a generous amount. "And where were you stationed for the event? Did you see them run?" He lifted his glass in a toast while Jabez left his drink on the table. "We brought Southern Rights to Lawrence with a vengeance, we did, and the scoundrels ran like rabbits. Did you see it?" He downed his drink.

"I didn't," Jabez said. "I arrived only this morning. I saw the aftermath."

"You saw what we can do, then, eh?" Atchison puffed himself up. "It was the happiest day of my life! We made them bow to the law, eh?" He poured another shot. Behind him, a door banged open and a rotund serving woman bawled something unintelligible.

"Whether they're obeying the law or simply avoiding cannon fire and muskets may still be a question," Jabez said. "They will answer you, I'll stake my horse on it."

"Well, sir, you may be right." Atchison's words were slurring now. He smiled sloppily and tapped a tattoo on the scarred table. "Them rogues'll sure as hell come up with something to pester us with. They don't give up easy." He poured yet another shot.

Jabez picked up his glass and sipped. Monongahela rye. Trust Atchison to drink only the best.

"Of course," the big man said, eyes narrowing, "if you'd convinced Robinson to turn back like I asked you to, we wouldn't be in this goddamn mess."

"Senator," Jabez said, "you well know Charles wouldn't turn back once they reached Kansas City. They believe, as you do, that the stakes are too high."

Atchison twirled his glass, looked at the bottle. It was nearly empty. "Wil Bigelow was supposed to stop them if you didn't. Don't suppose you know anything about why he never showed up?"

Jabez snorted. "I have better things to do than play hide-the-stooge with your gunmen." He sipped his drink, keeping his eyes on Atchison's. "If our friend Wil hasn't been fulfilling his assignments, maybe you should get someone else."

Atchison studied him in the flickering light of a badly trimmed wick. "Stooge, is it," he said. "Best not be letting Bigelow hear you say that. That one's a bad enemy to have, Doctor." He downed the last of his drink and stood, his good humor back. "Well, sir, I'm that pleased to see you here among us, Robinson. Remember, we're the winning side. You're a smart man. I see you choosing the winner." Jabez stared at the man, twisting his glass on the table in front of him. Atchison bowed and turned into the barroom calling for another bottle.

Cannonballs pounded the earth, ricocheted off trees and walls, spewed dirt and dead leaves and debris. Someone shrieked his name and the sound echoed across the valley. The pounding faded into hammering, the steady hammering of carpenters nailing coffins, rows and rows of them, stretching across the landscape, up a hillside, out of sight, nail after nail after nail, each coffin embracing a body, torn and bloody, and he knew if he watched the coffins long enough, the bodies would sit up, one by one, and turn their dead faces toward him.

"Robinson, wake up, open the door."

Jabez shook himself out of the nightmare and into consciousness, recognizing by the gray light of early dawn the shabby hotel room, the lumpy bed, the threadbare blankets. Whoever pounded on the door must have awakened the entire establishment by now. He rubbed his hand over his head and down his beard, rolled out of bed and into his trousers. He recognized the voice, now. It belonged to Albert Boone, Atchison's partner. Boone pushed his way into the room without invitation, his bulk shrinking the already tiny chamber.

"Get your clothes on, Doctor, you're needed." Boone looked around the room, saw Jabez's coat and shirt slung over the back of the single chair and flung them at him. Jabez, never at his best first thing in the morning, flung them on the bed with a snarl.

"The hell I am," he said. "If you need a medical man, get your pal Stringfellow out of bed."

"Stringfellow's already out of bed and mounted up," Boone said. "We need you. You're known to be neutral. There's murder been done this night, and the abolitionists did it. You're needed to witness and tend to the wounded." He picked up the coat and held it out.

Jabez tucked in his shirt, shrugged into his coat, tugged at his bootstraps. They knew as well as he did that Stringfellow, if a medical doctor at all, risked doing more harm than good to anyone ill or wounded. If there were wounded, Jabez would have to go. Couldn't leave them to his "colleague's" tender mercies. "Murder done where?"

"Down to the south, place called Osawatomie, near forty miles. Men killed by night riders, hacked to pieces. Boy just rode in with the news." Boone headed for the stairs. "We've got your horse saddled. It's a long ride."

Jabez stopped to load his Colt, slid it into his pocket. He grabbed his medical bag and saddlebags and followed the man down the stairs.

They rode a hellishly long time, south of Blanton's Bridge down the California Road, across the prairie in the growing light. Eight riders strung along the trail: Boone and Atchison, Stringfellow, a major from the territorial militia, Jabez, and three men he didn't know. In Prairie City they rested the horses, ate, then pushed on. Jabez spoke rarely to his companions. Atchison, once again affected by drink, said not a word the entire day. The others kept whatever grim thoughts they had to themselves.

Early in the evening they forded Ottawa Creek and the Marais River and at dusk reached Mosquito Creek, horses blowing and stumbling with exhaustion. A tiny store perched on the verge of the road, along the stream's bank, surrounded by a hard-packed dirt yard littered with rusty equipment and trash. The store itself consisted of a rough cabin, its shelves half-filled with canned goods, tools, flour and grain, its windows broken. A dozen men and women milled around both inside and outside the store, several helping themselves to foodstuffs and goods. Lanterns lit up the yard, wavering over men with hunting rifles and sidearms, bowie knives and cudgels. A woman and a child huddled on the porch, wrapped in threadbare quilts, their eyes red and swollen. The child shivered under her quilt.

Jabez's party dismounted. The local men kept rifles pointed in their direction until Atchison identified himself and his companions. Then the story tumbled out, angrier and wilder with each telling. Five men dead, dragged from their homes and hacked to death, women terrorized. Jabez listened for a few moments, then turned his attention to the two on the porch. The child needed medical attention, she was in danger of falling so deeply into shock that she might not emerge. He lifted his medical bag from the saddle horn, took out a vial of laudanum. Sending one of the women for water, he knelt next to the woman and child.

"Ma'am, my name is Robinson. I'm a doctor. I need to know if you or your daughter is injured in any way."

The woman scowled. "Hell, yes, we're hurt. Them men killed my man and my two boys. What do you think, we're all right?"

He laid a hand on the little girl's forehead. "She's chilled. She needs hot food, then sleep." He added laudanum to the water and handed the tin mug to the mother. "Drink." He took back the mug and helped the child to drink and turned to the gathered knot of women.

"The child needs hot soup. And they need beds. If they can't get to their own home, make up beds in the store." He turned back to the mother. The laudanum was already having a calming effect. "What's your name?"

"Mahala Doyle. My man's Jim Doyle." She turned her head away, tears starting again. "Was. Was Jim Doyle." Jabez handed her his handkerchief.

"Robinson." Boone gestured, and Jabez left the two to the ladies, crossed the yard to where the men gathered lanterns and prepared to move down the road. "We're going to see what happened. You're needed to come along."

Jabez secured Jupiter next to a water trough, then grabbed a lantern and followed the group on foot. Behind him came a wagon driven by two of the local men. The road was heavily wooded, dusk had long ago faded into darkness. Beyond the circle of light thrown by the lanterns, the night closed in with a soft, velvety feel that comes with spring, a breeze blowing up the creek with a gentleness that riffled invisible leaves and echoed the music of running water. But it carried with it the acrid smell of blood and death. Jabez hated the scent.

First they saw a dog, a hulking bulldog that sprawled belly up, legs stiff, in the middle of the road. In the light of the lantern, its blood pooled black and sticky in the dust. Its head lay at an unnatural angle, and Jabez realized only the spine held it to the body. No ordinary bowie knife sliced that deep. As he studied the animal, a beetle, an inch long and iridescent green, crawled out from the neck wound.

Another hundred yards. One of the men called out, an answer sounded from ahead. "Jesus Christ, Martin," the voice said, "you know what it's like being here with them? I ain't going to volunteer for guard duty no more." The man's voice shook. The apparent spokesman for the locals, a man named Martin White, turned to Atchison. "We got men staked out at the bodies, so animals don't get at them. Wanted you to see where they lay, how it was with them." White turned back to the guard, said, "All right, Pete, we'll take it from here. You go on back and get some dinner. We'll be bringing them in once the Senator sees things." With obvious relief, Pete pushed past the line of men and scurried back toward the store.

The men formed a circle, lanterns illuminating the two bodies. They lay back to back, nearly touching. As with the dog, rivers of blood spread out from beneath them, soaked into the dust, congealed in rivulets in the ruts. Jabez knelt beside the closer body, held his lantern high, and his stomach tightened. Little more than a boy, early twenties maybe. He'd been chopped and hacked until his features disappeared. Open wounds gaped at the shoulders, the arms severed. One limb lay twisted under him, attached only by a sinew, the sleeve black and stiff with blood. The other sprawled nearly a yard away, the fingers and wrist mangled and sliced as if he had tried to ward off the blows with his bare hands.

The features on the second body remained intact, the bulbous nose and gray hair of an older man. This must be Mrs. Doyle's man, her Jim. Though slash marks covered the trunk, a hole in the right temple surrounded by powder burns indicated he may have died a quicker and more merciful death.

Jabez stood, blew out his lips and turned to Atchison. "These are saber wounds, obviously. Cutlasses. Sharp and heavy, not the type of ceremonial sword or even fighting sword the cavalry carries. Something bigger, maybe a broadsword."

Atchison cursed under his breath, staring down at the bodies. Boone and the major muttered, their faces in the lamplight ferocious. Stringfellow leaned down and turned the boy's head. Sightless eyes looked up at the men above them. "Goddamn abolitionists," he said. "We'll get them for this, by God we will." He kicked at a pool of blood and spat into the dust.

Martin White turned to his men. "Load 'em up, boys. We got others to look to." He turned toward the creek and headed down the slope. Here the trees thinned out. They felt grass under foot, the ground soft and damp. Another hundred feet and White stopped, lifting his lantern high. "Here's the young one. This one's Drury Doyle." The men parted for Jabez.

The body lay on its belly, dressed only in a nightshirt. The bare buttocks, legs bent and curled into the body, made the boy look young and vulnerable. His arms, too, were hacked away, a gash ran through the crown of his head. Again, the swords had been at work, there was no sign of a compassionate gunshot. Jabez carefully smoothed a lock of hair, matted and sticky with blood, covering a portion of the wound. He stood. There was nothing to be said. The group turned back up the slope, leaving two men to wrap the boy in blankets and place him in the wagon with his father and brother.

In grim silence, they walked another half mile down the road to a cabin lit by a blazing fire in the scrubby yard. A half dozen men and two or three women clustered in the shadows or tended the fire. Two men approached White and spoke in low voices, eyes shifting to the Atchison group of strangers. After a moment, White looked up, and he signaled to Jabez. "Miz Wilkinson's inside. She's sick, has need of a doctor." He motioned to the cabin. Jabez pushed his way through the throng in the yard and past a trestle table, flush up against the house, on which a body rested. Dressed in trousers and stockings, no shoes, no shirt or coat, the head and side showed gashes, the throat had been slit ear to ear. An old woman dipped a cloth in a bloody basin and washed the man's wounds. Two three-dollar gold pieces weighted down his eyelids. Jabez paused to look for a moment, and a deep sadness welled up in him. He turned and stepped into the dimly-lit interior. The cramped front room held a bed, pushed against the back wall and covered with tumbled bedclothes. A pungent smell of unwashed bodies and sickness mixed with the oily smell of a lantern and the scent of death. On the bed huddled a woman and two children, all three disheveled and dirty.

He found a stool lying upturned and set it beside the bed, his medical bag on his knees. The woman shrank against the wall, squeezing the young ones to her. Lank, dull red hair hung in strings over her face. She wore a nightdress, the shoulder seam ripped, a faded ribbon hanging undone from the neckline. The children, like terrified wild cubs, clutched at her, great dark eyes fastened on his face.

Jabez clasped his hands together over his bag, his voice low and gentle. "Mrs. Wilkinson, my name is Doctor Robinson. I understand you've been ill."

For a moment, there was no response from the woman, then she nodded, a quick jerk of the head. With the movement, her hair swung back from her face, and Jabez saw nasty pustules covering the skin of her cheeks, forehead, neck. She cheeks glowed red, her eyes shone with fever. "How long have you been broken out like that?" he asked, laying a hand on her forehead. She was burning.

"Two days. Three days. I don't rightly know."

"Are you hurt anywhere else? Were you wounded by the attackers?" He held her thin wrist, counting the beats of her blood through dry, papery skin.

"No, no, nothing like that." She didn't pull away her hand, even loosened her grip on the children.

"You have the measles, Mrs. Wilkinson." He set her hand carefully on the coverlet. "Have the children suffered from them yet?"

"No sir, they been sick before but never with this rash."

"Well, they will undoubtedly get it, too." He opened his bag, pulled out a tin of salve and a bottle of powder. He cast about the cabin for drinking water and a mug, mixed in an amount of powder and handed it to her. She drank as he smoothed salve over the pustules on her cheeks and forehead. "Now, you do it, while I watch. Don't get too much." He indicated the spots on her neck and breast, and she haltingly dabbed at them.

The light from the doorway dimmed, as the stout form of David Atchison filled it. "Miz Wilkinson," he said, his voice too large for the room, "sorry to bother you, ma'am, but I need to know what happened here." He lowered his bulk onto the end of the bed. The children, who had begun to calm at Jabez's quiet words, cowered against their mother, terrified all over again.

Others crowded into the cabin—Boone, Stringfellow, the militia officer, Marvin White, a couple of neighbors—and Jabez glared at them to keep a respectful distance from the frightened family. One or two had the grace to look abashed and stepped out the door. Atchison paid no attention.

"Who was it, ma'am? Did you see the men?"

Mrs. Wilkinson plucked at the quilt over her legs with a shaky hand. But when she spoke, her voice was sharp with bitterness and her eyes flashed in the lantern light.

"I did. They was five or six of them, and the old man was in charge. He was the one who told Al to get himself out of the house. Wouldn't let him even put his boots on."

"The old man," Atchison said. "Did you know him?"

"No, I never seen him before," she said, "but I'll know him if ever I see him again." She pulled the littler one close and rested her chin on the top of his head. "He was tall, had to stoop to get in the door there, taller than Al by a head. Al had to look up at him." Her eyes teared up. "Didn't seem fair, him so much bigger than Al." She swiped a hand across her eyes and shook her hair back. "Had a long narrow face, kind of horse-like. Filthy clothes, all black, dirty old straw hat."

"Did you see any of the others?"

"Naw, one of them came in to get the saddles, they stole both the saddles, but they'd taken out the light and I couldn't see him much. They called him Owen, though, I did hear that."

Atchison turned to Boone and Stringfellow. "Owen Brown. This is the work of old John Brown and his boys," he said, "just like you thought." He nodded at White. "Here's proof."

He stood and patted Mrs. Wilkinson on the head, an awkward gesture. "We'll catch the killers that did this, ma'am, and when we do, you can be the one to send them to the gallows." He turned to the local men. "Take care of the little lady, boys. We'll need her testimony." He grinned, wholly without humor. "Unless of course they somehow don't make it alive to trial, hey?"

There were mutters of agreement and approval from the men in the room. Jabez stood, put the powder and the salve on a ledge above the headboard. Back outside the men loaded Wilkinson's body in with the Doyles, and a second wagon pulled into the yard, bearing yet another mutilated corpse, the fifth victim of the past night's work. Jabez glanced at this last body and turned away. Torn flesh, the evidence of uncontrolled anger and madness, of vigilante justice. He settled his hat on his head, grasped his medical bag and a lantern, and started back up the road without waiting for the others.

22

Summer 1856

"Agnes, I'm to be married," Billy said, leaning forward tentatively in Agnes's new-bought Salem rocker. Elbows on knees, hands twitching together restlessly, he peered at her from under heavy black brows.

"So I hear tell." She smiled at him, wondering why the nervousness, and ceased snapping beans. "I know little of Julia, but I very much like what I've seen." They sat in the evening shade on the vest-pocket front porch of Agnes's very own little house.

He grinned a quick, pleased grin and sat back. "Well, that's that then. I wanted your approval."

"My approval?"

"Well, sure, you always seem to know what's right, so I figure if you say this is a good thing, then it is."

"Would you jilt her if I hadn't approved?" she asked.

He laughed. "Nope."

"Well then." She set down her bowl and leaned forward to give him a hug. "I offer you my heartiest congratulations and think you've made an admirable choice."

Agnes had yet to meet the girl, Julia, who lived in Forest City, but Sam and Rachel approved, and Billy beamed with satisfaction. He'd returned from California a full-grown man, broad-shouldered and thick-chested like his father, opinions and disposition tempered by variety and experience. Agnes took pride in him, and valued his opinion as much as he valued hers.

She picked up the bowl and snapped another bean. "How do you like my house?"

He glanced around as if he'd not noticed there was a house.

"Pleasant," he said. He grasped the porch post and shook it. "Seems sturdy."

She wrinkled her nose at him. "Much better than that. Only five years old and solid." And all mine, she thought. Chosen by me, paid for by me.

"A little small," he said.

"There's only one of me. I have an indoor kitchen, a parlor and a bedroom. And a storeroom. And a fruit cellar."

"All the comforts, then. Maybe Julia and I can get something like this."

"You and Julia will have something much nicer than this. You'll need room for the babies."

He raised his brows at her.

"They'll come soon enough. You'd best be planning."

He cleared his throat. "Well." He gazed down the street, not much more than a trail, that led into town. Her view consisted of the back door of the Baptist church and the chicken pens and apple trees behind houses on Jefferson Street. A top-heavy white pine crouched at the corner of the lot, and dried mud and ruts cratered the front yard where John had unloaded her small possessions. She thought it lovely.

"Agnes, don't you think you'll be lonely here?" Billy leaned forward again and lay a hand on the arm of her chair. "You're used to Nancy's house, all the children...."

"A little too used to them," she said and patted his hand. "A woman can be lonely in the middle of a crowded house or she can be lonely in her own home. I've always been beholden to someone else, and I don't intend to live out my life that way."

"But a woman alone." He waived his hand as if that explained all.

"What about a woman alone?"

"Well, it just ain't safe," he said.

"I can't imagine what isn't safe about it. No one's going to attack a spinster living nearly hand to mouth. It isn't as if I have a pile of cash money under the floorboards."

"But you might still marry."

She put down the beans. "Billy." She fixed him with her best school-marm look. "I'm thirty-one years old. And a half. I'm too used to managing my own affairs without subjecting them to the control of a husband."

"I thought maybe you and Doc Robinson....."

Her face flushed furiously and her tongue refused to work properly. She bent over to place the bean bowl on the porch. "Doctor Robinson and I are friends. We talk politics and books, and that's the extent of it."

"Politics and books can lead to all sorts of things." His smile broadened.

"Mostly to arguments, if political talk these days is any indication." She tucked a loose tendril behind her ear, stood and smoothed her apron. "Besides, the talk among the ladies is that he's sparking a widow in St. Joseph."

"You might ask him yourself," Billy said, settling back in his chair. "Here he comes."

She sat with a whoosh of skirts and looked up the street. Sure enough, there came the doctor, on foot, a smile splitting his beard and a bundle of pasqueflowers and prairie roses in his hand.

"Sparking the widow, huh?" Billy said softly.

"Manifest destiny," Billy said. "This country can spread from one coast to the other, we'll be the most powerful country in the world. But not if we let any state that wants to break away whenever they get a burr up their ass."

"Destiny be damned," Jabez said. "Is that what you learned in California? What you've got is a powerful set of fanatics like John Brown who're bound and determined to exterminate a society. First the south, then the natives, then the Mexicans. It's all economics and who'll control the purse."

Agnes stood in the shadows of her tiny parlor, coffee tray in hand, listening through the open window. The argument was repeated again and again on church steps, in the dry goods store, at dinner tables all over town and, she supposed, all over the state and the country. From where she stood she could see Jabez's profile. He leaned forward in his chair, black brows drawn in a furious scowl, fists knotted. Billy had no chance against him in argument; he was a master. Whatever had happened to him in Kansas during the spring, his arguments, angry and bitter now, usually attacked the radicals of the north.

She stepped to the door, and the conversation stopped. Billy jumped to take the tray. He held it while Agnes poured, then dropped to the top step with his cup. "Agnes, how'd you like to live in the new country of Missouri? Aristocrats telling you what to do. Maybe we could elect a king."

"That's a bit far-fetched," she said. "I don't yet know my mind on secession. But Doctor Robinson has a point about what's worth fighting for. It's slavery I care about—I don't see any civilized country can make any progress at all until it's gone."

"Well it ain't going to die out of its own," Billy said. He looked off toward the setting sun. "They can grow cotton in Texas and use slaves in the mines out west. We're either going to be a slave country or a free-labor country. No in-between."

Jabez harrumphed. "You can't force slavery on people who're unwilling to have it. Douglas had it right, let legitimate settlers vote on slavery and they'll vote no. You see any slaves in Kansas now? Or Nebraska? It won't happen."

"But you want to break up the country anyway."

"What I don't want is war."

"Will you fight if it comes to war?"

"I'm too old." Jabez poked at Billy with his toe. "Leave it to you young fellows. I'll be the one patching up the wounded."

"I'll fight. I'd sure hate to fight against you, Doc."

"Not against me. I'm not on one side or the other."

"Aldo Beaton says you're a secessionist. Rufus Byrd said you ought to be run out of town."

"Rufus Byrd is a pea-brained trouble-maker," Agnes said. "No one's going to listen to him."

"My pa says you're one of Atchison's men."

Jabez thumped his coffee cup down. "You can tell your pa—"

"That's enough." Agnes stood. "I won't have my family and friends at each other's throats. Billy." She jammed her fists at her waist and glared at him. "You're too smart to listen to drivel. And you, Doctor." She scowled at him. "Your temper will get you into more trouble than it's worth. You're a leader in this town. You have a duty to calm people down, not rile them up."

There was silence for a moment, then Jabez stood and bowed stiffly. "I beg your pardon, Madam," he said and stalked off the porch.

Agnes sighed. "Well, I suppose now he'll go back to sparking the widow."

Jabez's spate of temper was short-lived, as always, and Agnes saw him often that terrible summer of killing and burning along the border. By fall, an uneasy peace settled in, and the town's factions took a breath before the upheaval of the November elections.

Late in September, trees brilliant and grain harvested, Lick Creek's townsfolk gathered on the courthouse square. They clustered around long trestle tables, indulging in chicken salad, roasted corn, green bean casseroles, beet root and eggs, drop dumplings, squash pie, pound cake. Conversation flowed with a conviviality sparked by a successful growing season for a plump and prosperous community.

The Zooks sat companionably with the McIntoshes, their commercial rivalry set aside for the afternoon. Mr. and Mrs. Moodie and the Reverend Fuller hovered about old Mrs. Finley. The Irvines, proclaimed Unionists, sat next to the Caytons, leaning secessionist, so their daughters Annie and Margaret could put their heads together and whisper. Aldo Beaton paid court to Miss Baxter, who wore the widest crinolines in town and whose mama continued to view Jabez as a prospective son-in-law. Cyrus Cook talked school business with Mr. Collins and John Jackson, and Jabez lowered himself next to Agnes with a smile and a nod in their direction.

"Your cousin John appears to be recruiting old Cyrus into the education business," he said, digging into a plate of glazed ham, mashed sweet potato and biscuits.

"John's thinking ahead," she replied. "The good folk of Holt County are producing young ones like rabbits. Someone needs to educate them."

Agnes studied her cousin's husband. John's rugged profile was still handsome, his graying hair distinguished, blue eyes intense.

"Old flames die hard, eh?" Jabez said. He glanced at John, slanted a sideways look at Agnes.

She wasn't surprised. It seemed natural that Jabez knew her so well. "I gave over that infatuation many years ago. Very childish."

He mixed a forkful of butter into his sweet potato. "He's a good man. None better."

"He's always been my standard. But I don't compare every man I know to him." She inspected an ear of corn. "Just most."

"I'm delighted to hear that," Jabez said, cleaning up the last of the sweet potato with a chunk of biscuit. His attention strayed to the street, where a buggy rolled to a stop. "What do you think of Mr. Cundiff and his wife? I hear he's taken on the newspaper."

"He's printing Mrs. Stowe's new book in serial. It's called *Dred*."

"Fatuous and sentimental, isn't she?"

"Not at all," she protested. "It's a riveting story and I'm enjoying it immensely."

"Any better than Uncle Tom?" he said, waving at a fly.

"You haven't read it, then?"

"Haven't had the time, I guess." He attended to another biscuit. "You'll have to tell me how it ends."

"No, indeed, you'll have to read it for yourself. How can you judge when you haven't read it?"

"I just know a woman of her background wouldn't know what she's talking about."

"You don't think any of this is true, then? She isn't authentic?"

"Oh, I think she's authentic as far as it goes. But she never lived it, did she?" He leaned on one elbow, turned toward her. "I prefer Mr. Whitman. *I am the hounded slave, I wince at the bite of the dogs.*" He flashed a smile.

"Whitman is one of those forbidden fellows, isn't he? Young ladies aren't supposed to read him."

"I think that's the case, yes. Especially the part about *I clutch the rails of the fence, my gore dribs....*"

"Well, good thing I'm no longer a young lady, then, isn't it? Do you have a copy I can borrow?"

"Of course, my dear Miss Canon. I wouldn't want it said that I hadn't grasped every available opportunity to lead a lady to imprudence. Young or not." He set aside his plate and pulled out a cigar.

Jabez loaned Agnes his Whitman, and she loaned him her Margaret Fuller. She learned a great deal from him about politics and governance, and she taught him history and literature, subjects he had neglected.

"You find me a poor pupil, I think," he sighed when she'd read the latest installment of *Little Dorrit* from Harper's magazine during an after-dinner gathering at the Jacksons'.

"You learn well enough when you're interested," Agnes said. "It's just that I persist in boring you to distraction."

141

He smiled at her and reached out, as if to tuck a strand of her hair away, then sat back and took the coffee cup Nancy passed. "No," he said. "Impossible."

23

Agnes never expected to marry, nor at the advanced age of thirty-two did she think much on it. And she did all she could to resist the tempting idea that a good friend might become something more. She had her own home, her independence, no one to direct her thoughts and activities. But when the rumors revived concerning Doctor Robinson and the widow in St. Joseph, she suffered.

He spent a great deal of time there. As November and the presidential election neared, he published articles in the newssheets in support of the Democrat Buchanan, praising his experience and temperament and cautioning against the new Republicans. His tone was moderate, and she complimented him on his ability to keep his temper under wraps.

"It's a struggle, Agnes," he said, shifting in the rocking chair on her front porch. She couldn't remember when he first began addressing her by her Christian name, but he fell into the habit when they spoke seriously. When he teased her or displayed his fearsome wit, she became "Miss Canon" again. "There's so much hyperbole in the press these days my inclination is to tell them all they're fools and dogs. But someone has to appeal to the minority who show some intelligence, and that's what I try to do."

She was at that moment little interested in his political writings. "Do you visit any particular friend when you go to St. Joe?"

"There's Governor Price's men, and there's Mr. Hall. Judge Treat from St. Louis has been there."

"And do you visit no ladies when you go?" She concentrated so intently on the embroidery in her lap, she pricked her finger.

He gave her an odd look. "Well, yes, I do visit about. Why do you ask?"

She looked up, sucking her finger, and laughed. "Oh, you know, the ladies here talk. Miss Baxter still hasn't relinquished her claim to you, but I believe if you let it be known there's someone in St. Joe, you'll convince her once and for all."

"I see." He studied her with an intensity that made her flush. "I do see a certain Mrs. Rawlings. She's the widowed sister of Mr. Hall, and she's usually at home when I call on him." He turned away. "She's quite attractive, young, intelligent." He took a long pull on his cigar and gazed across the street.

"Eliza would be so pleased."

He looked startled. "Whatever do you mean?"

"She would approve of your, well, of your getting out, meeting new people...." She tapered off, returned to her embroidery, concentrating on a featherstitch.

"So the ladies of Lick Creek have married me off to this mysterious St. Joe lady, have they?"

"No, no, not at all." She'd have given anything to extricate herself from the conversation. "I assure you I won't share your news."

"There's no news to share, Miss Canon. By the way, I see our friend Mr. Beaton's been escorting you from church lately?"

"I'll make a bargain with you, Doctor." She tucked the embroidery hoop into its bag. "I'll keep you apprised of my courtships if you'll tell me about yours."

He gave her an unreadable look, then his singular grin, a flash of white in the midst of the silky beard. "That's a deal."

Jealousy is a ready inducement to passion. Affection, friendship, solicitude for another may flourish, but when a potential rival enters the picture, serenity flies out the window, and one's peace of mind follows. Suddenly affection turns into adoration, friendship grows into love, solicitude mutates into possessiveness. Agnes spent the winter in the throes of resentful vigilance, tracking Doctor Robinson's trips to St. Joseph, tallying the days of his absence, teasing him when he returned. She surreptitiously gathered information on the odious Mrs. Rawlings and discovered, through the good offices of Mrs. Norman, who traveled often to St. Joseph and St. Louis with her husband, that the lady in question was much younger (by at least five years), possessed light hair and a delicate complexion (similar to Eliza), and controlled a comfortable fortune settled on her by her late husband. Whether Jabez showed any particular attention to her while in St. Joe, Mrs. Norman couldn't say, as she never saw both in company at the same time.

Agnes's distress continued long after the election ended and his trips to St. Joseph dwindled to no more than every two weeks or so, though she managed to greet him with aplomb when they met on the street or he dropped by to loan her a pamphlet or borrow a book. He honored her by sharing a letter from Maine announcing the death from consumption of his sister Mary. He even allowed her to read it. His old father expressed his grief for his lost children and his fondness for those who remained in the artless and florid style of a by-gone generation. Agnes warmed to him as she read his letter. Knowing even a little of the father helped her know more of the son. She suggested to Jabez that he might want to visit Maine when the weather cleared, and he allowed as he might do that. But he never did.

As the wet and dreary spring of 1857 advanced, Jabez stayed close to Lick Creek. Mud clogged the nearly impassible roads, and spring storms swept out of the western plains in sheets, accompanied by battering thunder and formidable lightning, gale winds and icy sleet. Farmers feared for the spring plowing and sowing. Not until June did true summer appear, and then it dropped in all at once like a curtain let loose on a stage. One morning the sun rose at six, and the temperature climbed by thirty degrees. The hazy, soporific days of a Missouri summer were upon them, the rich scents of fields and meadows and creeks permeating the town, and the rumbles of trouble seemed far away. Kansas continued quiet, the occasional burning, a contested election or two, nothing unwonted.

School adjourned for the summer, and Billy and Julia set up housekeeping toward the Missouri River bluffs in sight of the steamboats heading north and west. Elizabeth grew large again with child—once she got the way of it she enthusiastically kept it up—and Tom added on yet another room to their farmhouse, more acreage to their prosperous orchards.

Jabez, who spent the stormy spring months medicating the county's ague, flux, grippe and rheumatism-ridden citizens, contracted a lingering fever himself. For much of June he languished, shut up at home. Agnes visited him as often as was decent without raising eyebrows, and they talked. He told her about his sister Angeline, suffering from consumption. "She always wanted to do whatever Mary did," he said with that graveyard humor doctors often favor. He spoke of his brother in Texas whose wife had died over the winter, leaving him with an infant. He'd begged the brother to come live in Missouri and made the same request of his father, but both refused to leave their homes. Canny men, they foresaw the conflict between north and south centering on the middle of the country, with Missouri and Kansas the focal point. Both in turn implored him to take up residence with one or the other of them, but "I too am attached to my home here," he said, "and don't want to move on. Perhaps I'm getting too old—" he smiled at her— "or maybe there are other incentives." His smile disappeared. "But there may come a day when I'm no longer welcome here, depending on the swing of political opinions."

"If you're driven out, then half the town must go with you," she said. "It appears to me the town's evenly divided."

"I seem to have a propensity for offending both sides somehow," he said, arching an eyebrow at her.

"Maybe it won't come to that after all. It's been quiet this summer. We may be over the worst of it."

"It's the quiet that precedes an earthquake, I think." He took her hand. "I wish you were right, Agnes, but I wouldn't stake the farm on it." They sat there as dusk fell, not speaking, holding hands, rocking in the sultry evening.

24
Late Summer 1857

The hush of a September evening surrounded her—the first, tentative calls of cicadas and crickets, the last, sleepy trill of song sparrows and cardinals. The willow trailed languid, yellowing fronds while the brook, exploring its banks and sheltering its trout, moseyed along, indifferent to human troubles.

"Agnes."

She jumped and whirled, taken by surprise. Jabez had been gone for weeks, and she'd missed him.

"I brought you a few things from New Orleans." He held out a basket filled with packages: oranges, pralines, the newest book by Melville, a glorious flowered shawl.

"Doctor Robinson." She looked not at the gifts but at him, knowing full well her face showed everything it shouldn't. "How very kind of you to think of me." Foolish thing to say.

"Miss Canon." His smile softly mocking, his dark eyes laughing. "I have been thinking of nothing but you." He set the basket down, took her hand and drew her into the shelter of the willow.

They married in November, a few days before her thirty-third birthday. She traded her new house for a husband. Independent as a hog on ice, she thought, as she closed her front door and surrendered the key to the young man who bought it. But she knew in her heart it was time—she was ready—to move on.

The ladies of the town took over the creation of her bridal costume. She refused to be decorated in white silk and rows of lace and instead fell head over heels for a pattern featured in Godey's in rose tarlatan, with skirt flounces edged in black velvet and guipure lace. Nancy and Mrs. Norman cut and measured, Elizabeth and Mrs. Watson stitched and fitted. Most of the town turned out for the wedding dinner, whether invited or not, and the bride and groom both delighted in their company. When they slipped off in the late afternoon for St. Joe, they left their guests dining on roast goose with sauerkraut, venison steaks and potato balls, corn pudding, sweet potatoes, brandied cranberries and raspberry pie. And drinking their fill of ale and cider and the last of the lemonade.

They cruised to St. Louis by steamboat, Jabez apologizing that it was not New Orleans or Chicago, but Agnes didn't care. A city with shops and theater, restaurants, even a mediocre opera thrilled her. They settled in the Planter's House Hotel at Fourth and Pine, and made it their object to discover the sights. As the weather favored them with unseasonably warm days—termed Indian Summer for reasons Agnes could not fathom—they explored Washington Square, Hyde Park, and St. Louis Place. They traveled an hour by carriage to the new fairgrounds to see the vast amphitheater, the racetracks, grandstands and water features, the fine arts hall, the mechanical hall and the three-story Chicken Palace, all quiet now and empty of fairgoers, but magnificent even so. They rode omnibuses and marveled at the length of the levee and the number of steamboats, and shopped and dined above their income. Agnes convinced Jabez to escort her on a tour of Lemp's Brewery, the limestone storage cave, and the tavern on the riverside where they enjoyed their first glass of a new beverage called a "lager." Agnes developed a decided taste for it.

Jabez laughed and joked, took Agnes coffee in the morning and chocolates in the evening, forsook all newspapers and pamphlets and public speakers, and concentrated his attention on her. They browsed the booksellers and argued vehemently over Smollett's work—she couldn't abide satire, he loved it—and purchased an entire set of Walter Scott's books to replace those she had sold to come west. Her husband's ease and lightheartedness gratified her, and she understood, finally, how it felt to love and be loved. And by January, she sensed new life growing within.

The pregnancy had progressed smoothly, and Jabez assured her that as her water broke before pains began, labor would be eased. After the first racking pain, she invited him to trade places with her, and he promptly left to fetch Doctor Norman. Big as a barrel of fall apples, she lay for a few precious moments in solitude, thinking she wouldn't go through the next few hours if she could choose, knowing she had no choice. A woman facing birth resembled a man facing imminent battle: no way under heaven to avoid the inevitable. A man, of course, could cut and run. For a woman about to birth a child no such option exists.

A spasm seized her, and she screeched. As the sultry September evening progressed, Jabez encouraged her to use her vocal cords as often and as loudly as possible to relieve the pains. She took him at his word and later, she came to understand, the neighbors gathered up and down the street to listen and place wagers as the evening wore on. She remembered Rachel buzzing in, her work-worn hands comforting, stroking, Sarah following her with a basin of cold water. She remembered hours of bearable pain and a single hour of almost unbearable wretchedness. She remembered the lamplight on Jabez's tense, frowning face, and Doctor Norman's peaceful, amused expression. Agnes had insisted on Doctor Norman's attendance—if anything went wrong, Jabez would never forgive himself—but Jabez adamantly refused his colleague's suggestion that he wait in the front parlor throughout. Agnes recalled someone's hand on her belly, and Doctor Norman counting with her, and Jabez saying impatiently, "My dear, you're not pushing right." She snarled up at him, asking how in the blue devil he knew whether she pushed right or not; he'd never done it, had he? And as she was doing the best she could, he had no call to be so high-handed. And she remembered Jabez chuckling and Doctor Norman choking back a guffaw. Then someone said "There's the head" and blackness, then Jabez, a smile wide as the Missouri splitting his beard, held high a wet and wriggling body, still attached. And her husband said, "A boy! Agnes, we have a boy!"

Much later, toward dawn, she lay propped against the headboard, the babe nestled to her breast and sucking with vigor. Jabez, washed and filled with coffee, dropped next to her, a look of supreme contentment on his face.

Agnes laughed, adrenalin running high.

"You can be proud of your accomplishment, Papa," she said, kissing his cheek.

He wrapped her with an arm and squeezed. The baby wriggled, mewed, waved his fists in the air at his father and smacked his lips. Jabez took him, tightened the blanket around the tiny limbs and tucked him into the crook of his arm. "No, my love, I know who did the work here." One long finger stroked the wrinkles from the child's forehead. "I've delivered so many of these, but this one is mine." He leaned his cheek against the top of her head. "And yours. It's very different."

They christened their son Charles Wetmore, after Jabez's mentor. Agnes suggested the name and Jabez was pleased, knowing that it honored both Eliza and her father. He proceeded to plan for Charlie's medical education, beginning with a recitation to him of the Latin names of medicinal herbs in their garden. Charlie gurgled and laughed and grew like a healthy puppy.

25

November 1859

Jabez spooned a dollop of mashed butternut squash into Charlie's dish. Charlie immediately dropped his spoon and clutched a handful, cramming it mostly into his mouth. His eyelashes wore orange goo. Agnes tore off a piece of bread, took a sip of wine, and pushed away her plate. Her stomach roiled at the smell of roast pork. And roast turkey, beef, and ham, to say nothing of vegetables.

"Only you, my dear, could turn morning sickness into dinner-time sickness," Jabez said, swiping at his son's face with a napkin. "I believe you're going to be very uncomfortable for the next few months."

"Very funny," she glared. "You are now in charge of both feeding and diapers."

"Papas don't do diapers," he said solemnly. "Papas are in charge of playtime. And maybe lessons."

She looked at their child and shuddered. The moment passed. "I do believe this confinement promises to be more of a trial than the last."

"Well, then," he said, moving the plates to the sideboard. "I have a suggestion." He poured her more wine and filled his own glass. "Let's give you a little vacation now while you're still of a size to be mobile"—she threw a napkin at him—"and get you away from this monster for a time." He lifted Charlie from his high chair and set him on his lap. Charlie grabbed a waistcoat button and rammed it into his mouth. Jabez disentangled him.

"And where did you have in mind? With the weather coming on winter."

"How about a week in St. Joe? You can shop, we can see the new railroad, enjoy restaurant meals. A second honeymoon. What do you say?"

"In St. Joe? Second prize is two weeks in St. Joe?" But she smiled at him.

"Now, Agnes, don't be cranky. There's a new hotel. We can leave Charlie with Sarah Jackson, and it won't be too far for you. Besides, there's a political speaker scheduled just across the river that I think you'll enjoy hearing." He rubbed his nose into the back of Charlie's pudgy neck, making the boy giggle.

"Who is it this time?" She retrieved her napkin and wiped Charlie's tray.

"That lawyer from Illinois we've been reading about, Abe Lincoln. He's speechifying in Ohio and Illinois for the Republicans. Remember? He ran against Douglas for the Senate last year." He deposited Charlie on his special blanket in the corner and handed him his stuffed dog.

"Oh." She stopped what she was doing. "You know he's a cousin of mine. Our grandparents were related."

"I understand he resembles an ape." He slipped up behind her and wrapped his arms around her waist, still small enough, thank goodness. "It's a good thing you don't look like him." He nuzzled her neck. "He might even run for president next year. How would that be? Your cousin in the White House?"

She turned in his arms. "That would mean the abolitionist Republicans in charge, wouldn't it? And that would mean secession." As soon as the words were out of her mouth, she felt his playful mood die. He released her and dropped into a chair, lit a cigar and sipped from his wineglass.

"Yes, and probably war."

They traveled to St. Joseph the following week, leaving Sarah installed in their home with Charlie, and took a room in the Patee Hotel on Penn Street, a luxurious place with velvet settees and an indoor water closet, bell pulls for the maids and flocked wallpaper. Jabez suffered through a day of shopping, carrying Agnes's parcels, treating her to lunch at O'Brien's.

On the second evening, they dined at the home of Will Hall, whom Jabez met back in '56 during the presidential campaign. To Agnes's delight, the Widow Rawlings, tiny, white-blond and delicately complexioned, and once her imagined rival, held court at table, acting as her brother's hostess.

She displayed a quick tongue, a sharp intelligence, and a deep knowledge of music, drama and literature. She spoke not a word of politics, however, which dominated the evening's conversation. She and Agnes were the only ladies among the diners.

Their host, Mr. Hall, a short, stout lawyer with pronounced ears jutting from a mass of gingery hair, welcomed Jabez with warmth and obvious affection. He seated Agnes to his right at table and she found she liked their host very much, especially since he spent much of the evening extolling her husband's talents as a pamphleteer.

"The work of European agitators." The gentleman to Agnes's right said to Jabez. The man worked as an aide to Governor Stewart, but Agnes never did catch his name.

Doctor Lowry, a physician from Jefferson City, paused in his dissection of orange-glazed roast duck. "Pah," he said. "Ain't agitators at all. It's the whole North. They want to kill our cotton trade with tariffs and make us pay for their railroads."

"Us, sir?" Mr. Hall asked. "You align Missouri with the cotton growers? I continue to maintain Missouri must be neutral. We arm ourselves, but we keep our head down."

"Impossible," said a diminutive aristocrat named Jo Shelby. "Hiding your head under the covers won't be helpful to Missouri or anyone else." His mustache collected bits of food as he ate. He wiped long fingers on a linen napkin. "War's the answer and we're to be in the center of it."

"You've certainly done your part in dragging us all into the fighting, Shelby," Jabez said. Agnes noted that that her husband and Shelby were obviously already well acquainted. "Your adventures in Kansas got the blood flowing."

Shelby's smile was not pleasant. "No, sir, those northern invaders began the argument and my men did only what was necessary." He set down his knife and fork and leaned on his forearms. "Don't tell me you think John Brown's a hero?"

Hall stepped in. "Now, Jo, no call to insult the man." He surveyed his guests. "Do you know," he said, "that Waldo Emerson likens that man to Jesus?"

Jabez reddened. "I saw what Brown did. Saw it with my own eyes. Brown and his boys are killers and deserve to hang, but pray God that's the last of the killing. The north and the south should agree to separate and go in peace."

"Won't happen," Stewart's man said. "The abolitionists are on a mission. They won't stop until slavery's vanished from the face of the earth."

"I still say slavery will die of its own accord, given time," Jabez said, "though I fear time's running out."

"You're wrong, sir," Shelby said, pointing a forefinger in Jabez's direction. "Slavery is the African's natural condition, the best thing for him. Our entire society rests on that truth, the Negro isn't the equal of the white man."

"I don't claim equality for the Negro," Jabez said, "but it doesn't follow that slavery is his natural state. Or the natural state of any human."

"Do you mean to say, sir," Agnes jumped in, turning to Shelby, "that slavery is actually a social good?"

Shelby appraised her coolly, as if considering whether to respond. Then he bowed in her direction, awkwardly, as his short stature put him chest-high to the table. "Madam," he said. "I do indeed believe slavery is the right thing for the African race. Hence my support for the current legislation in the statehouse." He turned away from her.

"And what legislation is that?" she asked.

Doctor Lowry set down his wine glass. "A bill that requires all free blacks in Missouri to be seized and sold back into slavery."

Agnes drew back, eyes wide. "Surely they're considering no such thing?"

"Yes, Madam, they are," Stewart's man answered. "The Governor, however, is not supportive. If it passes, he'll exercise the veto."

Mrs. Rawlings, serving potatoes from a silver dish held by a Negro steward, stepped in. "My dear Mrs. Robinson, you can't have lived among them." She nodded to the serving man, and he moved on to the next diner. "They're like children, and a condition of servitude is the only way they'll survive."

Agnes bit her tongue. Mrs. Rawlings had the right of one thing, Agnes knew nothing of the race.

Jabez smiled at her through the flower arrangement between them, but the other men appeared discomfited, either with her opinions or simply because a woman had spoken up.

Mrs. Rawlings smiled. "Try the baked eggplant, Mrs. Robinson, do. It's a recipe Mrs. Davis gave me. I'd be happy to share it with you."

Mr. Hall turned to his left. "You mentioned tariffs, Lowry. I believe you've hit on it. The North's business is to prop up New England manufacturing and that means driving the South's cotton trade into the ground."

"Tariffs aren't all that bad," Shelby said. "I can support the hemp tariff."

"Can't have it both ways, Shelby," the Stewart man said. "If the southern states break away you won't have the power of the federal government to back your tariff."

"We don't need them to prop us up." Shelby sipped his wine, and his face bloomed red.

"I fear we do," Hall said. "The north has monopolized the shipping, the manufacturing, the banks—the southern states need to start from scratch if they want to compete."

"So where does that leave you, sir?" The Stewart man turned back to Jabez. "Still think the country can split itself in peace?"

Jabez set his knife diagonally across his plate and leaned forward. "I hold little hope of that, I assure you. I believe there was a time when the two sections might have negotiated their differences peacefully, either as one nation or two. I think self-interested men with a greed for power have put us all in a position where negotiation is an impossibility." He rubbed a hand over his beard and stared at Shelby. "My only hope now is that the fighting ends quickly."

And so it went. Agnes grew increasingly cross, relegated to the role of observer. And what she observed disturbed her: emotion ruled among these men who led Missouri's government and society. Sober judgment fled as the evening droned on and the wine flowed, and even Jabez allowed his temper to flash, as he debated Jo Shelby on point after point. The future loomed dark indeed.

"Do all those men at dinner yesterday own slaves?" she asked.

They huddled in the lee of the ferry boat cabin, crossing the Missouri into Kansas. Sleet whipped over the riverbed with needlelike intensity, lowering gray skies met foaming waves in fierce opposition to the needs of her tender digestive system. Agnes yanked her cloak more tightly about her neck and huddled against Jabez. He seemed immune to the elements.

"A couple of them have substantial farming operations. Jo Shelby is the largest slaveholder in the state. The others probably have a few house servants, at the least."

"But you've never supported extending slavery. Why do you associate with them?"

"I wouldn't associate with Jo Shelby if he didn't turn up everywhere. The others I find to be intelligent, thoughtful men. I don't happen to agree with their views on that subject. These are some of the men who will determine which way Missouri goes when war breaks out. I'd like to be a part of that."

"Mr. Hall didn't appear to agree with that Shelby man. I was quite disgusted with him. Shelby, I mean." The boat dropped into a deep trough, and Agnes gasped, burying her face in the rough cloth of Jabez's greatcoat.

"Hall's a Union man. I think he invites Shelby to keep a finger on the pulse of the radicals who're always looking for a reason to kill and maim their neighbors. That's what Jo Shelby wants, by the way, which is why I detest him." He tugged her hood more closely about her face and wiped a drop of rain off her nose. "I much prefer free labor, but I worry less about slavery than about the federals sticking their noses in the state's concerns. If I have any impact at all on prevailing opinion, it'll be to raise the threat of invasion from the north."

Her head jerked up. "Invasion? What makes you think they'd invade?"

"Haven't they already? You know what John Brown did, he butchered and murdered. And now he's a hero up there." His voice hoarsened. "What Emerson said, and Thoreau and those soft headed ... for the love of God, they call that man moral and humane? And there'll be more like him, it's a holy war to them." The boat bumped against the western shore, and Jabez pulled her to her feet, muttering. "They think they're Michael and his angels fighting the dragon." He shook his head and said no more.

They hurried down the ramp and joined a line of people waiting for a hack. After a mile's drive, they reached the town of Elwood, which fought a continuous battle with St. Joe for the overland trade. It boasted a dozen stores, sawmills, printers' and land agents' offices, and a hotel, the Great Western, three stories high. Its dining room, the largest space available in town, served as the scene of this lecture. Tables stood stacked in the lobby and the hallways, chairs and benches lined the room without consideration for the width of the ladies' crinolines, and a narrow corridor of standing room accommodated the overflow. Jabez wedged Agnes through the chattering crowd to a seat on a bench half the length of the room from the speaker's stand, while he stepped against the wall to stand for the duration.

Early dusk seeped through the few windows, and the crowded hall soaked up the gloom from outside. Coal oil lamps strained to pierce the heavy shadows. At the front of the room a platform stood, lined along the front edge with lanterns and along the rear with a dozen upholstered chairs and their occupants, none of whom Agnes recognized. The crowd grew quiet as a bewhiskered fellow with exaggerated collar points moved to center stage and began to speak. Agnes paid little attention to him but studied the men on the platform. None showed the slightest evidence of being a renowned orator, much less the possible next president. Perhaps he'd been delayed? If he'd canceled, their miserable journey through the sleet would have been for naught.

But the speaker with the whiskers introduced Mr. Abraham Lincoln, and a clean-shaven man seated on the far right rose and moved to the forefront. In his chair, he appeared no taller than average. On his feet, he towered over every other man on the stage, probably anyone in the room. His ill-fitting black suit complemented his mussed black hair, and his arms and legs seemed to move without reference to each other. A very broad forehead over deep-sunk eyes and high cheek bones framed a magnificent hooked nose, and his ears roosted on his head like wings.

He started with a story, his voice a high-pitched twang, something about having been labeled two-faced by a political opponent, and said, "If I had another face, would I be wearing this one?" The crowd laughed and Agnes joined in, a clever beginning.

He gazed about the room, sharp eyes lighting on first one then another of the audience. "I should not wonder," he said "that there are some Missourians about this audience, or if not, that by speaking distinctly, some of the Missourians may hear me on the other side of the river." More laughter, and from the back of the room a nasal voice shouted, "We're here!"

"For that reason," Mr. Lincoln continued, "I propose to address a portion of what I have to say to the Missourians." He drew himself up. "The issue between you and me, understand, is that I think slavery is wrong, and ought not to be outspread, and you think it is right and ought to be extended and perpetuated."

The same voice called out, "Amen!" and Mr. Lincoln flapped his big hand. "That is my Missourian I am talking to now." The crowd hooted.

"My friend Senator Douglas never says your institution of slavery is wrong. He never says it is right, to be sure, but he never says it is wrong. At the same time, he molds the sentiment of the north, by never saying it is right."

As he began to speak of slavery, his face commenced to light up, as if from within, his eyes sparked, his inelegant limbs became almost graceful. "He said upon the floor of the Senate, and he has repeated it a great many times, that he does not care whether slavery is voted up or voted down, that it is simply a question of dollars and cents, that there is a line drawn by the Almighty on one side of which slavery must always exist." He strode to the far edge of the platform and pointed a long forefinger at a paunchy gentleman in the front row. "I ask you, if this is true, that a man may rightfully hold another man as property on one side of the line, you must then admit he has the same right to hold his property on the other side." The crowd roared.

Agnes found his countenance captivating, astoundingly ugly in repose but transformed by zeal and candlelight into something resplendent and powerful.

"Douglas's great principle, popular sovereignty, gives you, by natural consequence, the revival of the slave trade whenever you want it. He says that it is the sacred right of the man who goes into the territories to have slavery if he wants it. Is it not then the sacred right of the man that don't go there equally to buy slaves in Africa, if he wants them? Can you point out the difference?"

Heads nodded, several people applauded.

"I often hear it intimated that the people of the south mean to divide the Union whenever a Republican or anything like it, is elected president."

A new voice, from among the crowd at the door: "That's so."

"That is so, one of them says. I wonder if he is a Missourian?"

Another voice: "He's a Douglas man."

"Well, then, I want to know what you're going to do with your half of it? Are you going to split the Missouri and Ohio Rivers down through, and push your half off a piece?" Applause and laughter. "Or are you going to keep it right alongside of us outrageous fellows? Or are you going to build up a wall some way between your country and ours, by which that movable property of yours can't come over here anymore? Will you make war upon us and kill us all?" He bent his knees, then straightened them forcefully, at the same time throwing out his arms. "Why, gentlemen, I think you are as gallant and as brave as any men alive, you can fight as bravely in a good cause, man for man, as any other people living, that you have shown yourselves capable of that upon various occasions, but man for man, you are not better than we are, and there are not so many of you as there are of us." Loud cheering to a background of yips and rude shouts. "You will never make much of a hand at whipping us!"

Agnes glanced over her shoulder at Jabez. He slouched against the wall, one booted ankle crossed over another, restless hands turning an unlit cigar end over end. His expression remained bland.

Mr. Lincoln threw down a challenge, an invitation to bloodshed, to these southerners so consumed by the poison of affronted honor. He next repeated a phrase Agnes had read several times about a house divided against itself not standing, that a government cannot endure permanently half slave and half free. Then he said something that took her by surprise, as his whole speech until that moment seemed so opposed.

"I will say—" he stuck his bony hands in his pockets as if to keep them out of mischief—"that I have no purpose directly or indirectly to interfere with the institution of slavery in the states where it exists. I believe I have no lawful right to do so, and I have no inclination to do so. I have no purpose to introduce political and social equality between the white and the black races. There is a physical difference between the two which in my judgment will probably forever forbid their living together upon the footing of perfect equality. This is the whole of it, and anything that argues me into the idea of a declaration of war is a specious and fantastic arrangement of words, by which a man can prove a horse chestnut to be a chestnut horse." And he drew a laugh from the crowd again, to soften the import of his words.

Mr. Lincoln slipped a watch from its fob and a kerchief from his pocket and mopped his brow. "Allow me to close with an observation," he said, his voice quiet now and sad. "John Brown will on the morrow be executed for treason against the state. He has shown great courage, rare unselfishness, but we cannot object to his execution even though he agreed with us in thinking slavery wrong. That cannot excuse violence, bloodshed, and treason. It could avail him nothing that he might think himself right." He replaced the watch and the kerchief and lifted his arms, and the shadow cast by the footlights resembled a monstrous hovering bat. "Treason," he said. "And if the south attempts to destroy the Union, that too shall be treason, and that treason will be dealt as old John Brown has been dealt."

For a moment the crowd held its breath, and then the room erupted in cheers, shouts, whistles, stomping feet, jeers and hisses. Jabez slipped his arm around Agnes's waist, elbowing his way through the crowd and out the wide double doors, and onto the street, where icy rain drove like shards of glass, and the hacks waited. They procured one all to themselves, and as they made their way to the ferry slip, the spell of that candlelit room and the stunning orator began to wear away.

"Well?" Agnes said. "What did you think?" And without waiting: "Amazing man—astonishing speaker! Everything so simply put, so well construed. He has a wisdom that we so seldom see in our great men."

"He is exceptional, I grant you that," Jabez said, adjusting the carriage robe over her lap.

"Don't say you didn't like him. Do you take issue with him?" Jabez seemed to Agnes to be unduly obstinate.

"No, I liked what he said, for the most part. I believe he has an uncommon grasp of the problems we face. Few men I've heard or read express themselves so clearly."

"Then what didn't you like?"

"I believe he'd do whatever is necessary to keep the Union in one piece, and that means attacking the south. Douglas will be the Democratic candidate, and if Lincoln is the Republican candidate, then a vote for Douglas would be a vote for peace. A vote for Lincoln would be a vote for war."

"And why would a vote for Douglas be a vote for peace?"

"He'd negotiate, try to compromise. The south will trust him, at least more than it will trust any Republican."

"A compromise similar to the one he made that started the Kansas war?"

"Well, you surely have a point there." He sat back in the hard seat and grinned at her. His teeth flashed in the light of the buggy's lanterns. "He's a manipulator, it's true, and will say what his audience wants to hear, but if he stretches out the negotiations long enough, slavery will collapse of its own weight, and the South's society will change in the natural course of things."

"And that's the solution? Continuing procrastination until something changes?" Now she was thoroughly irritated with him.

"Agnes, anything is better than all-out war."

She said nothing, listened to the beat of water against the canvas roof and pulled the lap robe closer about her. He turned away, his shoulders sagging. "If you'd seen what I've seen. Bodies torn to bits, infection, dirt and pain." His voice cracked. "Young lives ended miserably, boys left to die in muddy gore, alone and in agony. Nothing can be worth that. Nothing."

They rode to the ferry in silence, boarded in silence, crossed in silence.

Back in St. Joseph, the rain settled into heavy, steady drops, and the slimy clay path into town sucked at their boots. Agnes ducked her head against the weather and tucked in behind Jabez, her hand in the crook of his elbow, and so when he stopped abruptly at the steps of the hotel veranda, she crashed into the sodden wool of his greatcoat. The veranda was empty but for a single figure leaning against the clapboard wall, hands in pockets, a thin cigar tucked in the corner of his mouth. A subtle aroma rose from him, and Agnes drew back slightly, turning away.

"Miz Robinson." The man stepped forward and dropped his hand on her arm. A swollen purple scar slashed his left cheek, but she recognized his silver eyes.

"Willard Bigelow," she said. "How came you here?"

Willard's eyes narrowed. "I can be wherever I please, ma'am."

Jabez moved toward him, glowering. "Bigelow, step back from my wife," he snapped and shoved the man's hand from Agnes's arm.

Willard backed up a step, a derisive smile on his bristled face, hands held out in front of him. "Now, Doc, I just thought I'd say hello to your lady, seeing as we're friends and neighbors."

"We're not friends, and I'll thank you to move along," Jabez said.

"Hey, this here's a public walk, and I got a right to be on it," Willard said. He turned to Agnes and bowed from the waist. "Ma'am, happy to see you again after all this time. My brother Jake speaks highly of you." He turned to Jabez. "Your husband might've told you we ran into each other in Kansas City some years ago. He loaned me his knife. Right thoughtful of him."

Agnes shivered and stepped back against her husband. Jabez took her arm, keeping his eyes on Willard. "Agnes, if ever you see this man in our vicinity, get out the shotgun."

"Don't be giving her bad ideas about me, Doc." He flicked the end of his cigar into the street. "I still got that knife. I aim to return the favor some day."

"You do that, Bigelow." Jabez steered her toward the hotel door. Willard pushed in front of them. She smelled whiskey on him and wrinkled her nose. He laughed in her face and leaned in.

"I mean it, Doc, you come down on the right side in this thing and you and the missus'll be left alone. You come down on the wrong side and you'll see more of me than you ever bargained for." Willard held his ground another moment, eyes fixed on Jabez, then stepped back. Jabez, without another look, handed Agnes through the door and closed it in Willard's face.

26

August 1860

It was mid-afternoon, the heavy air simmering and pressing down like sweet sorghum, when Sarah Belle arrived, squalling and punching tiny fists. Doctor Norman attended Agnes's labor as Jabez was away from home, and it took a full three weeks for her to forgive him that dereliction. While Agnes labored, Jabez spent that day, as well as the preceding week, in Kansas City, conferring with a group of men—Governor Stewart, Mr. Hall, Sterling Price—in an attempt to save Missouri from being crushed between the sectors. Not a valid excuse, in Agnes's mind. True, Sarah presented herself ten days earlier than anticipated, but her temper rose with each day he absented himself.

When he did appear, he trailed along with him a farm wagon loaded with bedding, rough furnishings and two Negroes.

"You did what?" she said, once she'd snapped her jaw back in place. The man and woman stood just inside the kitchen door, expressions identically impassive.

"I bought them," Jabez said, a silly grin aimed at his daughter, who stared up at him, or wherever a two-day-old stares, from her nest in his arms. Sarah Belle slowly turned red, puckered up her brow and howled.

"You bought them." Agnes caught the woman's eye. The Negro held the gaze two ticks, than lowered her eyes toward the floor. "Jabez Robinson, you are no slave master."

Jabez held Sarah away from his body and wrinkled his nose. "Whew, never could understand how so much smell can come from such a tiny body." He laughed and turned. "Here, Rosie, we'll break you in right." And he handed Agnes's daughter to a total stranger.

"Oh, no," she said and snatched her away. Agnes lowered the baby to the stand in the corner where she kept a basin and a stack of linen triangles.

Jabez rubbed a hand over his beard. "Aren't you pleased? I thought you'd be pleased."

"Pleased that we now own two people?"

"No, pleased we'd have some help. You'd have some help." He fingered a diaper, patterned in red squares. "With the children. And the laundry." He leaned down to peer into her face.

Agnes crumpled the soiled cloth and dropped it into its bucket. "Stand here," she said. "Don't let her wiggle off." She fetched the kettle from the stove and filled the basin. "Where did they come from?"

"They're Maggie O'Day's, from the hotel in Kansas City." Jabez stroked Sarah's scalp, fuzzy with a hint of black hair. "She's selling up, moving to St. Joe."

Agnes set the kettle on the floor and whirled to study the couple. Neither looked the least familiar, but it had been seven years, and she hadn't paid much attention at the time. The girl was slightly built, her wrists protruding from blue calico sleeves, head wrapped in a brown kerchief. The man stood no taller than Agnes, but his ropy forearms and thick neck hinted at strength. He straightened under her gaze, his eyes on hers. Agnes thought she caught a glint of amusement in them.

"What are your names?" she asked.

The man stepped forward and bobbed his head. "Dick McDonald, ma'am, and this is Rose. My wife," he added. Agnes noted the emphasis he placed on those two words, as marriages between slaves weren't recognized in Missouri and many people simply disregarded the idea. Rose dipped a curtsy, and her husband placed his hand on the small of her back.

Agnes flushed and turned back to Sarah Belle. "What did you pay?" She realized they were talking about them as if they were two new plow mules.

"Sixteen hundred. A thousand for him and six hundred for her."

"Where do you propose they live?"

"Out back. Dick and I'll section off the stable, make a cabin."

"Jabez," she said, sliding a pin through Sarah's diaper and tucking the point into a fold. She turned to him. "I will not own people."

"She would have sold them south."

"So you're telling me this was an act of charity?"

A tinge of red bloomed on his cheeks. She knew well the signs of incipient vexation.

"It seemed at the time, my dear, to be a winning solution for everyone." He rapped his knuckles once on the stand, next to Sarah's kicking legs. "We'll discuss it later." And he stalked to the door.

"We must manumit," she said.

He glared at her, hand on the door jamb. "I'll take care of it," he said, and disappeared into the yard.

August melted into September, September slid toward winter. Jabez and Dick built a cabin attached to the stables behind the house, and as Jabez wielded the pen more skillfully than the hammer, he acted as general dogsbody to the Negro. Dick's talents as a carpenter manifested themselves early. Maggie had hired him out over the years, just as she'd hired out Rose as a wet nurse following three stillbirths. Agnes's heart ached for the girl at the same time she appreciated her natural felicity with the children. Often, as she watched Rose bathing or feeding Sarah Belle, she saw a mist across her eyes as if the girl were lost in the past.

The presidential election approached, Sarah Belle smiled her first smile, and Jabez spent his time writing and speaking throughout the state in support of compromise, or in the last resort, peaceful disunion. But all for naught. On a dreary day in early November the election went to the Republicans, that strange, cadaverous man became president-elect, and South Carolina seceded from the Union. Gunshots and shouting shattered Lick Creek's morning calm. At the time it all started, Agnes and Elizabeth were strolling down Main Street, their little ones wrapped in blankets, en route to a hen party at Mrs. Norman's. Beyond the courthouse a crowd converged on a buckboard moving through the streets behind two raggedy mules, Jacob Bigelow at the reins, Willard wedged behind the seat, revolver pointed to the sky. Braced in the bed stood a structure that resembled a gallows, the effigy of a man dangling from the crosstree.

The figure's long legs flopped over the wagon's side rails. Its flour-bag head, leaking straw and topped by a black shock of ropy hair, canted to one side like a broken-necked chicken. On its breast fluttered a sign lettered "Old Abe," and tacked to the tailgate hung a banner scrawled with "Death to Black Republicans."

Laughter. Cheers

"Secession is our watchword, our rights we will demand," someone sang.

"Traitors!"

"Pukes!"

"Nigger lover!" A big man Agnes didn't recognize pushed Mr. Baxter, the tailor, and someone else took a swing at the stranger and missed. Hands reached up and clutched at Willard who landed a telling kick, which Agnes later learned broke Earl Kunkel's nose. Jake slapped the reins against the mules' rumps, and they broke into a trot, then a run, wild-eyed, scattering bodies in their path. Agnes and Elizabeth retreated to the steps of the Presbyterian church as the buckboard rushed by, Jake grinning and Willard whooping like a crazed bullfrog. Down the street Aldo Beaton clutched a fistful of Galen Crow's coat, elbow pulled back to deliver a punch. Levi Zook gave Beaton a shove, and he toppled. Zook took Mr. Irvine by the arm and yanked him away from Mr. Cayton. The two continued to shout insults at each other as their friends dragged them to opposite sides of the street.

By the time Agnes and Elizabeth arrived, the ladies at Mrs. Norman's were clustered on her front porch prattling like a flock of geese, as fierce, though less physical, as their men. Agnes noticed several women missing who should have been there—Sarah Hill and Mrs. Cayton were normally of their circle, and Mrs. Foster, the attorney's wife. Women whose husbands supported secession and opposed Lincoln's election. Several ladies refused to acknowledge Agnes, and the party dissolved before it began under a cloud of tension and distress. That was to be Agnes's last visit to Mrs. Norman's home.

In the outside world, states continued to secede: Mississippi, Florida, Alabama, Georgia withdrew soon after Christmas, and the bombast ratcheted up to fever pitch. One sleepy afternoon in February, Agnes sat at the kitchen table with Rose, Sarah Belle napping in her basket by the warmth of the stove. Charlie stood on a chair next to her, his sturdy forearms on the table, the wooden alphabet his father had carved for him spread out in front of him. Agnes spelled out "Charlie" and looked to Rose. "Kar?" she asked, wrinkling her forehead.

"No," Agnes said, pointing to the H. "Remember C and H together say ch."

"Char? Charlie?" She flashed a bright smile.

"Me!" Charlie squealed, beaming. "I try." He scooped up the letters, knocking the L to the floor.

Agnes bent to retrieve it. "I suppose I could be arrested for teaching you to read." She tilted her head at Rose. "What was it like? You know, I mean how you grew up."

Rose pushed aside the C and the A, roamed through the other letters. "Didn't know nothing else, Missus," she said.

"But now you do," Agnes said, leaning an elbow on the table, cheek in her hand.

"Yes ma'am." She picked out the T, added it to her word and smiled.

"Excellent," Agnes murmured. "Now do BAT."

"I can!" Charlie shouted and reached for the B.

"Isn't there a difference?" Rose looked at Agnes, liquid eyes holding a question. "I mean, there must be something that says to you, inside, you're safe from … well, from beatings. Or worse."

Rose took the B from Charlie and replaced the C. "Don't know that we be safe, Missus. Mostly I just scared of the slave catchers."

"Well, that's understandable." Agnes sat up and pulled Charlie onto her lap. "As long as you stay with us, you're safe."

"But that means we ain't free, whether we got papers or no." She smiled a small smile at Agnes who nodded in return.

"My man feels it more than me," Rose said. "He say it in your head and in your soul, being free." The stew pot on the stove hissed, and Rose stood to give it a stir.

"In your soul." Something Maggie O'Day said, a long time ago, another kitchen. They tried to make a slave out of me and I wouldn't let them. And Agnes thought of the Irish boy who sang at the barn dance years past. He's chattel, Jabez had said.

"Main thing," Rose continued, sitting back down and jabbing at the letters, "when you free can nobody sell us away from one another. My momma was sold south. I was only a child, about big as Charlie." The mask had lifted from her face, her eyes deep with generations of pain. "That's why

I don't want no babies of my own, not 'til we get to a place where they can't be sold."

Not Maggie nor the Irish boy nor any white man or woman can be free, Agnes thought, until this abomination is ended. She clutched Charlie so tightly he whimpered and pushed her away.

The back door opened onto a rush of cold air and a gentle snowfall, and Jabez came in, shedding hat, coat, muffler and gloves in the back alcove. Rose stood and poured him coffee from the pot simmering at the back of the stove, and he sat with them, warming his hands on the mug.

"What news now?" Agnes asked, standing Charlie on the floor.

"The returns are final," he said. "The state's gone overwhelmingly for the Union." He referred to a referendum to settle once and for all the question of Missouri secession. "Not a single secessionist elected. So we'll continue as we are. Caught in the middle." He slumped in his chair.

Agnes was stunned. "But the Governor—that's a tremendous defeat. Couldn't he sway anyone?"

"Claib Jackson's a weasel. He'll go whichever way the wind blows, as long as he's in office and in power. Just like he did during the election." He picked up the M and tapped it, brooding, on the table. Rose lifted a lid to stir, and the aroma of rich beef stew filled the room.

"So now what happens?"

"Hall was elected, which is good news. We can get our planks into the convention platform through him. I hope this sends a message that we don't want war, and the legislature will quit trying to arm everybody and his brother." He sat up, put the M down in front of Rose, who was refilling his coffee, added the I and the S, and lifted his eyebrows at her.

"Mis?" she asked. He nodded, dug through the other letters until he found the O, then the U and the R and lined them up next to his first word.

After a moment, she said, "Our."

"Right." Charlie watched his papa keenly. Not much could keep the boy standing still, but his father always held him entranced.

Jabez added the I at the end.

"I?" Rose asked, perplexed.

"Put them together," Jabez said.

Rose moved the three words together. "Mis. Our. I. Mis-sour-i." She looked up. "Misourl?" She replaced the I with the A. "Misoura." She grinned.

Jabez laughed. "That's the way it sounds." He replaced the I. "But this is the way it's spelled. Things are not always what they seem."

"He'll teach you bad habits, Rose," Agnes said. "There are two esses in Missouri, he's just too lazy to whittle another set."

Jabez snorted, stood and patted Rose on the shoulder. "You're coming along well, Rose. Keep it up. You'll be teaching Sarah to read in no time."

Rose flushed and scraped the letters into her apron, to Charlie's loud objections, depositing them in his toy box. "Hush, now, child, you be waking the little one," she said and shooed them all out while she set the table for dinner.

Jabez swung Charlie onto his shoulders, the little head dangerously close to the ceiling. Agnes picked up the coffee cups and trailed after them. "What else will you put to the convention?"

"Stewart wants armed neutrality. Neutrality's fine as long as the federals understand they have no sovereignty over us. They can't tell a state what to do with its property rights, and that's the crux of the argument for slave-holders." He sat in his armchair, Charlie on his knee, and took a cigar from the box on the side table. "I don't hold with slave men, but unless the north leaves property rights alone, we'll be fighting them alongside Georgia and Alabama."

"And you think they'll actually pay attention? Lincoln and his friends, I mean?" Agnes pulled a brand from the banked fire and lit his cigar.

"No, love, I don't think that. I think we sit on the road between the Union and the Confederacy, we control two of the rivers both sides need, there are free states all around us—the northern army will have to march through Missouri to get to the enemy, and that's going to be interpreted as invasion. It'll force us into the war whether we secede or not." He took a long pull, blew smoke over Charlie's head. "We don't stand a chance."

Sarah whimpered in the kitchen, sleepy kitten noises that signaled the end of her nap. Charlie sat on his father's lap, crooning to himself and watching the glowing tip of the cigar. "Do you think there'll be fighting here?"

"Probably not, not close to us. There's nothing strategic here. You should be safe enough."

She turned her gaze on him. "Doesn't that mean you should be safe enough, too?"

"There will be a great need for doctors. I don't know where I'll be or what I'll be doing."

Rose carried the baby to Agnes. She settled onto her chair and unfastened her bodice, putting Sarah Belle to her breast. "What kind of world have we brought them into?" She murmured, not expecting an answer. Jabez stared moodily into the fire.

Not long after Missouri voted against secession, Jabez found himself, much to Agnes's chagrin, in possession of a newspaper.

Jace Biggers, the banker, turned up at their door one evening after dinner with a business proposition for Jabez. The editor of the Holt County *Courier & News*, Mr. Conklin, after a three-month tenure in which his customers smeared his office with old eggs and offal following the printing of a pro-Unionist piece, was ready to sell. Biggers wanted to buy, and he wanted Jabez to buy in with him.

Agnes thought Mr. Biggers' proposal a parlous idea, and firmly believed that no other instrument advanced strife in their community so forcefully as that paper. Whenever an editorial appeared to be slanted toward one faction or another, fistfights erupted outside its offices like mushrooms in manure. "You can bludgeon everyone in town at once with your ideas, now," she said, jabbing her needle into the hem of a new diaper. She knew he wanted to do it. "No more begging someone to publish you. You can sneer back at old Conklin and his friend, and we'll have rotten eggs thrown at our house, thank you very much."

Jabez laughed. "You do carry grudges, my dear. I don't much want to bludgeon anyone. But I don't mind saying it would be useful to have a forum." He turned to Mr. Biggers. "Price and Stewart are trying to get control of papers across the state. If we can control the press, we can guide what people think. And maybe keep us out of this war."

"Or bring the war into our home," Agnes said, but the men ignored her.

"That's why I came to you, Doctor," the banker said, rolling his whiskey glass between his white palms. "I'm truly tired of what this paper's been putting out these two years. There's just no sense in keeping folks constantly in turmoil. I like what you have to say, and I'm ready to put my money behind it."

"We'll offend someone sometime," Jabez said. "What do you think, Agnes?"

Biggers didn't give her time to answer. "It's your opportunity. You have things to say, and they're the right things. It's worth a little risk to get them said."

Jabez turned away from her, and she soon removed herself, leaving them to talk costs and equipment and editorial points of view late into the night. The next morning Jabez accompanied Biggers to the bank to draw up papers, after which they owned half of the Holt County *Courier & News*.

Trouble started immediately. First, the printer's boy quit, and Jabez and his partner searched all the way to St. Joseph before finding an employee who knew the workings of the press machinery. Then he penned a long opinion piece on the legality of secession and supported Missouri's neutrality, which served to antagonize those factions holding radical opinions in either direction, to satisfy but a few centrists, and to alienate his friend Mr. Stewart, the former governor.

The Robinsons became pariahs. No one spoke to Agnes on the streets. Levi Zook refused to take her money at his general store and sent her to his competitor, Mr. McIntosh, who sold to her most unwillingly. And Sam and Rachel avoided them, hiding behind the excuse that the weather kept them on the farm and out of town. Elizabeth, bless her heart, continued to visit Agnes at every opportunity.

In March, a Missouri convention asserted the state's autonomy and demanded the federals withdraw their troops from the state, a timely and gratifying statement of Jabez's position. The hostility towards them tapered off some, but Jabez continued to voice his opinion on the wisdom of allowing peaceful separation.

And then everything changed.

Book Three

"What woman needs is not as a woman to act or to rule, but as a nature to grow, as an intellect to discern, as a soul to live freely and unimpeded, to unfold such powers as were given her when we left our common home."
~ Margaret Fuller, *Woman in the Nineteenth Century*, 1845

27

May 1861

Jake Bigelow poked the fire tentatively, stirring the coals and sending sparks spiraling into the treetops on a soggy spring breeze. Late May and the nights continued chill, the Noddaway River running heavy with snow melt, the broken land that rolled away from the river's canyon harboring patches of frost in the early mornings. Stinging rain spit down, stabbing at his face and the backs of his hands, running off the brim of his slouch hat, seeping inside his collar. A mosquito whined past his ear. He wished he'd brought his old work gloves from home, but his kid brother used them for plowing, and he surely needed them more. The camp lay quiet this evening. Two days ago Willard rode off with some of the men on the rumor that the jayhawker Jennison headed north from Liberty toward St. Joe, leaving a trail of burning farms and hanged men in his wake. Jake figured the rumor to be bogus. Most of them turned out so, ever since he'd joined up with this crew. The boys had yet to light on any of the nigger-stealers who invaded Missouri down along the river, and Jake didn't expect them to show up now. They never got this far north. Jennison and his pack of abolitionists hit Independence and Blue Springs. They didn't cross the Missouri and didn't give a shit about the northern counties.

Jake jammed a sharpened stick through the rabbit carcass he'd gutted and propped it between two rocks. He knew Willard spoiled for a fight, and the longer his brother cooled his heels the more squirrelly he got. So when Joe Reilly rode into camp a few days ago and said he'd heard from the blacksmith at Helesburg that marauders marched north out of Liberty with the intent of subduing the secesh along the Missouri River, Willard corralled the two Little brothers, Dave Powers, Ora Juwitt, and Alfred Zerbin and took off south to see what was up.

The rabbit wasn't going to be enough. Jake's belly had growled ever since he left the farm. Not that he fed good there, either. Why his pa's farm skimped along while all the farms around grew fat as a rich man's wife, he never could fathom. Too many mouths to feed, for one. Even with the money he brought in hiring out to Sam Canon and some of the others, there was never enough. He watched Hank Jansen pluck a chicken he stole from a farm up north on the river. No way Hank'd share. Every man scrounged his own meals in this outfit. Willard set down the rule at the beginning. Jake thought that just pit them all against each other, but Willard was the boss, so what the hell. Jake and Willard, at least, watched out for each other.

The sucking sound of hooves in the sticky sludge of the path signaled new arrivals, and the four men in the clearing jumped for their guns. But Willard's voice called out "Hullo the camp" and they relaxed. Willard and two other horsemen showed dim in the last light, silhouetted through the trees against the open sky over the river. Wil tethered and unsaddled the big black he stole from Sam Canon on their way out of town last month. Jake didn't think it right to take from Sam. The man was friend to their pa, but Wil said he was a stinking abolitionist and a northern invader, and duty called them to take what they could from him. Jake rode the mare his pa used for the buckboard. The old nag wasn't good for too many more seasons, anyway. He needed to find something else pretty soon before she dropped dead under him.

Jake squinted at his brother hunkered next to him. "Only got one rabbit," he said. "You can have some, but we got to get something else or I'm going to die right here of hunger." Wil grinned, reached into his knapsack and dragged out two chickens, tied by the legs, heads hanging limp. "Had to kill them already, but they're still fresh enough," he said, and tossed them at Jake. "Got them from a place down to Easton, long side the railroad. Old lady there all by herself, man gone to fight." He produced a bottle. "Got this, too." He drank, and the sweet smell of whiskey rolled off him.

"What side?" Jake asked.

"What you mean, what side?"

"What side is her man fighting on?"

"Don't know don't care," Wil said, settling back on his elbows. "Everyone contributes."

"Any sign of Jennison?"

"Naw, nothing. We got all the way to Plattesburg. But he'd been there all right. There was two farms along the Barnesville road that was burning. And two dead men, shot down by jayhawkers their women says." He rolled up on an elbow to face Jake and watch him pluck. "One of them was kin to the Stringfellows. Their sister's kid." He scowled. "Someone's got to pay for that."

He took a chicken from Jake, held it over the fire to singe the pinfeathers. "I'm thinking about taking a little revenge for him, over along Barnesville way. Idea come to me when we was riding back. They're some Union families down there." Wil pulled out his knife and cut the chicken into pieces, dropping them into the fry pan Jake dredged up from their gear.

The light dimmed under the trees, and Jake couldn't make out Wil's eyes in the shadow of his hat. Good. He knew that look and hated it. He remembered that look from when they were kids, and Wil threw a rope over a stallion Pa'd bought to stud. He scrambled up on the beast's back and tore over the pasture and the stallion stepped in a rabbit hole and broke a leg and Pa had to shoot it. Or when they broke the lock on Zook's store in the middle of the night and stole cigars and the little bit of cash left in the drawer. Wil never seemed bothered by what happened after those tricks. No one knew about the Zook thing, but Pa nearly killed them both with his horsewhip after the thing with the stallion. No botheration to Wil. And here Jake was now, following his big brother into what promised more trouble than a sack of swamp rattlers. But he'd do it, because he always had.

Jake set his chicken to fry and pulled a haunch off the rabbit. He offered it to his brother, then cut himself a piece. "When you planning on doing that?" he said through a mouthful. He reached for Wil's bottle and took a pull.

"Tomorrow we ought to get on down there. I want them feds to know why they been hit. I sent the Little boys and Powers back to Easton to find us some horses. We meet them there tomorrow night. Maybe we can stop by the old war widow's place again." He snickered.

"So you want me to go with you?" Jake wiped greasy fingers on his pants, picked up a chicken leg. "Who else you taking?"

"Everyone." Wil waved a hand toward the campfires. He'd come back with Juwitt and Zerbin, and with the other three, Irving, Jansen and Godsey, that made five, plus the Bigelows. And the Little brothers and Dave Powers. None of the men was more than twenty-two or twenty-three years old, except that stupid Alfred Zerbin who took orders and smiled and nodded all the time. There wasn't much up there between those two jug ears of his. They all followed Wil without question, Jake thought. Wil always had ideas.

Next morning, Willard kicked the whole bunch of them out of soggy bedrolls and hurried them through a quick meal of cold meat and leftover coffee. The rain tapered off during the night, but the trees dripped and clouds tumbled across the sky. The trail along the Noddaway grew thick with beech and maple and twiggy ash, and sodden branches slapped at horses' flanks. The men's heavy canvas leggings were soaked through within the hour.

At noon, when they dismounted on the west bank of the Prairie River to finish off the last of the meat and rest the horses, Irving and Jansen were grumbling, and Carl Godsey openly rebelled. Willard, squatting by the river filling a canteen, paid him no mind for a couple minutes. Then he stood, fitted the plug back in and swung the strap onto his saddle horn before he turned to Godsey. Hands on his hips, he strolled over to the boy—Carl was no more than seventeen, if that much, slight of build with a downy jaw—and before the kid saw what was coming, took a swing. Godsey sprawled on his back with a yelp. Blood gushed from his nose, which was cranked over to the side and plainly broken.

"So don't go," Willard said and give him a half-hearted kick in the shin. "Get on your horse and head back to your mama." He turned his back on the boy and mounted the black. "Anybody else want to back out?" He stared around the group. Most of them had amused looks on their faces. Jansen and Irving no longer grumbled.

"All right, then, let's move out." Willard swung his horse around and headed for the ford in the river. The other men followed while Godsey pulled himself to his feet. Jake never saw the boy again.

By nightfall the boys stumbled onto the railroad tracks and turned toward Easton, the first stop on the Hannibal and St. Joseph line. The tracks ran south of town, right off the main street, which boasted half a dozen newly built establishments. Livestock corrals huddled at the west end where farmers brought their beef cows to be shipped to slaughterhouses in St. Louis. The war widow's farm sat outside town, in the middle of fields newly plowed for spring planting. It boasted a two-story brick farmhouse and a cluster of outbuildings, all dark and silent. Willard sent Juwitt ahead to see if the Little brothers and Dave Powers made it through, or if, since his visit the other day, the woman had set up a guard.

Juwitt returned quick enough. The men hid out in the barn with six new mounts. The old lady had disappeared, leaving her place unprotected. Willard grinned. He intended to clean the place out. The barn hulked big and drafty in the dark, empty of livestock, but chickens and ducks ran wild, and the boys helped themselves. Dick and Harlan Little broke in the back door and hauled out jars of pickles and preserves from the kitchen, and a jug of beer. They stuffed themselves, their cook fires hidden inside the cavernous barn. Then they were ready for fun.

They emptied out the house first. They loaded up on all the tinned goods and fresh early vegetables and dried fruit. They stuffed bacon and smoked hams into their saddlebags and stashed away all the coffee and flour and sugar they could carry. They poked under mattresses and dumped out drawers. No money or jewelry, but Jake found a Colt stuck behind the flour bin in the pantry and an old squirrel musket by the back door.

At Willard's order, Irving and Zerbin piled curtains and bedclothes in the front room, which was too fine anyway, with its horsehair settee and heavy carved tables and oil paintings of dark old men on the walls, and doused it all with kerosene. Dave Powers brought in a brand from the dinner fire, smashed in the porch window and threw the brand inside. The fire caught with a whoosh and heavy black smoke boiled up and out the broken window, flames licked up the inside walls, and the sound of breaking glass and exploding windows set the boys to whooping and cheering. Dick Little ran out of the barn laughing, followed by a wisp of smoke that soon exploded in an eruption of flames eating hungrily at the dried straw and duff.

Jake sat his horse and watched, stomach churning, but feeling good about it. This was war, Willard had told him, and this is what you do. It wasn't just sneaking into Zook's and stealing a handful of peppermint drops. He'd never had this sense of power before, power to cause other people, total strangers, to sit up and take notice. Even if they never knew who did this to them. Agents in the night, they swooped in and disappeared without a trace, their victims even more terrified because they were the unknown. Bigger than life. Grand. Really grand. He let out a sudden whoop and pounded his fist overhead, and the new mare he rode, already dancing at the flames, reared at Jake's sudden movement. He dug his heels into her side and raced down the road after his brother.

28

June 1861

Holt County *Courier & News*, June 6, 1861— "Sign anything, ratify anything, pay anything ... There never was a good war or a bad peace." That was the advice of Mr. Horace Greeley. That he penned it in 1848, on the eve of the war with Mexico, makes no difference. Its sentiment holds today, on the eve of an even more vicious, more costly, more deadly war, a war that threatens the American experiment in democracy. That experiment was built upon revolution, the casting off of a tyranny of foreign powers. Our founding fathers rejoiced in their separation from the "Mother Country," an unnatural mother surely, one who subjected her children to laws legislated from afar, to armies quartered on her citizens, to taxes imposed without consent. And so the founding fathers declared that it becomes necessary for one people to dissolve the political bands which connected them with another.

Now the states of the south have declared those bands null and void, and are attempting to assume a "separate and equal station," as did those thirteen colonies eighty-five years ago.

But what is the response? The northern tyrant resists lawful secession and seeks to impose by force its will on the new nation. Is this Union of ours a confederacy of states able to be dissolved when oppression demands? Or is it subject to a general government with the ability to enforce laws contrary to the needs, the desires and the traditions of a vast section of its territory?

Mr. Greeley also wrote, in that same year of 1848: "Our country right or wrong is an evil motto—what if your country be in the wrong?" Mr. Lincoln, your country is in the wrong. Let the southern states go, peacefully, quietly, without the hideous bloodshed and massive cost in lives and property that will accompany a war. Let lawful, peaceable secession take place.

- Jabez Robinson, ed.

The morning bloomed cool and fresh, June's warmth and humidity at bay, the breeze gentle and redolent of fresh-turned earth and fruit blossoms. Agnes and Charlie were on their way to church. Charlie, not quite three years, walked alongside her, tall for his age, and important with his hair slicked back and in his dress-up coat. Jabez, not a church-goer, remained in his study writing, always writing.

Not long before, the Reverend Mr. Rozell, whose church now dwelt in its own brick building complete with steeple and bell, broke with the Methodist South conference and joined the North conference, leaving his south-supporting parishioners without minister or sanctuary. Sectionalism spread like contagion among the town's congregations: the Presbyterians separated into New and Old School factions, and a small knot of Baptists withdrew from the Southern Baptist Convention. The Reverend Rozell displayed no qualm about preaching politics from the pulpit.

Since the April battle in South Carolina, tension in Lick Creek mounted daily. Governor Jackson raised a pro-south army under Sterling Price, while the federals awarded a general's commission to Nathaniel Lyon, who had slaughtered civilians in St. Louis. Jabez's most recent article instigated a mob in front of the offices of the *Courier* just three days earlier, and his visibility made him the focus of the town's resentments. But Agnes continued to hope for as normal a life as possible for their children, and so she maintained her usual Sunday morning ritual.

On the steps of the church they met Nancy, who knelt and cooed to Charlie, and John, who shook her hand. "Agnes, do you think you should be here?" he asked without preamble.

"This is my church too, John."

He hesitated. "Feelings are running high. Jabez's last piece stirred up a hornet's nest."

Nancy stood. "Oh, pshaw, John. It's Jabez they target, not Agnes. No one can be so uncivilized as to plague her." Nancy had grown plump, her hair dulled with gray, but her complexion was still smooth and creamy, her blue eyes gentle and complaisant. Politics passed her by. She lived one step removed from the animus seething through town. She slid her arm through Agnes's and steered her through the door.

"I'm just saying the mood in town is dangerous. You must be prepared, cousin," John said.

"A few snubs won't inconvenience me," Agnes said, guiding Charlie down a side aisle. She stepped into a pew, moved along to make room for Nancy and John, and nodded to the Irvines, seated at the other end.

They refused to smile back. In truth, they made no pretense of civility. Their daughter Annie, long a student of Agnes's, leaned forward, and Agnes thought she meant to say hello. Instead she whispered to her mother, and her mother shifted to block Agnes from her sight. And then Mr. and Mrs. Irvine and Annie stood and left the pew. A buzz circulated among the congregation as the Irvines made a show of the business, quite unnecessary, Agnes thought. She settled Charlie into her lap, doing her best to pay no mind. But the murmurs continued, and as she looked about the room, she caught furtive glances and quickly averted eyes, heard a few audible sniffs, and someone behind her muttered "The nerve!"

One family after another bypassed their pew once they realized who sat there. Then Sam and Rachel paused, and Sam grasped Rachel's elbow and propelled her up the aisle. Agnes's eyes blurred, and she ducked her head, nuzzling Charlie's hair. Rachel cast back a look of deep sadness, but Sam stared straight ahead. Charlie said, loud enough to be heard in the painful silence of the tiny church, "Auntie Rachel?" Finally, to her vast relief, Elizabeth and Tom slipped in next to her, and Elizabeth squeezed her arm.

The Reverend Mr. Rozell entered from his tiny office and stepped to the pulpit, but the murmurs continued. He said nothing, looked puzzled, finally caught the direction of the black looks. And then he did a most cowardly thing. He stepped back from the pulpit and nodded to J.W. Moodie, the most prominent lay leader, in the front pew. Mr. Moodie understood and rose slowly, turning to face Agnes.

"Miz Robinson," he said in a voice that carried across the sanctuary. "You are not welcome here, and you must leave."

She stared at him and refused to move. No one stirred. Charlie shrank against her, his eyes wide. Moodie turned to Sam. "Sam, you tell her."

Agnes stood, holding Charlie to her shoulder. "J.W. Moodie, what in the name of God can you mean? Reverend Rozell, I've been a member of this church for nine years."

A voice called out from behind her. "We'll have no secesh here!"

She considered the friends and neighbors she'd known for so long. No one met her eye. Sam rose and said, "Agnes, you'd best go on back home." Rachel clutched his sleeve. He shook her off. He scowled, at himself or at Agnes, she didn't know.

John growled, Nancy's face paled. Elizabeth, though, would not be still. Features twisted with disdain, she jumped to her feet, hands on hips, and fairly spit. "Sam Canon, how can you?" She skewered the minister with a look. "Mr. Rozell, is this your Christian charity?" She turned slowly and glared around the sanctuary. "For shame, all of you!" Then she grabbed Agnes's arm, and tugged her into the center aisle and out of the church. Tom followed, then Nancy and John. Charlie cried against her shoulder. Agnes trembled so with rage that she threatened to drop Charlie, and John eased him from her arms. They walked back to her home in silence.

The Bigelow brothers, Buck Sypes and the Pugsley's eldest boy disappeared into the bush. The Moodies' son and Earl Kunkel marched off to join the federals. The county emptied out. Throughout that muggy, sultry summer the news of skirmishes and depredations flowed into Lick Creek by dispatch and rumor. Doc Jennison from Kansas marauded up and down the western counties, murdering and plundering. In Cass County, he captured seven men, blindfolded them next to their grave, and shot them, then burned the town. Union cavalry burned homes, federal soldiers shot southern sympathizers in front of their wives and children.

In June, the horrid red-bearded General Lyon took Jefferson City, chasing the Governor and his men to the Arkansas border. Jabez's friend, Sterling Price, declared for the south and fought battles down toward Springfield, back and forth, no one really sure who won and who lost, knowing only that men died. Late in summer they learned the Confederacy soundly beat the federals outside Washington, and they hoped that would end it, but it was not to be.

Holt County *Courier & News*, July 12, 1861—The government of Abraham Lincoln and his minions has decided that it is not possible to carry on a war in the presence of a free press, if that press is in opposition. If our institutions are on trial, the free press being among those institutions, then already have they been judged wanting, incompatible with the condition of civil war. The federal government has deemed that "the reckless maundering and hysterical vituperation of the rebel newspapers" must be silenced.

We now find ourselves in the position of being invaded by an oppressive and reckless tyranny, in the midst of a war of aggression that must overthrow the federal system. The United States government, regardless of all moral, legal, and constitutional restraints, throws its hosts among us, belittles the character and intelligence of the people of our state, murders and imprisons its citizens, confiscates and destroys its property. This invasion is an attempt at coercion that may lead to consolidation or despotism but cannot lead to union. Union, as our founding fathers envisioned it, must be just, equal and voluntary. And it must be founded upon free expression through a free press.

Already, the *St. Louis Herald* has been suspended. The Lexington papers have been destroyed by jayhawkers or shut down by military order. Papers in Cape Girardeau, Hannibal, Independence, Franklin County, Platte City—all destroyed, closed down, taken over by the army. Who is to be next?

The great statesman George Mason declared that "The freedom of the press is one of the great bulwarks of liberty, and can never be restrained but by despotic government." Here in our state the press is being forcibly, violently restrained. It is the duty of all patriotic citizens to fight that despotism.

- Jabez Robinson, ed.

They had just finished dinner when the federals clattered into town. Agnes sat on the front porch with the children, enjoying the summer evening. Charlie toddled about snatching at the first fireflies, and Sarah Belle practiced her new skill of hauling herself to her feet, using the porch railing, dark ringlets damp in the lingering warmth. Jabez kissed the top of Agnes's head and headed to the newspaper office, visible across the square from their home.

They trotted in, a whole troop of them, twenty or thirty, foreigners to the people of Lick Creek. They rode in on horses sleek and fat from foraging on the rich pastures and prairies of Holt County's farmlands, armed with carbines and sabers and revolvers, brimmed hats pinned on the right side, sleeves and collars trimmed in yellow. They sported beards and mustaches or fresh downy cheeks, long hair and short hair, all of them young and arrogant. They thundered down Noddaway Street and drew up on the square before the court house, raising clouds of dust and powdered horse droppings that sifted lazily into yards and open windows, coating shrubs and furniture with the soft silt of summer.

People filtered out of shops and homes, the bank and the saloon, to gawk. A half dozen riders remained mounted, carbines relaxed but ready. The others slid off their horses, ignoring the growing crowd, and loosened girths, drank from canteens, swabbed sweaty foreheads and generally stood at ease. Agnes could see Jabez watching from the door of the building that housed his print equipment, his arms crossed over his chest and imagined the black scowl on his face, the danger in his dark eyes.

Within moments the federals organized into groups of twos and threes and spread out along the shops and homes lining the square, carbines clutched casually before them. No one attempted to gainsay the troops, and no one begrudged them entry to the establishments they wished to visit. Two soldiers emerged from George Baxter's tailor shop carrying piles of clothing. They dumped the booty onto the courthouse square and returned for more. Others hauled crates and sacks from McLaughlin's, one carrying a silver-chased saddle that Joe McLaughlin particularly prized. Levi Zook's store remained untouched.

Agnes bundled the children into the house, told Rose to keep them out of sight in the kitchen, and set out to cross the square to stand with her husband. Perhaps in her presence he'd clamp a lid on his temper—a fanciful thought but she must needs try.

When she reached him, he was standing in the doorway, one shoulder propped against the jam, a sardonic smile on his face, addressing two federals.

"Sorry, boys," he said, "paper's closed for the night."

"Step aside," snarled one of the soldiers, aiming his carbine at Jabez's midsection. "Don't take much for us to shoot you down."

"You do and it's cold-blooded murder," Jabez said. "Have we come to that already?"

"It ain't murder if we kill vermin," the other one said, pulling his Colt from a hip holster.

A tall man with crossed sabers on his hat stepped onto the boardwalk from the dust of the street. "Albert Peabody, First Missouri Cavalry," the captain said to Jabez. Jabez didn't reply. "I have orders to confiscate this newspaper."

"You have no call to," Jabez said. "This is a free press, guaranteed under the Constitution."

The officer nodded to one of his men, and the trooper slashed the butt of his pistol across Jabez's temple. Agnes froze as he folded slowly to the boardwalk, blood trickling into his ear. She screeched something unrepeatable and planted both hands on the captain's chest and shoved. He stumbled backwards, and she dropped to her knees next to her husband. Jabez groaned and rolled, groggy. A hand grasped Agnes's shoulder and jerked, and she sprawled into the street in a tangle of skirts, spitting words she didn't know she knew. She watched in horror as the pistol rose again and dropped with a hideous thunk on Jabez's skull. He dropped again to the ground and lay still. Agnes crawled to him on hands and knees and slid her fingers over his head, sticky with blood, felt for his pulse and found it, weak, under her fingers.

Someone loomed over her. Reuben Bigelow grasped Jabez by the collar and dragged him into the shelter of the bank's entrance. Agnes scrambled to her feet and scuttled after, watching as soldiers heaved the printing press into a wagon, strewed lead type into the street as if it were confetti, piled rolls of newsprint in the doorway along with ledgers and back issues and the gingham curtains she had stitched. She crouched in the doorway, Jabez propped against her, the tail of her skirt pressed to his bleeding head. With a start she realized his eyes were open. He shifted, winced, swayed and steadied himself. Reuben slipped away but Jace Biggers, Jabez's partner, cowered inside the bank. Agnes was sure he hoped the federals knew nothing of his complicity in the newspaper, and she vowed never to acknowledge him again.

There was nothing to do but watch as Captain Peabody touched an oiled torch to the pyre of newsprint, and flames licked up the summer-dry siding of the office. Jabez leveraged himself against the door jamb and dragged himself to his feet, reaching down a hand to her.

"Agnes, go home," he said. "I don't trust these men to destroy only the paper." He nodded across the square at their home. The children. And Rose and Dick. Federal troops were rumored to "liberate" slaves, impressing them into the army, selling them for profit, setting them free to be preyed upon by slave-catchers.

"Go straight there," he said. "I'll be along as quick as I can—I need to go round about for fear they'll follow me." He motioned north of town, then kissed her. "I'm the one they're focused on." He gave her a push and disappeared through the bank and out its back door.

Oily smoke boiled across the street, the night lit with an evil glow. Agnes threaded her way across the square, through the knots of soldiers and their horses, straining to catch sight of her home in the dark. She started to see her front door open, flickering lantern light spilling out. A man wearing a kepi jumped from the porch with a bulging flour sack and headed for the courthouse. She ignored him and dashed through the door, flying from room to room, sick with fear. No sign of the children, or of Rose or Dick, but a smooth-faced youth in an immaculate dark blue blouse rummaged through the linen press in the bedroom, her single silver candlestick poking from a pocket. He shrugged her off like a whining mosquito, and she let out a stream of invective and slammed down the lid on his fingers.

He hollered and snatched at her wrist, twisting her arm behind her back. "Secesh whore!" he snarled, breath hot on her face. He rammed her against the wall, kicked at her ankles, then he was out the door and gone. Quiet settled over the house. No flames. No shots.

They'd been thorough. Bureau drawers hung open, floury footprints tracked across the kitchen floor. Jabez's surgery suffered the most, the glass-fronted cabinet shattered, the shelves emptied of medicines, patient records scattered and trampled by muddy boots. Agnes stumbled through the kitchen and out the back and vomited into the rosebush.

A rustle sounded from the direction of the stables, and Dick emerged from the blackness of the stable yard, Jabez's rifle in his fist. He took Agnes's elbow and led her back to his cabin, shrouded in the shadows. Rose huddled on the bed, Sarah Belle in her lap, Charlie under her arm, and both children reached for their mother with whimpers that broke her heart.

"Mama!" Charlie's whisper was hoarse and loud. "We played a game. Rose said we was to play hide and seek and be real quiet."

"And you did, didn't you?" She snugged him to her and kissed his bright hair. "You were a brave boy to help Rose and Dick and take care of Sarah, too, weren't you? Mama's very proud."

Tears dampened Sarah's cheeks, and she hiccupped while Agnes rocked her. Dick stood watch at the window, the rifle cocked, keeping an eye on the stables. Someone had organized the fire brigade lest the entire town burn, and the clamor of the bucket line and the steady thump of the hand tub's pistons sounded in the distance. For an hour they watched until the glow from the fire faded. Jabez should have been back long before; surely he'd know to search for them at the cabin. By the time the children nodded off and the distant shouts died down, Agnes had determined to seek him herself. Dick urged her to let him go instead, but the risk to him was too great. She left him to guard the children and slipped back into the heavy night.

Jabez would have circled the town in the shadows north of the square, losing himself in the commotion of the fire. She crossed the stable yard and slipped up Monroe Street by Ross's saloon where the doors stood open, the shelves behind the counter empty of liquor bottles. Ross himself sat at his own front table, along with Reuben Bigelow and a bottle, watching the scene in the square. If they heard her, they showed no sign. Soldiers milled about at the other end of town. Too late she wished she'd asked Ross and Bigelow if they'd seen Jabez. She rounded the corner to the north side of the square and worked her way into the alley behind Sterrett's store. At the far end a pile of rubble and glowing coals marked the remains of the newspaper office, sparks settling like St. Elmo's fire on tree branches and grass blades before winking out. The smell of wet ash hung heavy over the streets.

A smothering blackness choked the alley, made impenetrable by contrast with a darkened lantern halfway down. Lit by a lurid glow, shadows jerked and grunted in what, to her disoriented mind, appeared a macabre dance. An apparition lifted the lantern and a beam of light flashed across the face of her husband.

Three men, hooded, crouched in a circle, swaying. One clutched Jabez's arms behind his back, a second let fly a fist into his ribs. Jabez kicked, and the third jumped in with a snarl and caught him across the cheek with a thud that made Agnes retch.

"Damn you bastards!" She hiked up her skirts and bolted toward them.

All three heads jerked in her direction. The man holding Jabez dropped his arms, the others stepped aside without haste. Jabez sank to the ground, caught himself on one hand. Agnes skidded to her knees beside him.

A man laughed, a short, sharp bark. *"All yours, Missus,"* he said, and the three masked forms melted north into the darkness. Aldo Beaton. She was certain.

Jabez sat, knees up, head in his hands, blood running through his fingers. He swayed, his breathing rough and unsteady. Agnes peeled his hands away from his face. Purple bruises, evident in the dim light of the smoky lantern, circled his eyes. His cheek bloomed under a scrape, and his lip and nose trickled blood, a great wash of it drying over his shirt front.

"Easy, love," he said. "I think I've cracked a rib or two." She drew an inadequate hanky from her pocket and dabbed at his nose.

"Can you walk? We need to get you home before they come back."

"I don't think they'll be back," he said. He groaned and pressed a hand to his side. "They weren't the soldiers, Agnes. It was someone from around here. Three men in civilian clothes with hoods over their heads."

"I know," she said, straining to keep her voice even, the rage tamped down. "I think I recognized the voice." She smoothed his hair away from the gash above his right eye. "Did you? Did they say anything?"

"No, not a word. They just hit me." He inched up, leaning on her shoulder, and ventured a step. "I think they were waiting for me, but maybe I only fancied that." He winced, stopped, closed his eyes. "I got in a few good licks, though. Someone's going to be walking around town almost as sore as I am."

"Sit back and let me fetch Reuben."

She propped him against the rear wall of the bank and raced to the saloon, uncaring whether she encountered soldiers or jayhawkers or any of their despicable neighbors. Reuben jammed a half-full bottle of bourbon in his pocket and followed her back. Between them, they shuffled Jabez home, inflicting a great deal of pain, and eased him onto the bed. Bigelow pulled the bottle from his pocket, set it on the nightstand, wordlessly patted Jabez on the shoulder and left. The first order of business was a shot of bourbon for Jabez and a shot for Agnes, then she helped him out of his clothes and into bed. Rose found ointment for the bruises in the ruins of the surgery and concocted a mustard plaster for the cracked ribs. Agnes mixed up a headache powder, and he finally slipped into an unquiet sleep.

Agnes slept little the rest of the night. Rose tucked the children into their beds. Dick stood guard in the dark living room, rifle to hand behind the locked front door. Rose brewed tea and set about bringing order to the mess the Union soldiers left behind. Agnes slumped next to the bed in the dark, holding Jabez's hand and watching the activity on the square. Long after midnight the federals stamped out their cook fires and mounted up, Peabody lifted his hand and motioned them forward. They rode southbound out of town, heading who knows where and leaving behind a pile of ashes and plundered stores. In their wake lay a town ever more suspicious, ever more polarized.

29

Fall 1861

Autumn arrived double-quick that year, and Jake Bigelow was cold. The nights were cold, the water they washed with (when they washed) was cold, the coffee, more often than not, was cold. And not yet the middle of October, leastwise, he didn't think so. Easy to lose track of the days, living the way they lived, camping in the woods or up on the prairie, sometimes in a barn or even a house. He enjoyed himself then, hunkered down in the straw out of the wind, listening to the boys talk. But sleeping rough wore on a man, and he shuddered at the thought of winter coming on.

At least the rain held off, the sky hung blue and bright, leaves glowed brilliant with reds and orange and gold. They ate good, too, what they didn't pick up from farms and isolated stores they shot in the woods. Deer and wild turkey, mostly, though turkey required a keen eye and a steady hand, not Jake's strongest suit. Alfred Zerbin, the one not quite right in the head, showed real skill with a Kentucky rifle, though, and he never begrudged the other boys a share of his takings. Willard preferred to help himself to whatever supplies he lit on from whoever lived in their path, he cared not a whit where they stood on the war. Jake fretted about that, but Willard said they deserved anything they found as pay for the job they did, so he kept his mouth shut.

It'd been a good run, too, the summer had. Anybody'd be pleased to serve under Wil Bigelow. Jake took pride in his brother. All the top leaders in this war, Martin Green and Price and Shelby and even Atchison, knew Wil and listened to him when they talked strategy. And he got information, God knew where from, he figured out which civilians were Union men and who held for the south. He thought up good ideas, too, like the time he stole a stack of Union coats and hats. He and some of the boys dressed up in them and visited a farmhouse where he'd heard jayhawkers hung out. Sure enough, once those farmers saw Union uniforms, they proclaimed themselves hard and fast Yankees, and that's all it took for them to get themselves beat up and their goods donated to the southern cause. The boys laughed about that one for days. They stowed away those uniforms in their saddlebags in case the opportunity to pull off another sneak raid like that came up again.

Jake and Willard and the men ranged back and forth across the northern counties all summer long, harassing any federals who dared show themselves north of the Missouri. Hank Jansen caught a slug in the shoulder during a dust-up in Audrain County, and up in Athens, they danced around the edge of a skirmish, laid in wait and picked off some of the federals chasing Martin Green's state guard men. Jake himself winged a man with the carbine he scrounged from a dead federal lying in a ditch. Then they fought their way to the western counties, tangled with a company of Indiana cavalry up in Harrison County—how those Yankees got that far west no one knew—and holed up along the Grand River. When they woke to a skim of frost over their blanket rolls, Willard raised the idea of going home for a visit.

"I been thinking about old Frank Kunkel," he said, stirring a mess of venison and potatoes in the fry pan. "He ain't never give up on that bottom land he stole from Pa. Maybe it's time we taught him a lesson."

"You think we can scare him into giving over claiming that field for himself?" Jake said.

"Don't see why not. I hear Earl's gone off with the militia, so there's nobody there but Frank and his old lady." Willard picked at the venison, burned his finger, swore. "We need new horses, anyway. Frank always had a good eye for horseflesh."

"They'd know in town who did it, if we was to hit the Kunkel place," Jake said. "Sheriff'd be after us for sure. I ain't so sure we should shit in our own nest."

"This is war, son." Willard flashed a feral grin at his brother. "Kunkel's the enemy. No one's going to say nothing about it for fear they get hit, too."

"Maybe," Jake said. "Before we hit the Kunkel place I want to go home and fetch some warm clothes." He dished up a plateful of stew. "And I sure wouldn't take amiss having some of Ma's biscuits and chicken for a change."

Willard snorted. "Soft-ass. We'll just take a little vacation, go on home for a good meal, sleep in a soft bed, then go visit old Frank." He guzzled from his pocket flask, always full, Jake didn't know for sure how that happened. "I'll tell the boys we're taking a breather."

Retreating to the bush again might present a hardship, Jake thought, seeing how his ma fed him three hot meals a day and plied him with sweets. Pa expected him to help with chores, and the old man didn't want to know what his two oldest boys had been up to. But the younger kids hung on every word and every story, and Willard spun some tales that Jake knew stood tall, but he fancied playing hero.

Pa himself, not Wil, brought up the Kunkel problem one evening after dinner. Most all the family paid no heed to Reuben when he got up his wind about Frank Kunkel and the boundary dispute, they'd heard it so much. But this time Jake and Willard joined in, goaded on by a new aggravation, the fact that Frank Kunkel pastured his sheep on the bottom land and proposed to fence it.

"He ain't got no call to be building a fence down there," Reuben said, bracing a pipe against his stump and tamping tobacco with a flat-headed nail. "I'm going have to go out there and tear it down, and he knows I'll do it, too."

"Let him finish it first before we tear it down," Wil said, "and he'll of wasted all that time and money."

"You can take some of those damn sheep too," the old man said. "Treat your boys to mutton."

"Hey, there'd be a feast, Wil, what do you think? I bet the boys'd be mighty pleased to see something besides venison," Jake said.

"Oh, we'll take more than sheep," Willard said. "I don't aim for Kunkel to get off that easy."

His pa threw him a sharp look from under heavy gray brows. "What you planning, boy?"

"Don't worry, Pa, when I'm done he won't want that bottom land no more."

Bigelow took the pipe from his mouth, stared at it. Never did draw right. "Don't you go doing nothing to come back on me and your ma," he said. "We got to live here."

"I'll take care of Kunkel, Pa. You take care of you and Ma and the kids."

Bigelow glowered but dropped the topic and didn't mention Kunkel or the fence again before the boys left. Jake felt a sadness in his pa when he and Wil packed heavy coats and the gloves their ma had made for them and mounted up, Jake on the little gray mare he'd picked up on the farm in Easton, Willard on a roan horse he'd borrowed from Juwitt. It wouldn't do to ride home on Sam's stolen black where Pa might recognize it. Jake swiveled in his saddle and waved a hand. He thought maybe Pa waved back but he couldn't be sure.

Dusk settled in fast, the late October afternoon faded by heavy overcast and a chilling wind that stripped the last leaves from the maples and white oak. When they reached the junction where the road branched toward the Grand River, Wil turned the wrong way.

Jake jerked the mare's head around. "What the hell?"

"Taking a detour," Willard said over his shoulder. "Canon's place, then Kunkel's."

Jake grimaced. "Not Sam, Wil. Come on."

"Hey, man's for the Union. He's fair target."

"What about the boys? They'll be waiting on us up at camp."

"Nope, they're meeting us here. I told them before we left. Should be camped over to Hog Creek."

Jake didn't like it, but he shrugged, reined the mare around, and followed his brother.

Jake was surprised at how many of the men waited for them in the hollow along Hog Creek north of the road to Richville. Both the Littles showed up, and Ora Juwitt, along with Dave Powers and Hank Jansen. He'd half thought they'd seen the last of a couple, at least of Hank, whose whining about his wounded shoulder got worse with the weather.

The men joked and laughed among themselves. Everyone looked rested and well-fed and anxious to get on with the night's work. Willard and Juwitt talked low between themselves, then Willard yanked on the bridle and motioned his men out of the creek drainage and to the southeast, headed for Canon's farm.

Night, crisp and deep, blanketed the farm, the unlit house a silhouette against the paler eastern skyline. The Canons must have gone to town, and no hired men stayed on the place this time of year. Jake was relieved, but Willard, furious at Sam's absence, rode the roan onto the porch and slammed his boot through the door. Jake started when Sam's old shepherd, hovering next to the barn, set up a furious racket behind him. Wil whirled off the porch, lifted his revolver and silenced it with one shot. The old dog flopped once or twice before it lay still. Jake remembered it trailing after him when he worked for Sam and headed into the fields after one of Miz Canon's breakfasts. She always made the best flapjacks.

Juwitt and Jansen ransacked the house, scrounging up a revolver, a rifle and ammunition, as well as cash and old lady Canon's jewelry. The Little brothers disappeared into the barn and returned with Sam's saddle horse and plow mules, while Willard directed the operation from horseback. Jake sat his horse in silence, disregarded or forgotten by the others, and watched Powers twist together a length of straw. Dave lifted it toward Willard, who touched a Lucifer to the tip, then threw it through the barn door, crackling into the duff on the floor. The terrified scream of an animal rose, a cow, Jake thought. Dick Little sprinted back into the barn, and in seconds three milk cows trundled out, eyes wild and rolling, and disappeared into the blackness. Jake wondered what the hell he was doing there. Then Willard slid out of his saddle, picked up another twist of straw, lit it, and steered for the house. Jake shook himself and leaped from the horse.

"No." He grabbed Willard's hand. The mad look in his brother's eyes terrified him, he'd never seen them this wild before. "No, Wil, not that. It ain't worth it. You done enough here."

Willard's eyes stared beyond him, glazed, then focused, swung back to Jake's face. He laughed and threw down the torch. Jake stepped on it, grinding out the flame with the heel of his boot. Willard punched him on the shoulder, laughing. "Just testing you, little brother." He grasped the saddle horn and swung onto the roan and laughed again.

"So this is just practice, boys," Willard shouted. "Now for the real show."

The fire in the barn swelled and crackled as dry straw caught. The gray mare pranced, and Jake hopped in circles before he managed to mount. His brother wheeled his horse around and tore up the road at a dead run, a triumphant howl trailing back. The others pushed their horses to keep up, drunk on destruction, and Jake galloped along side, shouting with the best of them, trying to drown out the doubts.

Frank Kunkel must have heard them coming over the fields well before they'd got within pistol shot. Jake spotted him right away, standing in the shadows of a big elm next to his porch, musket rifle aimed directly at Willard's chest. The overcast had blown itself into frayed clouds, and a half moon shone bright enough to light up the riders. Jake shivered, felt like he had a target painted on his chest.

"You there, Willard Bigelow, you stop where you are," Frank called before Willard reached the steps. "What you think you're doing, running around in the middle of the night disturbing decent folks' rest?"

Willard guffawed. "Hey, Frank, ain't you gonna give a welcome to old neighbors? Why you got that gun on us?"

Moonlight flashed off the rifle barrel. "I've heard what you boys been up to this summer, and you ain't welcome here and you know it, so just turn that horse of Sam's around and take yourselves out of here."

Willard grinned as he reined in the gelding at the porch rail, Powers and Jansen ranging up alongside him. "Now, Frank, if you heard about us you know what we're here for. We want your guns and your ammunition, and maybe your cash. You stay out of the way and you ain't going to get hurt, you and Nellie." He pulled back on the reins. The black chuffed and pranced. Willard got him under control and started to dismount.

Frank raised the rifle, aimed it at Willard's head. "Stay where you are, Bigelow, or I shoot."

Willard eased back into the saddle, his chuckle a trifle nervous now. Everyone knew Frank Kunkel for a dead shot, but no one expected he'd pull the trigger on a man, especially a man he knew.

"Frank, don't cause no trouble. You don't put that gun down I'm going to ride right up on the porch and through that door without getting off, then there'll be a real mess."

Powers sneered. "He ain't going to shoot." He threw his leg over the saddle, slid to the ground. "I'll go get that gun and we can get on with this," and he started up the steps.

The gun boomed, and Powers screamed like a banshee. His horse whinnied and jumped, shying away from the sudden noise and the smell of powder. The other horses plunged and snorted. The dark stain on Powers' left shoulder glistened in the moonlight. He stumbled backwards and fell in the dust. In an instant, chaos erupted. Men jumped off their mounts and sheltered behind them, screaming oaths, pistols cocked.

"You killed him! Son of a bitch you killed him!" Jake heard Willard's shriek, and he cringed, waiting for the next shot. But Frank threw down the rifle and backed to his door, and Jake stood in his stirrups craning to see. Willard rushed the porch along with Hank and Ora Juwitt while Dick and Harlan Little danced around hollering like red Indians. From the darkness of the porch came the soft thud of fists pounding into flesh, the crack of bone. Frank cursed. Jake heard a woman's voice, high and hysterical, raising a chill along his scalp. Juwitt swore, and Nellie Kunkel spun off the porch and onto her backside in the moonlight under the dancing hooves of the horses.

Something inside Jake tugged at him, urging him to turn tail and run for it, but that would mean the end of it between him and his brother. Instead, he reined up and watched. In a moment Hank and Willard dragged Frank from the porch by both arms. Kunkel's head wobbled as if it pained him to hold it up, blood covered the front of his white nightshirt, his trousers hung ragged over bare feet. The old lady sprawled sobbing in the dirt.

"What do we do with him, Wil?" Juwitt asked, his voice excited and sounding happy to Jake.

Wil's voice drawled. "What do you do with someone murders one of our boys?" He looked around the circle.

"Why, you hang him," Hank said.

Frank's head jerked up, and Jake felt the terror coming off the man from a dozen yards away. He almost laughed out loud, the idea was so preposterous. Nobody's going to hang Frank Kunkel. Sure he and Pa had their differences, but mostly everyone considered the feud entertainment, nobody got hurt. So Kunkel's a Union man, but in war you shoot a man's trying to shoot you, no call to go hanging neighbors.

But something about Wil's lazy, intoxicated swagger scared Jake, and he almost smelled the boys' excitement. He realized Harlan Little twirled a rope from his fist, and then Harlan flung it over a branch of the elm, a noose dangling from the end. Frank trembled so bad that Willard and Hank had to hold him up. Nellie sat on the ground where she'd fallen, legs splayed out in front of her, keening a single high note. They tied Frank's wrists behind him with Hank's neckerchief, Juwitt led his own horse to the tree, they boosted Frank up. Ora held him in the saddle.

Jake watched, numb. Surely they wouldn't do this thing. They'd give the old man a scare he wouldn't forget, then they'd leave him and Nellie rethinking their Union loyalties and go make camp and have a drink and laugh about it. But then his brother, mounted on the black, sidled up to Frank, settled the noose around his neck.

The sound of a smack on the horse's hindquarters raised a shout from the men gathered around the tree, and Jake squeezed closed his eyes and felt his face wet with tears. When next he looked, Frank dangled from the bough of the elm. His feet still kicked, his upper body twitched, and it seemed an eternity before those spasmodic movements finally stilled. There was no sound in the farm yard except the low, quiet sobbing of the woman. Jake thought sure they'd kill her too, but Willard dismounted, leaned over her and said something, then stood and laughed.

"That's a night's work, boys," he said. "Let's go." He swung into the saddle, the rest followed suit and trotted down the road in single file. Jake gaped at the still form hanging from the tree. Now there was no going home. Now it was truly war, and he was in for a pound. Nothing to do but follow Willard, go where he went, fight when he fought. Maybe it didn't really matter.

30

Winter and Spring 1862

The day after Sam's barn burned and Frank Kunkel was murdered, Sam moved Rachel into the Jacksons' house, while he and Billy barricaded themselves at the farm and began to rebuild. Rumors circulated that rebels massed at Albany, seventy miles away in Gentry County, and that the Yankee General Prentiss advanced on them from Chillicothe. And then the word was a fight on the Grand River forced rebels and bushwhackers to retreat west. So the good folk of Lick Creek locked their doors and hid away from one another in the dark winter nights.

They never discovered who was responsible for Jabez's beating, though Aldo Beaton appeared to limp for several days following. He claimed a horse trod on his foot, but Agnes heard his voice in her head. *All yours Missus.* The sheriff refused to hear her arguments. But most troubling to Agnes was the change in Jabez. His fire and anger about the war, about politics, his restless energy in debate and argument, his passion for interposing common sense on chaos devolved into something uglier. A slow recovery from the beating, a recovery more dilatory of mind than of body, brought on a dark, brooding quiet in both action and word.

He neglected his medical practice, closeting himself in his surgery writing pamphlets and tracts and articles and sending them to distant papers. Whether they were published Agnes never knew. His eyes no longer flashed, his quick laugh disappeared, and his sessions with Charlie and the alphabet dwindled away. And the debates and discussions, those long conversations of events and literature and ideas no longer seemed to interest him.

He first talked about sending Agnes and the children away a few weeks after Christmas. Whole families packed up and left the county, husbands sent wives and children to safety in the north. Abandoned farms and desolated towns dotted the countryside. Jayhawkers and bushwhackers on the prowl often found houses deserted, contents ripe for the plundering. Jabez wanted to send them to Pennsylvania, to her family, and her refusal sparked one of their first arguments.

"No," she said. "I'll not leave you behind and run." She dropped her book in her lap and glared at him.

"Then send the children away," he said. He slumped in his reading chair following dinner. Charlie and Sarah, both suffering from croup, finally slept, and the day of freezing February rain, fractious children and a brooding Jabez waned all too slowly.

"I'll do no such thing," she said. "They're perfectly safe here in town with family about." She knew that wasn't strictly true after what happened to Sam and Frank Kunkel. And the dispatches reported bad news daily: the Confederacy retreated in Kentucky, the federals pushed Price out of Springfield, raiders operated north of the river, close to Lick Creek. She wondered what was happening to her family? To all the families in Lick Creek? Rachel's home violated, Sam confused and angry at the chaos he saw around him, Billy preparing to march off to war. John clinging to unreality, evading a declaration of loyalty to one side or another. Faces, like images flashing from a magic lantern, appeared before her. Annie Irvine, whose father sent her and her mother to Ohio. The Cottiers, who deserted their farm and disappeared to the southwest. Galen Crow, gone to fight with Price. In normal times, a rural town countered boredom and grinding labor with an almost humorous daily dose of bickering, petty feuds, and entertaining litigation, mixed with a liberal portion of loyalty and friendship. Now it plunged headlong into disorder and destruction, and Agnes found herself alternately terrified or numb, cynical or enraged, accepting violence as a way of life.

"Just associating with us puts your family at risk," Jabez said. His long fingers picked at the material of his trousers in short, angry jerks. "We can't raise children in a town filled with hate. You need to take them away." He pulled off his reading glasses and dropped them to the floor.

"Then give up your editorializing and your speeches. It's you who make us unsafe with your secession and your politics."

"I? Do you think we'd be safer if I was to turn Unionist? Fat lot of help it was for Frank Kunkel." He pushed himself from his chair and threw his book on the table.

"Of course not, but you might keep your opinions to yourself. Maybe then they'd leave us alone." She knotted her fists and tapped the window sill, scarce knowing what she said.

"That doesn't sound like you, Agnes." His voice was quiet. "You've never been shy about either of us expressing opinions before."

"I wasn't a mother before, in the middle of a war. It's different now."

"That's why you'll go to Pennsylvania."

"I don't want to go. I want to stay here, in my home. With my husband." She swirled to face him. "John does it. He doesn't take sides. He manages."

She knew that was a mistake as soon as she said it, but she couldn't take it back. Jabez's brows drew together, and one side of his mouth lifted in a sneer.

"John is it?" he said. "Yes, John the saint. You still have a fancy for John, do you?"

"Jabez—"

"No," he said. "You'll go to Pennsylvania and you'll stay there until I call for you. And madam, I can assure you, it won't be before this war is over. And if we survive it, I'm taking my children away from your infernal family and this god-forsaken town."

He yanked his coat from the stand by the door and stormed out, and Agnes snatched up the first thing that came to hand and flung it after him. Her precious dictionary. It crashed against the closed door and fell to the floor, spine broken.

31

Spring 1862

Captain Billy Canon's rear end hurt more than he thought possible. He hadn't spent this much time on a horse since his summer trip to California, years ago. He thought maybe he'd buy a better saddle in Kansas City. The militia promised to outfit him and his men, but the regular Union army got first crack at equipment, and anyway he figured private outfitters supplied better tack than the army. He could afford a new saddle, storekeeping paid well enough.

He twisted in the saddle to size up the men. Three rode horseback but the rest straggled along the road afoot. No one wanted to donate a horse to the cause unless necessary, and they'd left their draft animals, saddle horses and buggy nags at home. He congratulated himself for recruiting so many, even if they were a disorderly band of devil-may-cares. He'd raised nearly seventy-five, almost a full company. A fellow he knew over in Andrew County scrounged up no more than fifty. Most of Billy's boys—and that's what they called themselves, Billy's Boys—hailed from Forest City, some from Lick Creek, a couple even from up in Atchison County, all men and boys whose families he knew, men he trusted to jump into a fight with vigor and stick it out to the end.

He faced ahead again and winced at the sting where the raw place rubbed on the inside of his leg. He'd outfit them and mount them up in Kansas City, and they'd shine as well as any company. They sure as hell couldn't feel any better. They rough-housed and tussled each other like a litter of pups. The mid-May weather spoke to the blood with its high blue skies and fresh breezes, and the two-day trek to join up with their regiment turned into a camping lark. They'd chattered last night around the supper fires about the secesh they'd kill as if they hunted buffalo or snipe. Some of them even targeted particular names, bushwhackers who'd stolen from or burned out a friend of a friend.

Billy Canon nursed a grudge himself. The Bigelow boys had torn Lick Creek apart, put his folks in danger. Nellie Kunkel gave witness against Willard Bigelow's gang, and clearly the same bunch had burned Sam's barn. And shot the dog. Sam truly loved that old shepherd. Its killing wounded him as much as the loss of the barn. Billy stoked a fury to find those boys and serve them the way they'd served Frank Kunkel. But he never talked about that to anyone, not even Julia, because arbitrary hanging sickened him. There were rules. Maybe those boys would hang, but only after a legal trial. If the Union men lynched, they'd sink to the level of the bushwhackers. But he hankered to lynch them anyway. Hankered to see Wil Bigelow swing.

He expected he'd not have the pleasure. The regiment would most likely march down south, where the real army fought, far away from Bigelow's territory. Since the federals won at Pea Ridge and pushed Price back into Arkansas, Missouri became officially Union territory, and the militia's job was to keep it that way. If he couldn't have at the Bigelows, Billy hoped he'd get into the fight against the raiders invading the western Missouri counties, Quantrill and William Anderson. He thought of Julia and his daughters, as he did probably no more than once every twenty minutes. They should be safe enough in Forest City, with her folks, and with Sam and Rachel nearby. But the threat of the Bigelow gang raiding Quantrill-like through Holt County boiled his blood and left a stone of fear in his belly that stayed with him night and day.

Billy's company camped out for three weeks in Kansas City collecting equipment and electing the rest of its officers. Billy found a saddle he liked at Whistler's Saddlery and paid more than he could afford, but the pain in his back, and his rear end, eased. He spent the time jawing with the other captains in the regiment, Jim Donnell and Henry Davis and Joe Roecker, second-guessing their superiors, and passing the time of day with his own men. Mostly they drilled. They learned formations and how to wheel and where skirmishers should ride. And how to follow orders. Those boys grew up damned independent and following orders wasn't high on their list of importance, but Billy recruited a couple good sergeants in Barney Holland and Willis Freeman. They'd served in the Mexican War and knew how to look a smart-ass kid in the eye and make him do what he should do. Billy never let on, but he learned everything he knew about command from Willis Freeman and followed the old soldier's lead those first weeks while he grew his army legs.

The best thing, the men agreed, was the rifles. The governor, the new Union governor, since Claib Jackson scuttled off to Arkansas the year before, convinced the federals to provide Sharps for the militias, and Billy's company thought they'd died and gone to heaven. They learned to shoot and load and reshoot within a minute, and they challenged the men in Company C and Company E to competition. By the end of the three weeks, Billy was proud as a new daddy of his boys—they'd best the devil himself for him and the Union.

Good thing, too.

The Little Blue River flowed south out of the Missouri and east of Independence, and Billy's orders were to scout among its limestone bluffs and rocky defiles for a gang of marauders that had ambushed the mail escort from Pleasant Hill. The escort, a squad from Company C, lost three killed and seven wounded, and its captain, Joe Roecker, rode with Billy in a white heat, talking nonstop about killing rebels. Independence wallowed in secesh, sneaky and dangerous, and the Union militia quartered there fidgeted, alert and on edge. The two captains led a column of fifty of Billy's men, the track winding through wooded outcroppings heavy with the warmth and ripeness of early summer, leafed out in a lethal curtain of vegetation that might hide any number of enemy.

Billy deployed outriders to comb the woods on either side of the track throughout the rough terrain, and the column of untried men maintained silence but for the creak and jingle of saddle and bridle. A heavy cloud cover muffled the morning, and the muted gurgle of a creek, the bedeviling buzz and hiss of flies and mosquitoes rose about them. The information they'd cajoled from a farmer three miles back indicated the bushwhackers camped on the east bank of the Little Blue, but Billy suspected the farmer fabricated his story, unreliable as most everyone else in that county, speaking Union to the federals, secesh to the rebels. So though Roecker, experienced on the scout, itched to forge ahead, Billy insisted on caution and convinced himself he was being sensible and not fearful.

But when the first shot sounded, fear ripped through him. The trees had thinned and the river's bank lay ahead of them, the bridge off to the right about fifty yards. Roecker's horse sank to its knees with a quiet grunt, blood spurting from a hole dead center of its front legs. Billy gathered himself long enough to shout the order to dismount and take cover. His men scrambled from their horses and dove for the underbrush, and Billy swung his carbine in the direction of the shot and fired.

His aim was off as much as ninety degrees, he soon realized—the echoes distorted direction. But his first shot of the war worked a strange magic on him, it removed him from the immediacy of the scene. He found himself looking on as a spectator, watching himself duck into the brush and yank his revolver, and he calmed and wondered what the script called for next in that instant when the forest hovered, quiet with the promise of storm.

The storm broke. A fusillade of shots burst over them from the high ledges overhanging the river. Bullets sliced through the trees sending a shower of leaves and twigs and bark raining down on the men of Company B. Roecker was nowhere to be seen. When his horse collapsed, he dove for the north side of the road and into the brush. Billy crouched behind a tree trunk, his carbine in one hand, his revolver drawn, and caught his breath.

Someone screamed from over by the creek but the sound passed over him without catching his mind. He marveled that the horse holders behind him gathered up the animals and led them back down the trail, out of range, just as they'd been trained to do. But what the devil was he supposed to do next? He ought to order something but what the hell was it? And where in God's name was the enemy? Their guns had ceased, and it occurred to him that it had all been a chimera, and he'd imagined the noise and confusion of moments ago.

But the smell of gunpowder and the now-soft mewling of the man in the creek were real enough. The thick mat of dead leaves behind him rustled, and he jumped, revolver swinging around. Sergeant Freeman pushed the barrel aside, amusement glinting in rheumy eyes.

"Just me, Captain," he said. "Direct that thing toward the river." He knelt, waved his rifle north. "See that crease in the bluff over there?" He pointed three hundred yards upstream where the river curled around the toe of a hundred-foot cliff scarred with rockslide and clefts. "That's where they dug in. Couldn't tell if any of them shots come from the other side of the river, but I'm betting they got the bridge covered on both ends."

"So what do we do?" Billy said. "Unless we crawl back down the trail on our bellies, they've got us pinned down."

"Well," Freeman said, "once in Monterrey we had them holed up like this, and we sent a round from a couple dozen rifles straight into the notch. Got enough of them to even up the odds and the rest of them ran." He rubbed a horny forefinger along the side of his nose. "Course, they was Mexicans."

"Let's give it a try," Billy said, moving into a squat and casting about for his lieutenant.

"Asa!" he hissed, and Asa Wagmann lifted his head from a patch of hawthorn bordering the river bank. "See if you can get Heintz and Glavin and a half dozen of the others, the best shots, aiming at that notch up there. Have them blast it all at once, see what we can flush."

He turned back to the bluff and wondered vaguely how the hell the rebs climbed into that crease in the first place and whether there was a back way out. Maybe he ought to send some men through the woods in that direction, be sure the rebs couldn't circle around behind. He suggested the idea to Freeman. The sergeant allowed as it was a good idea and duck-walked off through the brush to take the men himself.

Wagmann lifted his head and got a shot launched at him for his trouble. He disappeared again, and his disembodied voice rose through the underbrush. "Ready, sir."

"On my order," Billy said, eyes straining to see movement on the cliff face. "Fire!" he roared, and a dozen carbines barked at once. Chips and sparks flew off the bluff, and something bigger tumbled down the slope in a cloud of dust to lie still at the river's edge. The boys sent up a hurrah. Their first kill. Billy smirked, astonished at how pleased he felt, like when he brought down one of those wily cock turkeys. The kill brought reality back to him and with it confidence.

He commanded his men to reload and fire. An answering round burst from the cliff, and a man to the right of Wagmann yelped and dropped. He heard calls to his left, over by the creek, Roecker's voice shouted orders, and gunfire popped from that direction. Leaving Wagmann and his sharpshooters to pin down the rebels on the cliff, he scuttled across the head of the trail and dropped over the bank of the creek.

Matted vegetation barred the way, and drifting smoke from the guns stung his eyes. Murky figures appeared among the trees and underbrush of the slope, and Billy tried to pick out the uniforms of his men in the flashes from revolvers. Grunts and thuds and revolver shots echoed on all sides, and occasionally a man screamed or swore. Billy discovered Otis Morgan pulling himself behind a tree trunk and nursing his leg, though Billy saw no blood. Morgan waved him on. Then others, unidentifiable, thrashing on the ground, or lying still. Two of the dead men he stumbled across wore civilian clothes. He knew them to be bushwhackers and checked them for weapons, but they'd already been stripped. The sounds of the chase and the fight faded up the hill, and Billy stood alone, not sure of his direction, hearing the roar of Wagmann's riflemen from a distance. He shook himself and peered into the gloom as forms, dirty and breathless, materialized grinning, stunned, stumbling and choking in the smoke.

It occurred to him that it was up to him to bring order to the tumult. This was his company, these were his men, and somehow someone had put him in charge. Strange, as he hadn't even fired his weapon since that first wild shot, in fact his carbine was somewhere back by the river, and all he carried was his revolver. He gazed around at the faces in the shadows and realized they stared at him expectantly, figuring he knew the right thing to do next. So he shook himself, raised his voice and called "Company B, to me!" Oddly enough it worked. More men emerged from the shadows of the trees and clustered around him. Sergeant Holland appeared at his elbow, muttering "Form them up on the trail, Captain, don't let down your guard." So he barked out an order to form up on the trail, eyes sharp, and count heads.

The troop that gathered in the shelter of the trees at the edge of the river's bank included Wagmann's men, who'd raised no answering shots for half an hour or more. There were forty-four of them. They included six wounded, two severe, one shot in the breast and one in the belly, and two dead. Billy stared at the dead men, Private Darren Thompson and a boy whose name he should know but couldn't remember, and felt a piercing stab of pity that passed almost as soon as it hit. The belly-shot would probably die, too, before they got back to Independence, a viciously painful death. The company's assistant surgeon, who'd waited with the horses during the fire-fight, wrapped a cloth around the man's torso but the blood flowed too fast to be stanched, and he soon gave it up and turned to the lesser wounds. These boys died in the blink of an eye, Billy thought, and it might have been me. He shrugged it off, this wasn't over yet, and the men watched him for an indication of their next move. He thought about it a minute.

"Sir." Harlan Dow, corporal, stepped up. "We're missing Sergeant Freeman and the men he took to clean out the snipers."

That's what it was, that's what he had to do next. Find the missing men, account for them, collect the secesh wounded and bodies, see what else waited out there in the woods. Seemed as if a hand-to-hand fight would serve to chase the bastards off, but they had a way, he knew, of slinking into the woods and the rocks and disappearing, so no one really knew how many skulked out there or whether the job was finished.

He detailed a dozen men to go with Wagmann and sent Barney Holland with him, to spread out along the west bank of the river and smoke out any remaining marauders, clear out the nest on the cliffs and locate Freeman and his men. He planned to detail men to cross the bridge and test the east bank, see if the secesh escaped in that direction, but the cliff had to be secured before he'd expose his men. So he posted lookouts and set his men at ease to catch their breaths and scrounge a meal from their haversacks.

By mid-afternoon, the glowering sky loosed a steady drizzle, and Wagmann returned with three of the five men who'd left with Freeman, one dazed and half out of his mind, two with wounds that would heal if they didn't fester first. Freeman and the other two were nowhere to be found, but neither were the bushwhackers. The high ledges of the bluff stood empty, the woods quiet. Billy's Boys collected three dead bushwhackers, which they piled on remounts, and four live ones, two wounded and two feisty. Billy sent a squad of men across the bridge to scour the east bank. They rousted no secesh, but they did find a camp, and liberated six horses with tack, foodstuffs, blankets, a coffee pot and two frying pans.

Time to head back to Independence. The rain and chill intensified, and every man shivered and grumbled, wrapped in a cloak if he owned one or ducked down into his collar. The euphoria from being under fire dissipated fast, Billy discovered, and the men eyed the dripping forest with misgiving, cast baleful looks on the prisoners. More than one smashed a fist into the dead bushwhackers before mounting up. A wrenching exhaustion settled deep into Billy's bones.

The troop moved off through the curtain of wet, retracing their trail of the morning in the early evening gloom. The drizzle soaked into Billy's trousers and ran under his collar, down the back of his neck. The trail turned to muck under the hooves of scores of horses, and even Roecker clamped his jaw and said nothing. They'd traveled no more than five miles when hoof beats pounding toward them signaled the outrider coming back fast. Billy held up his hand to stop the troop and swore under his breath. Corporal Degroat rounded a thicket and sawed on his reins, white and shaking, his eyes red-rimmed. "Captain, you got to see this," he said. He bent from the saddle and retched.

Billy looked at Roecker, whose face was grim, and they kicked their horses ahead. What Degroat found lay not far beyond the next turn and when Billy saw it, he too, felt his gorge rise and bile fill his mouth.

Sergeant Freeman sprawled across the trail, his naked body partially buried in mud, the top of his head bloodied and raw. His eyes stared, his mouth gaped, a look of horror twisted his features. A hole pierced the center of his forehead, powder burns framing it in a starburst. Roecker slid off his horse and dropped by the body, and Billy followed. They knelt, one on either side. Roecker gently turned the head from side to side.

"They scalped him and cut off his ears," he said, his voice quietly ferocious. He raised the arms, tied in front at the wrists. In the dim light they saw bruises swollen along the arms and across the chest. By the angle of the left leg, they knew the knee had been broken, the leg doubled up unnaturally beneath the body.

"Christ in heaven," Billy said. He rested his trembling hand on the shoulder of what, just that morning, had been a man, a good man. Roecker closed the jaw, pulled the eyelids down. The jaw sagged open again, and Roecker tied it closed with his kerchief. Billy, a wild fury in him, leaped up and wheeled on Degroat. "Bring a couple of men," he snarled, "and a blanket. Be quick about it. Something to carry him." Degroat whirled his horse and whipped it back to the column.

They found the other two men a hundred yards up the trail. Both had been beaten. A dozen revolver holes punctured one man's body, as if he'd been used for target practice. Billy wondered why he and his men hadn't heard the shots. The other man's head looked like a pumpkin dropped from the hayloft. Powder burns scored the sides of his neck, and Billy and Roecker figured they'd stuffed gunpowder in his ears and blown it.

Billy glanced around him, into the darkening woods, shadows long, mist rising. He wondered if any of the butchers hid out there, watching the reaction to their handiwork, and his fury settled into a hot hard hatred that flowed through him like magma. He turned to Roecker. "Take some men into the woods and see if they're out there still. I've got half a dozen trackers and hunters who can find anything in the woods at night. Take Degroat." He dragged himself into his saddle and wheeled his gray around. "I don't want the men to see this."

Roecker grasped the bridle. "Billy, that's the wrong thing to do. They got to see this. It'll mean the difference between seeing this war as a game and turning these boys into fighters."

Billy stared down at him. It was a cruelty to put his men through that, but he knew Roecker was right, and he nodded once. "Set it up," he said and started back down the trail.

By the time the last of the company filed past the bodies of Sergeant Freeman and his two men, who lay uncovered and repulsive along the trail's edge, not a man wanted to return home before every secesh, every bushwhacker, every civilian sympathetic to the southern cause, was driven from the country or strung up on a gallows. Roecker's strategy was good, Billy thought. He brought up the rear of the file, said a quiet prayer over the bodies, ordered them wrapped and loaded on horseback. Dozens of men volunteered to go with Roecker into the woods to search, and Billy named his best woodsmen. But Roecker wasn't ready to go.

"Just a minute, Captain," he said, putting a hand on Billy's arm. "We got something else to do before we go looking for those boys." He gestured to the men watching the prisoners.

Billy'd clean forgotten them, the four men they'd captured. They were tied, as Freeman had been, wrists in front of them so they could ride. Now their guards pushed them to the center of the trail with gun butts, none too gently. Billy's men muttered. Somebody spit, and the gob splatted on a prisoner's shoulder. Billy studied the faces of his men. The sight of the brutalized bodies had done more than turn them into soldiers, it had turned them into killers. He looked at Roecker. The man's face was contorted, he wanted the kill as much as anyone. Billy stepped into the circle, grabbed the butt of a carbine aimed for a prisoner's kidneys.

"No," he said. He lowered his voice, mustering all his authority. "That's enough. We take them into Independence and turn them over to the regiment."

"Captain, these here vermin ain't worth the food they'll eat," said one of his men, a farmer from Atchison County. "They're just going to take the oath and go back to killing us."

Billy stared at the man until the farmer's eyes shifted away, and he muttered and stepped back. Billy turned slowly, looking each man in the eye until they all subsided. When he swung around to Roecker, the other captain grimaced, his look pitying. "You'll get over it, Canon," he said. "This ain't a war for justice and honor. It's a war for survival. They got to be exterminated." He turned and motioned to his crew of trackers, and they melted into the gathering dusk of the forest.

Billy watched him go, then swung into his saddle. "Mount them up, corporal," he said to Dow, and Dow shouted the order. He glanced at the prisoners. The looks on their faces varied from fear to relief. But one smirked at him and had the balls to wink. "He thinks I'm weak," Billy thought, but all he said was "Get this scum out of here."

Roecker and his men caught up with them an hour before dawn. They'd turned up nothing, and Billy took his men, his dead and wounded, and his prisoners, on into Independence.

32

Summer 1862

Jabez proceeded with his plan to send Agnes away, regardless of her wishes, and booked passage for her and the children on the railroad out of St. Joseph. Rose was to go, too. Arguing did Agnes no good and frightened the children, so she dropped into gloomy silence and promised herself they'd return at the earliest opportunity.

And then just a week before their departure, she received word of the death of her father. *Our father passed to his reward,* wrote Mary, the eldest sister, *on Friday last, the 3rd day of May,* and one more thread to the past was severed.

Her father was in his sixty-ninth year at his death, and she didn't mourn him. He was difficult and distant during her childhood, bewildered by the way her mother raised their daughters, distressed by his inability to mold his children to his way of thinking, disappointed at the lack of sons-in-law and grandchildren. She wondered if he'd left any word or held any thought of her, but the letter mentioned nothing. She didn't regret him, but she did regret the idea of him.

Mary's words struck her as cold and stilted. She'd not written at all in the ten years past, though Agnes wrote to her, often through their younger sister, Mattie. Their mother would have hated their distance. A memory flashed, Mama's laughing eyes lifting to Agnes over the infant she cradled, one of the boys, William or Samuel, who passed on young. She'd have loved to have seen Agnes's children, to know they continued her line. *The family gathered to lay him to rest. All the sisters attended, as did all the aunts,* Mary wrote. Everyone but me, Agnes was sure she intended to point out. Past, to present, to future. For so long she'd considered only the future, only what lay ahead. Now the present tilted, the future hid, shrouded in war and uncertainty. And the past tugged insistently.

Late in May, Jabez and Dick McDonald took Agnes, Rose, and the children to the train station in St. Joseph. Jabez and Agnes had spent the last ten days in cool formality. They'd apologized prettily to each other, then did their best to absent themselves from one another's company. So by the time the trunks and valises were piled into the borrowed wagon, she was more than ready to leave.

St. Joe appeared as desolate as Agnes felt. Despoiled by secessionists, plundered by federals, its businesses shut down, broken into, looted and burned. The train station, once the symbol of an ambitious town's future, bristled with the guns and hostility of its Union guards. At the last moment, while the train stood chuffing black smoke and cinders and Rose and the children climbed into the carriage, Jabez pulled her to him and held her tight, the rough wool of his waistcoat against her cheek. She drew in the faint fragrant odor of cigar smoke, and could see the strands of coarse gray that invaded his silky black beard. For just that moment they were close again, holding each other as they had at the beginning. Then he released her, and they parted.

She returned to that moment again and again as the train chugged slowly and carefully across Missouri. They boiled like plum duff during the day, even though the weather held cool and overcast, but when the windows were open, soot and cinders surged in from the engine's great stack. The stoves at either end of the car smoldered all day long until the dinner stop, when a crewman filled their bellies with fir and oak and the pungent smells of sap and pine tar blanketed the train, along with thick clouds of smoke. Then the stovepipes began to draw, the engine to move, and the miasma drew off with the speed of the train.

The journey consumed well over two days, with meal stops and train changes along the way. One of the trains they switched to somewhere in Ohio towed a sleeper car, which they explored during a meal stop, the berths no more than bare mattresses on wooden platforms stacked one above the other. They rode that train only in the daylight, though, and slept in much discomfort on the stiff-backed benches of the passenger cars. Agnes had never ridden a train before, and Rose and the children turned the experience into one long adventure. Even Sarah Belle, sitting wide-eyed on her mother's lap, found much to contemplate, in her solemn manner, in the sounds and sights of the belching monster in whose belly they rode. Charlie was in his element, tearing up and down the aisle woo-wooing with the whistle and chugging with the clack of the wheels. He enchanted all the civilian passengers, avoiding only the Union soldiers, asking his mother in a stage whisper if that was "really a Yankee," and staring with large dark eyes that held a touch of fear.

Agnes was fearful herself as they traveled through Missouri. Not too many months since, bushwhackers had burned a bridge east of St. Joe, and the resulting wreck of a passenger train killed dozens of civilians. The burning of bridges and destruction of tracks evolved into a kind of deadly game between the bushwhackers and the federals, with the federals declaring that anyone caught destroying the railroad would be summarily hanged. General Price decreed such actions permissible within the rules of war, and travelers hazarded their lives as they would. Agnes never adjusted to the thought of war as a game with rules and protocols, as if each side tallied deaths like points on a cribbage board, money wagered, lives traded, one team the victor to be celebrated with a round of ale at the local saloon. She continually cast about for a means of quick escape or a place to take cover if the cars suffered an attack and formulated plans in her mind for protecting her children from gunfire. The exercise kept the fears at bay until they left the train for the ferry across the Mississippi.

Once in Illinois, and then across Indiana and Ohio, the journey began to pique her interest. The countryside rolled by, prosperous and peaceful, the war far away, farmhouses and barns intact, villages bustling, businesses open, in stark contrast to the Missouri countryside. As the miles slipped by, she thought of them as a skein being re-rolled, a thread that had unraveled ten years before as she headed west, now being rewound as she reversed. She was uneasy at the thought of returning east, when she'd turned her face to the west so decidedly. In quiet moments she tried to capture the memory of the feeling that drove her west so long ago, the feeling that clogs the throat, quickens the heart—anticipation, newness, endless possibility and promise.

All she had left was that memory, really only a memory of a memory. Time and daily cares had diminished high hopes and muted the excitement. She'd traded her sense of adventure for marriage and children, a very different gamble.

"Welcome."

With that single word accompanied by a solemn smile, Mary received Agnes home. She and Isabella, the next eldest, lived in the old farmhouse, the land leased to a second cousin who farmed the land much the way their father had done. Mary continued as stiff and distant as Agnes remembered, her hair iron gray, her eyes heavy lidded, her long face setting off a bony nose and a mouth surrounded by small, tight lines.

"Come in, then, out of the rain," she said and stepped back from the sill. "Isabella regrets not being here for your arrival. She has teaching duties." The warmth of baking steamed up the windows, going a long way toward relieving the coolness of their reception. Agnes stood a moment in the doorway, light spring rain at her back, and absorbed.

"So," she said at last. "Little is changed." She reached a gloved hand to the dresser just inside the door. "Mama's violet dishes, every one. New curtains, though." She glanced at Mary. "These are nice. Cheery."

Mary dipped her head and flushed, looked up at Agnes, then away. "Thank you, made them myself."

Agnes realized her sister was embarrassed, didn't know what to say. She must have appeared exotic to her, a traveler, adventurer. And one with that most precious of commodities: children.

"Mary, these are my children. Charlie, shake hands, please. This is your Aunt Mary."

Charlie's little face was alive with want of the pies he smelled, but bashfulness ruled, and he hid his face in Agnes's skirt. She gently unwrapped him and guided him by the shoulders toward his aunt. Mary reached a hand to him as one would to an unknown dog, and he touched it tentatively.

"And this is Sarah Belle." This time Mary did smile and smiled sincerely. She reached for Sarah Belle and held her close for a moment, but the baby would have none of it, and she wriggled and scowled until her aunt set her on her feet. Sarah Belle promptly stuck a finger in her mouth and gazed up, fascinated, at the stranger.

Rose flustered Mary. A Negro in her kitchen presented a discomfiting situation, and she appeared at a loss whether to invite the woman to sit or whether to shoo her back out into the rain. "This is Rose. She helps me care for the children." Sarah nodded abruptly and Rose, after a moment's silence, said "I'll unpack the children's things, missus, if you tell me where they're to stay." Mary gave her directions, and Rose disappeared up the back stairs.

And then a whirlwind flew in the kitchen door in a swirl of serge and cotton, spraying raindrops and shrieks of delight and wrapped Agnes in a bear hug that lifted her off her feet. Mattie, the youngest sister, who glowed with delight in everything and everyone, was their mother in her high-spirited youth reborn. Already she'd become Aunt Mattie to half the county, though scarcely into her thirties, and she lit up the quiet farmhouse like a roman candle. Even Mary grew good-humored and fond in Mattie's jolly presence and folded her into her arms as she hadn't done with Agnes.

Mattie squealed over the children, and, before ten minutes elapsed, Charlie nestled into her lap, pie smeared over face and fingers, chattering to her about his home, his wooden letters, his papa, his imaginary pony. His aunt was tall and strong and superbly proportioned, and unlike the rest of the Canons, her hair was a honey brown, eyes hazel and full of merriment. She lived in town with two other sisters, both of whom taught, but Mattie refused to settle for teaching and invaded the world of business as a land agent and the half-owner of a woman's ready-made shop. She had written to Agnes faithfully over the years, until the war interrupted the post, and Agnes had long worked at convincing her to leave Fayette County for Missouri, but she always demurred. Her roots sank deep into the Pennsylvania countryside and she flourished like an oak where she was.

Charlie and Sarah Belle enchanted the family and the old neighbors who remembered Agnes from long ago. Charlie's tow head often loomed over a cousin's graying crown from a perch on his shoulders, Sarah Belle's dark curls regularly rested on the shoulder of one aunt or another. Agnes doubted either child set a foot on the ground for most of the length of their visit. Mattie's broad acquaintance entertained them with picnics and church socials, teas, quiltings, dinners, even a dance or two. The constant round of visiting and entertainments astonished Agnes and jarred her system. She'd slipped through a distortion of time and space out of a society that no longer functioned, away from folks who would not trust and could not enjoy, into a

216

community where life flowed the way it used to, as though no war, no young men dying, no horrible mutilations, no thievery or burnings or treachery haunted them.

Mattie's friends talked of household issues, raising children, the welfare of the Canon relatives in Missouri, but rarely of the war. It was as if the fighting took place in a far-off land, something to be read about in the papers, clucked and tsked over, but not allowed to interfere with the daily business of country life. Occasionally word arrived of the death of a young man of the county, or that someone's son had enlisted and marched off to fight the rebels, and the ladies gathered to roll bandages or knit socks for "our boys at the front," but no one discussed the reasons for the war or its progress or politics. Perhaps the men did, but in Fayette County, women took no part in such conversations. If word of Jabez's political leanings had preceded Agnes, as surely they must have through Rachel and Nancy's letters, no one gave an indication. But they slanted sideways glances at Rose, Agnes's "darkie." Very few Negroes appeared in Fayette County, and Agnes believed they looked at Rose and wondered how they would cope when slavery ended and the darkies came to live among them. The idea didn't sit well with the good people of the county, and Agnes judged many of them hypocrites.

"You miss him," Mattie said, fanning her flushed face with the tail end of her apron. "I know something's wrong, but you miss him."

They sat on the grass at the edge of the apple orchard, the shade of the ancient trees providing the smallest bit of relief from the early July afternoon. Both children lay on a blanket, napping in the warmth.

"The children cry for him when they're tired," Agnes said and stroked Charlie's hair off his damp forehead.

"No, I mean *you* miss him." Mattie ducked her head to peer into her sister's eyes. "Don't tell me you can do without him."

"I don't miss his black moods and his temper."

"He loves you. He must, to send you away to be safe."

"I worry about him. Always."

She laughed. "He'll get into trouble if you're not there to watch over him?"

"Very likely. He has strong opinions and a short temper."

"I wish he'd come with you," Mattie said, adjusting Sarah Belle's sun bonnet. "I'd like to meet him."

"Come home with us. It would be a comfort to have you there."

"So you can avoid confronting whatever it is about your marriage that's eating at you? No, I thank you kindly." She gazed off over the valley. "I'm not like you, Agnes. I have no hankering to go off to strange lands. My world is here, and I'll die here. But you need to go back to your husband."

Agnes said nothing. No breeze stirred. Leaves dangled, limp and exhausted. The hum of fat bumblebees and the flutter of white fairy butterflies sent the barest ripple through the still air. The world held its breath, waiting, waiting for the war to end, waiting to right itself again, waiting for the future.

"Yes," Agnes said. "Yes, I do."

Mattie lay her hand on Sarah's cheeks. "She's warm. Maybe she needs a cool bath?"

"They've both been warm, too warm these past two days. They should be under Jabez's care." A pang of fear sprung from deep inside, taking her unawares. "He'll keep them well." Sarah's eyelids lifted sleepily and her mouth puckered into a whimper. "You're right. It's time to go home."

They arrived home after an interminable journey, during which the children coughed and cried with the effects of summer colds, jostled on stiff horse-hair benches filthy to the touch, amid smoke and dust and the melting heat of late July. The sense of adventure from the trip east was long gone. Even the sight of war-ravaged Missouri villages and deserted farmsteads brought relief because it meant they were close to home, to comfort for her wretched little ones, and to Jabez. She feared he'd be angry at her leaving the safety of Pennsylvania—she had no way of knowing if he'd received her telegram—but there he stood on the platform of the station in St. Joseph. The sight of him, a head taller than most of the crowd, neatly brushed coat and clean linen standing in contrast to stiff Union blue wool and the patched and dirty shirts of army hangers-on, put a hitch in her breath, and sent her pulse pounding. He welcomed them with a joy he'd not shown since the night the newspaper shop burned. Charlie threw himself at his father, and Jabez pulled Agnes and Sarah Belle to him, too. "My love," he whispered into her hair, "I was a fool. If ever I insist you must go away again, do all you can to resist me."

"I'll defy you with all my heart," she said, her lips on his throat, soft with his beard.

He chuckled. "You have no qualm there, and that's why I love you." In the midst of war-ravaged Missouri, Agnes found peace and safety in the circle of his arms, more peace than she'd ever known in Pennsylvania. She was home where she belonged.

33

August 1862

Reuben Bigelow rapped on the Robinsons' bedroom window in the dark early hours of the morning. Jabez, accustomed to being summoned in the night by expectant fathers or worried mothers, looked out to see the big man silhouetted against the dim light of a quarter moon, the empty sleeve flapping in the night wind. Agnes woke and sat up.

"It's Reuben," Jabez said without turning. Agnes muttered something and pushed a curl off her forehead. Jabez struck a match, touched it to the wick of a candle.

The man outside drew great gulps of suffocating air, sticky with August's humidity. His mount stood in the shadows of Agnes's lilac, blowing with exhaustion. "You got to come with me, Doc," he said, his voice hoarse. "My boy's been hit bad." He leaned against the window sill with one hand, dropped his head and spit. "It's Jake. Jake's hurt bad. He'll die if he don't get help."

"Where is he?" Jabez was up, pulling on his trousers.

"Up on the Noddaway, up toward Skidmore." Bigelow paused, his breath slowing. "They fought the federals up along the border. Wil come to get me." He glanced over his shoulder. "He's gone on, can't be seen around here. I'll be waiting, Doc. Up yonder"—he waved—"north end." And without waiting for a response, he slipped into the night.

Jabez buttoned his shirt. "I've got to go, Agnes." She said nothing. "Can't let that boy just die."

"No, you can't." She raised her knees up under the sheet and wrapped her arms tight around them. "I know it's evil, but I wish it'd been Willard, not Jake." She settled her chin on her knees and stared at nothing.

"I'll take the buggy—may need to bring him back. If they'll let me."

"I'll call Dick and heat up the coffee."

Jabez checked Nellie at the river bank, where the road disappeared into the ford. Gnats tormented him and horseflies buzzed the old mare's ears as she snorted and shook her head. The Noddaway River, in the northern part of the county, rolled out of broken country into a broad and marshy plain. Scrub ash and cottonwood lined its banks, along with seedling maples that would drown before they matured. Withered purple spikes of indigo, round soft heads of buttonbush, chokecherries, elderberry and willow crowded against each other and blocked the buggy from proceeding any farther. Reuben, leading the way perched on the back of a meaty plow mule, located a trail, invisible to Jabez, and pushed into it without a word.

Jabez batted at a persistent blue-bottle fly, climbed down from the buggy, and looped the reins around a willow branch. He lifted his medical case from under the seat and followed the mule on foot, boots sinking into the soft earth of an old deer trail as a grass snake wound silently into the underbrush and grasshoppers snapped and whirred under his footsteps.

The trail led away from the river and up a rise, where the brush thinned and a stand of walnut and elm clustered at the head of a ravine. By the time Jabez reached the trees, his shirt clung with sweat, and his neck stung from mosquito bites. He set his case on the ground next to the smoking embers of a breakfast fire and shrugged out of his coat. Reuben slid off his mule, ignoring the men who clustered around the campsite among a litter of equipment and cast-off clothing. There were at least twenty, maybe more. He recognized Richard and Harlan Little from over Forest City way and Ora Juwitt but none of the others. Several sported bloody bandages on an arm or a thigh. They crouched grim-faced, tin coffee cups or a plate of eggs or a hunk of hard bread to hand. Some cleaned weapons, an old squirrel musket, Colts, one even had a Springfield rifle. What conversation Jabez heard was carried on in low voices, truncated phrases. Someone back in the trees hummed, a soft, monotonous sound that might have been a cicada's song.

"Over here." Reuben grasped the medical case and nodded toward the shade of the trees, where Jake sprawled on a blanket. The boy's right calf lay propped across a saddle, a coat folded under his head, his trouser leg split to the groin and rolled above a filthy and blood-soaked strip of shirting wrapped tourniquet-style around the thigh. Angry streaks of red shot from beneath the bandage toward the knee, and the smell of the wound cloyed in the heavy air, already oppressive with August heat. Jabez squatted next to him and pressed his fingers against the inside of his wrist. The beats raced beneath his touch. Jake gazed at him through sweat and fever and grinned.

"Hey, Doc," he said, "What you doing here? You joining up with us boys?" He choked the last word, a spritz of bloody spittle moistening his lips.

Jabez laid his hand on the boy's forehead. It burned. "Just visiting this morning. Looks like you got yourself into a fix here."

"Damn Yank caught me just as we was winning the day. I got him, though, shot him right in the chest." He closed his eyes and winced. "Didn't see him fall, though."

"I'm sure you got him," Jabez said, long fingers probing at the fiery skin between knee and bandage. "How long ago did this happen?" He looked up at Reuben.

"Wil says it's been two days," Bigelow said. "He dug out the bullet but it don't seem to want to scab over."

"I think it's beyond that now. Get some water heating up and if there's whiskey in camp, bring it. Bring everything you've got. And we'll need three of those men over here to help out." Jabez sat cross-legged on the ground and opened his medical case. He pulled out clean pads of cloth, untied the bloody strip of bandage, peered into the wound, probed and pressed, and applied the new bandages to stanch the blood that immediately began to well up.

"You going to let me keep my leg, ain't you, Doc?" Jake said, trying for another grin. "I'm kind of fond of it. Can't go after no more Yanks without that leg, you know." He raised himself on his elbows, pain shot across his face, and he squeezed his eyes. "Got anything in that box to kill the hurt?"

"Laudanum, that should help." Jabez pulled out a small black bottle, drew the cork, measured an amount of liquid into a silver shot glass. "Drink that. We'll combine it with whiskey, and you should be a little easier here soon."

While his patient downed the medicine, Jabez lifted a tray from his

222

case. Sunlight glinted off a set of five steel blades cradled in a bed of red velvet. Four were long and narrow, double-sided sharp, the fifth was a fat rectangular saw with tiny serrations along one edge.

Jake looked at the box, then squinted up at the doctor. "Hey, mister, you ain't going to be cutting on me, are you?" He laughed, a nervous, high sound. "Because I ain't in a mood to let you do that."

Jabez lay a hand on the boy's forearm. "Jake, there's nothing else to do. I'm going to need to take that leg off, or you won't live through the day." He touched the thigh, just above the knee. "See these red streaks? That's poison. It's already killed your lower leg. If it shows up above the wound, there's nothing I can do to stop it." Reuben knelt next to him, carrying a kettle of hot water, a bottle of whiskey under his stump.

Jake's breath came in little gasps. "Pa, you ain't going to let him take my leg, are you?" Tears rolled through the grime on his cheeks, into the stubble on his jaw. He jerked away from Jabez's touch, rolled onto one hip toward his father, clutched the old man's shirtfront. "Pa...? His voice weakened, the laudanum taking hold.

"Here, son, take some of this." Reuben tipped the bottle to Jake's lips. "I ain't going to let you die, but we got to take care of this leg." Surprisingly gentle, the big man pressed his son back to the ground, stroked hair off his forehead, positioned himself, kneeling, at Jake's head. He gave him another drink, while Jake cried quietly.

The Little brothers and a third man Jabez didn't know gathered, shuffling and looking ill. Jabez looked up at them. "You boys ready to help?"

Harlan Little shrugged. "I guess so."

"Well, then, each of you take an arm, and you there, you take the other leg. Pull it out of my way, there. He'll thrash, even if he's out, and I want you to keep him still."

They took their places, and Jabez swabbed the wound with a wet cloth, scrubbing away dirt and grime. He rose to his knees for leverage, tied the canvas band high up on the thigh to clamp the femoral artery. He rested one hand on the thigh above the wound, drawing back the skin to leave a flap when the cut muscles retracted. With the other hand, he grasped the longest-bladed knife. He willed his heart to slow, took two deep breaths, visualized the procedure. A circular cut around the leg, through the integuments and the loose superficial muscles, all at once, the least painful way. A second cut, dividing the deep muscles. Remove the pressure on the thigh, allow the muscles to retract. Finish the cut on the deep muscles.

Jabez shook sweat out of his eyes. He bumped up against the bone, and the cut looked good. Jake had lost consciousness. Richard Little retched and loosened his grasp on the left arm. Reuben hovered like an anxious bear. Jabez concentrated, took the scalpel, finished the last cuts to the muscles. His scalpel scraped bone, and he slipped in the linen retractor to tie back the flesh, reached behind him for the saw. He pressed his thumb into the wound, nail against the bone to mark his place, set the blade against his thumb, drew back once, lifted it, drew back again, then gently back and forth, back and forth, until the teeth began to pinch as the cut bone came together. He lifted the thigh from underneath with his left hand and released the blade, pulled back again, then again. The saw dropped through, the bone splintering as it separated, and Jabez swore under his breath. Jagged, not a good cut. He snarled to the man on the other leg to push the dead limb out of the way, picked up the nippers and snipped off the splinters.

The whole thing took no more than three minutes, an age to Jabez. Though he'd performed the operation many times before, he never managed to still his racing pulse or prevent his jaw from clenching so it pained him for days afterwards. He stared at the mass of blood and skin, bone and muscle, lying discarded in the dust, once alive, responsive, pumping with life. He shook himself and turned his attention to the stump. Tie off the main artery, then the vein, probe for other vessels to be ligated, smooth skin and muscle over the raw end of the bone and stitch, pack with lint and wrap with flannel, and it was over.

"For the love of God," Reuben said, his voice almost lost in his thick beard. Richard Little heaved up his breakfast in the underbrush. Harlan, without a word, returned to the campfire and poured himself a cup of coffee. Jabez stood and dabbed at his bloody arms with a grimy kerchief. Jake's stump twitched as if searching for its missing half. Disgusted and half sick, Jabez threw his bloody tools into the kettle of water and went to the river to wash.

Late afternoon. Jabez dozed next to his patient in the warmth of the summer stillness, a buzz of insects the only sound. Jake moaned. He hadn't regained consciousness, fever burned beneath skin still hot to the touch.

Jabez held out little hope for him. Reuben wanted to haul him back to Lick Creek, but Jabez advised not moving him until the morning, so they made him as comfortable as possible, taking turns swabbing him with cool water, brushing away flies. The others in camp avoided Jake, casting sideways looks in his direction but not offering to help with the nursing. Jabez had doctored the wounded men, two flesh wounds from Minié balls, a saber cut, a couple of severe scrapes and bad bruises. Children playing a deadly game.

He shook off the drowsiness and stirred himself to check on Jake. Nothing more he could do, he may as well go home. He'd leave his supply of laudanum, show Reuben how to change the bandage, though there was no point. By the time the bandage needed changing, Jake would be in his grave. But concerning himself with the bandage would keep Reuben occupied.

A shadow passed over him, and he looked up at a figure silhouetted against the sun.

"Well, well, it's the good doctor," Willard said.

Turning back to Jake, Jabez took the cloth from Reuben and rinsed it in the kettle of lukewarm water. Reuben sat back on his haunches, looking from his eldest son to the doctor, eyes glittering underneath heavy brows.

"Willard," Jabez said. "About time you showed up."

"He's been here," Reuben said. "Back in the trees, watching."

"Figured you was still aggravated with me," Willard said. "Didn't want you taking it out on Jake here."

Jabez lifted Jake's wrist, counted the fluttering pulse. "Your brother's in a bad way, thanks to you."

"He done a good piece of fighting the other day," Willard said. "Nothing to be shamed for." He pulled a plug of tobacco out of his shirt pocket, bit off a hunk. "Lots of boys going to die before this war's over." He chewed, spit. "So this mean you're on our side?"

"Wil, for the sake of God, shut up," Reuben said. "Don't matter, long as Jake's all right."

"I doctor whoever needs doctoring," Jabez said, heaving to his feet and dropping the cloth into the water bucket. "Doesn't matter which side."

"I hear you was printing secesh in that paper of yours."

"How the readers interpret my opinions is up to them."

"Got to be on one side or the other, Doc. There ain't no middle."

Jabez turned his back on Willard, squatted to brush the flies from Jake's face, tested his pulse once again.

225

"Reuben." He stood again. "I'm leaving you a bottle of laudanum. Give him a swallow every two hours, be careful not to overdose." He pointed to the stump. "These bandages should be good until tomorrow. After that, change them if there's blood showing through." He looked up. Jake's eyes, open and clear, were on his face.

"Well, son, you've come around."

A corner of Jake's mouth lifted. "Yes sir, I guess I been sleeping the day through." He tried to raise himself on his elbows. "My leg itches something fierce, Doc. You got anything for that?"

Jabez smiled at him. "Afraid not, boy. You'll just have to grit your teeth and bear it. You've been through a lot worse today. Itching is a good sign."

Jake rolled his head, saw his brother. "Hey, Wil, got some tobaccy? I could use a smoke." He wiggled. Jabez and Reuben lifted him by the arms, settled his back against the trunk of the elm. Willard reached into a coat pocket, pulled out a cigar, bit off the end and spit it out, lit it with a brand from the fire. He handed it to his brother, who drew deep and with a satisfied sigh leaned against the tree.

"Hoo, but my leg itches." He surveyed his stump, covered with a blanket. He appeared not to realize there was nothing there. "Nothing like a good smoke." His head dropped back, and his eyes closed, lips turned up in satisfaction. To Jabez he looked to be twelve years old.

Jabez settled his knives, which had been drying in the sun, back into their velvet nests and closed the lid of his case. "Nothing more I can do here." He turned to Reuben and held out his left hand. "Good luck, my friend. When you get him home, let me know. I'll come out." To Willard he said "Any of your other boys need doctoring, try Caldwell, down in Liberty." He started across the clearing.

"Hey. Robinson." Willard's voice followed him. "I ain't forgetting."

Jabez turned, fixed the flat silver eyes with his own black-eyed scowl. "I don't expect you are, Bigelow." Jabez moved off through the brush.

34

August 1862

Jabez arrived home near midnight, but the household was astir, lamps lit in the kitchen and the children's bedroom. Sarah Belle had fussed and fretted all day long, and at first Agnes thought Jabez's absence disquieted her, but now she tossed in her crib, the sheet damp, her small body hot to the touch. Agnes and Rose hovered, swabbing her with cool damp cloths. Rose brewed a catnip tea, and they slipped it between her lips, but she fought them and more tea ended up on the bedclothes than in the child. Agnes held her, rocked her, but she wailed and writhed, her features contorted, and only when they lay her down did she hush. She'd learned a few words, but nothing that might tell them where it hurt, and by the time Jabez returned, both Agnes and Rose stumbled with exhaustion.

Charlie huddled against the wall, awakened by the hubbub, the covers clutched under his chin though the room steamed. His frightened eyes took in a scene that must have appeared fantastical to him, the lamp flickering in the late-night darkness, the shadows of his mother and his nurse growing and shrinking on the bedroom walls, his small sister crying in creaky, high-pitched wails. When Jabez strode into the room, disheveled, fatigued, still clutching his medical case, Agnes moaned in relief and dropped onto Charlie's bed, gathering him in her arms, letting her frustrated tears drop onto his bright, sleep-scented head.

Without a word, Jabez set down his case and leaned over the crib, laying his hand on his daughter's forehead. Looking up, he told Rose to bring him hot water and soap and to make a poultice with the echinacea he kept in a sealed canister in the surgery. Agnes leaned against the wall with Charlie in her arms, watching her husband with dumb eyes, feeling the weariness roll off him. He picked up the lamp and held it over the crib, lifting Sarah's arms and legs one after the other, pulling down her lower eyelids with the utmost tenderness. While he examined he crooned to her, a low and tuneless song he often sang to her at bedtime when she claimed her place in his lap and he rocked her to sleep. She quieted for a moment, her breathing gentled, but when he stroked her neck, bent her head from side to side, she started up again, a distressed cry that squeezed Agnes's heart like a vise.

"Take Charlie out of here," Jabez said, without raising his eyes from Sarah. "Put him to bed in our room and don't let him back in here."

Whatever her illness, it was contagious. Agnes didn't question him, but scooped their son, now nearly asleep, and hurried out of the room, passing Rose with the water basin. She tucked him into their bed and stroked the damp strands from his forehead as his eyes closed and his breathing steadied. Once he slept, she sat for a moment longer, studying his features, the smooth childish skin, the small sturdy limbs, thinking how vulnerable he was, how defenseless. She kissed him on the forehead and returned to Sarah's room.

Jabez met her at the door. "Leave her," he said. His voice croaked with exhaustion. "Rose will sit with her for now. I've put a poultice on her. The tea will ease the fever as much as we can expect." He looked over his shoulder, where Rose leaned over the crib, stroking, gently, softly, with a damp cloth, and murmuring words I couldn't make out. "We'll take turns watching, but first you need to rest, and I need food."

She followed him down the stairs, loathe to leave her daughter with anyone else, even Rose. In the kitchen, he splashed water over his face at the wash basin, shed his coat and waistcoat, and dropped wearily into a chair at the table, face in his hands. She opened the door of the cook stove, stirred up the coals, threw in more wood, and set the coffee pot to the front to reheat. Then she turned to Jabez.

"What is it?"

"Maybe influenza, maybe a kidney infection." He rubbed his hand over his eyes, down over his beard. His eyes were red-rimmed, his hair askew. "But I think it's more likely meningitis."

She dropped the frying pan she'd picked up with a clatter on the sink board. There was a buzz in her head, a tingle to her breath that clutched at her throat. "No," she said. "No, don't tell me that." She leaned over the table, over him. "Jabez, tell me what it is. What's wrong with Sarah?"

He stood, reached for her across the table, hands on her arms. "I think it's meningitis," he said again. "We have to face it, Agnes." His grip tightened. "I need you to help me." He was silent a moment, eyes fastened on hers. "I just need you," he whispered.

They stood there for what seemed to be a lifetime. "It's not always fatal," he said finally, dropping his hands and sinking into his chair. "But we must be very careful not to pass it on to Charlie."

She turned back to the stove, broke eggs into a bowl, added milk, and shaved off cheese from the slab tucked under a glass cover. A glob of preserves smeared the cover, it needed cleaning before it attracted ants. She found a whisk in the cutlery drawer and mixed together her ingredients. Counted the strokes as her mother had taught her—one-two-three-four—not too many, keep the omelet light and fluffy. One-two-three-four. She dropped butter into the frying pan. Poured in the egg mixture. Stared at the setting mash and wondered what it was, what she should do with it next. Then Jabez was next to her, spatula in hand. He flipped and stirred, and she found herself sitting in a chair, staring at the floor, her mind empty, while Jabez slid his eggs onto a plate, poured himself coffee. She thought, as if from a distance, that he probably hadn't slept for twenty-four hours and had faced who knew what during that time, but it didn't matter. She couldn't raise her head, or lift a hand to help him.

Later, she remembered being carried up to bed, tucked in next to Charlie, Jabez slipping in on the other side. She woke to find her son curled against her, Jabez gone, light drifting in past the heavy curtains carrying with it the street sounds of the village beyond. She lay there for a moment, wondering why Charlie slept with them. And then memory flooded in, and she curled in on herself, the hurt clawing red hot through her as if her blood were on fire.

They took turns watching beside the baby's bed, fighting the disease with unavailing baths, futile poultices, useless teas. Dick attended to the chores, including the cooking, while his wife nursed someone else's child with the devotion of a mother. Nancy and Rachel and Elizabeth slipped in and out, providing food, whisking away laundry, entertaining Charlie. The days merged into nights and back again to day. Rash invaded Sarah's small body, light from the dawn tormented her eyes, she refused all food. Agnes and Jabez watched their daughter die by inches. On the sixth day, at eight in the evening, as the sun set behind a bank of bruised clouds, Sarah Belle slipped away.

The house sank into a bottomless hush, her wails silenced. Agnes held her and felt her tiny heart still, Jabez and Rose and Elizabeth clustered with her in the small bedroom. She stroked the smooth forehead, pushed back the dark curls, touched the soft lips, straightened the damp shift. The door squeaked open, and Charlie pushed his way in. A shaft of light pierced the room and caught him in its glare as the sun sent a last beam across the prairies and into the room. Charlie stopped abruptly, rubbed his eyes and whimpered. "Mama. My eyes hurt."

Jabez looked at him dully, rose and knelt before his son, put his hands on the boy's shoulders, then carefully unfastened the tiny buttons on his shirt. Red spots speckled his small chest, the rash ugly and cruel. Jabez turned and looked at Agnes and, at that moment, they knew they would lose both their children.

They buried them next to Eliza, on the hill above town. The elegant monument Jabez had erected to his first wife cast a gentle shadow over the two tiny graves, and Agnes comforted herself with the fantasy that Eliza watched over them. The night before the funerals, Jabez sat up with the children, the two miniature coffins in the front sitting room where he'd so often played with them, told stories to them, loved them. Agnes's heart and mind craved unconsciousness, and she slipped into sleep just after sunset that last evening. In the morning she found him dozing in his reading chair, the lid of Charlie's coffin propped open, his wooden alphabet scattered across the blue satin coverlet.

By the end of that summer, the war waxed frantic in Missouri, threatening Holt County itself. The Confederate colonel Joe Porter ranged across the northern counties gathering bushwhackers and southern sympathizers to his command. They heard that Wil Bigelow's gang, minus Jake who, Reuben confided to Jabez, had not lasted through the day, joined up with Porter and raided as far west as Cravensville, three counties east of Holt. The rebels took Independence and its arsenal, and killings, lootings and battles buried the countryside around Kansas City in ash and corpses. Skirmishes were reported south of St. Joseph, and federals from Fort Leavenworth invaded and killed civilians and guerillas alike. Swarms of southern sympathizers left Price's losing army and clogged the roads, exacerbating the tensions between neighbors, driving levels of distrust to dizzying heights. And killing, so much killing.

Agnes and Jabez ignored the news from outside their home. They lived as if sealed in a bell jar. Death meant nothing to them; they knew death. They owned it. The autumn crept in with its riot of colors, its rich smells of ripeness and rot, and they spent hours on the porch or lying by the stream beneath their willow tree, talking about nothing and everything. They kicked through fallen leaves, hand in hand, when they visited the cemetery or walked to the Jacksons or the Kreeks. Jabez's medical practice languished, and instead of paying house calls, he and Dick built a smokehouse out back, and they smoked a hog and venison against the uncertainties of the coming winter. Rose and Agnes preserved and dried fruit, baked, cleaned and sewed and immersed themselves in mindless toil.

But something happened to Jabez in December, and with the approach of Christmas, he began receiving patients again. One day he slung his medical bag onto his saddle horn and made his rounds. He appeared to have passed through the pain and emerged on the other side, to a place Agnes couldn't even imagine existed. It wasn't callousness on his part, but a detachment that encouraged calm and peace of mind. And though the pain still had power to twist her soul at unguarded moments, Agnes was soothed. Her husband's sense of quiet acceptance eased the days for her and made the nights bearable.

35

April 1863

"Waa-wooo-yeeaaaay-yee!" Willard Bigelow threw back his head and howled the Rebel yell. Flames, feeble to the eye in the bright spring sunshine, licked out of the windows of Turner's Mercantile. He sawed hard on the reins, and the mare settled on her haunches, snorting and wild-eyed.

"Look there!" He waved his pistol at the burning building, and Ora Juwitt, clutching a bulging gunny sack, swung into his saddle and wheeled his horse around.

Ned Turner bolted from the side door, head shrouded in a towel and a cloud of smoke. Wil aimed his Colt but the roan skipped, and his shot went wild.

"Missed him," Ora said and yanked his own revolver from its holster.

"Damn," Wil said. "I got a mind to put a bullet in this mare. Sure do miss the black," and he shot again.

Ora let off a streak of shots, and Turner dodged, blinded, in a tangled dance that dumped him ass first in a pile of horse shit.

Wil roared. "I got him! Got him! He's mine!" He squeezed the trigger again and yet again, and the man, untouched, threw himself flat on the ground.

Ora's horse held fast, and his next shot raised blood. Turner had shed the towel, and he shrieked, scuttling on hands and knees toward his burning store. Another shot from Ora, then a fusillade from both riders, and the man leaped in the air and dropped, one foot twitching.

"Weeee-hoooo-eee!" Juwitt hollered. "Did you see that? Lifted him right off the ground!"

"I'd a got him first shot if this damn horse'd hold still," Wil muttered. "Fucking black had to go get himself shot."

"Joe Porter's fault," Ora said. Excitement over, he swiveled in his saddle to jam the gunny sack into a saddle bag. "He should never a charged that artillery. Maybe Dick Little'd be alive if he hadn't."

"The black's a bigger loss than Little," Wil said. "Dick was always puking whenever he saw blood. The black kind of liked blood."

Juwitt snorted. "Tell that to Harlan. He's right pissed about his brother."

"Well, Harlan'll just have to get used to it. My brother died, too. I'm thinking of taking a little revenge anyway."

Wil finished reloading his pistol, shot once in the air and waved his arm at the rest of the boys. Harlan, down the street firing a stack of hay bales, waved back, launched his torch through the door of a barn and kicked his mount down the road to the south. Alfred Zerbin followed, leading a string of captured horses, and Jansen and Irving tumbled out of the saloon, arms filled with bottles.

"What kind of revenge?"

Wil nudged the roan into a walk. No hurry now, the rest of the townsfolk would hide behind closed doors and curtains until Wil's men were long gone.

"Thinking about going back to Lick Creek. We never finished up there."

"Jake always said don't shit in your own nest."

"Well Jake's dead, ain't he? And I aim to make sure Lick Creek don't forget."

36
May 1863

Captain Billy Canon rode through the spring sunshine at the head of his column of militia, next to Joe Roecker. Joe's Company C men marched with Billy's Boys. Death, disease and desertion had taken their toll, and neither command mustered full strength. Their regiment spent the winter in Jefferson City, its companies vying for the honor of bedeviling the bushwhackers who raided up toward the Iowa line. Billy and Joe rode out in early May with fifty-some men, expecting to be gone a month or more. They traveled light and foraged, an art Joe Roecker excelled at. His command pilfered liquor and horses, saddles and household goods throughout the countryside, and nobody believed his men took only from southern supporters. Billy didn't hold much with thieving from Unionists, but his men required provisions, and who could tell a Unionist from a secesh anyway? So he looked the other way.

One thing he knew, he'd rather shoot prisoners than steal from civilians. The prisoners he'd captured on the Little Blue swore the oath and promised to go home, and now he and Joe stalked one of them, by name of Ferd Scott, who'd run right back to the bush and raised up a gang of his own. Roecker nagged Billy that he ought to have shot Scott when he had the chance, and he believed it. Sometimes he thought about it, late at night, and wondered about the slow change that worked on a man, day by day, in time of war. Like growing old, he imagined, one day you look in a mirror and your hair's thin and gray and your face is creased, and you don't really remember it happening. You've become a different person.

The first couple of weeks in May, they saw no action, though Joe heard Scott's marauders were holed up around Macon. By the time Billy's Boys arrived, the gang had disappeared, leaving behind little in the way of forage or food for the militia and lots in the way of burned towns, abandoned farms, boarded up stores and businesses. Inhabitants of the countryside peered out at them between the cracks of shutters as they passed or looked up from a plow and put a hand on the shotgun strapped to their backs. No one challenged them when Billy and Joe commandeered what little supplies they found.

One day Billy rode up to a farmhouse to find a detachment of his own men butchering a hog in the parlor. Blood soaked into the thin carpet, mud and filth splattered sofas and walls. He lost his temper, shouting and threatening his men in front of the homeowner, a woman who sat, mute and stricken in her kitchen, clutching a toddler to her sagging chest. The men dragged the meat into the yard muttering to each other and finished the job there. No one offered Billy a cut, and he'd have refused it if they had.

Another day they encountered a troop of eight men in Union uniforms riding out of a steep defile into the Charlton River bottom where the militia had bivouacked for a full day's rest. The strange men hallooed the camp, and Joe invited them in for coffee and a share of fresh rabbit pie. The men tied their horses, squatted at the campfire, chatted, passed news, asked for and received a thousand rounds of shot, and rode off. The next day Joe and Billy happened on a group of farm women, grieving dry-eyed and burying their men and discovered their visitors had been William Quantrill and his men, traveling in Union uniforms and taking what they pleased from local farmers. Billy and Joe, in a foul mood at letting the worst bushwhacker in Missouri make fools out of them, vowed someone would pay.

Payment came two days later. They forded the Locust River and crossed the prairie toward Princeton, trailing Scott who'd been reported harassing Union families in the area. The night before, in the middle of a heavy downpour that soaked the fuel and defeated any hope of a hot evening meal, a Mr. Vandever came to their camp and reported two drunk men claiming to be with Quantrill showed up at his door demanding food and liquor. Billy took his first lieutenant, Walt Lefever, and three privates with him to check out the story.

Vandever's house, nothing more than a shack, squatted in the center

235

of a dark clearing, its door open and outlined in firelight. The first round of shots burst from brush to the north of the yard, and Lefever and Private Rapp dropped. Billy and the remaining two yanked back on their reins as men poured out of bushes on foot yodeling the unearthly yell Billy'd come to associate with rebels and battle. In the rain and the darkness, he shot his pistol into the melee and wheeled his horse back down the road. By the time he'd returned to camp, gathered his men and surrounded the cabin, Lefever was dead, shot three times at close range through the head. Rapp had been shot twice at close range, and his pockets turned inside out, but he lived. Vandever and the attackers had disappeared.

So this morning both Billy and Roecker craved a fight. The rain eased up but the sky hung low and threatening, the light murky and dim. They sent out scouting forays at first light, and by mid-morning were gathered in the foreyard of a tavern standing at the edge of a fenced cornfield. Corporal DeGroat trained his carbines on three civilians, one of them Vandever. Roecker ordered his men to surround the tavern and the cornfield, and push into the woods alongside the road, and the men scattered, leaving Billy and Joe in the yard with the prisoners and their guards. Ralph Mooney, a blacksmith from Platte City, jammed the butt of his rifle into Vandever's kidneys. The man moaned and sank to the ground, and Mooney kicked him for good measure.

Billy leaned over the pommel of his saddle and looked down. Vandever, face blotched with purple liver spots, huddled in the mud, moaning. The other two civilians were younger, and their eyes shifted with the wary look of feral dogs.

Vandever's eyes opened, and he shifted to a sitting position. "You ain't got no call to hurt us, Captain," he said. "We ain't with them 'whackers."

"And they forced you to lure us to your cabin last night?" Billy's horse pranced, and he drew it in.

"They had my boys here, said they'd kill them if I don't play along."

"I can almost believe that, Vandever. Except you were gone when we got back. All I found was a dead lieutenant. Shot dead after he was down. Where're the men who did it?" He nodded at Mooney, who kicked the old man again in the kidneys. Vandever cried out, and one of his boys swore and shoved an elbow into the belly of his guard.

At that instant shots sounded, far enough away to sound like popguns. They came from the cornfield, and Billy saw men running on foot from the woods, clambering over the rail fence and ducking among the newly planted rows, dodging shots. After them rode men on horses, his men and Joe's, jumping the fence or plowing through it. The riders surrounded the field, galloped ahead of the running figures and penned them in, and shot, again and again. One horse reared back, its rider flinging up his arms and sliding off over the rump, and Billy watched as another horse collapsed with a scream. Then it was over, and the riders milled around, one or another taking a last lone shot at whatever moved on the ground. The tender shoots of the cornfield had been trampled into a muck of blood and mud, the rail fence scattered. Billy glanced back at Roecker, who watched the field, nodding in approval. Then he lifted his head toward the group at the tavern's door.

"Guess we don't need you, now," Billy said. "Shoot 'em." He whirled his horse and trotted into the road without looking back.

Two days later, Billy, Joe and their men marched into Carroll County, planning to reach the Missouri River and circle back to Jefferson City by the end of the month, when an officer from McNeil's regiment brought news of guerilla attacks all across the northern counties. He mentioned that, among other places, Holt County had been hit and there'd been killings in Lick Creek and Mound City. Billy gathered up a hand-picked crew of Holt County men from Company B, left Roecker to return to Jefferson City with the rest, and headed west.

37

May 1863

John and Nancy's brood gathered on a lovely May evening for a birthday celebration. Agnes and Jabez were invited, but he attended to a birthing over toward Forest City, so she walked alone to the house by the school. Elizabeth and Tom, Sarah and her new husband crowded around the table. Rebecca and Johnny, the only two Jacksons left at home, took charge of the young Kreeks. Everyone sorely missed James, off in Kansas City learning to shoot a Sharps rifle and to march in formation, hoping to join Billy's company for the summer.

They ate on a trestle table in the yard, shaded by a maple John had planted when they'd first moved in, and watched the sun set in a riot of orange and gray-purples, fat clouds hovering on the horizon gilt-edged and magical. Fireflies winked on outside as candles and lamps winked on inside, and when mosquitoes began to bite, they hustled the Kreeks' little ones into the house over their objections. The men gathered in the front room and lit up cigars, the women clustered in the kitchen finishing the dishes, brewing coffee, serving up deep-dish pie made from the last of the winter-stored apples, tart and spicy and still hot from the oven. Agnes sat in a rocker in the kitchen with Elizabeth's newest child, Harry, at eight months a husky little thing with a powerful pair of lungs, a frizz of red hair and an appetite like a fledgling hawk. The children clattered overhead in one of the bedrooms, playing some game that involved romping on beds and frequent screeching, overseen by the resourceful Rebecca. The adults chattered among themselves, relaxing among friends for a few hours of peace and comfort, shutting out the chaos beyond the walls.

Nancy saw them first, out the kitchen window, as she bent over the dishpan to rinse an empty pie plate, and she screamed. The women froze, but the men leaped to their feet and crowded into the kitchen. John peered into the darkness over his wife's shoulder, and his face hardened. He stood more than a head taller than Nancy, his silvering hair glistening in the lamplight, a scowl deepening the creases in his forehead and the laugh lines around his mouth, his always-gentle eyes stormy.

"Tom," he said to his son-in-law, "lock the door in the front room. Jim,"—Sarah's husband—"fetch the shotgun from the bedroom. It's under the bed." Agnes heard horses now, shying and dancing in the back yard, and voices calling one to another.

John yanked the curtains over the window, turned the key in the back door lock. "Sarah, take the baby upstairs and keep the children quiet. If there's fire you may need to go out the window." Someone pounded on the front door. Agnes handed Harry to Sarah, and John touched his hand to his daughter's cheek. "I'm counting on you. Use the front bedroom, keep the children out of sight." They crept out of the room as John blew out the lamp. The room plunged into gloom, shadows thick in the corners, only the front room fireplace throwing a flickering light against the ceiling.

Nancy clutched Johnny who insisted he would stand with the men. His mother insisted he would not. The pounding on the front door increased, and a voice Agnes thought she recognized called for John Jackson to open up. John lifted the shotgun from Jim Ramsey and stood to the side of the door.

"Willard Bigelow," he shouted.

"Open up, John," Bigelow called. "My boys're in need of food, and I hear tell Mrs. Nancy's a right good cook."

"We don't have much, Willard," John said. "Had a family dinner and ate everything." He glanced around at us, at the untouched dishes of pie. "You men dismount and lay down your guns, we got some pie here. And coffee."

"No, John," Nancy said, clutching his arm. "Don't open that door, they don't mean any good."

"I know that. Stay back now, away from the window." He gestured to Tom Kreek. "Get into the bedroom, see what you can see."

The first-floor bedroom faced the town. Surely someone had noticed a band of horsemen riding up at dusk. But the good citizens of Lick Creek learned early in the war to lock their doors, close their blinds and keep their heads down, and no one stirred on the dark street. Agnes followed Tom into the bedroom and peered over his shoulder. Four riders pranced on skittish mounts in the front yard, and she thought she spotted another stationed to the side of the house, almost beyond view.

"Well, now, family dinner is it?" Willard stepped off the porch and scanned the second floor windows. "So you got all your men in there?"

"What is it you want, Bigelow?"

Agnes heard the back door crash open, and the next moments passed in the slow motion of a dream, a dream in which her body refused to obey the commands of her mind. Someone cried out—Nancy—and another swore. Figures swarmed into the dark kitchen, bringing with them the acrid smells of rank bodies and unwashed clothes, horses and bad tobacco. A man pushed past Agnes, drew back his arm, and she heard a crack like a tree limb snapping, and Jim Ramsey collapsed in a heap at her feet. Elizabeth stood at the foot of the stairs, spewing invective and swinging an iron fry-pan. An explosion, a flash, a groan, then another shot, and in the wavering light from the fireplace, Agnes watched John drop to his knees, shotgun clutched in both hands. A stranger, face hidden behind a matted beard, snatched the gun and smashed the butt into the lock on the front door. It swung open and more dark figures pushed their way in. One carried a lantern whose glare washed over the carnage and seared Agnes's eyes. She flattened herself against the wall and stared.

Jim lay stretched across the kitchen threshold. Tom Kreek pressed a fist to his shoulder, blood dripping through his fingers. Nancy planted both hands on the chest of a man who stood before her grinning, and pushed so hard he stumbled backwards with an oath onto an upturned footstool. She dropped to her knees at her husband's side, scrabbling at his hands, his cheeks, wadding her apron into the sticky pool gathering between his shoulder blades.

A fist closed on Agnes's elbow and wrenched her around until she stared into the scarred face of Willard Bigelow. Behind the stubble and greasy moustache, his lips twitched, and he laughed a low, raspy sound. He waved a revolver in his other hand, and she smelled powder and oil when he brushed it against her cheek.

"Well, if it ain't Missus Robinson," he said, his breath like spoiled eggs.

"Where's the good doctor?"

"Not here." She twisted in his grip.

He tightened his hold. "You tell him for me this is payback." He pointed the revolver at John. Agnes snatched for his gun hand, and he whipped it back, pointed at Nancy, said "Bang!" and tipped the gun to the ceiling. He tittered like a schoolboy, dropped her arm and shouted an order. Within moments they disappeared, slipping out the doors, calling to each other with a laugh and a whoop, mounting up and thundering past the schoolhouse, up the road to the north.

An instant of deadly quiet settled over the house, then Sarah clattered down the stairs, hollering to Rebecca to mind the children. Jim moaned and struggled to sit up. Elizabeth knelt beside Tom, ripping his shirt open, blood on her bodice. Johnny lay where they'd kicked him, curled around bruised ribs. Agnes dropped beside him and stroked a hand over his wet check.

John Jackson was dead. The bullet lodged in the center of his back, and he'd dropped to his knees and died without a sound. Nancy, blood smearing her face and hands, lay across him, her plump figure heaving.

"Damn! I should have been there." Jabez thumped his fist on the wall, then covered his face with his hands.

"What good could you have done?" Agnes wheeled away from the stove and jabbed her hands on her waist, too tired for tears. It was four o'clock in the morning following the attack, and she reeled with exhaustion. "You would have been killed too. Or instead."

"Better me than John."

"Oh, don't be a hero." She glowered at him and turned back to the sizzling skillet.

Jabez dropped into a chair and tipped his head back, eyes on the ceiling. "I know Bigelow. I know how to handle him. It was me he was after. I could have talked him down."

She wrapped her hand in her apron, hefted the skillet and dished eggs onto a plate. She poured coffee, carried the plate and mug to the table and set them in front of him. He straightened, hands on knees, staring inward and far away, and Agnes realized his cheeks were wet. She'd never before seen him cry, not even when they'd buried Sarah and Charlie. She sank down on the chair next to him, grasped his hands in hers.

"My darling husband," she said. "It does no good to blame yourself. This is senseless, this is insanity. You were busy birthing a new life while another was taken. A good man's life was taken, and I can hardly bear it. But you can't be responsible, you can't allow yourself to think that way. That's the road to madness."

"He was my friend."

"I know. And mine."

He turned to her then, leaned his forehead against hers, his eyes closed. "Agnes," he whispered. "I'm sorry." They stayed that way for a moment longer and then he drew in a deep breath and swiveled back to his food, lifted the fork, ate a bite, lay down the fork. He dropped the napkin next to his plate and pushed back, stood. "I should have been there," he said and left the room.

Billy arrived with a contingent of militia the week after John's funeral. Agnes thought again about the killing yet to come. Maybe Billy would die, maybe James. Maybe if this infernal war continued, even Johnny would march off to slaughter. Death had taken her children, no future generation would follow her or Jabez. So many men and boys dead, so many still to die, as if the neck of the hourglass had constricted so that only a single grain might pass at a time.

The Holt County supporters of the Union, led by Rufus Byrd and Aldo Beaton, rushed to the defense of the Jackson widow and orphans, dispensing their own brand of justice for the murder of their friend. Miranda Bigelow, Wil and Jake's mother, watched with tears on her cheeks, her younger children clustered about her, while Byrd and Beaton arrested Reuben. They convicted him by court-martial of harboring and provisioning bushwhackers and shipped him to a typhoid-ridden prison in Cincinnati. Within five months, the big one-armed man who'd been a friend to all was dead and buried.

38
May 1863

Billy rode into Lick Creek for an afternoon, stayed through dinner and rode off again to search for Bigelow without taking the time to visit his wife and daughters in Forest City. The evening he left, the women lined the Jackson front porch like a row of crows on a clothesline, black mourning dresses whipping about their ankles in a brisk damp breeze, their men behind them in the shadows, the younger children subdued and frightened. Jim Ramsey, revolver on his hip and carbine over his shoulder, had joined Billy's company as a civilian, and he and Sarah walked apart, saying their goodbyes.

Billy shook hands with the men. Tom Kreek's arm nestled in a sling, the bruises on his face the color of pea soup. When Billy reached his father, he held out a hand, and Sam grasped it. Billy pulled the old man into his arms and held tight. Sam pushed away and looked abashed. Billy grinned at him and punched him on the shoulder.

Jabez leaned against the porch rail, and Billy hesitated before he stepped over to him. The doctor had aged since Billy'd seen him last—he'd lost weight, and his cheeks were sunken, a thick web of lines creased his forehead and shot out from the corners of his eyes. His beard, once black and soft, bristled with gray.

"Doc," Billy said.

"Billy," the doctor said. He said nothing more, and Billy flushed. He stared over the yard toward the old schoolhouse, turned back to the man in front of him.

"Maybe," he said, fixing on a spot over Jabez's right shoulder, "maybe if your friends come back to town you can get them to lay off the family."

Jabez let out a breath, his eyelids drooped, then raised, and he looked straight into Billy's eyes. "Billy, they hate me as much as you hate them. That's all they are, is hate. They believe nothing, they stand for nothing."

"All the same," said Billy.

"You're after Bigelow."

"And his gang, yeah."

"I may get him first."

Billy's eyes narrowed. "How's that?"

"If he's still in this area, I'll find him. That's one thing I can do with my connections. And if I find him, I'll take care of him." The doctor spoke softly.

Billy regarded him for some moments. He stuck out his hand. "Here's to us, then, Doc," he said, and they shook.

Rachel, white and drawn, said nothing when Billy put his arms around her and kissed her cheek. Nancy sobbed and shook. She held James to her, her head no higher than his new stiff blue collar. Billy's new recruit. He'd resisted signing up James. The boy was nineteen, plenty old enough, the same age as maybe half of Billy's Boys. But he was James—the rambunctious boy under everyone's feet, the one who never went to bed when he was told, who grabbed life with both hands, everyone's favorite—and Billy ached at the idea of putting him in danger. Billy glanced at Agnes. Her eyes brimmed with tears she couldn't hold much longer. She caught his look and sent one back: I'm holding you responsible. Keep him safe. Billy nodded, a quick jerk of his head.

James stepped back, jammed his kepi on his curls, plunged a hand into his pocket. Withdrew his black shiny arrowhead and held it high. "Kiss it, Ma, for luck," and Nancy did. "We'll be back!" He gave it a toss, caught it and swung onto his tall sorrel with the white blaze. Ramsey climbed into the saddle, they waved and were gone.

The Bigelow gang had a ten-day head start, the trail old but clear. After hitting Lick Creek, they murdered two men in Mound City, then burned their way east over the prairie. Billy, James and Ramsey, joined by a dozen men from B Company, followed them through a countryside lovely with meadowlarks and warblers, wild strawberry, shooting star and vetch. At dawn, they rode to the faint peent of the woodcock and the booming of courting prairie chickens. At noon, red-tails soared overhead, and at dusk the owls began to call, trumpeting a kill. The prairie lived on, oblivious to the doings of men, intent on rebirth, unmindful of blood spilled, heedless of fire and death. And in turn, Billy and his men galloped through its beauty without seeing it, noticing only the ravished homesteads, the unplanted fields, the unburied corpses.

By the time they crossed the Thompson River into Mercer County, exhausted after twelve hours of hard riding, they'd encountered no enemy. They reined in at Modena, a raw settlement not far from Princeton where Billy and Roecker had operated earlier in the month. Bigelow had passed through three days earlier, revenging the shooting of George Vandever and his sons by gunning down the mayor of Princeton, his son and his nephew. According to one source they'd ridden south toward Trenton. According to another maybe it was east into Sullivan County. The people of Mercer County appeared indifferent to the militia's search. They looked up out of eyes weary and glazed, from shoulders that slumped. They were dog-tired, the proprietor of the general store told Billy, and wanted no more part of a conflict that made no sense, that no longer concerned them. They wanted to be left alone.

Billy's men slept through the night and ate courtesy of the reluctant Modena storekeeper, then saddled up and headed south. In Chillicothe, they rode up to a farmhouse south of town where Bigalow's gang had apparently been welcomed by the farm wife. Billy's sergeant wanted to arrest the woman for harboring bushwhackers, but Billy eyed the bigger prize, and he pushed on to Carrollton.

As dusk fell they topped a rise on the north bank of the Missouri. The river flowed to the southeast, the setting sun lighting up its surface as if a lake of fire nestled between the high bluffs. To the northeast the early evening lights of Carrollton glowed through smoke from a hundred chimneys. To the west, across a basin not more than a half-mile wide, a thicket of trees ran up the slope of the opposite hill, steeped in the dimness of coming night. At its crown, firelight flickered and men moved around a campsite, finishing the chores of evening bivouac. Billy and Barney Holland sprawled on their bellies, watching.

"That's them," Billy said and Holland grunted. They slithered backwards off the crest and re-joined their men, clustered out of sight on the down slope. Billy whispered his orders, and Marcus Degroat led three men into the dusk on foot, revolvers in one hand, bowie knives in the other. They'd take the sentries first. Billy wanted Bigelow alive.

"You're with me," Billy said to James, and the boy, eyes glinting and face flushed, didn't argue.

Billy waited ten minutes, unsheathed his sword and spurred his mount straight up the front of the slope. The rest of the company spread out across the valley and curved into a crescent as they rode, sweeping up the flanks of the hill. Their quarry froze in the firelight for an instant, then the hilltop erupted in confusion, oaths, a wild shot. DeGroat appeared across the clearing. Rebels burst from the trees on foot, mounted militia ran them down. A pistol shot exploded next to Billy, and he whirled to see Ora Juwitt pitch face first into the dust. Billy's men pounded through the campsite now, scattering cooking gear and bedrolls, clubbing and slashing with saber and rifle.

It was over in moments, the forest floor littered with dented pots and torn clothing, bodies stretched out unmoving or huddled and moaning. Holland and Ramsey dismounted and herded the conscious into a cluster in the flickering light of a campfire, while DeGroat and his men slipped off to collect the bodies of the sentries they'd killed. Six bushwhackers were dead. Billy dismounted, slid his boot beneath Juwitt and rolled him onto his back. His mouth grimaced in death, his eyes partially open. Billy spat and strode off to view the rest of the dead.

The Holt County men recognized Harlan Little and Alfred Zerbin among the four yet living. Billy examined the bodies twice, holding a fire brand to each face, then threw it down, fuming.

"Not here," he said. "Bigelow's not here. Either he slipped out when we came in, or he wasn't here to start with."

Little spoke up. "You ain't going to get him. He's too smart for you fuckers."

Billy kicked Zerbin in the chin where he sat, hands tied behind him, and the simple man crashed back with a howl. He turned on Little. "You're next, boy," he said. "Where's Bigelow?"

"Gone off," Little said, refusing to raise his eyes to Billy. "Been gone for couple of days."

"Gone off where?" Billy glared at the other prisoners. Each shook his head and glared back.

"Not going to get anything out of this lot," he said. "Load up the prisoners. Leave the dead."

They rode into Jefferson City at noon the next day, and Billy surrendered his prisoners to Colonel Hall. Before two in the afternoon all four were convicted by court-martial of treason and murder and sentenced to death. Harlan Little cried. Alfred Zerbin appeared dazed and without understanding. Billy's Holt County men won the privilege of leading them to the gallows, erected early in the war along the river below Capitol Hill, nooses dangling in anticipation of multiple executions. Zerbin, Charles Skelton, from Andrew County, and the fourth man, who refused to give his name, were prodded up the stairs, hoods drawn over their heads, nooses settled about their necks. Billy grasped Little by the elbow.

"One more time. Where's Bigelow? You've got nothing to lose," he said.

Little, hands bound behind him, twisted out of Billy's grip and shook his head.

Billy slashed his pistol butt across Harlan's face, bloodying his nose.

"I don't know," Little said, his voice rising into a squeak.

Billy jammed his pistol into his holster. "Get him out of here," he said, and Little was yanked up the stairs, his feet dragging, his trousers wet and stinking where he'd pissed himself.

Zerbin keened in a singsong voice, swaying as if the gentle breeze stirred him. Skelton muttered, the nameless man shouted curses muffled by the heavy hood, each oath punctuated by a mad giggle.

Every man in Billy's company vied to be a member of the shooting squad. "You," Billy said and jabbed a finger at Marcus Degroat. Degroat whooped and grabbed a rifle out of the teepee stack. "You and you. You." Charlie Koch, Emil Haas, Joe Weber. Four more. He stopped in front of Ramsey. "Jim?"

"Yes sir, Captain," Jim said, his face bland, and he chose a rifle.

"James." Billy eyed his cousin. The boy stood tall and lanky, a head above Billy. His arrowhead hung from a leather thong outside his jacket.

"No one'll think any less of you if you don't do this."

"I want to."

"Grab a rifle." James chose a Burnside.

The men raised their rifles to their shoulders. Billy lifted a hand to the hangman, slashed it down, and all four bodies dropped. The gargling of choking men sounded loud in the sudden silence. The drop, set intentionally so the prisoners' plunge wouldn't break their necks, left the bushwhackers alive, kicking and gagging.

Billy raised his voice. "Ready! Fire!"

Ten carbines exploded in smoke and flashes of fire, and the bodies twitched and jerked as bullets plowed in and through. By the time the last shot sounded, Harlan Little's body hung so riven with the broad wounds of Minié balls that one arm dangled by a shred of coat sleeve, and Billy swore light shone through the man's midsection. Skelton and the fourth man swayed, but Zerbin moaned, until a single shot boomed from the firing squad, and the moaning stopped. A sudden swirl of wind caught the acrid smell of powder and the reek of filth—the dead men's bowels voided at the end—and blew the stench into Billy's face.

James lowered his weapon and looked back at Billy. "For Pa," he said.

39

Autumn 1863

Billy never did track down Bigelow that spring. James enlisted in the regular Union army and boarded a train for St. Louis and points east, and Jim Ramsey returned to Lick Creek silent and hard-eyed, unwilling to talk about what happened, saying only that Bigelow's gang was dead. Willard Bigelow himself vanished like the smoke demon. His mother, the Widow Bigelow, packed up and moved to Texas with the younger children, and that, Agnes thought, marked the end of the Bigelows in Holt County.

The second week in July, reports filtered in of a massive battle in Pennsylvania, a battle that repulsed the southern army's invasion of the north and killed unspeakable numbers of men. And immediately after, the news arrived that Vicksburg had fallen to the Yankees, and they began to hope once more that the end was near.

"I never thought I'd say this," Jabez said late one evening. The heat stifled any hope of sleep. They sat on the front porch, Jabez in his rocker, Agnes on the top step, surrounded by Rose's citronella candles to ward off mosquitoes. "It doesn't matter any more if the north wins. It just needs to be over."

Agnes said nothing because he was right. A chorus of crickets filled the quiet spaces in their conversation, punctuated by the soft creak of the rocker. She leaned against his knees and searched for Vega, the only star she knew.

"I wonder," he said softly and stroked her hair. "I wonder if there ever was a time when we might have avoided it."

"You did everything you could," she said. She found Vega and began tracing the lines of its constellation. "Everything one man can do."

"No one was prepared to listen."

"It's men's nature to kill first, talk later." A white streak sped across the blackness above, so fast she thought perhaps she'd imagined it. "Shooting star."

"An old miner in California told me a shooting star meant death."

"Maybe in California. My grandmother said it meant life. And change."

"I think we can take our pick."

Agnes swiveled so she could lay her cheek against his knee and wrap her arms about his legs. "I choose change. Let's run away."

He stroked her forehead with his thumb, smoothing away the lines. "Not a bad idea. What do you think of Idaho?"

She looked up at him. "You're serious, aren't you?"

"Deadly serious," he said. "Hand me my cigar case, would you please?" She reached it down from the rail.

He chose a smoke, clipped the end and lit it at the flame of a candle. She leaned against him again and studied the profound mystery above. "Milky Way's bright tonight."

"It would be primitive. Frontier living."

"There are gold strikes out there. I read something in the paper a few weeks ago. Poplar Gulch or something like that."

"Alder Gulch. And Grasshopper Creek last year."

She turned again to look at him. "You've been paying attention, haven't you?"

"There's a lot of bad blood around here. I don't think we'll be welcome when this is over. You still can't go back to Rozell's church."

"I don't want to go back." She stood, and he pulled her into his lap. She lay her head in the hollow of his shoulder and took in the sweet, heady aroma of the cigar. "When the children—" She stopped a moment, let the emotion well up, and then started again. "I began to think about going west again. The way I did when my mother died. I think that's when I first began to dream about doing it. Really doing it. And then the children. And John. And now the old itch is back." She touched her lips to his jaw, just under his ear. "I may only be running from death, but I still wonder what's out there."

His arm tightened around her shoulders, and he rubbed his beard, still soft, against her cheek. "Then let's find out."

They next heard of Bigelow the first week in September. The town—Unionists and Confederates both—breathed a collective sigh of relief at reports of the death of Joe Hart, guerrilla chieftain of Andrew and Gentry Counties. Willard Bigelow was rumored to ride with Hart over the summer, when Hart shot and wounded Harrison Burns near Fillmore, just twelve miles from Lick Creek. They killed Burns' son-in-law, robbed the neighbors, and ran off whooping a rebel yell. Hart swore to kill off all of Andrew County, every last devil, but he himself was shot to pieces over by Chillicothe, and Bigelow inherited his men. Witnesses reported seeing him in Daviess and Grundy counties, and south along the Missouri River. Then Quantrill burned Lawrence, Kansas, and the sentiment against guerrillas grew so ferocious that even Bigelow went underground for weeks.

Jabez found him early in October. He returned home late one evening from a call to a family with measles on the Mound City road, and without a word disappeared into his surgery where Agnes found him checking his revolver. He glanced up when she slipped into the room. Shadows from a single candle flickered across his features.

"What is it?"

"Bigelow," he said.

"Where?"

"Holed up at the Henderson farm south of Graham. Word is he's alone."

"Take me with you."

"No." He poked about in a bureau drawer.

"You can't go alone."

"Dick's coming with me." He dug out a box of ammunition and shoved it in his jacket pocket. "I'll bring him back to trial. You can bear witness."

"Not good enough. And I don't believe you'll bring him back."

"Agnes...." He glared at her, but she lifted her chin and held his eyes.

"I'll just follow you."

He huffed and rubbed a hand over his eyes. "Suit yourself."

The road out of Lick Creek was wide and hard-packed from the summer's heat, autumn rains not yet churning it to muck. It wound between gently rolling hills and through patches of woodland, lit so brightly by a half-moon that each pebble cast a shadow. They rode on the verges as much as possible, in the shadows of the hills and trees, and in the softer earth of the ditches in an attempt to muffle the sounds of the animals' hooves. Jabez led, Agnes's mare Juno following Jupiter placidly. Dick brought up the rear on Nellie. No one spoke. Agnes felt no fear but rather exhilaration, like a child who slips into the night when she should be tucked in bed. And a sense that finally she was accomplishing something, that this war would not pass without her making a mark, however small.

The air carried the first chill of autumn, and Agnes was wrapped in Rose's worn wool cloak, Jabez's rifle resting across the saddle in front of her. She knew how to shoot it, Pa had taught all his daughters to hunt squirrel and rabbits, but she'd never pointed it at a man. She'd be able to, though, when the time came. So many things were different now.

She couldn't say what drove her to insist on joining Jabez. Clearly, they planned to do murder. Willard Bigelow deserved to die, and they were the ones to do it. Whether they acted as angels of a just punishment or demons bound on the simple pleasure of revenge, Agnes didn't care. The idea that any one man's life was sacred had become almost laughable. The bonds that tied her to that way of thinking had long ago rotted away. Their intended actions seemed to be the natural consequence of all that had gone before, the evolution, or devolution, of their lives, their thoughts, their principles, their consciences.

The highway stretched empty ahead; they met no other night travelers. South of Maitland, they left the road to avoid the town and picked their way through a stubble field, recently harvested, then followed the line of the Noddaway River to the bridge west of Graham.

Jabez dismounted and motioned Dick and Agnes to follow. "We walk from here," he said. "Dick, tie the horses in the shadows there. We're going up the bank and through those trees. House is just the other side."

They hiked into an apple orchard, the pungent, rotten smell of wind-fallen fruit sharp in the shadows under twisted branches. The Henderson farm covered the valley, a sizable white clapboard house squatting in the faint glow of the now-setting moon. Large, gracious oaks lined the path to the front porch, dead brown leaves clinging to their branches and cloaking the drive in deep shadow. They were all that remained of the once lovely plantation. Fire had gutted the west wing of the house, the barn door hung askew, heaps of rubble marked the locations of outbuildings. The Hendersons had chosen the secessionist path, and they had paid dearly for it.

Firelight flickered through a window on the ground floor.

"We go in from three sides," Jabez said. "Agnes, I want you at the head of the drive, just inside the oaks. Keep the rifle trained on the front door." He motioned to the north. "Dick, circle around to the back, cover the rear entrance. I'll go in through the burned-out wing."

He turned back to Agnes, the moonlight sparking in his eyes. "I'm glad you're here." He took her hand and raised her fingers to his lips. "Be careful."

They separated. The men disappeared into the dark, and Agnes slipped back through the orchard to the road, down the road to the drive. She worked her way through deep shadow until she reached the end of the row of trees and raised the rifle to her shoulder, trained on the front door. She clenched her teeth and held her breath, listening for gunfire, for shouts, for signs they were discovered. But when a shot exploded from inside the house, she started and let loose a yelp. The gunshot seemed to bounce off the trees, to surround her, and she ran, rifle at the ready, toward the house. She heard angry voices and curses, Jabez's among them, and she thanked God he lived and remained undamaged enough to curse. She climbed onto the veranda and tried the front door. It swung open with a squawk. Jabez's voice boomed from a back room, issuing orders. Someone laughed, high and nervous. Out of the dimness of the interior, Bigelow pushed past her and stumbled out, hands bound behind him, falling to his knees in the dust of the yard. Jabez followed, and behind him Dick dragged a second man by the collar whose rear end bumped across the porch and down the steps. Jabez raised his arm, pistol in his fist, and Agnes waited for the shot, but instead he smashed it down on the back of Bigelow's head. Willard fell in a heap and lay still. Jabez turned to Dick and pointed at the second man.

"Tie his feet and get a fire going. I'll take a look at his wound."

Dick gestured at Bigelow. "What about him?"

"In a minute."

Dick secured the wounded man and disappeared behind the house in search of kindling. Jabez pocketed his pistol and turned my way.

"Bring in the horses and get my surgical kit. I need to doctor this man."

The moon had set behind a bank of clouds, and after several false starts in the intense dark, she found the horses. By the time she returned with them and the medical case, Dick's fire lit the ravaged yard. By its light she saw a wet stain spreading across the injured man's left shoulder. He breathed in shallow gulps, his forehead bright with perspiration.

Agnes handed Jabez's instruments to him while he probed the wounded shoulder, dug out a chunk of lead, applied a bandage and tied it off. The blackness of the night had begun to slip into a misty gray, and objects in the farmyard emerged gradually into relief. Dick propped himself against the porch, busy with a rope, tying, untying, with a nervous intensity she'd never seen in him before. The wounded man floated in and out of consciousness, a shine of fever on his cheeks. He might make it or he might not, Agnes didn't know and didn't care. Wil Bigelow groaned and struggled to a sitting position, flat gray eyes shifting from Jabez to Agnes to Dick, never still. Wrapped in her cloak, she crouched by the fire and stared across the flames at the man who had killed John Jackson.

Let it end here, she thought. A long-forgotten memory flashed: a woman swinging in the breeze, her neck oddly tweaked, her skirts billowing.

She felt Jabez behind her, though he did not touch her. Dick's nervous hands stilled. She concentrated on the face across from her, white, framed by fire, eyes like the sloughed dead skin of a snake. *Let it end here.*

They watched each other, and time stretched. She stood and nodded to Jabez. Light grew, and birdsong burst forth, a watery trill that pierced the morning air and faded to silence. Agnes stared up through black oak branches silhouetted against a wrinkled sky. The breeze had turned sharp, a promise of rain. When she turned back, the killer sat mounted atop Jupiter. She climbed on Juno's back, and Dick tossed one end of the rope over a limb of the nearest tree, dragged at it to test its strength. It held. The noose dangled.

Willard's eyes danced, liquid and deep and fixed on Agnes. His face flushed, the scar a deep throbbing gash. Slowly a smile curved across thin lips.

Jabez led the horse beneath the oak tree, and Agnes followed, guiding the mare with her knees. She grasped the noose, smooth and supple in her hands. Willard reared back when she reached out to him. Jabez, mounted on Nellie, cuffed him across the ear. He reeled toward her again, and she slipped the noose over his head. He slumped, eyes narrowed now, and hidden. Agnes snugged the noose against his neck, spit in his face, and backed the mare away. Dick let loose a *hi-i-yaaa*, and Jupiter jumped and whinnied and ran. Bigelow dropped and kicked and finally hung still.

They watched him dangle there. They had broken past society's ultimate law: Thou shalt not kill. But thanks to men like Bigelow, there wasn't much society left, anyway.

40

December 1863

Billy stood at Sam's graveside and watched with dull eyes as gravediggers shoveled frosty dirt onto his father's coffin. Clods landed with a steady *thump, thump* that reminded him of distant guns in battle. Lucky winter arrived late—in spite of last week's blizzard, the blizzard that killed his pa, the ground wasn't yet frozen so solid it couldn't be dug. Sometimes in Missouri winters, Holt County's single mortician stored up a dozen bodies in an unheated shed, waiting for the spring thaw.

Dusk had settled in, early dusk thanks to the heavy cloud cover and because it was two days before Christmas, the darkest days of the year. A dampness touched his cheek, snow starting up again, another heavy storm from the looks of the ugly sky to the west. The rest of the family had returned to Nancy's house, Rachel leaning on Sarah's arm, looking so much older than when he'd seen her last. He wanted Julia, but she'd stayed in Forest City with the baby, sick with a cough. No one left in the cemetery but Agnes.

Billy resettled his hat on his head, tugging it down so the wet didn't get in his eyes. She stood next to a young fir tree, the one shading the graves of her children and Eliza Robinson, but she wasn't looking at those graves, she was watching him. Good old Agnes. Always there for him, as long as he could remember. Teaching him things. Listening to his dreams. Those rambling conversations they had on the flatboat, long lazy days on the river. *There's a good time coming, boys.* A snatch of song one of his men used to sing. *Good time coming.* The good time came and went, and then there'd been these last two years.

He leaned over, scooped up a handful of dark crackly earth and dropped it into the half-filled grave. "So long, Pa," he said aloud. "Sleep well." He turned away.

Agnes walked to meet him, and he pulled her into his arms and held on. He'd forgotten how tall she was, almost eye-to-eye with him. It was a clumsy hug, through her thick cloak and his greatcoat. He still wore his Union blue, hadn't yet sorted out civilian clothes. Still looked the soldier.

"Can't believe he's gone," he said. He released her and stepped back. She slipped her hand into the crook of his elbow, and they wandered up the slope toward the path.

"Were you right with him then?" she asked.

"Don't know. I wonder if you ever know, especially when it happens fast like that."

"He was proud of you, Billy. Proud of what you were doing."

"Well, things were simple for him, weren't they? Black and white. Right was right and wrong was wrong." Billy stopped and looked out over the town, spread at the foot of Cemetery Hill. "It's not like that in this war, that's for damn sure."

"You're going back?"

"No. No, I'm not. I resigned my commission, turned over my men to Joe Roecker. What's left of them. You know, it's strange, Pa dying a natural death. Men're dying all over the place, young men, men who should have lived long lives. Gunshot and saber wounds and disease. Then here's pa keels over with a heart attack, just like he's supposed to. Trying to get to the barn in a snowstorm." He pulled off his hat, ran his forearm over his face, jammed the hat back on his head. "A natural death for once." The corner of his mouth raised in a one-sided smile.

"We've had so much death. Even here, in town. First them"—she motioned to the two tiny graves beneath the hemlock—"then John. Now Sam. And all the boys from town who've died fighting."

"The Bigelows," he said.

"The Bigelows," she agreed. "That's a tragedy too. I always liked Jake, thought I might make something of him."

They reached the gate, and Billy held it for her. "If anyone could, Agnes, you could. You sure made something of me."

She didn't answer. In silence, they negotiated the downward path, fast becoming slippery.

"What does Nancy hear from James?" he asked.

"Nothing since before Thanksgiving. Last we knew he was with Sherman in Tennessee."

"I hated to see him go into the regular army. Wanted him to stay close to home."

"We're breaking up," Agnes said. "The family that came out on the flatboat." The snow fell heavier now, thick and white, and the town dimmed around them in a soft swirling fog.

"We are. Guess it just happens. Everyone making their own families."

"Speaking of that." Agnes turned her face to him with a smile that held in it a deep and quiet happiness. "We'll be adding to our family next summer."

Billy stopped dead in the middle of the street. "A baby? Agnes, that's amazing news!"

She laughed. "It is amazing, given my age, but it's true. I haven't yet told your mother. Only Jabez, of course. And Elizabeth." Billy pulled her arm tighter into his, hugged her to him, started off again.

"No one deserves it more. I don't always agree with your husband, but I admire him. You need a family. Does this mean you'll be staying in Missouri?"

She hesitated. "No," she said. "No, we won't. We'd hoped to go west this coming spring, but Jabez won't hear of it until the baby's come and is old enough to travel."

"God willing this war will be long over by then."

"Who knows, but in any event, we'll go."

"Do you want to? Go west, I mean? The way we used to talk about?" He tipped his head to peer beneath her bonnet.

She turned her face to the sky while the flakes settled thick on her lashes. "I do. You know I've always wanted to see what's out there, go exploring. I'll miss you all, you and Elizabeth especially. Miss seeing your children grow up. But the land is settling fast and soon there will be a railroad and who knows? Maybe you can visit." She laughed. "Not that I know right now just where you might be visiting. I still have very little idea where we'll be."

"Idaho, I thought."

"Wherever the gold strikes are. My husband never did get that gold fever out of his blood, ever since California."

"He's a restless man."

"One of the reasons I love him." They opened the gate to Nancy's front yard, where the snow already coated bare branches and dead winter grass.

"In the midst of all this death...." He looked at Agnes and smiled. "A baby."

41

Summer 1864

Jabez's restlessness grew throughout the spring and early summer of 1864, while Agnes simply grew. Her waist disappeared, her ankles swelled, her hair thinned, and sleep was a nightmare of discomfort. Her temper shortened accordingly.

"This is no longer home to you, is it?" she said one evening. "You can't wait to leave Missouri." The temperature registered over ninety degrees, the hottest July in memory, and the air dripped with the sticky humidity only Missouri can produce. A single lamp burned—any more seemed to raise the heat level unbearably—and as a consequence of the darkness both her hands and her mind idled. She rocked and fanned, fanned and rocked and fumed.

"Hmm?" Jabez said. He hunched beneath the lamp with maps and reports and news articles spread about him.

"What have you decided tonight? Texas? California? Oregon?"

He looked up, amusement flitting across his face. "Montana. Just like we've talked about."

"I thought it was Idaho."

"Montana, now. Virginia City's the capital." He watched her a moment, then stood, went to the sink and pumped water into a basin.

"Wonder if it's cool there."

"I imagine it's cooler than it is here." He knelt in front of her and unbuttoned her shoes, slipped them off, then her stockings. "Think of this, Agnes. Mountains as high as you can see. Snow on them year around." He dunked a cloth in the basin, gently swabbed her foot. "A clear river rushing over rocks, not sluggish and brown like here."

She closed her eyes and twitched her toes. The water, cool from the well, soothed like sweet music.

"I talked to some folks in St. Joe," he said. "Couple men come back to retrieve their families." He often talked to folks in St. Joe. More and more, Agnes caught the look in his eye, the excitement in his voice, glimpses of the young man who had long ago shipped for California, wandered the southwest, explored the gold fields.

He dunked her other foot in the basin, and her temper ebbed. "It does sound nice."

"It'll be rough. A cabin at first, nothing so grand as this." She opened an eye and raised a brow. "But then there'll be wildflowers and antelope. Grasslands for cattle. Like Missouri used to be."

"Before the war. Before all the blood."

"Yes," he said. "Before the war."

"When?"

"In the spring, soon as the snow clears. Once the baby's healthy."

"Rose and Dick want to go."

He looked up. "Do they?"

"Talk to Dick. Rose says he wants a business of his own and his own homestead. They seem to think color's not such a burden out west."

"That would be useful, having them along on the trip. Dick's a good hand with just about everything."

"And Rose can help with the baby." She snapped the fan closed, dropped an arm across her belly. "There's a lot to do," she sighed. "So much to do."

So they made their plans for the spring, but they hadn't counted on the war. Once again the fighting intruded, and their plans changed.

The baby arrived on the twenty-fifth of July, robust and alert and full of demanding cries. They named him Harrie Lee after the Revolutionary War hero, father of the Confederate general. Agnes admired the father greatly, and Jabez admired the son. Harrie ate well from the beginning, and Agnes soon started him on corn-meal mush and mashed tinned peaches. By the middle of August, when she took him to Peter McIntosh's store to be weighed, he'd plumped up to nearly twelve pounds.

For a time that summer, the war seemed far away, and weeks passed soft, dreamy, and quiet. She suffered little from childbirth and managed the lighter housework, weeding and culling the kitchen garden, cleaning the lamps, baking. Rose cheerfully laundered on her own, a challenging task with the baby's cloths and linens, but Agnes ironed and sewed as much as the child would allow. It was a peaceful time, an interlude, and the Robinson family was self-absorbed, giving little heed to the tensions and mistrust around them.

Then the rumors began that Sterling Price, still leading a band of ragged Southern fighters, planned a raid into Missouri, surely a hopeless, fool-hardy bid born of despair. The south had lost the war, and even if it drifted on in blood and destruction for months or years yet, Missouri was already a conquered land. But the Unionists left nothing to chance, and when Price's army invaded from Arkansas, their old acquaintance Captain Peabody rode out of St. Joseph, placing southern sympathizers and those suspected of secessionist views under house arrest. They heard his troops ride into Lick Creek late one night at the end of August, and when they woke the next morning, a sentry stood posted outside their door, another at the entrance to Ross's saloon, a third at Galen Crow's house. Since Crow marched with General Price's army, Agnes couldn't fathom what might be the purpose of standing guard over his household.

Jabez was forbidden to visit his patients, and he prowled about the house snarling at no one in particular for the best part of the day. Agnes worried he might seize the sentry by the throat and thereby cause no end of problems, but he checked his anger, though he demanded and received an audience with Peabody. That discussion appeared to serve no purpose except to rile them both and ended with the captain threatening to haul Jabez off to prison and a trial for treason. But the following morning the troops withdrew, and no one knew why they'd pulled out, or why they'd intruded in the first place. The incident emphasized once again the senseless aberration of an insane war and served to disrupt the small interlude of peace they had manufactured.

The episode also convinced Jabez to leave Lick Creek sooner rather than later.

"You and Harrie will never be safe as long as I'm here," he said. It was the morning the sentries had disappeared, and he pocketed his watch and buttoned his waistcoat in preparation for his medical rounds.

Agnes stopped in the midst of clearing the breakfast dishes, set down the coffee pot, and sank into her chair. "What exactly does that mean?" She distrusted the look in his eye.

"It means I need to leave for Montana right away. Before the weather turns bad and closes the road." He reached for his coat and shrugged into it. "The boy's too young for such a trip. I can't take the two of you now when I have no home for you at the other end and winter coming on. But I have enemies here. They turned me in, and Peabody's made a target of me."

"How will we come to you? Will you come back to get us? It could be months or years...." She stared at her hands, her head buzzing, not quite sure what it all meant. She looked up at him, heart pounding.

He pulled out his chair, sat, took her hands and stroked them. "If I were to go to prison, I would never come back, you know that." One hand lifted, brushed back the tendrils that had escaped her bun. "I'll find a new home for us, scout the situation, get things set up, then when you and Harrie arrive there'll be a place for you to come to." He took her chin in his hand, and kissed her softly on the lips.

"The steamboats don't run this time of year, and the wagon trains have left."

"I'll either take a coach or ride. Jupiter's well up to the trip. Maybe take a pack animal and travel light. Then next spring you and Harrie can get the boat the way we'd planned and bring the luggage."

He looked up. Rose stood in the kitchen, listening. He smiled at her. "Dick and Rose can come along with you. You'll be as safe as if I were with you, and we'll meet up next spring at Fort Benton."

She shook, her mind blank at the thought of a winter's separation and the uncertainties of those long months.

He stood and walked to the window, his back to her. "I don't trust the people here, Agnes, I haven't for months. You know that. Someone named me, and there's no telling when they'll do so again. Billy will protect you and Harrie, but not while I'm here." He turned back to her and smiled that rakish, come-what-may smile that she had loved from the beginning, probably from the moment she'd seen him in the book stall in Cincinnati, certainly from when he'd seized her by the waist and pulled her back from that mule. "So I'll just head off to the gold fields and relieve a few sick and injured prospectors of their poke."

He would, of course. He would doctor them and heal them, and they would pay him well for it, as they had in California, because they valued a skilled medical man above most others in a brand new land. And Agnes and Harrie would wait and worry the winter through without him.

He left three days later, riding Jupiter and leading two good Missouri mules loaded with woolen blankets, changes of clothes, two pairs of sturdy boots, his rubber coat and his heavy coat, the muffler, cap and gloves Agnes had made for him, camping equipment, oats for the animals and food for himself. And his weapons. And of course he took his medical cases and a supply of medicines. He crossed the Missouri River at Forest City, heading for the Platte River road, and Agnes heard nothing of him or from him for two months.

42

October 1864

Jabez stood on a high mountain pass where the Yellowstone River cut through a gap north of the Absaroka Mountain Range. The vista was breathtaking, remote, and primitive. To his right loomed towering sharp peaks, covered in crystalline snow brilliant in the noon sun. To his left, the Big Horn Basin disappeared south into murky blue, patches of pearly gray mist clinging to western slopes betraying a local storm of sleet or snow miles away. He'd spent thirty days on the trail that followed the Big Horn River up the valley, a new road dubbed the Bridger Cutoff after the man who led his party.

He hadn't intended to come that way, hadn't even known about it, when he reached Fort Laramie on the North Platte. The talk there was all about the gold strikes at Last Chance Gulch and the new road John Bozeman had marked out along the east side of the Big Horns, through Sioux hunting territory. It cut four hundred miles off the trip to the mines but that didn't do a man much good if his scalp was hanging on some warrior's lance. On the other hand, Jim Bridger was taking trains up the west side of the Big Horns, well away from Sioux country, but the grades were steep, the forage was sparse, the water bad. Jabez wasn't much interested in tangling with the natives—he shuddered to think what Agnes would say if she knew he'd considered it—and besides, no trains were leaving up the Bozeman road that late in the year. But he did encounter a gentleman by name of Major Owen, returning from the east to his home in the Bitterroot Valley with three freight wagons, who had determined to hook up with Bridger and trail up to the Yellowstone with the old mountain man, building the new road as he went.

So Jabez had joined his party. They left the Red Buttes area in the middle of September and headed up to Muddy Creek, which lived up to its name. The prospect was not auspicious, as there were dead oxen along the way and the grass had been eaten to stubble by the trains that had passed earlier in the summer. But once they entered the Big Horn drainage, the grass improved, the water was sweeter and they made some time; then the No Wood joined the Big Horn and they were into badlands again. Two of the wagons overturned and had to be abandoned. They laid up to grade road, and they spent hours and days hauling wagons up and down impossible slopes, they chased loose oxen, they rationed flour. They crossed the Wind River and the Gray Bull and the Stinking Water, and by the time they reached the Pryor, Jabez and two other men, all traveling on horseback, were impatient with building roads and muscling wagons, so they bid the others Godspeed and headed for the Yellowstone more rapidly.

Now he stood on what felt like the rim of the world. Before him spread a valley, broad and rolling, stretching far to the gleam of sun-lit water where a river wound its way through boggy meadows among wavy lines of cottonwood. The deciduous trees glowed yellow, the firs and pines were a deep green blanket. The prairie was covered in ragged patches of snow from an early storm, but the sun was brilliant and warm now, at noon, and promised melt. He reached into his coat pocket for the darkened spectacles he'd carried from home, and mentally patted himself on the back for remembering to protect his eyes.

His companions had left him two days before to ride ahead, while Jabez rested on the banks of Rock Creek where the Bridger Road met the Bozeman Trail. He was thin, he'd been cold and hungry and thirsty. He missed Agnes and Harrie terribly. Jupiter was scrawny, and the mules were battered and cranky. But as he looked to the mountains, across the valley to the river, up to the immense and searing blue of the sky, an eagle floated lazily on the breeze, and his spirits lifted as they had not for many years. This was what it meant to be alive, every sense alert, every nerve honed. It was what he remembered from his California days, from the months he spent roaming the deserts and high barren mountains of the southwest, what he'd wanted so desperately these last difficult years to know again. He wished Agnes was by his side to see it, to feel it. Soon, he thought. He nudged Jupiter's protruding ribs, yanked on the mules' lead rope, and moved onto the downhill trail.

Bozeman was three months old when Jabez rode in the third week in October of 1864, but it already consisted of a hotel, two general stores, a saloon and a half-dozen cabins. All were log, some even boasted a floor. The biggest had two rooms. The hotel was a substantial story-and-a-half, and Jabez checked in for his first night under a roof in nearly three months. He had a bath and a whiskey and a hot meal of rare beef, potatoes and onions, and Jupiter and the mules had hay in addition to the last of the oats they'd carried halfway across the continent. There were cheap cigars to be had at Fitz's store and Jabez lit up, leaned back against the rough interior of the hotel's common room, and stretched his boots toward the fire. The two men he'd traveled with were dead broke and had gone off to camp on the prairie, and as it turned out he never saw them again, but it was no matter. Companions came and went in that country and rare it was to form lasting friendships, even if you had trusted your life to them just weeks before.

The men who gathered around the fire for conversation and companionship in the early dark of an autumn night appeared to be locals; not many travelers passed through that time of the year. Jabez sat in his corner and watched the townsfolk gather, listened to their talk, recognized the age-old tribal tendency to form hierarchy, to band together in community, to sniff about a stranger with caution. Jabez smiled around his cigar, the outsider looking in, the insiders unaware of how predictable they were.

But he was enjoying himself and enjoying the conversation. Mostly these men sounded reasonable, some of them educated, all of them practical. There was talk of Bozeman the town and Bozeman the man, the latter apparently a local hero, though there were reservations. The man with intense eyes, high forehead, soft Georgian drawl, was a supporter and promoter of both man and town; the man named Burtsch was not but kept his comments low key and passive. The innkeeper was young, clean shaven and jittery, kept glasses filled and tapped his foot restlessly any time he chanced to come to a standstill. There was a Mexican named Merraville playing chess with a gnomish fellow with a Scots burr, and a gentle-eyed man with a ready smile, a potato farmer, who engaged him right away in a discussion on ranching in the Gallatin Valley.

That led the conversation around to farming and the opportunities to be made supplying the mining camps with potatoes and vegetables, flour, beef and butter. The winters are hard, the farmer said, the camps isolated when passes filled with snow and the steep grades iced up. Merraville allowed as how flour and forage and fresh vegetables would be scarce and dear well before spring opened up the freighting roads again, and if the Montana Territory were to survive it needed to be self-sufficient.

Jabez spent four days in Bozeman, fattening his animals, learning what he could about the ranching land and homesteading opportunities. He discovered there was a doctor in town who'd bought into one of the general stores and didn't much like the practice of medicine, and that his own skills would be welcomed. As it happened, he was called upon on his second day there to stitch up a gash on the instep of Caleb Fitz's boy. It would be a good place to sink roots, to raise his son, a good place for Agnes. They could learn together how to farm this country, take what they both knew and adjust it to the needs of the virgin prairie, be a part of a new-born community with the chance for a fresh start, and then to grow old here in the shadow of these magnificent mountains.

But first he needed to make some money, so on the fifth day he saddled up a rejuvenated Jupiter, packed his mules and headed for the sick and injured prospectors of Virginia City.

43

1865

November rolled in with its rimy winds before Agnes next heard from
Jabez, a letter mailed from a place called Bozeman, informing her he had
arrived. Then nothing. He haunted the corners of her mind throughout
those long winter nights. She lay in bed, wakeful, the drum of rain against
the window or the eerie wash of starlight reflected from waves of snow
brightening the dark, and wondered whether he slept, if he dreamed of her—
if he still lived. News reports mentioned that winter snows descended thick
on the plains and in the mountains. Mail to and from the mining camps
took months to wend its way along the trails, and she never knew if hers
reached him, but she wrote nevertheless, a letter every week. It comforted
her to tell him how Harrie grew, when he first smiled, rolled over, lifted
his head. When he first hefted himself to hands and knees, made scooting
noises, rocked his little body back and forth, wanting to roam, to explore.

Agnes wrote to him about the big and small happenings in town, how
Billy was building a good business selling horses and mules to the army, that
Doctor Norman's son presented him with a grandchild, that Jonas Watson
died fighting the federals in Tennessee.

She wrote to him at great length about her ideas on Lincoln's reelection,
on the emancipation situation, on the political atmosphere of the county
and what the newspapers said. She didn't describe her fears for him, or the
doubts she struggled with, whether she should take their small child and
embark on a dangerous and lonely journey with the very real prospect that

he wouldn't be waiting for them at the end.

But finally, the third week of a frigid February, a packet arrived from Virginia City with three letters together with a draft on the bank in Kansas City for three hundred dollars. Agnes read and re-read those letters until the paper wore thin at the creases and she'd memorized every word. He told her about the gold mines, and she was reminded of the letters he'd sent Eliza from California so many years ago. He wrote with vigor and excitement and energy, and she imagined his eyes flashing and his quick grin lighting up his face, the vitality in his step and the assurance in the set of his shoulders. The country captivated him, the variety of humanity fascinated him, and he thrilled at the thought of birthing a new society the way he delivered a new child.

Agnes, he wrote, *you cannot begin to imagine the clarity of the air here, how light and clean it is, the quality of sunlight on rapid rivers, the expanse of prairie and majesty of mountains.* He described feasting on antelope and buffalo, fishing for grayling and trout in wide rivers with deep pools so clear the ripples of sand etched along the beds cast shadows. He mentioned the characters he met, the prospects for a civil community where ideas blended and courteous discourse ruled. He referred to the stories of road agents and vigilante justice that filled the eastern papers and assured her the territory was now made decent for families and farmers.

He was prosperous. *I demand payment from miners who I know have a sizeable poke before I provide a medical service,* he wrote, *and I have come into a goodly share of the treasure that's being extracted from the gulch.* At the same time, he wrote about a family of parentless children whom he had treated for colds and sore throats and the pouch of gold dust he'd slipped to the eldest.

He filled the longest passages with plans for their family, with his ideas for ranching in the valley of the Gallatin River, raising wheat and vegetables and beef for sale to the mining camps. He sent lists of items to pack—tools and seeds, household goods, clothing and boots and pans for butter-making and milking—but instructed her not to bring furniture, as the freightage cost more than its worth. He mentioned several ladies in Virginia City had carried sewing machines across the plains and since they proved to be practical, suggested she buy one.

She bought the sewing machine, a Wheeler and Wilson for which she paid sixty dollars, as well as a new butter churn and a plow, disassembled and crated. She gathered barrels of nails and hand tools, a trunk filled with bolts of calico and muslin and wool. She packed her clothes and Harrie's and the things Jabez left behind, lamps with extra chimneys, paper, pens, pencils, ink. Their precious books, and the contents of his surgery. She made up a box of kitchen utensils, pots and pans and kettles, tucked her precious china in barrels of sawdust and rolled up the parlor rug and wrapped it in canvas.

She packed Harrie's clothes and his few toys and worried about how she would keep him safe on the long journey. She was haunted by visions of his tumbling off the deck of the boat or falling from a moving stage or being snatched by the Natives that she'd heard collected at way stations for handouts. But Rose, ever calm, assured her they would both be on guard. "That boy come to no harm, Missus, I promise that," she said, and Agnes was comforted.

She sold Juno, Nelly, and the buggy to Billy, along with the house, which he wanted for Rachel. What she didn't sell, she gave away, and by the first week in March they were ready to leave.

The twelfth of March, eighteen hundred and sixty-five, was Agnes's last evening in Lick Creek. Elizabeth and Billy left her at dusk at the foot of the trail into the cemetery. She wanted to be alone for this last ceremony. She watched them disappear around the corner in the direction of Nancy's house, heads inclined toward one another in conversation. The three were brother and sisters, bonded much closer than mere cousins, and her heart wrenched to see them off.

She climbed the hill, her cloak wrapped against the March chill, and settled on the ground next to Eliza's grave, where her monument stood watch over Agnes's children. She pulled from her pocket a letter she had received from Jabez's father, William, still alive and lonely in Maine, and read aloud. Her voice was quiet, and it seemed even the wind paused its rustling through the trees to listen.

I hope you will do me the kindness to follow up our correspondence as long as I live, for Jabez is so much engrossed in business that he has not written to me near as often as I think he ought to—

The old fellow must be nearing eighty. At last count, he'd lost seven children. I've lost two, she thought, and wondered if the pain multiplies with each new death.

He is the only son I have left that I ever expect to hear from. I was much surprised to learn by your letter that Jabez had gone into that country with the intention of settling there where he can promise himself nor his family anything but the roughest kind of a rough life the remainder of his days, and I do hope and pray for his sake and yours, if he lives to return, that he will forever abandon the thought. We are all born to suffer as well as to enjoy, but there is no fatal necessity of our running into trouble with our eyes wide open, and as for escaping trouble by shifting our situation, it is vain, and for you and him to move into that country will be to deprive you both of what little comfort is to be enjoyed in this life.

"Father William," she said to Eliza. "I've never met him, did you? He's probably an ornery old soul, maybe a complainer, but I think I'd like him."

… if Jabez returns, please say to him that I think he owes me one more visit since it has pleased God to spare my life to such an advanced age, and I shall look for it.

"How I wish we might oblige him. But here we are, running into trouble with our eyes wide open. I leave you behind, Eliza, to watch over them for me. Charlie and Sarah Belle. I leave Jabez's children in your care."

44

They took passage at St. Joseph aboard the *Deer Lodge* on the fourteenth of March, a gloomy day, the wind sharp out of the northeast. Leafless branches overhung the river, a skim of ice nestled in the shadows along the banks. Agnes watched Dick supervise the stowing of their freight on the lower deck, and she struggled with memories of her trip up the Missouri many years before, with their children and chickens, their baggage and their dreams.

Now the same river would carry her on the next leg of her journey, and as the sleek sternwheeler swung into the middle of the river and left St. Joseph behind, the throb of the engines matched the throb of the blood in her veins. When they passed Forest City later that afternoon and bid good-bye to Holt County, she had no regrets.

They stopped in Omaha and Yankton for supplies and struck the first sand bar just above Randall where they stalled for a full day and a half. The captain tried sparring off, a strange operation in which poles are pushed into the river bed and the boat is expected to leap ahead like a one-legged man on crutches, but the project failed, and they simply waited for the river to rise. Which it did, thankfully, when the next evening's rainfall set the boat afloat once again. The captain informed her that it promised to be an unusually low-water year for the river, and he cheerfully advised her to expect the trip to last an extra month while they negotiated sandbars and the ever-changing channel, dodged snags usually lodged well below the surface, cordelled over rapids normally drowned.

Agnes submerged her impatience and tried to keep busy. Each day, she and Rose settled themselves in the passageway outside Agnes's stateroom, sewing or reading. Harrie was crawling now, and managed to move with a rapidity that kept one or the other of the women on her feet whenever he was awake. Thank goodness he was not yet walking; what a nightmare that would be. When he slept, which he still did twice a day—he grew so fast he was worn out with it—they simply watched the strange and lovely world pass by. The shoreline daily presented new and varied landforms, fluctuating hues of cliff and vegetation, washed by the light and shades of sunrise and dusk, glowing in gray and mauve. Soon antelope, then buffalo, appeared on the riverside plains, and the men expended vast amounts of ammunition vying for trophies which were butchered and served for dinner. She enjoyed antelope, to her taste somewhat sweeter than venison, but buffalo was truly excellent, less fatty than beef. By the time they steamed into the upper stretches of the river, they relished any fresh meat the hunters brought in.

As March turned to April, they grounded again. And again. The wind often sent the boat scurrying into the lea of the bank, and thunderstorms crackled overhead, violent torrents of rain sweeping across the plains.

Then April faded into May, and they arrived at the farthest northern point. They followed the river as it swung west, leaving the Dakotas and entering the newly minted Montana territory, and she began to count the days. At a hundred miles below Fort Benton, a three-day journey when the river flowed well, they stuck fast on the monstrous Dophan Rapids. After a full forty-eight frustrating hours, they winched over only to repeat the operation at Drowned Man's Rapids twenty miles farther up. The three days stretched to eight and then to eleven, when they turned a bend and Agnes saw ahead a haze of smoke against a ridge of treeless hills. A cluster of buildings squatted along the wide plain of the river's bank, and the white adobe walls of the fort shone in the bright sun of a cloudless day. They had arrived. It was May 30, 1865, and they had been seventy-eight days on the river.

"I don't see him," Agnes said to Rose who stood next to her at the upper deck rail, a wide-eyed Harrie in her arms. She searched the crowds, listened to the babble, the shouts, the bawls of oxen, bark of dogs, crash of crates being unloaded. She'd dressed so carefully in her pearl gray poplin traveling suit and a never-worn straw bonnet. But Jabez wasn't there.

"Keep looking, Missus," Rose said. Her eyes flitted over the throng. "So many people!" Buckskin predominated, along with blanketed Indians and uniformed soldiers. Agnes spotted an assortment of women whose tricked-out gowns suggested their occupation.

Agnes was always and forever aware of his presence, and now she sensed his absence. She bit her lip in disappointment, shook back a treacherous tear, and looked around.

On the south side of the river the bluffs rose abruptly, crenellated on top like a great fortress. The town huddled on a flat bench along the riverbank which rose gradually to the north in folded hills, their contours soft and golden like the curves of a naked human form. Stores and saloons fronted the levee behind a street inches deep in muck. Massive freight wagons, yoked to a dozen oxen each, were being loaded with merchandise from the newly-arrived ship while the great stolid beasts stood patiently, tails twitching at a horsefly, drool and excrement mashed into the mud beneath their hooves.

Rose shifted Harrie to one arm and grasped Agnes's portmanteau with her free hand. "Let's find Dick, Missus, get out of this bustle." She shouldered her way through the throng on deck, leading the way to the stairs. With one last glance at the crowd, Agnes followed, and they plunged into the chaos on the docks.

They found Dick with ease, but a hotel room proved more difficult. After an hour's search, they settled their luggage in a cramped boarding house off a side street and procured an over-priced meal. Meanwhile, Dick canvassed three general stores, the shipping facilities and two hotels, finally unearthing a letter from Jabez that had arrived several weeks earlier instructing her to take the stage from Fort Benton to Virginia City. "Virginia City is an easy ride from our ranch," he wrote, "and I will have a comfortable home for you and Harrie by the time you arrive." *Our ranch? We have a ranch?* Agnes thought. Jabez had been busy.

Newspapers accompanied the messages, and six weeks late, they learned of the final surrender of the south and the death of President Lincoln by assassin. So jaded and frayed were Agnes's feelings about those long, sorry, sad years, that this ending seemed gruesomely fitting, an indication that in the midst of defeat and anarchy, her countrymen managed to sink still lower.

The next stage for Helena and points south was scheduled to leave the following morning. Agnes slept almost not at all, thanks to Fort Benton's all-night revelry, and they were up and ready long before the horses were harnessed. Leaving Dick behind to accompany the freighted baggage, Rose, Harrie, and Agnes traveled in a large Concord coach, which didn't prove large enough for the ten passengers inside and three on the roof. Gentlemen jostled the ladies for the best seats, and Rose and Agnes drew the center bench, their backs supported by a leather band hanging from the roof. In this uncomfortable manner, and with Harrie in their arms, they swung and swayed and braced themselves for thirty miles, until a stop at a home station for a change of drivers allowed them to snatch the rear seat from two mongers forced to heed the call of nature.

Twenty-five hours later they reached Helena. There they changed coaches, lost a few traveling companions, picked up new ones, ate a warm meal at a real hotel, loaded up and moved on, over the backbone of the continent, across the Jefferson River, along the foothills of the Tobacco Root Mountains, down the valley of the Stinking Water River, and finally arrived at the spectacle that was Virginia City.

"Lord a'mighty!" Rose murmured when they stepped down from the coach. She stared around her at the scene in the street. Virginia City's citizens didn't honor the Sabbath with rest and worship. Every prospector within fifty miles must have descended onto the town. The stores stood open for custom, the smithies banged away at their fiery business, the saloons burst with patrons, the dance halls rang. Hundreds of oxen, horses and mules stirred up the dust of a dry Montana day, all braying and complaining. Chinamen, dark-eyed and silent, slipped in and out of the crowds on the boardwalk. Children of both sexes ran barefoot and begrimed through the streets, chasing dogs, carrying packages, dodging deadly hooves and wheels. Three fancy ladies leaned out the second-floor windows of the Star Billiard Hall, smoking cigars and laughing at a street orator on the corner whom everyone else ignored. Agnes and Rose stood on a rough plank walk in front of the Oliver and Conover stage facility, their valises at their feet, the circus flowing around them.

Rose touched Agnes's arm, nodded her head up the street and smiled her soft, amused smile. "Look there, Missus," she said, and lifted Harrie from his mother's arms.

There he stood, arms crossed over his chest, leaning against a porch post and grinning.

Jabez—brushed coat, clean starched white shirt, dove-gray waistcoat, shined boots, freshly trimmed hair and beard. White teeth flashed in that wicked grin, his eyes danced, and Agnes's first thought was horror at how she looked. After forty-eight hours on the road, her fresh gray poplin had wilted, her new hat was jammed into her valise. Sweat marks stained her jacket, her hair tumbled loose from its pins, and the faint scent of Harrie's soiled cloths clung about her. But she cared not a lick. She picked up her skirts, ran the length of the block, and threw herself into his arms.

He buried his head in her neck, lifted her off her feet, spun her in a full circle and laughed.

"You're a sight for these old eyes, Agnes, my love," he said in a booming voice that caused a dozen people to stop and stare, and he kissed her squarely, a kiss which brought hoots from onlookers. She clutched him and smiled, attempted to control the tears, and then pulled him toward their son.

"He's grown so much, Jabez, you'll not know him. He's strong and healthy and he hated being confined in the coach; he's like you, always on the move." She babbled on and on, as Jabez lifted his son from Rose.

Harrie wrinkled his brow and pursed his lips like a Baptist minister and studied this big, strange man who held him high. Jabez laughed and swung the boy onto his shoulders, and Harrie sunk both fists into his father's hair and drummed tiny heels against his chest.

"Have you laundered your shirt every day?" she asked. "So you would be fresh and clean and upstage us?"

"You're always a beauty in my eyes." He held onto Harrie with one big hand, grabbed her valise in the other. "Rose, how are you, girl? How's your reading coming?"

"Fine, Mr. Robinson, just fine. We practiced on the boat." Rose picked up her own valise and Harrie's bag and followed Jabez.

"I have us rooms at the Fairweather, ladies, and there'll be a good meal waiting. Harrie here'll have to bunk in with Rose, Agnes. I want you to myself."

She linked her hand through his elbow and felt her ears grow hot. "Don't be crude in public."

He laughed again and leaned over to kiss the top of her head. "Where'd you leave Dick?"

"At Fort Benton. He was loading the baggage. They planned to leave the day after we did."

"So he should be here tomorrow or the next day. We'll need to wait for him. Did he get a cast-iron stove? There was supposed to be a shipment on your boat."

"Are there no stoves out here to buy? What do you cook on?"

"Most folks use a camp stove, or the open fireplace."

"Is it that wild out here? There're not even stoves?"

"You'll find there are many things we do without, Agnes, or we pay dear for them. But we're booming and where there's people, someone figures out how to sell them things. Now that the snow's out of the passes, there'll be freighters from Salt Lake coming through. We just need the cash to take advantage."

"And do we have cash?"

"We have enough to get us started, and wait until you see the ranch—good grassland, good water, cows can fatten and wheat will grow like you've never seen it."

"Is it ... is there a house?" She flashed back to Rachel's apprehension, when first they arrived in Holt County. She hoped for ... she knew not quite what she hoped for, but she wanted a solid roof over her head. As long as they weren't consigned to a canvas tent, she was determined to accept whatever came.

"There's a house." He looked at her sideways. "It won't be quite what you've been used to, love, but it's warm. Keeps the rain off. Not quite finished yet." He studied a display of wilted vegetables in front of a store, didn't meet her eyes.

Inside she sighed. Outside she squeezed his arm and said she'd be delighted with any place he made for her. He lit up at that and ushered them into the hotel.

They stayed for two days, and Virginia City fascinated her the way the insane of Bedlam, put on public view for the entertainment of the upper classes, must have fascinated their visitors. Compared with the tiny boat cabin, the hotel accommodations were luxurious. Carpets covered the floor and lace curtains hung at the windows, and though they slept on bare ticking because she neglected to pack linens in her small trunk, she felt like they honeymooned again, so pleasing it was to be together. She bathed and soaped her hair thoroughly for the first time in weeks and sent their clothes to a laundress who washed out the Missouri River muck.

Jabez had bought a farm wagon and driven the mules to Virginia City, Jupiter trailing behind, and they shopped for tools and household items newly arrived from Salt Lake or Fort Benton. The prices were outrageous, and the cost of stabling the animals, lodging at the hotel, and eating in restaurants and the better saloons disturbed her. But he answered two medical calls—one an arm crushed when a sluice collapsed, the other a gunshot wound to the foot when a drunken freighter attempted to demonstrate his shooting skills to the crowd at Madame Dumont's saloon—and earned enough gold dust to defray the costs. Gold dust and nuggets acted as currency, greenbacks were roundly scorned, and Jabez carried with him a small set of gold scales to weigh what he took in and what he paid out.

They bought lamp oil and molasses and salt, flour and sugar and coffee beans. And then they added whitewash and water buckets and a used adz and saltpeter and saleratus and a cake of precious yeast from the brewery. They searched for furniture but found none, no chairs or tables or bureaus. Jabez added an open crate with six hens and a raucous rooster. When Dick arrived with the baggage, he and Jabez loaded trunks and barrels and boxes, an iron cook stove and Agnes's precious new sewing machine onto the wagon, and they left Virginia City for home.

45

They traveled along the Madison River where it coursed lazily through open country, winding however its fancy took it, braiding and channeling, cottonwoods thick along its banks. The road melted into soft yellow hills, rounded in sweeping curves, from a distance appearing soft to the touch, a sprinkle of pines in their creases. Shadows floated over their flanks as feathery clouds danced across the face of the sun. They made thirty miles the first day and crossed the river at Blacks Ford where sturdy gravel bars formed a half dozen riffling streams. They camped on a wide bench of pebbled land where the high mountains gave way to squared bluffs, which in turn yielded to low broad grasslands, and ate trout from the stream and biscuits baked in a dutch oven buried in coals. They slept, exhausted, as the light faded and stars winked into sight far above.

Agnes awoke to drizzle. Jabez stirred in their bedroll, rolled over, stood, as she curled around Harrie's little body, the warmth trapped between them alluring. But Jabez had let in a draft. Half asleep, she scowled and grunted.

"Agnes," he said, "get up. Let's get you two under the wagon."

She poked her head above the blanket. Damp coated her face and hair, a trickle slid down into her shift. "Where did this come from? It was clear when we went to sleep."

"Weather changes fast out here. It may just be a drizzle or we may be in for a real storm." He squatted, lifted Harrie, tucked him against his shirt front and bent over to keep the rain off.

Agnes sniffled. Her nose was full, and her eyes ached. Their campsite wore that bleak look and feel of too-early morning when fog and damp and hopelessness permeate everything they touch. She felt the looming hills, heard the aloof flow of the creek.

She remade their bed under the wagon and slipped in, reaching for Harrie. A rock jabbed into her hip, the underside of the wagon was filthy with mud and dust. She rolled onto her side, folded around her son, sniffled. Sneezed.

Rose soon joined them under the wagon, while Dick and Jabez rekindled the fire. Agnes hung between sleep and waking for perhaps an hour, then sighed, tucked the blankets tightly around Harrie and scooted out. Coffee boiled as the rain spit into the flames. Rose was up soon after, and they ate cold biscuit and bacon, cleaned up and packed.

They left the Madison and followed a no-name creek across the grasslands toward the sunrise, which consisted of a slight lightening of the gray. The rain continued throughout the day, and Agnes's head grew stuffier, her mood more disagreeable with every mile. She and Rose huddled in hooded cloaks while Harrie alternately howled and fidgeted. Water dripped from the brims of the men's hats, and the trail disappeared in sodden grass and mud. Clouds obscured everything, but Agnes could hear the swollen stream rushing nearby and sensed vast spaces stretching away all around her.

By noon they'd traveled but fifteen miles, with another twenty to go. Once again they ate cold biscuits, cold bacon and a handful of precious dried apples while the mules rested. Judging from the hollowness in their stomachs, it was dinnertime when they reached the Gallatin River and Shed's Bridge, and she thanked the stars they needn't wade the crossing. The bridge appeared new and untried, but they chanced it and turned south. Three miles yet.

Jabez mounted Jupiter, reached down his hand to Agnes. "Give Harrie to Rose," he said. "We'll ride ahead and see our home, just the two of us." He smiled through the beating rain, and she swung up behind him, tucked her arms around his waist, and buried her face in his jacket to keep the rain off.

She dozed much of the way and missed what there was to see of the scenery along the river, which she later prized as the most beautiful she'd ever seen. At the time, though, she found nothing lovely. Her nose dribbled, and she sneezed again. An early dusk had descended by the time Jabez reined in and turned in his saddle.

"I thought you'd up and died on me, so still you've been." He put an arm around her. "Except for the sneezes. We're here, love."

She raised her head and stared with bleary eyes. They stood on a gentle slope a hundred yards above the river. Fading in and out of the mist on all sides spread grasslands, the vegetation shank-high on Jupiter. A shed of squared and chinked logs hunkered along the top of the slope, two rough-cut, empty openings piercing its wall, the roof bristling with sod. Beyond, the shadowy bulk of a larger structure loomed out of the murk, but half completed as far as she could tell, with no roof at all.

"Is that the house over there?" she asked, waving at the bigger building.

"That's the barn."

"Then where's the house?"

"This is it."

"This is it."

"Yes."

He swung out of the saddle and lifted her down, his eyes anxious. She stumbled forward and pulled aside the canvas flap that served as a door. The fading light intensified the gloom of the interior. She looked down. The floor was hard-packed dirt, and puddles gathered where steady drips plunked into depressions. She looked up. Roots and dirt hung from the ceiling, forming the uncovered underside of the sod roof. She looked to her left. A bedstead of rough cut logs with planed boards across rope, on which tumbled Jabez's damp quilt, sagged against the wall. She looked right. A small sheet metal camp stove, a wooden crate half-filled with wood and kindling, an array of battered cook pots hanging from hooks on the wall, a table tilted unevenly beneath them. A round of stump served as a stool.

She wandered inside. The cabin stretched nearly twenty feet in one direction, seventeen or eighteen in the other. She hadn't expected much, certainly not the clapboard home with parlor and washroom they'd owned in Lick Creek. *It isn't a tent*, she said to herself, *it isn't a tent*. This will do nicely. She sniffed, sneezed, blew her nose on a sodden hankie, sank onto the edge of the bed. Something scurried below her, tiny feet scrabbling against the hard earth below the bed, and she started. *I will not cry, I will not cry.* She pressed her fingers into her eyes, swallowed hard, bent over to hide her face in her lap and sobbed.

Jabez knelt on the muddy floor in front of her and slid his arms around her waist. He said nothing, rocking her like a child, stroking her hair, until the sobs abated into an occasional hiccup.

"I'm sorry, Agnes," he whispered. "I would have had it ready but the weather was so good, and I needed to get the spring wheat in. And the garden—we got in the peas and onions and turnips already. There were men here to help me, and I needed them on the barn more than on the house. I can do the house myself."

She nodded, scrubbed a fist over her eyes. He'd accomplished so much already.

"It's the rain makes it worse. We've got the window glass now and canvas for the ceiling. I'll fix the leaks and set up the new stove." His voice dwindled.

She lifted her head with a shaky smile. "I think I'm done now." She cupped his face in her hands and kissed him. "Just need a good night's sleep. We'll make it lovely," she whispered. "As soon as it stops raining."

He laughed, willing to think all was fine, squeezed her tight, and jumped to his feet.

"I'll build us a fire in the stove," Agnes said with a gulp and stood. "While you put up Jupiter. We'll give Dick and Rose and Harrie a warm welcome." She rubbed her hands up and down her arms. He kissed her and disappeared into the drizzle and she choked back another sob and set to work.

Agnes's spirits hadn't recovered by the next morning, though she dissembled as best she could. Her head continued stuffy, and her nose was red as a raspberry. She feared to pass the catarrh to Harrie, so Rose took charge of him while Jabez plied her with a tea he concocted from a large fuzzy white-flowered plant growing along the river. The rain abated, but a heavy overcast persisted, along with a chill wind that obstinately refused to dry the bedding. The mist obscured the world beyond the barn, and the bank of cottonwoods loomed hazy along the river.

Jabez arose before dawn and emptied the cabin—nearly moving the bed out the door with Agnes still in it—stripped the roof, draped canvas over the rafters and replaced the sod before lunch. It was a filthy task, and Agnes spent a grimy hour raking mud and vermin from the earth floor. Jabez tacked a tow cloth to the south wall of the barn and painted it with a paste made from rye. With several paintings and a month or two to dry, they'd have a decent oilcloth for the floor, but Agnes hoped that by then they'd find planed boards somewhere since a dirt floor in winter seemed both unhealthful and unwise. For now, she unrolled her lovely dark blue parlor carpet, and though it covered less than half the floor, it provided some warmth and introduced a touch of homeliness.

The third day, Agnes rose with the dawn, a sunbeam glancing through the newly cut and glazed east window. A fresh breeze had chased the clouds, and the world sparkled blue and yellow and green, filled with birdsong and earth scents and the sound of the river dancing over gravel bars.

She stepped from the west-facing cabin door and drank it in, grinned a silly grin, raised her arms and laughed and spun, then stopped in her tracks. The mountains were there—*right there!*—so close she believed she might reach out her hand and touch them. They had lurked there all along, hidden by the fog, silently waiting to be discovered. Though the foot hills started at least twenty miles away, they appeared in the crystal air to hover just over the cabin, rugged and substantial, swathes of dark forest on the lower slopes, patches of white higher up. They seemed to smile at her, sharing in the joke. "We've been waiting for you to find us," they seemed to say. She'd glimpsed mountains from the boat and the stagecoach, but never before had she felt so close, seen anything so massive. She turned to the south. More snow-topped peaks, hazy and distant. To the west, far-off peaks behind dry hills, the hills they'd crossed journeying from Virginia City. To the north rolled gentle yellow-brown highlands, soft and comfortable. The broad rich valley stretched from the toes of one range to the toes of the next. Agnes felt protected from the wildness beyond, nourished by the possibilities within, and from that moment, the joyful sense of belonging awoke and welled up deep inside her. She was at peace. She was home.

Within two days, the heavy strip of canvas that served as a door was replaced by a solid panel of planed boards fetched from the new Springhill sawmill north of Bozeman. The cast-iron stove dominated the south wall, its blacking a-gleam, its water reservoir full. Dick repaired the wobbly table and tacked together benches of split logs. They stowed trunks and crates around the edges of the room for storage and small tables, and the sewing machine dominated its own corner. "Curtains," Agnes thought, "the yellow print calico will brighten this room considerably." She stood with hands on hips surveying her little home and felt a rush of pleasure.

46

Agnes loved watching the wheat ripen. There were acres of it east of the barn, the acres that Jabez and two hired men plowed and planted back in the spring before she arrived. That Jabez could coax such bounty from the raw grasslands was an ongoing wonder to her; there was nothing, she concluded, that he could not do. They lost some to pesky grasshoppers; some of it shriveled with thirst. But by late August they had a respectable crop, and Jabez hired in men to cut and stook, thresh and sack, and haul it to the mill.

About that time, Rose and Dick struck out on their own. Dick filed claim to a town lot south of Bozeman, on the Sourdough Creek. He and Rose lived in a tent while he built his cabin of cottonwood logs, the first black couple in the valley, though several Negro men had settled around Bozeman. Rose took in washing, and she agreed to take the Robinsons', saving Agnes the labor of two full days. That arrangement occasioned a weekly trip to Bozeman, an excursion both Agnes and Jabez anticipated with pleasure. There she met several of the ladies of the area—there were not many—and he talked territorial politics with the men. Always politics. Agnes feared they would never put it behind them.

By that time, too, she had beans and cucumbers and onions ripening in the kitchen garden, melons and squash and potatoes coming along, peas dried in sacks stacked waist high in the barn. She loved digging in the rich river loam with Harrie toddling at her side, daydreaming. In her head she designed a home, a ranch house with parlor and kitchen and a study for Jabez and a separate room for Harrie and books, lots of books.

In the evening when supper dishes were cleared away, Agnes and Harrie would perch on a bench outside the door while Jabez read aloud by the fading light of the summer's evening from last week's newspaper or his favorite Whitman, or a new book borrowed from someone in town. As the song of peepers and the trill and clicks of the barn swallows closed down the day, Agnes's mind filled with the pictures Jabez's words painted.

Jabez seemed to have endless energy: he rose with the dawn, spent the days in the fields cultivating and harvesting and digging ditches, feeding the stock, cutting sod or finishing a shed or mending harness or sharpening blades. He found time to visit the next ranch to debate farming methods, to answer the call of an ailing or injured neighbor, and of course to spend his Saturday afternoons in Bozeman talking politics and weather and the merits of a local Masonic chapter. It was as if he were making up for the way time and forward movement had stopped for four years, when the war sucked the energy and vigor out of a body. There were weevils in the cabbage and deer in the lettuce, frost blackened the tomato starts, and mice fouled a hundred-weight of peas. But the sky was an endless blue, the showery rains were gentle and the breezes light. Life was good and both Agnes and Jabez were content.

"You'd think you were thirteen years old," Agnes said, dabbing a gooey mix of egg yolk, witch hazel, and arnica on the vicious bruise below Jabez's left eye.

Autumn had moved in, and Jabez's plans had expanded with the chill in the air, until one day in early October he came home with another hundred and sixty acres, a seat in the legislature, and a black eye.

Jabez flinched. "Stings like the devil," he said.

"Serves you right, scrapping like a boy with the neighbors." She inspected his scraped knuckles. Harrie crouched nearby, eyes big. He hadn't seen his papa hurt before.

"At the risk of sounding peevish, they started it."

"So you bought Richard Miller's claim, but Mr. Foster says he's claimed it for himself?"

Jabez touched a tentative finger to the swelling on his lower lip. "Foster won't believe a black man has the right to claim land, says the law doesn't recognize Miller's claim. So it follows that Miller can't sell his claim to me." He reached out a hand to Harrie, who scrambled onto his lap.

"But there are lots of Negroes with claims out here. Dick for one." Agnes stood back and studied her doctoring, leaned in to dab ointment on a cut at his hairline. "And why is Miller selling? What did you pay? How can you buy a claim that isn't proved up yet?"

Jabez stood, set Harrie on the table, examined a long tear down the front of his shirt. It would need to be repaired. They didn't have the shirt goods to make a new one.

"I paid a hundred dollars gold for the claim and the improvements he has on it. He's decided to take off to Confederate Gulch and try his luck there. Luke Donan's planning to lease the east section from me. Only makes sense he and I take it since it lies between our claims." He poured a cup of coffee from the pot that always simmered on the back of the stove. "Bob Foster's got no call to thinking he can steal it off Miller or me." The back of his neck flushed.

"Did you register the claim in Gallatin City?"

"I ran into Miller while I was there seeing about the election and when he offered to sell, we hunted up Campbell and transferred the deed right away."

"So you don't have anything to worry about. It's all legal, and Mr. Foster has no claim." Harrie's kitten jumped onto the table next to the boy. Agnes lifted both of them off.

"He doesn't see it that way. He was out on the property with the Emerson boy when Luke and I rode in to look it over. Had the gall to order us off."

"So you threw a punch."

"No, he did." Jabez gave her a pained look. "You know I don't start things."

"I know your temper. Why didn't you just go for the sheriff?"

"He and the boy were busy loading up lumber Miller'd stacked there for his house. I'd just paid for that lumber. Luke and I unloaded it."

"And they came after you."

"The boy doesn't know a thing about how to fight. Can't be more than seventeen anyway, skinny as a sapling. Luke took him down in no time."

"And you took down Mr. Foster."

"Wasn't hard. I've got about fifty pounds on him." He leaned against the table and sipped his coffee.

She sank onto the bench and sighed. "It's so disagreeable to be bickering with the neighbors. Folks tend to take sides. As we well know."

Jabez grinned, his face brightening. "Well, we can be pretty sure the neighbors are on our side. They just elected me to the legislature." He laughed like a little boy with a new pony. "Out of thirty-four votes I got thirty-two."

Agnes drew in a sharp breath. "You told them you'd stand?"

"I didn't say yes." He reddened and swiveled his eyes away from hers. "But I didn't say no."

"And when do you expect to have the time to farm your new claim?"

"I'm thinking of running beef cattle on that one. Won't take but some men to ride herd on them a couple times a year." He sat down across from her and reached for her hand. The kitten hopped into her lap, and Harrie pulled at her skirts. Jabez's face brightened again, full of enthusiasm and plans. "The sessions won't take much time. Month or two a year. It's a chance to forge something new, be in at the start of something, be in charge. I'm tired of being on the losing side, there're plenty of good Missouri men here and we can make this territory a showplace."

Politics would intrude again in their home. After its legacy of death and horror stretching over the past decade, Jabez continued in its thrall. In a territory without laws, with land free for the taking and the misuse, where gold worked its insidious evil. Politics, civilization, would intrude and threaten their happiness all over again.

Agnes squeezed his hand, stood, and turned away. "I'm very proud that your neighbors have honored you so." She fussed at the stove. "We'll have a special dinner tonight to celebrate our growing plantation and your rising star. Now take these two little animals outdoors"—she handed him the cat and gave Harrie a gentle shove—"and let me get to it."

Jabez tucked the kitten in the front of his torn shirt, swung his son onto his shoulders and threw her a kiss. She watched them duck into the bright October sunshine. Could there be a more aggravating man? And could she love him any more than she did?

The dying months of 1865 and the first of the new year brought snow, sleet, and below-zero temperatures. A quick trip to the privy was positively bone-chilling. Ice encased the river, wind swept the pastures clean, deep velvety nights descended by mid-afternoon. Those days passed in chores and contentment, evenings by the stove reading, sewing, talking, the three of them generating their own warmth.

When early spring rolled in at the beginning of March, Jabez left for Virginia City to attend the legislative session, and Agnes's mood turned dark. She grumbled at having to feed a half dozen strange hired hands who plowed and planted and cared for the stock, and she resented the milking and churning, planting and weeding, cooking and baking and mending without Jabez by her side. And chasing after a child of twenty months to be sure he didn't fall in the river or out of the hay loft or under the hooves of the mules didn't help. She was cross with everyone.

Jabez returned six weeks later and tried to entertain her with tales of the politics of the fledgling territory and the antics of Governor Meagher. He told her anecdotes and sad stories about the characters who peopled Virginia City, about the legislators and their wives, the connivances and personalities that drove the machinery of territorial government. And glad as she was to see him, she was not always entertained.

Within a week her snit evolved into full-fledged illness, starting with a cold and progressing to chills and fever. Jabez put her in bed with hot bricks, soaked her feet in warm water, dosed her with flax-seed tea and compound of lobelia and kept the cabin at boiling temperatures.

He convinced Rose to leave Bozeman and stay with them to care for the house, the meals and Harrie during her illness. Ten days passed before she left her bed, limbs feeling like wilted lily stems, her chest and throat achy and raw. Jabez pronounced her on the mend and immediately packed a valise.

Agnes watched him in dumb misery. "Where are you going?"

Jabez took her hand in his and touched his lips to her knuckles. "I must leave you to Rose's care for a time," he said. "I'm off to Virginia City to see the lawyers."

"But you were just there. Didn't you see them during the session?"

He shook his head. "They set a court date after I left. I've put it off as long as I could while you were sick. It can't be postponed any longer." He stacked the lunch plates and pushed them aside. "Bob Foster is determined to sue me over the Miller property, and if I don't respond right away I'll default."

"That's going to cost a penny." Jabez seemed to seek out controversy, and it put her out of sorts all over again.

"Dick's taking a wagon load over. We'll go together."

"Well, then go." She fussed with Harrie's damp curls and pouted.

"Don't overdo. Let Rose handle the housework." He leaned over to kiss her on the forehead. "Anything I can bring you from the big city?"

She lifted her eyes and studied him. Lines streaked his forehead, creased the corners of his eyes, his skin burnt by work in the sun and wind, his beard and hair shot with gray. She stroked his hand and whispered, "Just yourself."

"Always, love." He squeezed her hand, picked up his valise and the medical bag that went everywhere with him. "I should be back by Saturday."

Rose stepped in from the yard, and Jabez threw an arm around her shoulders, gave her a hug. "Take care of my girl." Rose smiled and nodded. "Make her get outside tomorrow."

"Yes sir."

He filled the doorway and for a moment, the house darkened as he shut out the sunlight. Then he was gone.

47

June 1866

Bob Foster and the Emerson kid declined an offer to settle the lawsuit, and Jabez foresaw an expensive and time-consuming fight, but he refused to stand by while they stole his land through the courts. He'd hired a raft of lawyers, and he steamed and grumbled to Dick and to himself all along the road. Then to add insult, before noon on the second day of the return trip Dick's left front wagon wheel dropped in a rut and cracked, and they spent a couple hours altogether cobbling it enough to get them home. Jabez wanted to speed Jupiter on ahead, as the patched wheel bumped and rattled and slowed the wagon even more than usual, but he hated to leave Dick behind.

Heat shimmered, flies buzzing through it like soot from a chimney. They moved slowly thanks to the bad wheel and by mid afternoon, hours behind schedule, arrived on the banks of the Gallatin, where the river was fordable in late summer. The trail itself swung north toward Shed's Bridge, across the southeast corner of John Nelson's claim. Jabez spotted John and his oldest boy clearing brush off to the north and waved them in.

Dick halted the team along the edge of a ditch flowing into the big river to let them water. Jabez jumped down from Jupiter to stretch, his legs cramped, his stomach rumbling. Nelson and his son trotted up, the boy on a mule, wiping sweat from their eyes. Jabez produced a new pack of cigars he'd picked up in Virginia City, passed them around, and the men lit up, smoked, talked about the prices Dick had got for the last load of freight.

Jabez took a pull on his cigar. His eyes roved over the river. The current tumbled over the rocks and gravel, fed by snow melt from the mountains to the south, but most times the bed here was solid. Another five miles up to the bridge, then three miles down the other side to home. He could cut that to two miles if he forded on Jupiter. He wanted to be home. He wanted Agnes in his arms and Harrie in his lap. He even missed the kitten. He tossed the butt of the cigar into the ditch and turned to Dick.

"I'm going to cross here," he said, gathering the reins of the big gelding and unstrapping his medical bag. "Cuts off six miles, and I want to be home before dark."

John Nelson looked at the river, studied it in his quiet way. "Don't know as you should, Doc," he said. "That current's real wild this time of year."

Jabez threw his bag into the wagon. "Jupiter can push through it and it's shallow enough. Besides, if we get into trouble, you'll pull us out, right?" He grinned at his friends.

"I'm taking the bridge," Dick said. "Get to your place real late I reckon."

Jabez looped the reins around his fist, hefted himself into the saddle and walked Jupiter to the edge. The sun, still high in the west a day after solstice, glinted off the riffles and blinded him for an instant. The big bay shied, hooves sinking into the soft muck of the bank. He urged him on with his knees, talking softly. The horse eased into the water, found his footing, moved forward. Jabez gauged the current. Graveled bottom spread next to the bank in a swirl, its far edge hidden by sun glare. Farther in the current strengthened, and the river bed darkened. He read it through the strong legs of his mount, and he pushed into the center of the stream.

Then the bottom dropped off, a hole scoured by the spring flood and obscured by the murk kicked up under Jupiter's hooves. The current eddied and foamed, and wavelets washed to his waist, filled his boots with icy snowmelt. Dick called from the bank, unintelligible. A fast-moving tree limb crashed into Jupiter's chest and the horse spooked, twisted and thrashed, now turned downstream, away from the landing place. Jabez saw the men running along the bank, mouths open but words drowned in the rush of the river. Dick was in the water up to his thighs, swinging a rope over his head. Jabez slid sideways and lost sight him, swiveled back around. He could feel Jupiter's frantic underwater paddling, his head tossing from side to side, his breath coming in snorts. Ten yards separated them from the east bank, ten yards of swirls and eddies invisible from the opposite shore.

Out of the corner of his eye, Jabez saw the rope snake through the air, the knotted end splashing yards short and floating downstream. Jupiter squealed and bucked, eyes rolling. His head smacked Jabez in the chin. Jabez dragged hard on the reins, momentarily blinded, and the big animal rolled, taking Jabez under. Jabez clutched with his thighs, twisted his body, and they flopped, both the horse's and the man's heads emerging. They closed in on the east bank and Jabez lunged for a tree limb, grabbed, caught hold. The horse's fear thrilled through him. Calm, calm, he thought. Panic now and you're done. The limb tore across his palm, slicing a jagged path, and snapped, and he watched the bank recede as they were pushed back into the center of the river.

Through a sheet of water he saw Dick wade into the river again, directly across from him, the rope in hand. "Throw it!" he yelled, his voice sounding hoarse to his ears. The rope whistled toward him, and terror speared through him at the thought of Dick being dragged in. The rope splashed down inches from the horse's nose, and he seized it, looped it around his fist. The movement startled Jupiter and he thrashed again, bucking and snorting water. Dick called to him, horror in his voice, to drop the rope, drop the rope, it was tangled, it would pull him under. Jabez let the rope slip from his hand, watched it twist away.

Water closed over his head. For an instant he melded into the big animal that screamed next to him, pinned to it, then he pushed himself free, a roar in his ears. He scrabbled for the bottom, but his boots found nothing; they were heavy and filled and he knew he should kick them off. Then something struck him in the temple and there was pain, but it seemed to be someone else's pain. The light here shone blue and green and silver, white-gold shafts caught in bubbles, lovely. He floated, though his limbs were heavy; trying to move them was like pushing through honey. The roar dissipated into a soft kind of quiet, the music of flowing water a vibration against his cheek. He turned, slowly. It was peaceful here, under the water, the light now far away. Figures appeared, dim, just beyond sight, people he thought he once knew. Were they in the river with him? Had they been there all along? He smiled to himself and let go.

48

1867

Agnes stood in the door yard, hanging laundered sheets on a line strung to catch the freshest breeze, the scent of new-turned earth sharp and tangy. She brushed a wisp of hair from her face and looked up into a clear and strangely empty blue sky, birdsong suddenly stilled. Movement to the north caught her eye—horsemen on the river trail, riding in her direction. Agnes's heart jumped, but Jupiter didn't appear. He was so big, so dark, she could always pick him out. There was a gray mare that belonged to John Nelson. John's boy, his oldest, followed on a mule. Dick rode on the big dun gelding he used to pull his freight wagon.

And that is the picture that lodged in her mind, the haze through which she would ever after view the world. Jabez was not with them. They rode closer and she ran toward them. Dick's dark, kind face was streaked with tears. And she knew.

The neighbors rallied around. Mrs. Nelson stayed with her for two days, watching Harrie, cooking meals, holding her hand. Her oldest boy, Marsh, the one who'd been there on the river bank that day, slept in the barn and managed the stock. He must have been there a full month; Agnes couldn't quite remember. John Nelson took her to the spot on the Gallatin where he and Dick had buried Jabez's body, in the field where they'd found him soon after he'd disappeared below the surface. She hated leaving him in that sad lonely place, Jabez, who loved company. To leave him in a grave that would soon be lost forever was just not right.

So Dick made a casket and she, Harrie, and Rose climbed into the wagon for the trip to Virginia City. She had decided Jabez would rest on the hillside above the town that would become the hub of Montana, in sight of the raucous machinations of politicians that so entertained him, the frontier's bare hills and rolling valleys spread on all sides.

They chose a spot with a beautiful view, and Dick dug, but the soil was such that he could not go deep, so he built a cairn of shaped rock and slab stone. His hands, rough as bull hide with all manner of work, were gentle, almost caressing, as he shifted the casket. He'd put much thought and effort into it, and it was a lovely piece of craftsmanship, the corners mitered, the joints dovetailed, a testament to his love for the man who had once owned him. It was a legacy, almost as much as the child she held close, a way to prolong a life long after the last breath has fled. She and Harrie together placed the last stone on the cairn and, with Rose's hand in hers, she turned and climbed back into the wagon.

It was easier in the summer and autumn, those months right after, when the ranch work needed to be handled, business affairs addressed. Dick and Rose moved back in and he took over the farm chores. The Nelson boy helped when he could, and she paid both of them with produce and meat. John Nelson took over the management of the lawsuit, that pesky trouble that Jabez left behind, the artifact of his temper that haunted Agnes. Mr. Nelson's expenses for trips to Virginia City, payment to witnesses, payment to lawyers, began to mount and her small stock of gold dust dwindled. But Robert Foster had stated boldly that now he dealt with a widow rather than the hot-tempered doctor, the case would fold, and he'd have the land on forfeit. She was determined to prove him wrong.

As the winter came on, though, and the weather ended the visits to and from neighbors, Agnes felt the hurt. She wondered if Harrie would remember that winter, maybe the scream of the redtail, or the moan of the wind through the chinks of the cabin. It would be a blessing if he forgot how they couldn't get warm at night even though they huddled together in the bed with all the blankets and the rug on top. He cried with the cold and the loneliness for his father, and so did she. Not in Harrie's hearing, of course. But in the afternoons when he napped, and the snow fell through blue shadows that wavered and danced about the cabin as if they floated under water. Or in the mornings when he bundled up in every scrap of clothing he owned and trudged with Dick to the barn to milk and feed the restless animals. But mostly in the deep nights when he snuffled himself to sleep, and she pushed aside the woolen drape from the window and looked out to the stars, distant and cold. She remembered those same stars from the porch in their Lick Creek house when they first discussed the idea of going West. The shooting star, she said, was a sign of change. Jabez said it was a sign of death. They were both right.

Her savior that first winter, and truth to tell throughout the months that followed, was Rose. Rose baked and they did laundry together when the weather allowed, made butter and sewed. And talked. She told Agnes tales of servitude in Arkansas, where she was born, and talked of her mother, of those she had lost and the courage she'd drawn from them. She taught Harrie songs that reverberated with the warmth and mystery of exotic places, and she listened while Agnes recounted bits and snatches of memories of her marriage.

In February, Mr. Nelson brought the news that the lawsuit was decided in Agnes's favor. The land was hers, but the suit had cost more than she ever might expect to recoup by selling it.

When he left, she sank into the only chair she owned. Rose looked up from the chicken she was flouring for dinner. "You'll manage, missus," she said. "Wheat's selling real good and we'll get a new crop of calves this spring."

"We need a new plow before spring plowing, and a new hog lot," Agnes said. She creased the tablecloth idly. "Thank God we replaced the threshing floor last year. I could never afford it this time around." She retrieved the bowl of potatoes and a paring knife and set to work.

"What would you think, Rose," she said, "if I were to go back to Pennsylvania? Would I be a quitter?"

"No shame in going back, missus," she said. "You don't got nothing to prove. Land sake, I believe you proved to any soul who might ask what you made of. You a brave lady a hunnert times over."

Agnes grimaced. "Thank you, Rose. I don't always feel brave. But I do wonder what Jabez would say."

"He'd say do what your heart tell you. Do what's right for your boy. He'd trust you to know."

"He would at that," she said. "He would at that."

Events in the spring decided her. In late April, John Bozeman was killed by natives along the Yellowstone River and word was that the Sioux would sweep down the Bozeman Trail and attack the Gallatin Valley. That strange little Irishman who was the Territory's temporary governor raised a militia and marched to the Yellowstone, to find only a few straggling Absaroka. His army, composed of once-high ranking officers in the Confederate Army and soldiers who needed a federal paycheck to stake their mining adventures, roamed the valley making nuisances of themselves and a fool of the Irishman. Agnes's taxes went to support this farce and once it ended, the Natives resumed menacing the settlements. When in August there were fights and killings along the Bozeman Trail, quite far from Bozeman but threatening none the less, she decided her son required a safe and civilized place to live. The irony of taking him back East to live among the people who had just fought the bloodiest and most dangerous war in history was not lost on her.

And she thought of Jabez buried on that hillside. She'd be leaving him behind just as she'd left Charlie and Sarah Belle in Lick Creek. But even though she wasn't a religious person—not in the church-going sense, anyway—she knew she'd be taking Jabez with her. And she believed she'd see him again, be reunited with him, after she breathed her last. For now, she needed to live, to provide for Harrie, to see him educated and raised in a way that would make his father proud. For now, she needed to go back, retrace her journey, and return home.

49

May 1868

On her last morning in the Gallatin Valley, Agnes spotted a sandhill crane, its red cap gleaming in the early sunlight. The lovely Montana spring had swept in, the rivers running free of their icy coverlet, the wild meadow grasses beginning to green, mallard and teal chasing one another in noisy arcs, after territory and mates. She would miss the mountains looming heavy with winter snow, promising fast rivers and full irrigation ditches for summer crops. She would miss the vistas, the clear air, the sky that seemed to go on forever.

Harrie, nearly four years old, ran on strong legs along the river bank, laughing in the early sunshine. He reached for a butterfly and squealed when it flitted away. He shouted to her to watch and planted his hands, heaved his bottom, and turned a somersault. Then he clambered to his feet, threw his arms wide, proud of his accomplishment. He'd inherited the dark eyes, the silky hair of his father, and Agnes liked to think the quick mind, too. Already he'd learned his letters and his numbers, and she hoped to enroll him in a fine school in Pennsylvania, but it was always hard for him to sit still. He was truly Jabez's son.

She tucked her last-minute items into the trunk that sat in Dick's wagon bed and snapped it shut. Rose stood in the doorway of the house, her eyes red-rimmed, a handkerchief held to her nose. The house was hers now; Agnes had deeded the claim to her and Dick. Rose was pregnant—freedom gave them confidence to begin their own family, and Agnes regretted she would not be there to hold the baby and watch it grow.

She threw her arms around her friend one last time. The sun crept over the shoulder of the eastern mountains, flashing off the waters of the river. The clear *whee-deer* of the flycatcher drowned out all other sounds. She lifted Harrie into his seat in the wagon bed and climbed to the bench next to Dick.

She and Harrie would take the coach south from Virginia City, past the Great Salt Lake, then on to St. Joseph. She planned to detour to Holt County, to close the book on its memories and see, once again, Elizabeth and Billy, Sarah and James. James who escaped the war unscathed, convinced of the protective qualities of his black arrowhead. And to visit the graves of her babies once more. Then the train to Pennsylvania.

She looked forward to the coming journey almost as much as she had looked forward to the trek west sixteen years earlier. It was another new adventure, this one internal—challenges not of place, but of character— making her way in the world without a husband, raising her son in Jabez's image. She looked forward to those challenges with an eagerness that surprised her.

She knew it wouldn't be easy. But she'd lived through the war, lived through loneliness, lived through loss over and over again. Lived through the killing. She remembered the roughness of the noose in her fingers, saw the flash of Wil Bigelow's silvery eyes, heard the report of the gun and the thud of John Jackson's body on the living room floor. She remembered holding Sarah Belle's fevered body and kissing little Charlie's forehead for the last time. And she remembered watching Billy ride off to war and then James, the arrowhead dangling from his neck.

It had been a very public and national war, but it had been a private war, too, a personal war for everyone who lived through it, suffered, learned, survived. She thought of her distant cousin, that odd, gangly man whose words had thrilled her so long ago, who did what he could, right or wrong, single-minded, to preserve what he believed in. She had come to believe that Lincoln had been right, that preserving the country without slavery was essential. But oh, the cost. He had lost battle after battle, but he had won the war.

And so had she.

She'd received a letter from Billy just weeks earlier with the news that Rachel had died after the first of the year and that Julia had presented him with another daughter. For every death, it seemed a new life was created in recompense. A life for a life. Jabez left her with Harrie, and she knew for a certainty that someday new life would flow from their son. She wished with all her heart that Jabez could be there with her, see Harrie grow, welcome grandchildren, and watch them grow in turn. There were times his absence splintered her heart, but she knew that even though the hour glass narrows, a grain of sand slips through and that's all it takes to carry on.

Author's Note

Agnes Canon's War is fiction based on lots of fact. I am indebted to Lida Holmes Robinson Morrow for putting down the facts in a manuscript that came to me in the 1980s. Agnes Canon was born in Fayette County, Pennsylvania, in 1824, one of nine children (one living male), none of whom married except Agnes. She returned to Fayette County in 1868, after living alone with a toddler on the Montana homestead, and raised her son alone. She never remarried, lived to be eighty-four years old and is buried in the Lincoln-Robinson Cemetery outside Uniontown, Pennsylvania. Harrie Lee became a lawyer, changed his name to Harold, married, sired eight children (seven boys and one girl) and built a mansion in Uniontown, which is still standing.

Jabez grew up in Maine, one of twelve children. Family lore says he went to California via the Isthmus of Panama, took a degree at Transylvania University (the records show he enrolled there, but never actually received a degree), and was elected to the Montana Legislature (he was elected but never seated—that's another story).

The Jacksons and Sam Canon's family were real people, though there were more children than appear in the novel; many of their descendents are living today, a few in Holt County, Missouri. The cemetery in Oregon, Missouri (the Lick Creek of the novel) holds the graves of many of the characters whose stories are told here.

The events that took place in northwestern Missouri and in Kansas are drawn from historical accounts of guerrilla warfare during the 1850s and 1860s. Jabez did own a newspaper, which was destroyed, did hold secessionist views, was placed under house arrest.

Though I don't know Agnes's and Jabez's true views on slavery and race relations, Dick and Rose MacDonald (her name was actually Mary) were the first black couple to settle in the Bozeman area. The fact that they must have joined the Robinsons in the move to Montana gives me hope that the two couples were truly friends.

The Bigelows—Reuben, Jake and the fish-eyed Willard—are fictional creations. Jabez's participation in the aftermath of the John Brown massacre is a product of my imagination, as is his connection to Senator Atchison and Charles Robinson, both of whom are historical figures.

Oregon, Missouri, a delightful town, looks much the same as it must have in those early years, with the addition of a new courthouse and a high school. The cemetery and the library are treasure troves of local history and the rolling hills and prairie land around it give rise to all sorts of fancies about how life may have happened back then. Agnes and Jabez, my great-great grandparents, lived and loved and suffered during their time there. I've tried to imagine how it all was—I hope I did them justice.

Discussion Questions

1. Jabez felt strongly that keeping the two sections of the United States together as one country was not worth the cost of war. In hindsight, knowing how many people were killed and maimed, do you agree or disagree with him? If the war had not been fought, would slavery have died out of its own accord?

2. Social institutions—schools, churches, fraternal organizations, political parties, for example—act as a kind of glue to hold a society together. How have those social institutions changed between the 1850s and today? What new organizations do we use to interact with our neighbors? How can social institutions affect an entire nation as opposed to a local society like a village or town?

3. A woman's role in mid-19th century America was usually seen as preserving the home as a domestic haven and providing children with a moral upbringing. How might that background develop into the role of activist in such areas as temperance and abolition? What might be the advantages and costs of expanding her role beyond the home for such women as Harriet Beecher Stowe, Margaret Fuller and Louisa May Alcott?

4. Do you think vigilante activity is justified in some extreme situations? Should Agnes and Jabez have turned over Willard to the authorities? How did Billy's moral compass change over the course of the war?

Acknowledgements

Finishing this project has long been a dream, and I appreciate all the help and encouragement I've received along the way. Thanks go especially to Lida Holmes Robinson Morrow and Irene Costello, both now deceased, who kept the story of the Robinsons alive and passed it on to a new generation. I am indebted to my readers/editors/supporters, particularly Toni Kennedy and Diane Robinson; Carol Kean and the IWW critiquers; and Mike Burgess, Marilyn Burkhardt, Donna Harwood-Martyn, Nancy Turner and Carol Doyle from the TBCC writing group. There are many other supporters who've had faith that I could finish this, and I thank them too.

Thanks especially to Kristina Blank Makansi and Amira Makansi at Blank Slate Press who believed in this book and made it so much better.

Thanks most especially to Dan, who cheerfully endured field trips to the midwest and all the other inconveniences that being married to a writer entail.

About the Author

Deborah Lincoln grew up among the cornfields of western Ohio, the product of farmers on one side, doctors and lawyers on the other. She earned a bachelor's degree from Michigan State University and a master's degree from the University of Michigan and doesn't really care which one wins the big game. She and her husband have three grown sons and live on the Oregon Coast.

CPSIA information can be obtained at www.ICGtesting.com
Printed in the USA
LVOW12s1956150914

404150LV00004B/209/P